Readers love the Warders

His Hearth

"Mary Calmes has once again struck gold. Her latest well plotted release is filled with passionate, charismatic characters that left me begging for more."—Fallen Angel Reviews Recommended Read

"...a worthy afternoon read..."—Literary Nymphs Reviews

Tooth & Nail

"...an action-packed love story so absorbing I could not put it down."—TwoLips Reviews

"...drew me right in from page one."—Whipped Cream Reviews

Heart in Hand

"Ms. Calmes has balanced this personal part of the story with the creepy... and she's done it with great creative flair."—Literary Nymphs Reviews

Sinnerman

"This is such a good story and such a fantastic series!"—The Romance Studio

"...full of intrigue, romance, excitement and hot steamy sex!"—Dark Divas Reviews

Nexus

"I loved every minute of this emotional roller coaster..."—Queer Magazine Online

"...a well written story with a great round-up of characters..."—MM Good Book Reviews

Cherish Your Name

"...what the Warders series is all about: hot sex, hot men, action, and romance."—Joyfully Reviewed

By MARY CALMES

NOVELS
Change of Heart
Honored Vow
Trusted Bond

A Matter of Time Vol. 1 & 2
Bulletproof

Acrobat
The Guardian
Mine
Timing
Warders Vol. 1 & 2

NOVELLAS
After the Sunset
Again
Any Closer
Frog
Romanus
The Servant
What Can Be

THE WARDER SERIES
His Hearth
Tooth & Nail
Heart in Hand
Sinnerman
Nexus
Cherish Your Name

Published by DREAMSPINNER PRESS
http://www.dreamspinnerpress.com

WARDERS

VOLUME TWO

MARY CALMES

SINNERMAN

NEXUS

CHERISH
YOUR NAME

Dreamspinner Press

Published by
Dreamspinner Press
382 NE 191st Street #88329
Miami, FL 33179-3899, USA
http://www.dreamspinnerpress.com/

The Warders Collection, Vol. 2

Cover Art by Anne Cain   annecain.art@gmail.com

ISBN: 978-1-61372-492-7

Printed in the United States of America
First Edition
May 2012

Sinnerman (June 2011), Nexus (October 2011), and Cherish Your Name (December 2011) were previously published individually in eBook format by Dreamspinner Press.

Thank you to all my wonderful fans
who asked when the boys would be in paperback.

Sinnerman

1

I WAS alone, and that was death for a warder. Fortunately I was not fighting demons at the moment but was instead drinking, which could be dicey in a few hours considering the mood I was in. But even as drunk as I was, I recognized my friend Ryan's boyfriend sitting with some guys on the other side of the bar. I wondered if he was out to pick somebody up, hanging with his friends until he spotted the one-night stand he would leave with. He was probably cheating on Ryan the way my hearth, Frank Sullivan, had been cheating on me. And my buddy would never know until it was too late, until he caught them. Yes, Julian Nash was out cruising—why wouldn't he be? What was his boyfriend's heart worth when leveraged against a hot body in his bed?

Sitting there, nursing either my fifth or seventh—I had lost count hours ago—scotch and water, I watched Julian laughing. All the guys with him were about his age, the camaraderie obvious, probably coworkers having drinks after work. I realized after a minute that I wasn't the only one watching the five men. I was used to scanning a room, in the habit of looking for threats, so I saw the man at the bar, three stools down from me, staring. I thought it would take me some time to see where his interest lay, but when Julian rose to get another round, the man studied his progression from the table to the bar with absolute unshakeable intensity. And I understood. Julian Nash was a treat to look at. A lot of men in the bar would have had him in their sights. Once they talked to him, the desire would be even greater to have him. He was funny and smart and, most of all, kind. I liked him immediately when I first met him. I really hoped he was just having drinks with friends and not looking to get laid. Even one more disappointment would be too much.

"What can I get you?"

I looked back down the bar and realized that the tall man I had noticed before had, as I suspected he would, leaned close to Julian and propositioned him. The hearth of my fellow warder smiled wide. My stomach flipped over with dread.

"I've got mine, thanks."

"Well, then have a seat, and the next one's on me."

"Actually I'm having drinks with friends"—Julian smiled warmly—"but I'm very flattered."

He was out with his friends and was not on the prowl. It was stupid how happy the little piece of news made me, but I was, as ridiculous as it sounded, still a romantic at heart.

"Have dinner with me."

"I'm having dinner with my boyfriend after this, so no, thank you."

The man suddenly seemed unsteady in his chair.

"Are you okay?" Julian sounded concerned as he picked up a martini with an onion in it and a highball glass that was halfway filled.

"I'm fine," the man told him, shaking his head like it needed clearing. "I'd just really like to have dinner with you."

"And I told you no," Julian repeated, turning.

The guy rose fast from the barstool and moved around in front of him. This would be the true test, because standing there, gifting Julian with a wicked smile that lit his emerald eyes, the man was tall, dark, and very handsome.

"Are you sure?"

"I am, but again, I'm very flattered," Julian said softly, stepping around him, starting back toward the table.

I snickered, and the man turned at the same time and caught me. It was not one of my better moments, and one I could have normally covered, but my reflexes were shot for now.

"Something funny?"

I coughed to clear my throat but couldn't help smiling. "Nope."

He squinted at me before he came toward me.

"Sorry," I apologized up front. Handsome really didn't do the man justice. "But"—I chuckled—"you never had a chance, man."

"No? Why's that?" he asked, his eyes sweeping over me, darkening, the hunger infusing them. I was not Julian Nash, but apparently I would do.

"His boyfriend is really hot."

He looked like I'd slapped him.

Nobody killed heat as quickly as I could. It was a gift, really, my sort of blunt blurting of the truth that no one ever wanted to hear. The very handsome man was appalled, and then he recovered.

"Is that right?" he snapped at me, the voice that had been interested seconds before now icy cold.

"You watch *Ryan's Rundown* on Channel 5?" I asked, trying not to slur my words.

"Sure. Everyone watches Ryan Dean," he said irritably.

And they did. The ex-model-turned-television-host was too charming and too hot not to have a religious following. He was also a very scary sword-carrying demon hunter. "He sleeps with Ryan Dean every night," I said, pointing after Julian. "You think you got a chance?"

His scowl was dark.

"Oh, what the fuck?" came a growl from behind the Adonis.

The look of utter disdain that washed over the man's face was very amusing. Watching him turn slowly to the voice, I nearly lost it.

"Malic," he said, his voice dripping with contempt.

"Graham," my friend said, the irritation right there for anyone to hear as he took a seat beside me.

They didn't even look each other in the eye, but the loathing, even without it, was overwhelmingly obvious. Graham made a noise in the back of his throat like just being in the same room with Malic made him sick. Malic's patronizing scoff was just as telling.

Graham turned on his heel and left. He threw a fifty on the bar as he walked by it but didn't stop even when the bartender called a thank-you after him.

"God, that guy hates you," Marcus Roth, another of my friends and a fellow warder, said as he took a seat on the barstool on my left.

"Like I give a shit."

Marcus's knee bumped mine, and I felt his hand on my thigh, patting me, just for a second. He was worried. They all were. "You need to work on your people skills."

"I didn't hit him. That's as good as it gets," Malic told him, a dark scowl on his face.

"But why do you let that asshole get to you every time?"

"I dunno. He just rubs me the wrong way."

"How long've you known the guy?" I chimed in with my innocuous question.

"Long enough. He's a dick," he told me, squinting at me. "And Leith was right—you look like hammered shit."

"Thank you very much."

"Hey."

I turned to Marcus, and I was instantly sorry I had. His dark eyes never missed anything, and at the moment he was concentrating his considerable powers of observation on me.

"Me and Malic are headed over to my place to eat and then go patrol. Come have dinner with us."

There was something wrong with that sentence.

"Jacks?"

I ran it back in my head, processing his words, trying for the life of me to figure out what was wrong with what he was saying.

There was something.

Come eat. Come eat…. Wait. "I thought Joey hated Malic. How're you taking him home?" I asked, realizing how long that had taken me. My brain normally worked a lot faster. I was really trashed.

He shrugged. "Apparently I missed the obvious. Joe didn't like Malic because all this time, he thought that Malic wanted me."

I squinted at him.

"Just don't say it."

"Huh. So for, what—five years now, almost six, your hearth, the guy you love more than anything, thought your best friend wanted to get down with you."

He nodded.

"What changed?"

"Dylan." Marcus sighed. "Malic found his hearth; Joe spent one night listening to the lovebirds together and confessed everything."

I did a slow pan to Malic.

He rolled his eyes before flipping me off.

"When did I say that that's what it probably was?"

"I think it was five years ago," Marcus offered from my left.

"And when did I say that you should just tell Joey that you love Marcus like the brother you never had but that's all?"

"Same time," Marcus chimed in.

"Uh, fuck you both," Malic told us, lifting his hand to get the attention of the bartender.

I leaned my head forward, raking my hands through my thick curly hair that now fell to my shoulders. It needed to be cut. I also needed to shave. I had gotten lazy about the stubble on my face, and now, after a month, maybe two, had a beard and mustache to show for it. Like it mattered. "You guys don't need to babysit me. I'm not gonna kill myself."

"Come eat." Marcus repeated his offer, hand on the back of my neck, massaging gently.

"No." I smiled. "I'll let Joe bond with Malic. They lost a lot of time."

"They bonded," he assured me, "and Dylan's the one my boyfriend's in love with now. Compared to him, Malic and me are both chopped liver."

And I understood that. Dylan Shaw, Malic's newly discovered hearth, was as close to candy as any man could be. At nineteen he was devastating; by thirty he'd have the world at his feet. What I liked best about him, though, was not his ethereal beauty but his loyalty. It was a trait I had come recently to admire.

I was a warder, and I hunted demons. Every city had a sentinel, and every sentinel had five warders, a clutch, that he commanded. Warders, because we basically lived in a cesspool of filth and evil, had to be able to come home at the end of each day to a sanctuary. The hearth of a warder, their mate, provided that. For two years the man I came home to was Frank Sullivan. He was it, my whole life, the guy who made my loft off 18th Street in Potrero Hill the place I wanted to be more than anything. And then, three months ago, I had tracked a demon, was racing across rooftops after him, and had come to a dead stop before I could vault to the next building.

"Aren't we running?" he had asked sarcastically, doubling back down off the ledge when he had realized I was no longer in hot pursuit.

I couldn't move at all. I was frozen where I stood.

"Warder?"

He was not a demon, specifically, but a creature I wanted to kill nonetheless. A being I had to slay in order to keep Malic safe.

"I...."

"What has you so mesmerized?"

My mouth opened, but no words came out.

"Speak."

But I couldn't. I could only stare.

I felt hot, wet breath on the back of my neck, heard him inhale deeply as I pointed with the tip of the ornate rapier in my left hand.

Across the chasm between the buildings, on a marbled, opulent-looking penthouse patio, stood my hearth, accountant Frank Sullivan, and his top client, Rene Favreau. The night had started out being about saving Malic, but now I was going to have to kill him for ever introducing Frank to his buddy.

"What am I looking at, warder?"

I couldn't even push air through my lungs as I watched the two men kiss. And it wasn't the tentative first kind but the one where you knew what you were doing because you had done it so many times before. Rene's mouth slanted down over Frank's, and he took possession, one hand fisted in his hair, the other cupping his ass.

"Oh, he's enjoying that."

The words tore me open. I whirled, swinging the rapier, ready to take the kyrie's head.

"Touchy," he said, leaping back and sideways, easily evading my hasty attack.

"Your kind killed my family!" I roared.

"No," he clarified, his voice calm, deep, and husky.

"Yes!" I snarled out my murderous rage. It was the only thing left in me as I thrust forward.

He maneuvered around me. "The day you pulled me off Malic, you screamed that obscene accusation at me, that a blood demon killed your family."

I advanced on him.

"And I grieve your loss, warder, but it has nothing to do with me."

"Kyries and blood demons are the same thing," I assured him, my tone icy as I swiped at him with roundhouse swings.

"Nope, wrong." He smiled wickedly, his extended canines glinting in the moonlight. "Kyries are born in purgatory, all demons in hell. Demons have no finesse; kyries know the difference."

I growled.

"And we're the savages?"

I lunged at him, the rapier swinging wildly, splitting the air with a whoosh of sound, fast as a whip. But he was an excellent swordsman and deflected me effortlessly with his Chinese *jian*, parrying, thrusting, and driving me back. I looked for a weakness, for a misstep, but his stance was solid, and I found no opening.

"Warder!"

His voice brought me from my murderous rage; my eyes flicked to his face.

"Again I say, I am sorry for your family, warder, but a kyrie is not a blood demon, and my kind had nothing to do with their deaths."

I rolled forward, ready to take his head off.

"I want you to acknowledge the truth, warder."

There were no words as I charged, but he moved fast, too fast, and my momentum carried me forward toward the edge of the twenty-four-story building. Before I could recover my balance, he had me.

I was shoved down to my knees, a hand fisted in my hair so that my head was yanked back hard, my throat bared even as he focused my gaze back across the yawning space to the patio.

They were inside, the sliding glass door closed now, the drapes drawn. But the light was on and made everything transparent. Rene Favreau, whom I had always liked, would not have thought to pull the blinds. They were up too high, and the building Raphael, the kyrie, and I were on housed offices. He would not have imagined that anyone was looking. But I was. I was looking, and when Frank, my partner, my love, stepped naked from the bathroom and was thrown down onto the bed laughing, I thought my heart would stop beating at that very moment. He invited Rene just as he had me, on hands and knees in the center of the bed.

"Is he wagging his tail, warder? What do you call that?"

I struggled, my hands on the thickly muscled forearm of the kyrie.

"Is he your hearth, warder?"

I would not cry in front of a monster, in front of a creature meant for killing.

"Is he?"

Something broke inside my chest; I felt a cog come loose as I dragged in air.

"Warder," he said, his voice thick, "when you pulled me from Malic as he lay in my arms and I drank his blood, I turned and sank teeth into you. Do you recall?"

I didn't, and as I watched the shadowy figures blend, combine, become one, I could not be made to care.

"I had thought to come back in the night and steal Malic away, drag him to the pit with me, have him see hell, chaos, the rings, and all the planes. I crave a mate, same as you, warder, need one perhaps even more desperately. I've heard that warders go mad, eventually curl up and die without a hearth, but kyries… we vent that madness. We share it. If we are unloved, we turn solely to hunting and find solace only in killing."

I heaved out a breath.

"And one day, we become that which we hunt."

The shadows parted, one rose, and the other extended arms as the room went dark. I wanted to howl in pain, but there was no air.

"But Malic's blood was not sweet; it gave me no sustenance, and taking it was not a joy. Had you not come when you did, I would have fulfilled my promise to him and taken little. But in your fervor, warder, in your panic to free your friend, your shoulder moved beneath my fangs."

I nodded because suddenly I did remember. I had found him drinking from Malic, and all I could do, all that mattered, was saving my friend from the fate that had taken my family from me. I had leaped forward but had missed Leith moving at the same time. When he tore the kyrie from Malic, I found myself between the two men. Malic's blood was pumping from the wound that I would admit that Leith created when he separated them, and I had enough time to roll sideways and take the impact of the kyrie's bite deep into my right shoulder.

"Your blood"—his voice rumbled deep in his chest—"unlike Malic's, is the sweetest I have ever tasted."

I had felt the kyrie's hands turn to claws as he clutched me tight. Arms and legs had wrapped around me as his mouth found my neck. I had been frantic to get away. I fought for my life, and even after we were separated, Ryan had pinned me to the bed so I wouldn't go after him. Marcus was holding Malic together, pressing his bloody shirt to the man's throat. Leith was calling for Jael. The room had spun, the images blurred as I separated my past from my present, not sure if the screaming was me or Marcus.

I hadn't told anyone what had happened; no one had seen the bite, too focused on Malic. They saw me struggling with the kyrie, but no one knew the blood was mine. I didn't want to worry Jael, my sentinel. He had been concerned that the kyrie would come back looking for Malic. I didn't want to add in the anxiety for me as well.

"It is you I hunger for now, warder."

Everything blurred as my eyes filled with hot tears.

My head was tipped sideways. A wet tongue slithered from shoulder to ear, tasting, licking, lips pressed to my skin before teeth. Even the bite did not move me, infuse me with the will to fight. The tug of skin, the first swallow—even then, I was frozen from what I had just witnessed.

My family had been taken from me by a blood demon, by a pack of them. The warder of the city I lived in at the time, I had grown up in, Knoxville, Tennessee, had found them and killed them. I was twelve when I went to live in San Francisco with my Aunt Gail. At sixteen I met Jael. One of his warders was sent to Paris, and he needed a replacement. I felt the call, his call, the stirring inside the moment I saw the man. He was like a surrogate father to me; I didn't want him worried that a kyrie wanted to drink my blood. I kept it to myself and hunted Raphael down alone. I would have killed him, but then I saw Frank.

"Is your heart so broken that you would gift me with all your blood?"

I would have *tried* to kill him at least. Kyries were preternatural bounty hunters; they were not the easiest things to dispatch.

"Tell me your blood is mine to take, warder."

His question brought me from my thoughts.

"You think you found me, but the truth is… I let you."

Let me?

"Of the two of us, I'm the true hunter. You protect; I hunt."

I couldn't think. His tongue slid over my punctured flesh, soothed it, and eased away the sting, the heartbeat of raw, pulsing pain.

"I wanted you to find me," he said softly. "I hoped."

Hoped?

"You taste like heat and life, warder." He breathed the words in my ear. "I will devour you, and you will be mine. I've never ached like I do now. Only speak the words, and I will take you from this place, from this pain. Only speak the words."

"What words are those?"

"'Take me'. Tell me to take you, and I will."

I shivered hard because it was tempting. Death and oblivion sounded okay. "You want me to let you kill me?"

"No, warder," he breathed over my skin, his nose slipping down the side of my neck. "You mistake my desire for you as a desire for your death. I don't want to kill you; I simply want you to be mine."

The darkness in him was the only thing I understood at that moment, but I wasn't ready to tumble into the abyss. Not yet. "Go away. Please," I begged him, screwing my eyes up tight.

When I opened them moments later, I was alone on the roof in the howling wind. I sat there even when the sky opened and poured down icy rain. I couldn't move. I was rooted there to the spot where everything I knew had come to an end.

"Jacks." Marcus bumped my shoulder and brought me from the past back to the present.

I turned to look.

"Have you even talked to Frank at all?"

"I have," I told him, coughing.

"And?"

What was I going to tell him? That Frank had said I was selfish and I had agreed that I was? That Frank didn't want to be the custodian of our relationship anymore? That the man I loved wanted and needed more than I could give him? "He wants to be happy." I shrugged. "Who can blame him?"

"What does that even mean?"

"It means that he should be able to count on me listening to him, not just the other way around. He said that all I ever did was take, that I never gave anything back."

"I don't follow," Malic told me.

"He wants more."

"More what?"

"Caring. I was dragging all my shit home to him day after day and never letting him vent, never listening for what he needed."

"And so fucking around on you, that was the way to clue you in?"

"He said he tried talking to me and I just never heard him."

"That's bullshit," Marcus growled. "When Joe wants my attention, he makes sure he gets it. And think about that for a minute. Joey is quiet and composed... but if he's unhappy, don't we all know it?"

There was no argument. "He hit me with a book the last time because he thought—just thought, mind you—that I wasn't listening to him."

Marcus smiled. "I always tell him I'm thinking so he doesn't poke me. But the man's blind, so he can't see you and check."

"Blind my ass," I grumbled. Technically Marcus's hearth couldn't see, but he was one of the most perceptive men I knew. Just by things I didn't say, he could assess my mood.

"Yeah." Marcus sighed.

Five, almost six years, and he still got the dopey look on his face whenever he thought about the man he loved. Not that Joseph Locke wasn't in the same boat; theirs was a love I actually still believed in, as I saw it all over both their faces whenever I saw the two men together. And the banter that went back and forth was a treat to hear. I liked walking places with them. I liked to watch them hold hands, see Joe reach for Marcus, not tentatively but knowing full well that his partner would be there. I missed it, the faith and the certainty. It was a blessing to walk through the day knowing that you belonged to someone else. To be let go was something I had never hoped to be.

"I should go home," I told my friends.

"Come with us."

"I'm shitty company," I assured them, "and I'm drunk. I need to go home."

"Hey."

The three of us turned to find Julian Nash leaning on the bar, gifting us with a smile that translated warmth and interest at the same time. The man looked like home, and I wanted one of my own.

"Julian," Marcus greeted him. "How are you?"

"Good," he said as he put a hand on Malic's back.

Most people were not brave enough to touch the man without being asked. He was scary, plain and simple, and just from looking at him, I could tell that Julian was not intimidated in any way.

"What're you guys up to?"

"Just checkin' on drunk as shit here." Malic tipped his head to me, not saying a word about Julian crowding him or touching him.

"Jackson."

My eyes flicked to Julian.

"Me and my buddy Cash are meeting Ry and Cash's wife, Phoebe, here, and then we're all goin' out to dinner. Why don't you come?"

"I—"

"Why don't you all come?"

"No thanks." Marcus smiled, unable not to. "Me and Malic are expected at my place, but I think Jacks going is a great idea."

I shook my head.

"Why not?" Julian pressed me.

"Because Ryan won't like it," I said flatly. He'd much rather spend time with you and your friends than with any of us. He hates us."

"Speak for yourself," Marcus told me.

"Oh c'mon," I groused. "I don't know a man that hates being a warder more than Ry, and because of that, he hates all of us too. You know it and I know it. There's no way he wants any of us around."

Dead silence.

Shit.

I leaned over and buried my face in my arms on top of the bar. I was hoping they'd all just go away.

"Actually," Julian said, his voice low, sensual, as his fingers dug into my shoulders. "You guys are the only family he has, and he kind of likes you."

I was going to argue, but he was kneading my tight muscles with his strong hands, and dear God in heaven, it felt good. I was used to having someone touch me. I had two years of hand-holding and hugging and leaning and quick pecks and wet kisses with tongue to get over. I was used to being loved physically and emotionally, and to go from getting a full-body hug at least once a day to nothing was heartbreaking. No one had touched me since Frank left.

"Ry would love if you had dinner with us."

I was going to start bawling like a baby if I did not get the hell out of there.

"Maybe another time," I said, quickly jerking up, almost knocking over Julian and the barstool as I stood. I shoved my hands down into my pockets. "I gave the bartender my credit card to run a tab," I told Malic. "Close it out for me, okay? And give him a big-ass tip. I'll see ya, guys."

I bolted around Julian, waved to his friend, Cash, who I recognized sitting at the table, grabbed my peacoat off the coat rack at the end of the bar, and was outside seconds later. Unfortunately I plowed right into Ryan Dean.

"What're you doing?" he snapped.

"Nothing, sorry," I growled. "See ya."

But he held on, and even though he was shorter than me by a couple of inches, leaner, less muscular, he was just as strong. So when I went to go, he swung me around to face him.

I stared at him, into his hazel eyes, and watched his brows slowly furrow.

"Don't get your panties in a bunch. I'm fine."

"You're not fine," he ground out, dragging me a few feet away, still under the awning of the bar so we were not standing in the rain. "You're drunk off your ass."

"I can't have dinner," I almost whined, my voice cracking. "Ry, I can't see Marcus and Joe or you and Julian. I just…. It's stupid but—"

"You need to shave this," he told me, changing the subject just like I needed him to. I could have kissed him, I was so grateful. He put his hands on my face. "All this—this isn't you."

I nodded, and his hand slid around the back of my neck as he leaned my head down into his shoulder.

"For fuck's sake, Ry, don't be nice to me."

"No, you're right," he said, shoving me away from him. "That would never do."

I tried to smile, but he was great and didn't stand there and make me. He just pulled the very confused-looking woman with the jade-colored eyes after him into the bar. I flipped up the collar on my peacoat and ran down the street to the next awning and the next until I crossed one street and then another. I saw a pub I liked and headed for it. Halfway there I saw Simon Kim, my friend Leith's hearth, get out of a cab and hurry inside. I would have gone somewhere else, but I was out of options this far downtown. Why was I suddenly awash in hearths?

When I looked back up from the ground toward the front door, I saw another man, and the hair on the back of my neck stood up. Slipping into the doorway of a closed real estate office, I got my phone out and called Marcus.

"Hey, Jacks, did you change your—"

"Didn't you get a restraining order on that guy Eric Donovan so that he had to stay, like, a hundred feet away from Simon at all times?"

"What?"

"Simon. Leith's Simon. How many fuckin' Simons do you know?" I asked irritably.

"No, I—oh, you're somewhere else and—oh. Oh. Yeah."

He had worked it out. "So if I just saw Simon go in a bar, and that guy Eric followed him, then—"

"Then tell me where you are, and me and Malic will be right there."

I told him where I was, flipped my BlackBerry closed, and crossed the street to the pub.

It was noisy inside. The game was on—*Monday Night Football*—and it was hard to get through the crowd. Even though I was not small at six two, two hundred pounds, it was still slow going. Being a warder, I could have plowed through them if I needed to, but there was no emergency. I saw Simon sitting at a small round table toward the back, the pitcher of beer on the table letting me know that he, like Julian, was meeting friends, and I spotted the guy I had tailed at the end of the bar. There was an empty barstool beside him, and I took it.

I lifted my hand to catch the bartender's eye, and he was there immediately, asking what I was having. I ordered a cognac and then leaned sideways and asked Eric Donovan what he was having.

"What?" He was startled when I bumped him and even more alarmed to have not only my attention but the bartender's as well.

"What're you drinking?" The bartender fired the question at him.

"I—I don't—"

"Can't sit at the bar if you're not drinkin'," I told him.

"That's right," the bartender agreed, smirking before turning back to Eric. "So what's it gonna be?"

"Uhm, wine, I guess."

"White wine spritzer?" I teased him.

The bartender snorted out a laugh. "Coming right up."

"No, wait. I—"

"Shut the fuck up," I ordered him under my breath.

His head twisted to me. "What did you just—"

"You're so fuckin' lucky it's me that saw you trailing Simon in here and not Leith," I said, leaning into him.

All the color drained from his face at once. His eyes got huge and round, and his mouth opened, but nothing came out.

"You're not supposed to be here, Mr. Donovan."

"No," he agreed.

I nodded, tipped my head sideways, and studied his face. "Do you want to hurt him?"

"No, I—"

"You just need him to listen to you."

"Yes," he exclaimed.

"Do you have a firearm on you, Mr. Donovan?"

The look I was getting was absolutely broken. I recognized it. I wore it a lot myself.

"Do you want to gimme the gun before Mr. Kim's lawyer, the one I just called, shows up and has you carted off to jail?"

He swallowed hard and nodded.

"Is it in your suit pocket or the pocket of your trench coat?"

"Suit."

"Okay," I soothed him. "Lean into me and drop it into my coat pocket."

"But—"

"This is the last time you're ever gonna see it. Wrap your brain around that."

"It's my father's, not mine."

"Then be prepared to explain things to him."

"I—"

"You're violating your restraining order, Mr. Donovan." I let my voice go cold. "Not to mention that even though Leith Haas is one of the sweetest guys you ever wanna meet, where Simon Kim is concerned, he can be kind of territorial. I heard he can turn into a real caveman."

His eyes, when they flicked to mine, were scared, and he didn't even know the half of it.

Four months ago Leith and Simon had taken an unexpected trip into a hell dimension. By all accounts the siphon world had changed the normally sensitive and articulate warder into a barbarian. The only way Simon had been able to communicate with him at all was because in any form Leith took, Simon was still the heart of a warder, his hearth. Even though they had only been dating for half a year, I saw their bond becoming stronger with each passing day.

"Mr. Donovan?"

He leaned into me, slid the gun into the large pocket on the outside of my peacoat, and stood up, staring down at me. "My father will want his gun back."

"I have no idea what you're talking about, Mr. Donovan," I said evenly, my gaze fastened on his, holding him there.

"Who are you?"

"I'm your guardian angel, obviously."

He took a shaky breath. "I don't know what to do."

"You need to understand that this is your last chance, Mr. Donovan." I sighed, turning to tip my head at the bartender as he deposited my Courvoisier and Eric's lightweight drink on the bar in front of us.

"I would never actually hurt—"

"I'm not a good man," I confessed solemnly, my eyes flicking back to his from my cognac. "Isn't this pretty?"

He nodded.

"I'm gonna drink mine and you drink yours, and we'll go out the back, and no one will know you were here."

He took the glass, and I watched him wrestle with his choice. Stay or go, fight or run, what to do, what to do….

I drained my glass, pulled out my wallet, and lifted my hand for the bartender. He was there fast, and I gave him a twenty and a ten. "Thanks." I smiled.

"Stick around," he told me.

I smiled my appreciation for the flirting, rose, and took Eric Donovan's arm. I saw Marcus and Malic outside and tightened my hand on his bicep. I suddenly wished I hadn't called them because I had no interest in seeing them for the second time that night.

I dragged Eric after me down the short hall, past the bathrooms, and out the back. In the thick air outside, I swung him around hard and slammed him up against the wall.

He clutched at the brick at his back.

I reached into the breast pocket of my peacoat and withdrew my business card. "I am in private security, Mr. Donovan. If your father wants to know where his gun is, he can call me. This is your last warning. If you go near Simon Kim ever again, I will be forced to put you somewhere you won't like."

He stared into my eyes.

"I know you met Leith's friend Malic Sunden, didn't you?"

There was a quick nod.

"And I know you met Leith's lawyer, Marcus Roth."

Yes, he had, and he let me know with another nod.

"I'm different from them." I exhaled, swallowing hard, feeling the anger well up in me. "Marcus is inherently good. So is Malic." I squinted at him. "I used to be good too, but I'm not anymore. I will hurt you, so if nothing else will deter you, if nothing else will scare you, let it be this."

He sucked in his breath when I put the switchblade to his throat a second later.

"I don't care what happens to me." I shivered, feeling how cold I was inside. "Don't make me hurt you, okay? Please."

My voice, my eyes, and the blade, all of it together were too much. I smelled the urine even before I saw it puddling beside his right leg. He was wearing a navy suit. He could walk away, and no one would know.

It took me a second to realize that I had him pinned against the brick wall. I stepped back, careful where I stepped, and he levered off the wall and ran. My phone rang a second later.

"Hey." I coughed, clearing my throat.

"Where the hell are you?" Marcus asked. "I'm here, Malic's here, and Leith just got here to meet Simon. Where the hell are you?"

"Sorry," I told him, starting around the side of the building back toward the sidewalk. "I don't know why I called you; I was out of it. I took care of it already."

"What do you mean?"

"I mean he had a gun on him and I need to get rid of it."

"Oh for crissakes, Jacks, we need to call the—"

"It's done, Marcus. I had no idea I was scarier than Malic, though."

"You have been lately."

I grunted. "I'll see ya later."

"No, wait. Where—"

"Gun. I need to ditch the gun, Marcus."

"Fine."

"I'll talk to you later. Who's patrolling tonight?"

"Leith and Ry."

"Okay," I said and hung up. As I slipped from the side of the building to the sidewalk, I wondered what I was going to do with the gun. If I went over to Rene Favreau's house and shot him and then Frank, everyone would blame Eric Donovan. Or his father. The idea had merit.

II

THE night I had found out that my hearth, the man I loved more than my own life, was sleeping with one of Malic's friends, I had gone home and sat up, waiting. When he came home at three in the morning, he had been startled to find me sitting in the dark in the living room. He flipped on the light, and I squinted, his appearance, not the light, hurting my eyes.

He had gasped. "Jesus Christ, Jackson, you scared the hell out of me."

"Sorry."

"What are you doing here?" He cleared his throat.

"Where else would I be but at home?" I asked, staring at his flushed face, swollen lips, tousled hair, and wrinkled clothes.

"Why are you sitting in the dark?"

What to say.

"I thought you were patrolling tonight."

"I was," I told him. "Downtown, close to Union Square."

He turned from hanging up his topcoat and suit jacket to look at me.

I stared back.

"Okay," he said, laying his gloves and scarf on the back of the couch, lining them up.

"So what are you going to do?"

"Meaning?"

"Meaning"—his voice was so controlled, so steady—"are you going to move out, or should I?"

My life imploded.

I yelled, I screamed, I tore the apartment apart until Frank threatened to walk out if I didn't calm down. When I did, making myself stand by the window and not move, he talked.

He loved me, but he couldn't live with me. I was a selfish bastard and I only cared about him for what he could give to me. I gave nothing in return. I was possessive and jealous and smothering, and how I could live every day in a black-and-white world without any gray, without any room for liking things, not simply loving them or hating them, was too much for him to handle anymore.

He could not be somebody else's everything; he needed a break. I loved too hard; I did everything too damn hard. I needed to throttle back on the passion; I was going to burn out on life if I wasn't careful.

It was exhausting being in a relationship with me where he had to give so much, was expected to be there for me, on for me, all the time. He wanted a friend; he wanted a lover who would cuddle and be gentle, not constantly maul him, manhandle him. Why did he have to be held down or fucked up against the wall in the kitchen? Why couldn't there be dinner and wine and snuggling on the couch? Why was all my communication done through sex? Why couldn't I use my goddamn words once in a while?

He said he needed normal. He told me he was tired of demons and fighting and seeing me come home covered in dirt and bruises. Watching blood run down the drain in the shower was not his idea of fun. It had been thrilling at first, had been a rush to be the man who created a sanctuary for a champion, but now, after two years, now it was too much to ask. He wanted a dog and a house and a yard and kids. He wanted his life to start, and Rene Favreau, with his kind heart and brilliant career, was just the man to give it to him.

I threatened to kill his new lover, and he was terrified enough to call Malic and tell him to protect his friend. And while I was warned not to go near Rene, my fellow warder severed all ties with his friend. I told him later, weeks later, when I could breathe, when I could think, when I could speak again, that he didn't need to lose Rene because of me, but Malic, being Malic, said that no friend of his would ever fuck the mate of another. The hearth of a warder was a sacred thing, and even though Rene did not know the magnitude of his trespass, he would still not be forgiven. He had still screwed someone who he knew belonged to another. Malic had no respect for a man like that.

"Malic should forgive Rene," I had told Ryan when we were patrolling together.

Ryan had turned and looked at me hard. "If it was me, and Julian had slept with Rene, I can't say what I would have done. Your constraint is admirable."

I was stunned because I thought the way I was calling Frank and e-mailing him and stopping by his office verged on psychosis. "I've been stalking him."

"But you haven't killed him or Rene," he said flatly. "Like I said, it's admirable."

I took a shaky breath. "You would never do that, you have too much pride. If Julian ever cheated on you I know that—"

"I don't know what I would do and I prefer not to guess. Let Malic do what he wants."

I never said another word about it.

One night I was standing out in the rain on Rene's balcony, not even realizing that I was soaked to the skin, my shoes filled with water, when Frank came out to see me in galoshes, under an umbrella.

"You're lucky he's not here," he told me.

"He can't hurt me," I told him through chattering teeth. "I'm a goddamn warder. I'll throw him off his own fuckin' balcony."

Frank nodded. "But what are you doing out here? How did you get here without me letting you in? That would be the question."

"Like I give a shit."

"I'm going to call Jael," he told me. "You're jeopardizing the rest of the warders with this behavior. You get that, right?"

I was shivering really hard.

"I'm sorry, Jackson," he told me. "I really am, but I don't love you anymore. I haven't in a really long time and I'm sorry I lied when I said I did. I was just too tired to make a change. Even though it was draining, even though it was like having a second job, I just—I was addicted to the rush of you needing me. I thought if I left you, you would fall apart, and then you'd make a mistake and maybe die. It just…." He exhaled sharply. "It was so stupid."

"No, it's not. I have fallen apart. You are my whole—"

"I'm not! My ego would not let me think that you could live without me, but that is such bullshit! I mean Jackson, c'mon, if you decide to go run in front of a bus, that is not my problem. And I don't want to hurt you, but that's the God's honest truth!"

"Frank, baby…." My voice cracked as I reached for him.

He stepped back, and I saw the disgust all over his face. It ripped through me, tore out my heart, and left me gutted and breathless. That he could look at me like that, like I was a pathetic loser, after looking at me like I was a god so many times before, was crippling.

"Listen to me," he demanded, his voice rising, roaring over the pouring, driving rain. "I can't make you do anything. I can't make you kill yourself or be happy, I can't make you the kind of man I need, and I definitely can't make you do anything that you don't want to do. I don't have that kind of power. You make the choices for you, Jackson, and you have to choose now to leave me the fuck alone, because my life that I shared with you, that I had with you, is over."

Two years gone because he fell out of love.

"I'm sorry I hurt you, and I'm so sorry for how it ended, but I had a chance to be happy and I took it. I wish you all the best, Jackson, but I don't want to see you anymore. I don't want to talk to you or go to bed with you; I just want you to be gone."

I looked at his soft blue eyes, saw the pleading, and finally heard the beseeching words.

"Go away. Please go away."

I shuddered, freezing, in the rain.

"There's nothing here for you anymore."

I turned and ran toward the edge of the balcony. There was no call of caution, no concern at all. If I died, I died. He had moved beyond me. And he said he was a prick because he had stayed with me even as he fell out of love, so that when he left, he didn't give a damn anymore. He didn't crave my touch—he abhorred it. He didn't miss my voice— just the thought grated. He had taken all he could. He was finished with me in every way. I had nothing to give him, and he wanted nothing from me.

As I soared through the downpour, flying from one rooftop to the next, I realized that I had never been so cold. I didn't even hurt anymore; there was only the lingering numbness. The next night I followed him but stayed out of sight. I saw him at dinner with Rene and their friends, his new circle. I watched him laugh and wipe crumbs from his new boyfriend's lips with his thumb, saw him lean in, press a kiss to the side of the man's throat, watched Rene throw an arm around him and tuck him against his side. They were all over each other on the way out of the restaurant. The catcalls and whistles from friends made them smile, and then they fell into a cab and were gone. I stood on a ledge above the building, like some psychotic Batman, and put my head back to howl.

Days passed, weeks, and I realized, finally, that there was nothing left to vent. I was cried out, screamed out, and just plain wrung out. The rage was gone; all that was left was a horrible hole where my heart used to be. I was empty. I felt nothing at all.

I went on patrol, and when I was attacked, I killed. I didn't think anymore, I didn't judge, didn't wonder about the meaning in the act of destruction. I just did it. I had always had an image of myself as a good man, a righteous man, but now I was simply dealing out death because it was my job.

"You're acting like this," Ryan had said as he hosed me off on Malic's back porch, "because there's no one to tell you when the end is."

"What are you talking about?" I asked as I stood there, letting him blast blood and flesh and muscle off my body.

The carnage of the night was all over me, in my hair, on my clothes, and Malic would not let me traipse gore through the home he shared with Dylan. I had to be rinsed off first. It felt like a riot hose had been turned on me.

"Did you hear me?"

"Yeah," I yelled back. "I just don't get what you mean."

He released the sprayer for a second and looked at me. "When I get home after I've been hunting, Julian feeds me or puts me in the shower or fucks me."

"Oh God," I groaned. This was not what I needed to hear.

He sprayed me in the face.

"Fuck, Ry!"

"You have nobody who loves you anymore, you stupid prick. There's nobody at home waiting, and so that's why you're doing what you're doing."

"What am I doing?"

He ignored me. "Think about Malic before Dylan showed up, and think about Malic now—night-and-day difference, right? A warder needs a hearth or their moral compass gets all fucked up, and that's why you're doing this."

"Doing what?" I asked again.

"Trying to get yourself killed!"

"I am not! I'm fine and—"

"You're not fine! You haven't been fine since you caught Frank and Rene together. Do you have any idea what you did tonight, Jacks?"

"I—"

"You leaped into the middle of a nest! Malic and I had to fight our way in there just to reach you!"

"And I was fine."

"You have the same death wish that Malic used to have, but with you it's worse because he was careless but you're suicidal."

"I am not! I—"

He shot me in the face again with the hose.

"Fuck!"

"I know you're not sure if you're a good man anymore, Jacks, because there's nobody you trust anymore to tell you."

And the last guy I had actually trusted to tell me what I was or wasn't had left me with the thought that I was a selfish prick.

"All you can see is the bad right now in everything."

Especially in myself.

"You gotta stop this."

I put my head back, starting to freeze with the water blasting away at me.

"That was insane tonight, Jacks. You just—you killed so many demons, and you were unstoppable, and that scared the fuckin' shit out of me."

I had not meant to scare him. I didn't mean to scare anyone, but it seemed to be all I was doing lately.

"Warder."

I snapped out of my thoughts, having drifted far afield as I strolled, and realized that I had taken a wrong turn and was walking in the Tenderloin district at night, close to Folsom. Not the best neighborhood, not that I was worried. I did have supernatural powers I could use if things got dicey.

"Warder," the voice called again.

Looking around, I saw no one.

"You would make a terrible ninja."

I looked up then and saw him, crouching above me on a window ledge, dark eyes glittering in the moonlight like the predator he was.

"What do you want?"

His smile, the one that showed off his fangs, made my stomach tighten. He was dangerous, and fighting with him, just to see what would happen, was the only thing lately that held any sort of interest for me.

"You wanna play?"

I stopped moving and stared up at him. "What are you wearing?"

It was not, apparently, the question he was expecting. He leaped down, falling the twenty feet to the ground, hitting hard, on stiff legs like I never could. I had to bend at the knee to take the impact.

I rolled my eyes and got a waggle of eyebrows in return.

"You don't like the leather trench?" he asked.

"It's stupid and very Hollywood and makes you look like a douche."

"Huh."

"Just sayin'." I yawned.

He squinted. "I should take fashion advice from a man who doesn't shave and who dresses like an out-of-work house painter."

I shrugged because he was right and turned away from him as it started to drizzle.

"Since when do warders carry guns?" he inquired, catching up with me easily, falling into step beside me.

"How do you know I'm carrying a gun?"

"I can smell the metal."

"Impressive."

"Kyries have good noses."

"I guess," I agreed, hands shoved into my pockets.

"Tell me about the gun."

It didn't matter, so I told him. And it was odd, would have been odd to other people, but I saw the kyrie a lot; our paths crossed constantly now when I was patrolling and he was hunting. We had developed a prickly, cautious ceasefire. Because I really had no interest in killing him anymore, and when we did fight, it was to injure, not kill. We stopped at blood being drawn. I knew the reason, and it was simply that after having my heart wrenched from my chest, not much else mattered. And he was not, contrary to my sentinel's belief, really dangerous. He was not a demon, either. His kind, kyries, had never done anything to me or anyone I knew, and honestly the man, creature, had saved one friend of mine, Malic, and had rescued another friend's hearth, Simon. Trying to separate his head from his body seemed like a big waste of time. Although, if he was going to start dressing like he belonged in *The Matrix*... it might be time to reconsider.

"Stop," he said suddenly.

I stilled and turned my head to see him.

"Aren't you going to attack me?"

"Why?" I asked. "Are you gonna attack me?"

"Perhaps."

I shrugged. "Lemme get rid of this gun first, and then I gotta go home and get my sword, and I'll meet you somewhere if you want and we can go at it."

He frowned. "You don't have a sword on you?"

"You can see I don't," I said irritably. "Can't you smell the metal or lack thereof?"

"That was snide."

I scoffed.

"Why not?"

"Why not what?"

"Why aren't you armed?

"I was drinkin'."

He made a face as my phone rang.

"Hold that thought," I said, darting under some scaffolding to get out of the rain that was coming down a little harder. "Hello."

"Jackson, this is Cal Thompson, how are you?"

Client. "Oh I'm good. Thank you for asking, sir. What can I do for you?"

He cleared his throat. "Jackson, I have a matter, a very personal matter, that I need your help with. I'm in Zurich on business until the end of the month, but I have a situation there in California, down in Malibu, that requires immediate attention."

"Of course, how can I be of help?"

"It must be handled with the utmost discretion."

"Always."

He sighed deeply. "I know, you've never failed me in the past, even with the scandal with Southland and the little misunderstanding there."

Misunderstanding my ass, it was corporate espionage. I had stolen back what had been stolen from him, but two wrongs did not make a right. I was still in deep shit if anyone ever figured out who had broken into a million-dollar facility. The security had been impressive, but I had gifts others didn't have. I didn't tell my sentinel about my nefarious activity. He would not have been pleased. We were always supposed to use our power for good. I didn't always adhere to the warder code of conduct; it just wasn't in me to be good all the time. It was exhausting.

"Jackson." He sighed deeply. "I will pay you double your usual fee as well as all expenses and a bonus commission that you can set yourself if you and your team can be at my son's home in Malibu by tomorrow afternoon."

It was already nine at night, but really, what else did I have to do? "Absolutely," I agreed, watching the kyrie come toward me.

The walk was a strut, fluid, graceful but with obvious confidence. Not the swagger that I had that pissed people off, this came from years of people staring, stepping aside for him, and reaching out to touch him. He was amazing-looking, and he knew it because he didn't have a modest bone in his beautiful, sculpted body.

"I'll be there, sir. E-mail me everything I need, and I'll be in touch in the morning."

"Excellent," he said, and I heard the relief in his voice. "I will be in your debt, Jackson."

"No you won't, 'cause you're gonna pay me." I smiled into my phone.

"I love your honesty." He clipped his words. "It's in rare supply these days."

"Amen to that." I chuckled as I hung up my phone.

Raphael's smoky topaz eyes flicked over me from head to toe, and I found myself caught in his heated gaze.

"So it looks like I can't play," I told him, my breath catching as he stepped closer. I was noticing things about him lately that I had not seen before—the hard, muscular lines of the man, his long aquiline nose, high cheekbones, and thick eyebrows. "Sorry."

"Where are you going?" he asked, lifting his hand, taking hold of the lapel of my peacoat, letting his hand just hang on it.

"I have to go to Malibu."

"That's terrible. What a tragedy for you."

I smirked. "Well, ya know, perils of the job."

He lifted his other hand and slid it around the side of my neck. I closed my eyes under his touch. It had been months since anyone had pressed skin to mine, and I had forgotten how good it felt. Not that my asshat friends didn't touch me, but that was different. This was different.

"I gotta go home," I told him.

"You're trembling," he said, leaning in, and I felt his breath on my collarbone.

"If you just want some blood"—I shivered—"go find a donor."

"I don't want blood," he told me before his mouth opened on the base of my throat.

"Fuck," I groaned, hands fisted on his ridiculous leather trench coat, making sure he couldn't get away.

His tongue swirled over the spot, and even though I decided that I didn't even care if he bit me, he began kissing a trail up the side of my neck to my jaw.

I let my head fall back against the hard brick wall and felt his knee wedge between my legs before his thigh was shoved into my groin. I hissed in agony.

"You're like a bow that's been drawn too tight and left," he whispered, kissing along the line of my jaw to my chin and up.

I leaned forward at the same time he drew back. Our eyes locked together, and I saw the heavy-lidded hunger, the dilated pupils, and then the man behind him.

"Shit," I yelled, hurling him off me, sideways, slamming him into the wall as a knife was buried in my side.

It was like a burning razor was driven into my flesh. I yelled as the man yanked it out of me and drove forward again. Raphael grabbed him, yelling in Spanish. I could tell the language—I had a working understanding of it—but the words tumbled out too fast, too clipped and guttural for me to catch them.

I saw the shadow to my left and pitched sideways before the man who swung at me with his katana could complete his killing stroke. Stretching out, lengthening my body even though it hurt like hell, I used both hands and caught his wrist, wrenching the sword free, holding it tight as I turned and waited for his next attack.

His jaw looked like it unhinged, his mouth opening to grotesque proportion, filled with hundreds of needle-like teeth. He snarled and lunged. I was concentrating so hard on him that I missed the creature behind me. Claws drove deep into my right shoulder at the same time the demon in front of me charged. I slammed my body as hard as I could back against the creature, ramming him into the side of the building. Pinned there, he released his hold so I could whip the katana up and then down, beheading the demon with a wide slicing arch. The hole in the sidewalk was instant, sucking him through a black-hole vortex so fast that I had to throw myself forward or be devoured by the darkness as well. Whirling around, I faced the demon that had taken half my shoulder with him.

"Warder," he gasped, shivering, horror all over his face.

I was startled. He hadn't been after me?

Head back, his body went dim and was gone, dematerializing right in front of me.

He had not been there for me.

"You fuck!"

I looked up and saw Raphael with his hand on the chest of the demon who had driven a long serrated knife into my side. He was shoving the blade into the throat of the creature inch by inch, strong enough to drive it through muscle and bone and into the brick-and-mortar wall behind him. The demon was hanging there, twitching for a moment, black blood pumping out of the wound before his head fell sideways, dead.

It was gruesome, not the death a warder dealt, not clean and tidy and fluid-free. I felt the bile rise in my throat before I went to my knees, clutching at my side. I saw blood seeping through my fingers as I tried to breathe.

Raphael rushed across the space separating us, skidding to a halt and dropping down beside me. I felt his hands on me, one on my back, the other on my chest.

"You should go," I told him, freezing suddenly, beginning to shake. "I have to call somebody, and I'm gonna hafta take a trip to see my sentinel. You don't wanna be here when another warder shows up."

The muscles in his jaw clenched. "I want to stay."

I reached into the pocket of my peacoat. "Do me a favor—hold onto this gun for me. I might need it down the road if that guy ever goes after Simon again, so if you could just put it somewhere that you could put your hands on it, I'd be appreciative."

He made a sound in the back of his throat as he took the weapon from me. "I can heal you if you let me, and then you don't have to see your sentinel."

The thought was appealing. "But I have to be in Malibu tomorrow. If you fix me up, can I do that?"

His brows furrowed, and he shook his head fast.

"See, I gotta be good by the morning." I forced a smile, closing my eyes for a second, letting the need flow through me and out, releasing the call for aid. "Okay"—I opened my eyes—"now you really have to get outta here. Whoever shows won't understand me bleeding and you here with a dripping knife."

"I fear no warder."

I was going to speak, but my body shuddered with the answering call of a fellow warder. It rolled through me, warm, comforting... Ryan.

"Go already," I ordered him.

"I told you." His voice cracked. "I fear no warder."

"But Ry's coming, and you really should be afraid of him," I said. "'Cause even though Marcus and Malic are bigger and Leith's smarter and I'm meaner"—I grinned—"he's the fastest. Ryan's a killing machine, and he's usually logical, but he's not gonna really see all this. He's only gonna see me."

"I too only see you."

It was crap, but it was flattering crap. "Go away."

"You don't want me hurt."

"Not today," I told him. "And get rid of your mess."

Clearly he did not want to go.

"Please."

He rose, and I put my head back and waited for Ryan Dean.

"I will see you soon, warder," I heard Raphael say.

But I would be gone in the morning. When was he planning to visit?

III

THE house was huge. As I sat beside Cielo Jones in the rented silver Lexus, I tried to find a position in the seat that would not put any pressure on my right side. It hurt every time I moved, and when I winced, my friend and business partner noticed.

"You should have stayed home."

"I'm fine," I lied for the tenth time in the last half an hour.

"You're not," he told me, guiding the car down the long paved drive toward the front door. "And this is some place."

It was. The house looked like a huge beach cabana complete with an enormous entryway, fans that ran the length of the wooden porch, and double French doors. Once we were out of the car and on the front steps, I found the panel beside the front door, punched in the code—my employer's late wife's birthday—and gave Cielo a nod. He used the keys that had arrived from private courier at the airport before we left San Francisco and opened the front door. The smell of marijuana hit me even from where I was.

"Shit.'" Cielo chuckled, waving his hand in front of his face. "Even I like to indulge on occasion, but, Christ."

I turned and looked over my shoulder at the six other men walking up the stairs behind Cielo. The looks on their faces, between annoyed and amused, made me shrug.

"For fuck's sake, Jacks." One of them, a man who had been with me for over three years, Miguel Andrade, shot me a look.

"What?"

Cielo moved to walk inside, but Miguel took hold of his shoulder, stopping him.

"Me first," he grumbled, brushing his suit jacket back to reveal his holstered Glock as he walked into the house.

The others followed behind him, with Cielo and finally me bringing up the rear.

It looked like a Roman orgy in the house. There were people everywhere in various stages of undress, the house itself looked like the morning after a raging frat party, and it smelled like pot and puke and piss and beer.

"Are you kidding?" Miguel snapped. "This is cleanup, Jacks; you didn't need muscle. You needed Chase and Brooke."

I usually brought Chase Holmes and Brooke Canellas and their teams when it was more of an intervention than security, but it was at that moment that a big muscular guy in boxers came charging down the staircase from the second floor. He had a gun in his hand.

"See," I told Miguel, gesturing at the gunman.

Six guns were drawn fast and pointed at the man with shouts to put the gun down and get on the goddamn ground. I had never seen a big macho guy come so unglued and move so fast. I thought he was going to pee his pants.

It was chaos after that as Miguel secured the guy, handcuffing him, and the rest of the team, three upstairs and two downstairs, started sweeping the house. Normally I would have gone, but I hurt, so I went out onto the vast patio and waited.

Cielo joined me minutes later, sitting down across the table from me, opening up his laptop and turning the Cincinnati Reds baseball cap around on his head, the bill backward as he began tapping away.

"You should have stayed home," he said without looking up.

"It's my company. Mr. Thompson called me."

"It's my company too. Just because you own 51 percent and I own 49 percent doesn't mean that me being here wouldn't be enough."

"He called me," I said again, rubbing the bridge of my nose. "And it's my responsibility. Shut up already."

"That's mature."

"Please shut up."

"Asshole," he barked, and I was surprised enough at his outburst to look up at him from the screen of my phone. "Without you, none of us have anything. You're it. You're the company. Please do not fuck around with your life."

"I'm not gonna die." I scowled.

"Or mine."

"I'm fine," I insisted, wanting him to actually believe me.

"But you did need stitches," Miguel said from behind me, shoving two men out onto the patio and down into chairs. "So just take it easy."

"I am," I told him, motioning at the two. "I let you do all the heavy lifting today."

He grunted and walked back toward the house. "I'm gonna clear everyone out. If you hear yelling, just never mind."

"Do I ever question you?" I called over to him.

I heard him make a noise before I turned my head to look at the two men sitting beside me. I lifted my sunglasses and looked at them both. "Good afternoon."

"Who the fuck are you guys?" The taller of the two men yelled, ready to lift up out of the Adirondack chair he had been shoved down into.

"Just calm down," I told him. "We work for Calvin Thompson." My eyes flicked over to the heavyset man beside him. "Your father."

The young man gasped. "We called the police."

"And they're not coming," I informed him. "We were there already this morning, giving them our credentials and contact information. Both the sheriff's department and your local police department as well as your private security company know we're here."

"Who are you?" the other man shouted.

"Do not yell at us," Cielo warned him, looking at both men, tearing his eyes away from the screen of his laptop. "We work for his father"—he pointed at Hayden Thompson—"and we're here to shut down Xanadu and rein in all this ridiculous spending."

Both men stared.

"I'm Cielo Jones, and this is my partner, Jackson Tybalt. Our company, Guardian Limited, provides security, accounting, and basic intervention and lockdown services to high-end clients. Your father, Calvin Thompson, has given us all access to your accounts, your home, and your list of employees."

He just stared at Cielo.

"How can he do that?" the other man asked.

"Because he foots the bill for the lap of luxury," Cielo informed him. "And as of an hour ago, all of your assets are frozen, Mr. Thompson. Your credit cards, every check you've written, absolutely everything is being scrutinized by our accounting team. A report will then be compiled and sent to your father's accountant, and at that time we will inform you as to what accounts will be terminated and which will be continued."

"Wait," he said, leaning forward, hands on the table. "I have people who work for me on vacation with their families who—"

"Mr. Campbell, your groundskeeper." Cielo cut him off. "We know about him. Of the people who work for you, as far as I can tell, he's the only one who actually does work. His trip to Disneyland with his family is the only secured payment that we approved."

Hayden was stunned; it was all over his face. "But Javier...." He turned and looked at the gorgeous man sitting beside him. The guy looked like a model, all smooth caramel skin and big brown eyes. "He has school and a club membership and—"

"It's called getting a job," I growled before turning on Javier de Souza. "Your tuition is paid for this semester, and that's it. Your expense account, your club membership—"

"Clothes allowance," Cielo offered.

"Clothes allowance," I echoed, "all of that is gone. You wanna continue to live here, fine. We don't get to say who stays and who goes, but to stay here, you have to submit to a drug test that includes hair and blood, and an extensive background check. If you wish to operate a vehicle owned by Mr. Thompson, you need to submit a driving record to us, an abstract, with proof of insurance. Once we leave, there will be an onsite handler in charge of security and all house and personal accounts who you will be able to obtain all your clearances from."

"He can't do this." Hayden gasped, looking at me. "My father can't just get rid of all my friends and—"

"I'm out of here," Javier announced, getting up and walking around the table.

"Wait," Hayden called, getting up, running after him.

We heard the begging, the cajoling, and the apologizing. I winced when Javier told him that the only thing he cared about was the money. It was the only thing that had made sleeping with a fat fuck bearable.

"Ouch." Cielo sighed, going back to what he was doing, closing more accounts, sending e-mails, basically turning off Hayden Thompson's life as he knew it. "I guess you shouldn't just live off Daddy."

"Nope," I agreed, sighing heavily, getting up and walking to the edge of the patio that looked out onto the Pacific Ocean. "God, it's pretty here."

"You didn't tell me."

"I didn't tell you what?" I asked, looking up and down the beach, waving at some women who were jogging by. Four sets of hands waved back, all tanned, blonde Barbie beautiful.

"You didn't tell me how you got hurt."

I turned around, putting my glasses back down over my eyes to regard my friend. "What do you want to know?"

"I want to know if the demon that stabbed you is the same one who cut clean through your shoulder."

"How did you know I was hurt?"

"I saw you in your office before we left this morning."

I grinned. "Why were you skulking around? Are you trying to catch me naked?"

He stared. "If we could be serious for, like, half a second, that'd be great."

I groaned and started to turn around.

"Jackson!"

I had no choice but to look at him.

"I know all about you, asshole, so tell me what the fuck."

So I told him about the kyrie and the demons and how pissed Ryan had been at me and how worried Jael had been and how I ended up going home alone to an empty house.

He sighed heavily. "I know you've been a basket case since Frank left but—"

"I don't wanna talk about that."

We stared at each other.

"Listen," he finally said. "You're in pain, I know that. But please do not have a death wish because you're inconsolable. I need you."

"Yeah, I know." I sighed, turning back to face the beach. "It smells good here, huh?"

"It smells like the ocean," he grumbled. "And I hate it."

"You're just bein' a dick."

"I need you alive and well, and I know that Frank tore your heart out, but—"

"Just let it go." I cut him off.

He was quiet, and after a few minutes, I relaxed when I realized he was actually going to do what I asked and drop it.

"You think that if you submerge yourself in violence that you'll stop hurting."

I rolled my eyes but didn't say anything.

"Frank's an idiot."

"Frank needed more."

"You would have turned yourself inside out to be whatever he wanted," he told me. "We both know that."

I couldn't argue, because it was the truth. Two years with Frank Sullivan and three months without him had told me, if I didn't know already, what I would have done.

"Just be careful. It's not just you."

And I knew that.

"Jackson."

I looked over my shoulder and saw Owen, another of my team, giving me a very pained look. "What?"

"He's crying."

I squinted at him. "I'm sorry?"

"The kid, the son, he's upstairs locked in his bathroom, and he's crying. Do you want us in there? Do you want the door down?"

"Yeah, I dunno what he's got in there."

"Will do." He began to turn away.

"Is the house cleared?"

"Yep, all clear."

"Great."

He left, and I was alone again with my partner.

"Did you hear me?"

And he meant from earlier.

"How could I not?"

"Okay."

Finally we were done.

"HEY."

Hours later I turned from the enormous television screen to look at Hayden as he walked into the living room. "Hi," I greeted him.

He rubbed his tousled curls and flopped down on the other end of the couch, away from me. "Where is everyone?"

"All gone except me." I sighed, realizing how tired I was. "And the security guards outside, of course."

"Why do I need security guards?"

"Because we're on lockdown here," I told him.

"I gave a ton of people the security code for my house, you know."

"It doesn't matter. We changed everything today."

"You sure as hell did."

I shrugged. "I can't be sorry about that. This is my job, not to mention you needed this bad. I have never seen someone with more people taking advantage of him. Your life should serve as a warning to others of what not to do."

"Gee, thanks."

"You're welcome."

"Have people been trying to get in?"

"Yep."

"Shit," he groaned. "All my friends are gonna be so pissed."

"As far as I can tell, you don't have any friends besides Maria Santos and some guy named Christian."

"Christian," he breathed out. "God, I haven't seen him in months."

I shrugged. "Well, so far, like I said, only he and Maria check out."

"God, they both probably hate me."

"Nope," I told him. "Cielo talked to Maria, and I talked Christian. They would both love to see you. Maria wants you to come back to school, and Christian says that you're welcome to come by the hospital and see him whenever you like."

"He's doing his residency. He's gonna be a pediatrician."

"So he said."

He shook his head. "I'm so stupid."

"You're young; you're supposed to be stupid."

"Oh yeah?"

"Well, to an extent." I chuckled. "But your quota for dumb-ass has been met. You're not allowed to be taken advantage of again. We're basically going to monitor you from now on. I'll see you once a month, Cielo will talk to you every week, and the security company will monitor your home starting from now. You can go wherever you want, of course, but all your credit cards have been suspended except the one for approved transactions."

"I could just get a job, and then I wouldn't be dependent on my father's money."

"And if you have to work, then we won't worry about what you're doing when you're not," I explained. "You get it, right?"

"Yeah, shit. It all makes sense."

"I mean, your father knows that he basically put you here by enabling this lifestyle, but now that he sees what you're doing with your wealth and privilege, he's gonna make you live how he wants or he's gonna make you want to have your own life by getting a job. Either choice you make, toe the line or strike out on your own and build from the ground up, he's happy."

"Fuck."

"What're you gonna do?"

"For now, until I decide what I want to do, I'm going to live here under lock and key."

"It's not like that. You get everything back tomorrow. There are just stipulations now. There are no more big wads of cash going out; there are limits on everything. You have a budget that you'll have to stick to, and if you go over it, then you have to call your accountant, who is now Cielo, and explain what you need and why."

"That black guy that was with you?"

"Just guy would suffice," I told him.

"Shit, I didn't mean—"

"It's fine."

"Christ."

"It sucks, but you made your bed. Lie in it."

"You're all heart."

"Poor little rich boy, you're breakin' my heart."

His eyes flicked to mine, and I saw the hatred there for a second. "How long was I sleeping?"

I checked my dive watch. "About nine hours."

"Holy shit." He gasped, eyes wide.

"I'm thinking you needed the rest."

He sighed deeply. "God, I don't even know what I need."

I smiled. "I think you need to take a vacation from your life here and figure out what the hell you want to do with it."

The hatred I saw had been replaced by weariness. He looked wrung out. The dark circles under his eyes, how bloodshot they were, his cracked lips, the stubble, all of it spoke of a man who was drained dry.

"Listen, I am sorry for the all-or-nothing approach that had to be taken here, but you were this close to overdosing on drugs, going to jail, or just turning up dead. You don't see it, don't get it, but I swear it's true."

His wounded eyes surveyed me. "You know, you don't look so great yourself."

"I was in a knife fight yesterday. I have an excuse."

"No shit." He perked up a little, probably wishing I had died.

"No shit."

He was silent for a few minutes. "Did my father tell you I was gay?"

"Yes, he did."

"Javier was supposed to be my boyfriend."

"I figured."

"You don't care?"

"Since I'm gay too, not so much," I told him.

His smile came slowly until I saw the first signs of life.

"I really did have a lot of deadweight in my life, huh?" he offered as a peace offering.

I arched an eyebrow for him.

His head fell back, and laughter bubbled up out of him. If he could laugh at himself, at the mess he'd made, he was going to be okay.

When the mirth had run out of him, after the tears were shed, the heavy sigh exhaled from deep down, he looked over at me.

"If I get your old man on the phone, will you talk to him?"

He nodded.

"You gotta know that this is love and not control."

"It feels like control," he told me.

We sat there together on his leather couch in the great room surrounded by opulence, and I understood that for all of it, for all the possessions, he had nothing without his family.

"It's love," I assured him.

"Are you sure?"

"I am. Your father wants to give you everything, and he almost gave you too much."

"I just want someone to love."

"Join the club," I told him.

IV

I STAYED three days, hired Hayden all new staff as well as a personal assistant and a personal trainer and a live-in maid. He looked different when I left than when I had arrived, and when I got back home to my office, Cielo informed me that the commission on the job put us squarely in the black. He had paid all our bills, the mortgage on the office, all salaries and bonuses, and even had money left over to get new software he'd had his eye on and more gadgets for surveillance. I had another new phone, and so did everyone else. Miguel held it up for me to see while Cielo gushed.

"Just because technology gives him a hard-on, do we all have to get excited?" Miguel groused.

I went back to answering e-mails and was still at it when Leith Haas came through the door at quarter to six that evening.

"What the fuck did you do?"

"About what?" I asked, looking up, leaning back in my chair.

He rushed across the room to stand in front of my desk. "Marcus says that you talked to Eric Donovan a week ago. He followed Simon."

"Yes."

"And you didn't think I should know that my boyfriend was still being stalked by a psychopath?"

"No."

"No?" he barked.

"No, I handled it, it's handled, case closed."

He stared at me with dark aqua eyes, deciding, and I held the gaze intently. After several minutes he took a breath.

"I know you wouldn't let anything happen to Simon."

"No, I wouldn't," I agreed. "I know what he means to you."

He nodded. "Do you know where Eric Donovan is now?"

"Yes."

"You do?" He was startled.

"Yes, I do. I'm in security and surveillance. I know where everyone is that I keep tabs on."

"Oh."

I rolled my eyes and got up from my chair and walked to the window that was getting pelted hard with rain. "He moved to Boston."

"Boston?"

"Yes. He's getting married and going to work for his fiancée's father. I don't expect him back."

"How can he get married if he's gay?"

"You can get married to a man in Massachusetts."

"You know what I mean! He's not marrying a man, is he?"

"No."

"Then?"

I turned to look. "Why are you asking me? You wanted to know where he is—that's where he is. Beyond that, I have no idea and I could give a shit."

He just shook his head.

"What are you going to get Simon for Christmas?"

Several seconds ticked by.

"What?" he asked finally.

"It's coming up, Christmas, I mean. What's your plan?"

"Oh."

"No idea, huh?"

"No."

I went back to watching the rain.

"Ryan said you were hurt before you went to LA."

"I went to Malibu, but yeah."

"And you're okay now?"

"Yeah, why?"

"Well, Marcus has some kind of fancy dinner he's supposed to go to tomorrow, tuxedos and everything, and he wanted to take Joe and go, but if—"

"That's fine. I can patrol with you."

"Are you sure?"

"Absolutely."

"Okay. I'll meet you down by the Federal Building after nine, then."

"After nine tomorrow. Got it."

He was at the door when he called out, "You're a good friend, Jacks."

At least I was something. "Thanks."

When he was gone, I went back to watching the dark-gray day turn into a black, starless night.

I decided to grab something before I headed for home because I knew there was nothing to eat, my fridge and cupboards were bare, and I didn't feel like stopping and buying groceries and then cooking. Doing all that prep for one person was just too much. So I ran through the rain and ducked into my favorite delicatessen after work to grab a sandwich. I was headed for the salad bar when I came around the corner and found myself suddenly face to face with Rene Favreau.

I froze.

He caught his breath.

We must have looked really stupid.

What was the appropriate thing to say?

Gray eyes locked on my face. "Jackson."

I exhaled fast and went to move around him.

"Wait."

I stopped, and he stepped back in front of me. It was only then that I saw the cut lip, black eye, and bruised cheek. "What happened?"

He cleared his throat. "Frank."

I scoffed before I could stifle it. There was no way.

He took a breath and slipped by me. I was going to go after him, but it hit me that it was truly none of my business. I had no more say in Frank Sullivan's life, and he had made his position on me being in his very clear the last time we had seen each other. It was strange that just the mention of the man's name had not put my heart in a vise. Maybe, just maybe, after three months, closer to four, I was finally starting to see my way clear. I hoped so.

The salad bar was calling, and as I picked what I wanted, I saw a woman eyeing the beets disdainfully. When she looked up, she caught me staring.

"I don't eat those," I told her.

She bit her bottom lip as she smoothed a hand over her very pregnant stomach. "I'm supposed to be eating light, but all I want is steak all the time."

I scowled at her, and she laughed.

"Just looking at all this salad makes me wanna hurl, but the beets are especially heinous."

"I agree"—I grinned at her—"about the beets."

"Beets taste like dirt," she told me.

"I'm sure the American Beet Growers would disagree."

She laughed and then tipped her head, studying my face. "I think I know you."

"Nice pickup line."

"I'm pregnant. Who am I gonna pick up?"

"Maybe I'm into that."

She rolled her eyes, lifting her hand so I could see the rock on her finger. "There's this too."

"That doesn't stop some people."

"Agreed"—she sighed—"but I'm still in love with the big dumb jerk."

Enjoying her phrasing, the banter, and her lovely voice, I let some of the tension drain out of me from seeing Rene.

"So…." She chuckled, and it had a nice sound, full and deep. "Who do we both know?"

I shrugged.

"Do you have kids in elementary school?"

"No kids."

"Not yet," she clarified.

"Do I look like I could be some kid's dad?" I scoffed at her.

"Yeah"—she nodded—"you've got the look."

And that was the most astounding thing anyone had ever said to me, that I looked parental. "Do I?"

"Yes."

Her tone, the look in her gorgeous jade-colored eyes, the laugh lines around them, her dimples, her high cheekbones—she was just radiant. "I think maybe you should come home with me anyway, married or not."

"That'd be a neat trick. Aren't all you guys gay?"

"All of what guys?"

"All you warders."

It was like she hit me—all the air slammed out of my lungs.

Her smile was huge. "You're one of Ryan's friends."

"Oh." I nodded, taking a settling breath, getting my bearings, remembering where I had seen her before—in Ryan Dean's living room. "You belong to Julian, who now belongs to Ryan."

"Yes." She beamed, walking around the salad bar to reach me. I was surprised. I thought she would stop, but she kept coming, right up to me, lifting up, reaching. "I'm Phoebe Vega, Cash's wife."

I bent so she could bring me down to her with an arm around my neck, plant a kiss on my cheek, give me a quick hug before she pulled back. It was nice. No one ever hugged me anymore, and I missed it like crazy.

"I—"

"Jackson."

We both turned, and there, no more than three feet from me, was Rene Favreau. Apparently he had not left after all. But why he was standing there looking like he was ready to start bawling was beyond me.

"What's with—"

"I need to talk to you."

"I don't have time to—"

"I need you to make time."

Shit.

"You're the only one I can talk to, and I know it—"

"Stop," I ordered him. "I'll meet you outside."

"Are you okay?" Phoebe asked gently.

He moved fast up beside her, and because he was acting so weird, I reached for the bright, bubbly woman I had sort of fallen in love with and drew her protectively to my side.

"Come now," he ordered, but it sounded more like a plea.

"I'll be right behind you."

He looked at Phoebe, looked her up and down, sizing her up, before he turned fast and walked away.

"What was that about?" She sounded worried.

"Nothing," I soothed her, passing her my sandwich. "Eat this instead; you'll love it. I swear. Get a salad and split it with your husband."

She opened her mouth to say something.

"It's okay," I promised, kissing her forehead before I whipped around her and headed for the door.

Outside, I saw Rene halfway down the street, standing in the rain holding open the door of a cab. I moved quickly along the sidewalk and reached him fast.

"You first," he said, his voice flat.

I slipped into the backseat, and then he was in behind me, barking directions to the driver and falling back with a deep release of breath.

"Tell me what's wrong," I said after we had gone several rainy blocks in silence.

"He's lost his mind."

I crossed my arms and waited.

He reached out to touch me but stopped himself and let his hand fall back down to his side. "He gets up in the middle of the night, and when I follow him, he's attacking people and grabbing them, and he used to just scare them, but now he's attacking them and—"

"Wait." I stopped his rambling explanation. "Frank is attacking people on the street? This is what you're telling me."

"Yeah, and the other night when I tried to stop him from going out we actually started fighting and—look at my face."

I had already noted the damage earlier.

He raked his fingers through his hair. "I don't expect you to believe me, but yesterday he finally came out and told me that he wants me to hunt demons with him."

Fuck.

"Demons, Jackson," he breathed out. "Holy shit. He's lost his mind."

In a sense. Hunting demons, for him, was insane. The demons themselves....

"I told him I wanted him to see someone, and he just started talking to me about warders and demons and hearths and...." He rubbed the bridge of his nose. "I don't know what I'm supposed to do."

I cleared my throat. "Have you talked to his family?"

"I don't know his family!" He blew up. "I barely know him, and now"—his head snapped up, and his eyes met mine—"I have no idea what to do!"

But I did. "Okay."

"Okay?" He was stunned. It was written all over his face. "This is all you have to say?"

"Until I see him, yeah. That's all I fuckin' have to say."

His eyes were locked on mine.

I turned to look out at the smeared world rushing by the window.

"Jackson."

I didn't turn.

"I'm sorry."

There was no answer I could be expected to give him.

RENE had to slide a key card into a slot in the elevator to get to the penthouse. Other people got on, and I was apparently of interest. I was silent as I shed my trench coat and scarf, raked my fingers through my hair, and took off my tie. I watched the numbers light up one after another and gave nothing else my attention.

"I never realized how intimidating you are."

"Compared to Malic, I'm a fuckin' Boy Scout," I said, stepping off the elevator when it stopped, the doors opening up into a living room. Amazing the nice digs money could buy.

The room was warm, and instantly I felt a twinge of loss for the home that Frank Sullivan could create. Fire blazing away, the muted Beethoven I could hear, the dinner I could smell, pot roast, maybe, and the touches everywhere that told me that Rene Favreau did not live alone. There were roses in a vase, the table was set for two, and the wine had been poured.

"Frankie!" Rene called out.

I swallowed down my heart and stood there and waited.

"I made Swiss steak and—Jackson."

If I could just keep breathing, I would really have something.

He came into the room dressed in black jeans and a pale gray Henley. He was barefoot, which I found odd in the middle of winter, but it was warm, so maybe it was fine.

"Can I talk to you a minute?" I asked gently.

His eyes were all over me, and I was uncomfortable for Rene for no reason that made any sense. Why did I care if my ex was checking me out in front of his current boyfriend?

"Please."

He looked over at Rene. "Why don't you go change out of your wet clothes?"

"I—"

"Please," Frank asked breathlessly. "I need a moment alone with him."

Rene looked at him a long minute and then turned to me. I could tell that for the life of him he had no idea what was the right thing to do.

"Five minutes," I told Rene. "That's all."

He was upset, and it took a lot out of him, but he left the room and us.

As soon as he was out of earshot—it was a massive space, so he had a way to go to actually exit the room—Frank turned his curious gaze to me. "What are you doing here?"

"I hear you're hunting demons," I replied softly.

His lips parted, and that tender mouth of his that had once kissed me so sweetly now hung open in surprise.

"Dangerous business, that."

He just stared.

"And you said you hated everything about it."

"I just want to help," he told me, coming out of his momentary trance, putting his wineglass down on the table behind the couch.

"You miss the thrill of it, hearing about it, knowing it was real."

"I felt important."

He had been the most important thing in my life.

"I mean"—he took a step closer—"because I was there, you could do what you needed to do. I made a difference because you did."

I nodded.

"And it's the best secret ever."

"Sure."

"I figured out how I can help, and I have been."

"But why would you want to?"

"Jackson, I—"

"Why not just forget all about it?" I felt my anger rising, but I was powerless to stop it.

"I can't."

"You told me you hated that I was a warder and you hated being the hearth of a warder."

He pressed his lips together tight.

"Maybe it was just me you didn't like." I calmed, the truth, finally, rolling through me. It was useless to get mad; it was over and done with.

He sucked in a breath. "I just want to help, like I said."

"By hurting them, the demons you come across."

"Yes."

"And you can tell because when you touch someone and it hurts, you know they're a demon."

He nodded.

"But it's fading already," I told him, because I knew. "You're not hurting them anymore."

His eyes, those soft doe eyes of his, got huge and round. "Yes. Why?"

"Why what?"

"I—my touch used to burn them and I could tell, just like you, said who was a demon and who wasn't, but it doesn't work anymore."

"Of course not."

"But why?" He closed in on me.

"You're no longer the hearth of a warder."

It was obvious from the look on his face that he had never once considered any of what I was telling him.

"Your house isn't sealed, Frank. You need to be careful that nothing follows you home."

His eyes filled with realization that turned quickly to fear.

I shrugged. "But why would it? You're just a man. And if anything ever scares you, you can call me, all right?"

His eyes narrowed as he stepped closer to me, but when he lifted his hand toward me, I moved back beyond his reach.

"Since when?"

"Since when what?"

His eyebrows lifted. "I don't get to touch you anymore?"

"Why would you want to?"

He seemed to consider that. "I thought that Rene being sweet and gentle at first would give way to heat and power and dominance," he told me slowly, confessing, moving until he was standing in front of me, in my space, staring up into my eyes. "It didn't."

"Sweetheart of a guy all the way through, huh." I smirked. "Too bad for you, since you like to be fucked up against walls."

His jaw clenched as he shivered.

"No, wait, that's not you anymore, is it?"

"I told you it wasn't all I wanted. I never said I didn't want it at all."

Apparently he had gone from me manhandling him all the time to none at all from Rene. He wanted his sex life somewhere in between.

"You do a lot of your communicating through sex."

He had never complained until the end. Or maybe I had just never heard him. Whatever the case, it was done. Rehashing was useless.

"You have nothing to say?"

"Make Rene use all your toys on you. That'll help."

Brows furrowed, and he could no longer keep my gaze. While I had never enjoyed the role-playing that Frank did, had not liked using his assortment of whips, clamps, and various restraints, I had done as he asked because it did it for him. The part I had loved was seeing all his barriers come down and having him come apart in my hands. His gratitude, that I would put aside my own discomfort for him, had been touching to see. I thought that my actions had spoken my love for him, but it turned out that he wanted words… and a penthouse view.

"So," I said, stepping back, realizing that his scent had changed from when he used to sleep curled into my side. He didn't smell like me anymore underneath everything else. I used to be able to press my nose in his hair and inhale our bed, our sheets, and my life. "No more demon hunting, because any second now, you're gonna get your head torn off."

"Jackson," he said under his breath.

"Think of it as no longer having armor."

"Jacks."

But he didn't want me. It was the high of the hunt he was in thrall to. He was an adrenaline junkie looking for a danger fix, and I had no idea when that had happened. "You're on the outside looking in now. Embrace this instead." I gestured around. "I would."

"I miss you," he said.

It was a lie. There was no way he missed his life with me, which was small compared to the jet-setting, high-class dream he had going with Rene. "Stop what you're doing, forget what you know, and buy a yacht or something."

He stared at me as I started to go.

"Jackson," he called softly, seductively, just the way he used to.

I didn't stop. I walked back to the elevator instead. When I hit the button, the doors whooshed open at the same time I heard Rene call my name. I turned to face out, and he was there, holding the doors open so I couldn't escape.

"He's fine now," I told him. "It's all done. Ask him."

He looked over his shoulder at Frank. "Tell me what's going on?"

"Everything's fine." Frank forced a smile. "I'm sorry for scaring you."

Rene was nonplussed, I could tell, at a complete loss to understand what was going on around him. And who could blame him? "One visit from your ex, and you're all fine?"

"I just needed some resolution," Frank lied, eyes flicking to mine.

I met them for seconds, wasn't sure what I saw—desire, hatred, hard to tell all of a sudden. I couldn't read him anymore because I no longer knew him.

"Jackson."

I looked at Rene, and there was pain all over his face.

"Don't think too hard about it," I cautioned him. "Move your hand."

But he didn't. He slipped into the elevator beside me instead.

"Wait," Frank yelled as the doors shut.

I didn't move, didn't speak, and was, in fact, doing a great impression of a statue.

"Please talk to me."

"He'll be fine."

"Look at me."

After a minute, I did.

"Was he always like this?"

"Like what?"

"Manic. He has such highs and such lows…. I had no idea."

"He's not manic. He's not schizophrenic. He's not anything but him," I promised. "My guess would be that he got overly tired, that ending things with me and starting them with you took more of an emotional toll than he was willing to admit. I think he just needed to see me and have his moment of closure."

It was a really good story. I was kind of proud of myself.

"I would have thought you would have had closure when you begged him over and over to take you back. When you stalked him and—"

"Closure for him." I cut him off. "I know what I did, and I know why he left, and I'm smart enough to know that he wants you and not me."

"But being with you was more exciting than being with me. You, your business, your world is much more prone to life and death than mine."

He had no idea.

"I think he misses hearing about the excitement, all your near misses."

The man was more perceptive than I gave him credit for, and I realized that in another life, where he had not stolen the man I loved from me, we could have been friends.

"Shit," I groaned.

"What?"

The truth was that Frank had wanted to go. It took two. Rene had stolen nothing from me. Frank had run away.

"I think he misses his life with you."

"He doesn't," I said, putting on my jacket and trench coat, wrapping the scarf around my neck. "And when he's in Paris with you, you'll both forget that any of this ever happened."

"How did you know we were going to Paris?"

One of the main things that Frank had thrown up in my face was that Rene was going to show him the world that I never could. So it made sense that when the globetrotting began, it would start in the place that Frank had always wanted to see more than anything.

"I know Frank," I lied.

He nodded. "You do."

"So will you," I told him, sighing deeply as the elevator dinged loudly and the doors slid open. "Good-bye, Rene."

"I'll see you around."

I really hoped not.

"Jackson!"

I pivoted around to look at him.

"I miss Malic."

I made the international sign for a phone with my thumb and pinky.

"He won't talk to me."

"I'll put in a good word for you," I said before I took a few steps backward and then turned, jogging toward the doors. The entryway felt immense, but when I was finally outside, I felt lighter, like I could breathe.

I pulled my phone from the inside pocket of my suit jacket and called my sentinel.

"Hello?"

"Hey," I said as I shivered in the damp, chilled night air. The rain had stopped, leaving that sheen on the road and puddles on the sidewalk. It smelled wet and cold, and I breathed it in deep. "I have to talk to you. Can I come by?"

"Of course. Where are you?"

"I'm in the city, but I can be out to Sausalito in an hour or so."

"Have you eaten?"

"No."

"Excellent," he said, and I could hear the smile in his voice. "I just made some borscht. Come over and have some."

And remembering Phoebe and how much she hated beets and how much I hated them, as well, I started laughing there on the street. I laughed until tears rolled down my eyes.

"For crissakes, Jaka, it's not that funny. If you don't like soup, you don't have to have any. You can have a sandwich if you want."

His comment didn't help, considering that I had started out my night with a sandwich being all I wanted.

V

THE risk, Jael had explained to me over dinner that night, which was maroon-colored soup for him and a roast beef sandwich for me, was that sometimes when a warder and hearth parted, the hearth went mad. Frank's obsession, from what Jael said, was on the healthy side compared to what he had seen and heard.

The best-case scenario, outside of a hearth and warder growing old together, was that the hearth left the warder, as Frank had done, and not the other way around. When a warder left, he or she left behind a broken heart and took away a whole other world at the same time. To be the hearth of a warder meant that you knew more than most people, understood that supernatural forces were real, and had to be, for another person, their whole life. A lot of hearths could not separate their warrior from the person they loved, and that was fine as long as the love remained. When it was time to say good-bye, it was a lot to give up.

Jael understood Frank's desire to hold on to the piece of power that he had.

"He probably does want you back, Jaka," he said, using my warder name, my call sign, handle, whatever it was, instead of my given name. "Paris is luminous, but how can it compare to the adrenaline rush of living with a warder?"

"I'm thinking Paris beats killing demons any day of the week."

"For you."

"For anybody with a brain."

He chuckled low and deep and reached out to put his hand on my face. "You'll make a very pragmatic sentinel one day."

"Me?" I laughed. "You've got me mixed up with Marcus or Ryan."

He shook his head. "Rindahl hates warding and does only what he must. It's why he keeps his life with Julian so separate. You can't lead what you don't even want to follow."

"I guess," I conceded. "But Marcus?"

"Marot's dreams are in the physical world with Joey, and he won't jeopardize those to lead." He lifted his hand to shut me up when I tried to interrupt him. "Leith is far too gentle for the job, and Malic is far too rash."

"Malic would get us all killed." I smiled at Jael.

"Not purposely." He nodded. "But yes. He thinks you are all as strong as he is."

"Aren't we?"

"No. Malic is strongest, Rindahl fastest, Leith is the most logical, and Marot is the caretaker. I have never seen anyone, even in the heat of battle, check and know where everyone else is."

"That's why he should be sentinel."

"If Marot were sentinel, no chance would ever be taken. He fears loss more than any man I know."

"And me? What am I good at?"

"Normally you're the one who leads, Jaka. Any of the others would follow you anywhere. It's a gift."

I thought about his words. "You said normally."

"Yes. You're not yourself. You seem to be in the middle of some crisis of faith that I can't help you with."

"I'll get over it."

"I hope so."

"But what if I never find another hearth?"

He shrugged. "I worry least about you even though the others fear for your sanity."

"Nice."

He smiled. "I have had many warders in my lifetime and been to many council sessions and met and trained warders from all over the world. I have to say that I would put the five of you—Malic, Marot, you, Rindahl, and Leith—among the best. A lot of warder clutches are stronger individually but not collectively. The five of you work better together than any I have ever seen, and I assure you that you balance each other out quite remarkably."

"If you say so."

"I do."

"Ask another question?"

"Of course."

"Why the damn warder names?"

He squinted at me. "Some of you have dealings with a large number of the people, others do not. Leith is a welder, Malic owns a club, both of which are more solitary professions. You, Rindahl, Marot, lead very public lives, and as such, if a demon were to discover you and scream out your warder names, those that are recorded at the Labarum, all would be well."

"I guess, though Malic owning a strip club would technically qualify as him seeing and dealing with a lot of people."

"He does not strip himself."

I scoffed. "No, he doesn't, thank God."

"That was very unkind."

Like I cared. I made a face watching him eat the borscht. "It looks like you're eating blood."

"That's charming."

I thought of something. "Hey, isn't next week when you take your trip to Scotland to see your intended?"

He scowled. "She's not my intended. She—"

"She's a sentinel too, right?"

"Yes, but—"

"And you know her family."

"Jaka—"

"It's in the bag, right?"

"You know you're the only one that actually listens when I tell you all these things, and I tell you because I have to, not because I want to, so it's quite disconcerting to have it all thrown back in my face!"

I shrugged.

"Which is why I say again, you will make an excellent sentinel when it comes time."

"Great." I dismissed him. "What's her name again?"

"Deidre." He breathed it out.

"Uh-huh."

He leaned back in his seat. "She might not like what she sees."

But for a guy in his midfifties, he looked pretty good. He looked great, in fact. The lady was gonna lose her mind as long as she didn't mind the stiff neck from looking up at him all the time. "Wait, how tall is she?"

"Why does this matter?"

I gestured at him to just tell me.

"I believe she's five eleven."

"Oh, you're lucky, 'cause what're you? Seven one?"

He squinted. "I'm six seven; I'm only an inch taller than Marot and two inches taller than Malic. You're six two, for goodness sake, you're not exactly small."

But he looked huge. We all thought of Jael as a giant. "Are you sure?"

"Am I sure what?"

"That you're only six seven?"

He made a face like I was *the* most annoying man on the planet and got up to go to the kitchen.

"So while you're gone, we shouldn't do anything stupid, right?" I called after him.

"If you could manage."

I would really try; I couldn't speak for anybody else.

JAEL told all the others about Frank, and the following night, when I was on patrol with Leith, he gave me the third degree. He wanted to know how I had handled things with him, and when Malic and Marcus joined us, I had to recount the story all over again.

I told Malic again that he needed to patch things up with Rene.

"You guys were friends a long time," Marcus told him.

He turned his bright blue eyes on his best friend. Malic's eyes were strange; they were this Technicolor turquoise that didn't match his somber disposition in any way. "If Rene was going out with Joe, would I be talking to him?"

Marcus was easily the coolest guy I knew. Ice water ran through him, and he was completely unflappable. Nothing ever shook him. Even in a fight he retained his precise outlook on things. He compartmentalized his feelings from his actions, and what worked in battle also worked in the courtroom. The word was that he would make partner at his law firm this year. All of that flew out the window, however, when you were talking about the man he had spent the last five years of his life with. Joseph Locke was the one singular piece of Marcus Roth's world that could shake him to the core.

He turned and looked at me. "Sorry, Jacks," he said quickly and then looked back at Malic. "Agreed."

"Good," Malic said, bumping him with his shoulder. "We have to go talk to my friend Adrian Chen tonight. He thinks he's got a *jiang shi* in his building and asked me to check it out."

"Christ, Malic," I groused. "Is there anyone in your life that doesn't know you're a warder?"

"Lots." He smiled wickedly. "But unlike you, I know who to trust."

"What the fuck does that mean?"

"It means besides Cielo, who have you ever told?"

I thought about it a minute. "Frank," I told them.

Leith laughed beside me, and we all turned to look.

"What?"

Marcus's smile was huge. "Maybe it's time to bust out of your comfort zone, there, Jacks."

Maybe it was.

VI

I WAS looking for him, and a week later I was finally rewarded with a glimpse of him. I followed fast, running, racing along the pavement to catch up. He flew behind three men into a vacant warehouse, and when I reached them, I was stunned at what I saw.

The men were on the wall, held there against their will by some invisible force that kept them dangling several feet off the ground. Raphael was in the middle of the room, frozen, head back, breathing hard.

"Why are you chasing me?"

I walked into the room, the leather soles of my dress shoes scratching through the dirt as I advanced. "I wanted to talk to you," I said softly. "What are you doing with these guys?"

He looked over his shoulder at me, and I was struck by how raw his eyes looked. "Why do you care? They're demons."

But whatever he had planned might actually hurt him more than them. It might take a toll on his soul. "I don't care, but tell me what you're going to do."

"I'm going to skin them alive and then transport them back to the siphon world they came from."

"Who are they?"

He turned to face me. "Ever since I helped your fellow warder's pet—"

"Simon. We're talking about Leith's hearth right?"

"Yes," he snapped. "Ever since then the demon lord Saudrian has put a bounty on my head, and since kyries are solitary and I have no patron, I'm kind of on my own."

He sounded almost sad.

"I'm sorry."

I got a shrug and a wry smile. "Not that it will matter soon anyway." He gestured at the demons held plastered to the wall. "My transformation is coming. I can feel it so—"

"What does that mean?"

He squinted at me. "That means that I'm going to change into a demon soon. Kyries do unless they're—kyries change."

"Unless what?"

"What are you doing here?" he growled, changing the subject.

I gave him a smile. "Well, I was thinking that I never properly thanked you for saving Simon."

"Simon saved himself and his warder."

"Yeah, but like you said, you helped. Without you they would have never made it out."

He was glaring at me.

"So again, I should thank you."

"Don't tease me, warder, I bite."

I arched an eyebrow for him.

"Go away," he muttered gruffly, and I could tell he was purposely trying to sound mean.

"C'mon, just let them go. I wanna talk to you."

He shook his head. "No. I don't want to talk to you."

"Please."

"No!" he snarled, flashing his teeth. "You use that word, that stupid, simple word, and you make me do things, make lots of people do things, and I hate it. You can't just say please and expect—"

"Why are you angry?" I asked softly, moving closer, reaching for him. "And why did you disappear? You've been so good at stalking me, showing up wherever I am, and then what? I lost my appeal after I almost bled to death on your boots?"

He sucked in a breath, and the demons fell from the walls. They started forward, the menace there in their slow stride, moving to attack us, but I lifted my head so they could see me, let a pulse of power run out of me and hit them. We could all do it, every warder, push a wave of energy through our own bodies and release it. And every creature from the pit knew what it was, what it felt like when it touched them and what it meant.

"Warder," one of the demons said under his breath before each of them threw their heads back, dimmed, and disappeared.

I returned my eyes to Raphael's and found him squinting at me.

"How can you say that to me?" he asked, furious.

"Say what?" I asked, reaching for the heavy black motorcycle jacket.

He meant to step away, but I grabbed and held him. "This is a nice change from the leather duster. It fits your bad-guy image without being over the top."

"Don't—"

"Don't what?" I asked, easing him closer, putting my other hand on his hip, leaning forward, inhaling his musky scent, letting it soothe me.

"You were almost killed because of me, and I made up my mind that night that I would no longer put you in danger. My life is filled with horrors that—"

"So is mine," I told him, moving my hands, one to the back of his neck, the other burrowing up under the cable-knit sweater he had on, under the T-shirt, until I hit warm skin.

The sound that came out of him, whine, moan, whimper all at once, told me everything I needed to know.

"I'm not afraid of your world. I live there already."

"But you—you don't, I'm going to change and—"

"Kyries only change," I said, sliding my hand over the small of his back, stroking his bare skin, "if they are not claimed. Isn't that so?"

He tipped his head back, offering, and I leaned in and pressed my parted lips to the pulse beating at the base of his throat.

"Isn't that so?" I repeated, smiling, kissing up the length of his throat and wedging my thigh against his groin at the same time.

The noises he made, the moans that came from the back of his throat as he clutched at my biceps, holding me tight through the zippered cardigan, made me smile.

"So then why run from me? Stick around."

"I don't want you to get hurt," he almost cried, shoving me off him, stepping back.

I saw it then, all his pain, all his desire, there in his ragged, red-rimmed eyes.

"Come here." I called him gruffly.

He pointed at me. "Because of me, you almost died. I don't want you to die, warder. I'd rather stay away from you than—"

"I want you." And I did. The desire for him, just to sleep with him, was nearly overwhelming. There was no one else I craved at all, no one else I really even saw. He was it, the only bright, terrible point of light around.

"You have no idea what you're saying."

"I do."

"You don't," he shouted. "You don't make idle promises to a kyrie. It's not like breaking up with your whiny-ass bitch of a boyfriend. It's a gift and grants you dominion, and once it's given, you can't take it back. I will always be there; you'll never be free. It's what your sentinel warned Malic about—the thrall of a demon."

"You're not a demon," I reminded him.

The muscles in his jaw corded with the effort it took for him not to yell.

"And I'm not afraid."

"You're not afraid because you place no value on your own life."

Perhaps.

"But soon you're going to pull free of this haze of"—he shook his head—"sadness or whatever the fuck it is, and then—"

"Why're you fighting with me?"

"You cannot take this pledge so light—"

"I'm not. I swear I'm not. Just c'mere."

"You are! You said you wanted me," he yelled, "and if you do, truly do, then I'm yours, Jackson Tybalt, but once given, once you take me once, have me once, it's done."

"So the thrall of a kyrie has nothing to do with blood?"

"It has everything to do with blood, but not me taking yours, you drinking mine!"

"Show me."

He rushed back to my side, and as he came, he pulled a knife from behind his back. There were hidden sheaths in the jacket, hiding all manner of weaponry, I was sure, but the knife, dragged across his wrist in one fluid motion, the knife he cut into himself with was the only one I cared about.

"For crissakes, don't hurt yourself."

His flickering smile was breathtaking. "You're worried... about me...."

"Don't cry," I teased him gently.

He shook his head and then grabbed me, shoving his wrist against my lips, clutching the back of my head tight, his hand fisted in my hair.

I had to open my mouth, I couldn't breathe, and the second I did, I tasted metal and felt the liquid warmth on my tongue. I swallowed, sucked, and swallowed again. I felt like a fiend and got my hands on him and wrenched free. I fell back, hitting the ground hard, and scrambled to sit up. He was on his knees close to me.

"I—"

"Look."

I lifted my eyes, and his wrist was pristine—no cut, no blood, nothing.

"Perfect," he proclaimed, and I saw that the soft, gentle look in his face was replaced by obvious hunger. The predatory look went right to my groin.

"Raphael."

"If the bond works, I heal."

"And if it didn't?"

"I'd be dead at your feet."

I caught my breath. "You stupid son of a—"

"I healed, warder."

He had.

"I'm yours."

I would have said something, but I was flat on my back with two hundred pounds of hard-muscled man on top of me, straddling my thighs, dragging his ass over my painfully engorged erection a second later.

"I belong to you now, warder."

The magnitude of what I had done, without thinking, hit me hard. And then I saw the flutter of eyelashes as he stilled above me.

"You don't want—"

"Oh, I want." I cut him off, hands on the granite thighs, pulling him forward, lifting my legs to support his back. "Come home with me."

His eyes were slits as he stared down at me. "This is not a romance, warder."

"What the fuck does that mean?"

"That means that you're not ready." He studied me, my face.

"Ready for what?"

He rose fast, dragged me to my feet after him, wrenched me sideways, and then drove me across the floor face-first into the wall. The impact pushed all the air from my lungs. As I stood, gasping for breath, he yanked and tugged at me, unbuckling my belt, working the button fly open, shucking my jeans and briefs down in a violent motion.

"What the fuck are—"

"Say stop," he whispered, his breath hot and wet in my ear. His chest was shoved against my back, and I felt his hands sliding over my ass, thighs, and hips. "Tell me to stop, even once, and I will, warder. I will."

His hands felt so good biting into my flesh, learning new territory, pressing, stroking, and then he fisted my cock, and I let my head fall back on his shoulder.

"What do you deserve, warder?"

I had no idea what he meant.

"Are you a good man?"

Was I?

"Jackson?"

I shook my head no. I was not a good man. I had driven away my hearth because I wanted too much and had nothing to give back.

"I will take as you did," he said, sliding two of his fingers into my mouth.

I licked them because I knew what was happening, coated them thoroughly, making sure they were slick and wet.

"I can hardly wait to feel that tongue on my cock."

My heart hurt, and then I felt a finger slip between my cheeks at the same time he stroked my shaft from base to head.

"Please," I begged him, my voice a throaty whisper.

I heard him spit, felt him working his fingers inside me, and it burned, the pressure, the opening not gentle but rough and jarring. My lips parted to tell him to get off me, but his hand tugging on my cock, pulling, eclipsed all else. The first throb vibrated through me, and I pushed back on his fingers, felt my muscles give a fraction, and caught the scent of precome before the head of his shaft was pressed against my entrance.

I was vulnerable, giving, which I never did, and his hand slid over my shaft, milking it as he sank slowly inside me. His cock was thick and long, and it felt like I was split in half as he pressed into me, stretching, filling, the tight rings of muscle resistant until he thrust hard and deep, buried to his balls in my ass.

It was agony until he pulled back and slid back in, slower, scraping his cock over my prostate at the same time he spit into his right hand and took hold of my still leaking shaft. He began a slow, sensual rhythm, in and out, thrusting, impaling, and the pinching sensation changed. I felt my balls tightening, drawing up, and the persistent edge of pain was finally replaced by sizzling heat as I let out a deep, guttural cry.

"Jackson," he whispered against my ear. "You're so hot and tight."

I trembled as he drove in and out of me, harder and deeper with every plunge, slipping an arm around my neck to hold me against him.

"My smell is on your skin."

The thought of him claiming me, cruelly, ravenously, of his hands on me, his mouth, his fangs sinking into my flesh, his shaft buried inside me, tore the orgasm from the base of my spine and dragged it though my body in a blinding release that had me writhing in violent ecstasy, screaming his name.

My muscles clutched around him, squeezing him tight, and he erupted inside me, pumping come deep into my clenching channel, his climax only seconds behind my own.

We stood together, shuddering with the aftershocks, pressed together, my forehead leaning into the crook of his arm as he braced it against the wall. As my brain cleared, the weight of what I had just done hit me on all levels.

"Should there have been a condom?" I asked breathlessly.

He shoved back away from me, and I gasped at the suddenness of the movement, the pain, the relief, all swirling together.

I was cold when he was gone, the warmth of his skin, his breath, sharply missed.

"A kyrie does not catch or transmit filthy human diseases, warder," he said disdainfully. "We are above such mediocrity."

I turned and looked at him over my shoulder as he scoffed. "You're a prick."

"Which you loved," he sneered, slapping my ass hard enough to leave a mark.

I faced the wall so he couldn't see my face, see that his words hurt and how true they were. To be manhandled and taken had been what I needed, what I deserved, what I craved, but I felt empty inside because nothing, none of it, had been anything but skin-deep. For the sex to hold meaning, the connection had to be there. I had thought that maybe he would be the balm for my broken heart since he was evil just like me, and we could be a horror together. But as it turned out he didn't want anything to do with my heart, broken or otherwise.

I pulled up my underwear and jeans, working the buttons, buckling my belt, eyes on my task, not letting myself look anywhere else.

"Don't even think about turning me away," he warned me, contempt in his voice.

When I finally lifted my eyes, he was halfway to the entrance, the swagger evident in his stride. I could not remember ever hating anyone more.

VII

I WALKED, I talked, but there was nothing inside. I just went through the motions. I went to work, went on patrol, but it seemed surreal. Days passed like that, and the only thing that broke them up were Raphael's visits. I dreaded seeing him and was anxious to at the same time. I got so I knew his walk, his scent, the wicked gleam of his eyes, and the sound of his breathing.

The night before, I had gone to a bar to meet Ryan and Julian for drinks and had seen Frank. He was there with Rene, and they looked happy. When they were joined by a third man, Frank rose and gave him a kiss that made me uncomfortable even from where I was across the room. Rene shook the man's hand, and interestingly, the man took a seat beside Rene and not Frank.

"It's none of your business," Ryan said as he slid into the booth beside me.

"What's not?" Julian asked, leaning forward.

As Ryan explained, Julian turned to study both men before his eyes came back to me. I was surprised at the smile I was getting.

"You're hotter than both Rene and that other guy."

I appreciated the compliment.

"Phoebe says that you and she bonded over beets."

Caught off balance, I chuckled. "I think I might be in love with her."

He nodded. "She has that effect. Ry and I are meeting them for dinner after. Why don't you come?"

"Oh no, that's okay," I told him, knowing that Ryan would not want me there. Jael was right. He liked his life separate and—

"I would like that," my fellow warder said, turning his hazel eyes on me. "Really."

So I went because I was truly invited, and when I followed them into the restaurant and we reached the table, Phoebe was up and out of her seat and around the table and in my arms before I could even say hello.

"Okay." Cash gave me a wide grin. "You're Jackson, right?"

I nodded as I hugged his wife. And she was still the only one hugging me lately. Because even though the kyrie and I were having sex, there were no kisses exchanged, and he never just held me. He pinned me against things—walls, tables, even bent me over my car in the garage. It was always desperate and jarring, but he had started carrying a small tube of Astroglide, which I appreciated. The thing was that I couldn't tell anyone what was going on between us, and that was hard. I needed to talk to someone, but I didn't know who.

"Oh, honey." Phoebe sighed, stepping back, grabbing my hand and leading me away from the table.

"Phoeb?" Cash called out to his wife.

"Be right back," she promised, not stopping, making a beeline for the front door.

I was led outside, and once we were there, she turned and pounced on me.

"Spill. You look like shit," she commanded, arms crossed, looking up at me.

"I—"

"Just tell me," she prodded, unwrapping her arms, taking my hand. "God, Jackson, something about you—I feel like I've known you a million years."

I felt the same.

"And—oh."

"Oh?" I was confused.

"Oh-oh," she said, hand on her swollen abdomen. "I think this kid is ready to come out."

"Are you kidding?" I gasped.

Her face said no. I scooped her up and deposited her on the bench in front of the building. I got a quick pat, an apology for how heavy she was, and an order for me to get Cash now.

I kissed her forehead and turned to go.

Her fingers dug into my forearm.

"Honey?"

"You're a good man, Jackson. Believe it."

I tried to leave, but she tightened her grip.

"Really." She winced. "A very good man."

I nodded and charged back into the restaurant and up to the table.

"Did you ditch my wife?" Cash teased me.

"No, you gotta go; she's ready to have your kid."

His eyes went round, but I got why Phoebe loved him. He was gorgeous, and that was apparent, but the way he rose, got his coat, and walked out the front door amazed me. Ryan, Julian, and I were right behind him. When he reached his wife, we could all tell she was scared. But he got there, told her things, asked about the contractions and how far apart they were. He then turned, gave Julian his keys, and gave him directions about where Phoebe's packed hospital bag was in their house. Julian was to get it and meet them in delivery. He then turned to Ryan and told him to go get his Jeep and drive them to the hospital. All his words were measured, his voice stayed level, and he held his wife in his arms the whole time. The man was a rock. I wanted one just like him. But I wanted Phoebe too.

I watched as Ryan kissed Julian before he left; I saw the smiles they exchanged, and my heart hurt. I saw the way Cash hugged his wife to him as they waited, heard her sigh of contentment as she nestled against him and was touched. When Ryan returned, the Jeep there, double-parked in front of us, Phoebe yelled that she expected to see me at her bedside at some point. I told her I would. And then they were gone, and I was alone.

As I was walking home, Raphael jumped me, and it was rough and bruising, like stone scraping over concrete, and I was raw inside and out. But I allowed him to treat me like a piece of meat, like nothing, because it was what I deserved. All that I deserved. I had not been able to go to the hospital; I didn't have it in me to face the love I would surely see.

In my office that night, I was getting ready to leave, and when I twisted left, I winced with pain. My whole body hurt. I was covered in scratches and bruises, and when the marks were being given, I could not have been made to care, but now that I was standing in front of my desk, packing my courier bag, the pain was another story.

A sudden scent made my stomach roll over. Turning, I saw him, sitting quietly like a spider in the corner of the room. I had not heard him come in. He stood, unfolding himself from the overstuffed chair, rising fluidly, rolling forward to his feet, and reached out and pushed gently on the door. It was heavy, so it slowly, inexorably, swung quietly closed. The tumbler in the lock clicked over at the same time. No one was getting in without me opening for them.

My mouth went dry. "You need to leave me alone."

His heavy-lidded eyes did not widen. Instead he simply watched me.

I forced a smile. "Seriously, Raph, don't you have people to hunt?"

A slow shake of his head, and he came closer, reaching out as I turned to face him, hand on my shoulder that I realized was less human and more animal. The claws dug into my shoulder.

"What do you want?"

"There's only one thing I ever want from you, warder," he said as he pushed me back against my desk.

I put my hands down on either side of me, anchoring myself, as his hands went to work roughly, greedily, on my belt buckle. I let my head fall back, wondering how I would take him pounding into me again so soon, and craving it at the same time. I was broken inside, and he was filth. It made sense that we would come together this way.

The cool air of the room hit my cock a second before my jeans and briefs were yanked down and he engulfed the long hard length of me in his hot, wet mouth.

"Raphael!" I shouted hoarsely, shoving forward, burying myself in the back of his throat on instinct.

He sucked hard, his cheeks hollowed out; his tongue swirled and laved my rigid shaft, and watching his lips drag from base to head was a religious experience.

"You taste so good," he growled, smiling around my cock, and I saw the canines that could have cut into me if he wasn't careful.

But he was careful.

The pull, the suction, was fierce, and his hand holding my balls, the other holding my ass, all worked together to push me closer to climax. When I buried my fingers in his hair, fisted and held tight, his moan of pleasure, the vibration on my throbbing shaft, was too much.

"I'm gonna come," I warned him.

He just sucked harder, faster, and I arched my back, plunging deep, emptying down the back of his throat.

My whole world was me coming, the orgasm that rolled through me, my shout of release. When he leaned back, licking me clean before he stood in front of me, I felt his hands on my hips as the claiming began. He was rough as he turned me, and I was bent down hard over my desk, mauled into place, manhandled.

My legs were parted as far as the corduroys around my ankles would allow. I heard the snap of the flip-top cap before the head of his massive dick nudged my entrance.

"You gotta be careful," I confessed. "I'm sore from last night."

I shouldn't have told him. He might have gone slowly if I didn't tell him. Instead, he spread my cheeks and drove inside me so hard, so fast, I saw stars. The pain, the burn, left me reeling for a moment before his cock, his amazing, thick, long cock, slid over my gland. The nerve endings ignited, and I was plunged into heat.

"Oh God," I moaned loudly.

"See," he said, impaling me, pushing deep. "Your body craves mine."

"I'll find someone who won't just wanna fuck me," I told him.

"Promises, promises," he said, one hand in my hair, yanking my head back sharply, the other splayed across my abdomen. "I am addicted to seeing you writhing around on the end of my dick."

I yanked my head free and slammed my hands down on the desk. "Just fuck me already, and then get the hell out of here!"

"As you wish," he said and impaled me in one brutal thrust.

His lube-slicked hand slid over my flaccid cock, but in his grip, it lengthened again, hardened. His talented fingers stroked until I was whimpering his name, hating myself and wanting him in equal measure. I matched his passion, his anger, his hunger, and when it was done, when the rage had alchemized into a flood of release, we were both left panting and sweating, heaving for breath.

The tears were of no consideration. This time I didn't give a damn.

"Get the fuck out and never come back," I ordered, pulling up my briefs and pants, tucking my T-shirt in, adjusting my sweater. No one would miss that I smelled like sex. Maybe I would stand in the rain and get it off before I got in a cab for home.

"You claimed me."

"What?"

"You claimed me. You marked me. You can't—"

"Fuckin' prove it," I snarled. "There ain't a mark on you."

His eyes were flat as he stared at me.

"Go away."

"No."

"Please."

His eyes narrowed. "You've found someone."

When would I have done that?

"Tell me," he ordered, his voice low and ominous as he moved forward, fisting his claws in my sweater.

"Why would you care?"

"Who is it?" he roared in my face.

I shoved him back, furious. "There's no one, but there will be. Fuck you and fuck this. I deserve better."

He was shaking hard, and his jaw clenched as he watched me.

"Get the hell—"

"Finally," he exhaled, and I saw his eyes fill, the tears there, but not falling.

I was dumbstruck. What the hell was going on?

"You know me," he said finally, sucking in his breath. "You know the kind of man I am. Think about me, look at me, really look, and remember who I am."

I had no idea what he was talking about, but when his breath hitched, caught, it took every bit of strength in me not to grab him.

I saw the muscles in his jaw working; his eyes were dark and turbulent, swimming as he bit into his bottom lip with one long fang.

"Is there another?"

I shook my head.

"Then I will be now what you truly need and deserve."

I was so lost.

He took a breath, and then he was gone. The door bounced open a second later, like a strong breeze had blown through my office. There was no sign of anyone but me. I had no idea what to begin to think, but I knew what to do. I had to take a shower.

BY THE time I got home, I was soaked to the skin. I peeled off my clothes, dropping them around me on my way to the bathroom, and when I stepped into the shower, I felt different. Better. My life that had been turned upside down had suddenly righted itself, or else I had made the adjustment to walking on the ceiling. Whatever had occurred, I was glad. I felt like me for the first time in a very long time, like I was back to living in my own skin.

In the kitchen I was scrounging for food, not wanting to go back out into the monsoon, when something moved out of the corner of my eye. When I turned, I saw Raphael crouched like some living gargoyle outside my kitchen window, safe from the rain under the overhang of the loft above mine. It was a tiny space to be sitting on. I couldn't have done it, and I was impressed, as always, with his balance.

I moved fast, opened the window out, and looked up at him from where I stood leaning over my sink.

"Well?" he asked, holding up a large paper bag. "I have pho. Can I come in?"

But I couldn't fight with him anymore; I didn't have it in me. "I—"

"Don't you like pho?"

He could not have known that Vietnamese soup was one of my favorite things in the world. "Okay, yeah, come in."

Fluidly, like he was boneless, he slithered in from the cold, stepping from the ledge to the counter and to the floor in front of me. I closed the window and then faced him. He was closer than I thought he was. The dark eyes were fixed on my mouth.

"What brings you back out in this weather, kyrie?"

He squinted at me. "If I stop calling you warder, will you stop calling me kyrie?"

"Yep."

"Done," he said, passing me the bag. "Will you eat with me?"

We didn't eat together. We did nothing together but fuck. "Sure."

"Good." He gave me a fleeting smile.

I watched him walk out of my kitchen, shedding clothes as he moved, like it was expected that I would pick up after him.

"Hello, not the maid."

He grunted as he dropped his parka, unzipped the heavy knit cardigan under it and pulled out of one sleeve and then the other, letting the sweater fall to the floor only to step over it. He was down to a pocket T-shirt and 501s by the time he flopped onto my couch. I put the bag down on the coffee table as he unzipped his ankle boots and let them clunk to the floor. His socks were peeled off and flung toward the fireplace that had wood in it ready to be burned.

"Dude."

He made a fist, and there was a sort of rise of heat in the room before I had flickering flames where there had been nothing moments before.

I smiled. "That's handy."

"That impressed you? Really? It's a parlor trick."

"Pretty neat trick."

His grin was wicked as he looked up at me.

I jogged back to the kitchen and got bowls and spoons, napkins, and two bottles of beer. I had liquor, beer, and milk in my refrigerator, and that was it. When I came back, he was lounging on the floor beside the coffee table.

"This was nice of you."

"I can be nice."

"Uh-huh."

"I can. Whatever you need," he said, leaning forward, elbows on the table. "I can be. You want bad boy with a chip on his shoulder, I can be him. You want poetry and flowers, I can be that guy too. You ask and you shall receive."

I nodded as I pulled the huge Styrofoam container of soup out of the bag. The broth smelled amazing, and as I unpacked all the items that were supposed to be added in—the grilled chicken, bean sprouts, mint, rice vermicelli, long-stemmed mushrooms, and green onions—he watched me.

"Tell me what you want in yours," I asked, passing him a beer.

"Just make it the same as yours."

Once I was done, we settled down to eat. It was good, and I was starving, and so, apparently, was he. We ate in silence until we both started slowing down.

"I like the music," he told me when he was finished, leaning back, arms braced behind him on the area rug.

"I always have something on; I can't stand a quiet house."

"Why not?"

"I dunno." I shrugged. "Feels weird, lonely."

"And that's not you."

"That is me. Why the hell do you think I need the music on to chase it away?"

He chuckled. "This singer, she sounds sad."

"It's jazz. They all sound like that."

He smiled, stretching his leg, sliding his foot along the side of my thigh. Even through my sweats, I could feel how icy his skin was.

"I should get you some socks," I told him, getting up.

"No, just sit on the couch with me. I wanna talk to you."

"Let me clean this up. Make yourself comfortable."

"I can help."

"You brought dinner. That was enough help."

"Nice to not have to do everything, huh?"

I didn't answer, instead concentrating on the task at hand.

Once all traces of dinner were gone, I brought him another beer, turned off all the lights except for the low ones in the living room, and took a seat on the opposite end of the couch from him. He immediately slid both feet under my right thigh.

"Christ, you're frozen." I smiled over at him, putting my hand on his calf, gripping tight.

He hissed out a breath and let his head fall back on the throw pillow behind him. "That feels so good."

I put my beer on the floor beside the couch, turned, and slid each of my hands up under the cuffs of his jeans. His legs were toned and strong, and he moaned out his pleasure as I kneaded the rigid muscles.

"I killed Saudrian," he said softly.

My eyes flicked to his. "What?"

"You heard me."

I went still sitting there, staring. "When?"

"Last night."

"You didn't tell me."

"We haven't been speaking."

And we hadn't. The sum of our communication had been me bottoming for him.

"Are you hurt?"

"No." He chuckled. "Do I look hurt?"

But around his eyes, he did. "Yeah, kinda."

His brows furrowed as he lifted his legs, pulling them free of my grip only to slide them over my right leg, down into my lap, and shove under my left thigh. "It was harder than I thought it was going to be, and his mate—a dark witch—she got away."

I was listening, but I was also watching, and the way he was fidgeting, his hands restless, picking at the couch cushion, made me wonder what he wanted. "Are you scared of her?"

"Not of a witch," he said, his eyes darting all over like he was getting ready to run.

"You wanna get in my lap?" I asked.

He didn't answer; he just moved. He rolled forward, fast, like he uncoiled, and shifted over, straddling my thighs, his long legs folded on either side of my hips as he shoved his groin into my abdomen.

My head tipped back, and I looked up into his eyes. "Are you hurt?"

He shook his head. "Are you?"

"From what, a little rough sex?"

He cleared his throat. "It was necessary."

"It wasn't necessary. It's your kink, and you loved it, and you would have gone on loving it if I would have—"

"No." He caught his breath, his fingers lifting, reaching, sliding over my chin to my jaw until he had my face captured in his hands and was staring down into my face.

I took hold of his wrists, realizing suddenly that the eyes that I had found so ferocious and feral were now soft and simmering with need.

"Jackson." He whimpered.

I lifted my head and he bent and took absolute possession of my lips. The whine that came out of him was heartbreaking, and he kissed me like it was the only thing in the world he wanted to do. All the hunger and need and craving was still there, but now it was tempered with a new, shivering anticipation that I felt tumble through me.

He wasn't pawing at me, pulling, or trying to rip off my clothes; he was instead intent only on my mouth, licking, sucking, his tongue pressing against mine, one kiss flowing to the next and the next, creating a rising pool of need in me.

I'd had no idea he would taste so good.

When I finally pulled back, breaking the kiss, he leaned forward to recapture my mouth.

"I wanna talk to you."

"Why?" He was breathless, hands on my shoulders, as he ground his mouth back down over mine, kissing me deep. His moan a second later was very sexy.

My hands slid the length of his arms, over bulging biceps and triceps to muscular shoulders, tracing his deltoids, marveling at the definition. The man was toned and beautiful, his frame strong and powerful, and having him in my lap was pure pleasure. My body was definitely ready to play.

He slid his wet, swollen lips from mine and looked down at me with heavy-lidded eyes.

"You're so pretty, Raph." I smiled.

He lifted his arms, and I pulled the T-shirt up over his head, revealing a broad, carved chest, dark-brown pierced nipples, a washboard stomach, and sexy lines on each side of his stomach that I traced with my fingers.

He jolted under my touch.

"You just expect to come over here and get laid?" I asked, leaning forward without even thinking about it, pressing my lips to his hot bronze skin.

"Oh, Jackson, please." His breath caught as he buried his hands in my hair.

I pushed up, and he made the most amazing noise at the same time he pressed his crease down over the hard bulge in my sweats.

"Wait." I looked up, confused. "You're a top."

He shook his head. "I'm whatever I want, just like you, so could you... please?"

I let out a deep breath as I saw how red-rimmed his eyes were, how hard he was working to hold himself together, and how the slight tremble was giving him away.

"Would you come get in my bed?"

He fell forward, arms wrapped around my neck, face buried down in my shoulder, and just breathed.

I felt the shudder run through him, felt him surrender, and felt the wall collapse. The faith he had to have, his belief that in this vulnerable state I would not attack him—I was humbled.

With the taste of him in my mouth, the warmth of his touch on my skin, and the deep sound of his exhale, I grabbed him tight, one hand on the back of his head, the other on the small of his back, anchoring him to me.

"Don't let me go." He spoke the words onto my skin. "Just keep me."

Amazing.

If there was anyone more stupid than me, I had no idea who that could be. The man in my arms had been right in front of me for months, waiting, watching, mine for the taking, and I had been crying over a man who didn't want me anymore. He had taken chances for me, killed for me, stood between me and death, and still I had persisted in not seeing him. And then when he had me, just a part of me that I would give him, because I would not recognize goodness in myself, he had met me, blow for blow, with only the cruelty and violence that I thought I deserved. But truly, in his deepest, most secret heart, the man wanted to be loved and cherished and to simply belong to me.

"I'm an idiot," I told him.

"Yes," he said, pressing even closer to me, his legs tightening.

I smoothed my hands slowly over his thighs because I really wanted to shove them down the back of his pants and grab his ass hard. It was a raw need that I couldn't shake.

"Get up," I ordered him, my voice deep, commanding.

His eyes narrowed, suddenly heavy-lidded, as he clasped his hands above his head, stretching his rippling muscles and smooth bronze skin for me just in case I was stupid enough to not see him.

"I get it, asshole," I growled. "You're a god, and I'm a clueless mortal."

"Good," he breathed out, rising up off of me in a seamless, fluid motion.

I rose beside him, leaned in, kissed his cheek, and was rewarded with a smile that would melt butter. "Just c'mere."

When I reached for his hand, he was there to take mine and hold tight. Halfway down the hall, he shoved me into the wall, ground up against me, and pressed his groin to the inside of my thigh. His hands went to my waist, burrowing up under my T-shirt.

"God, your skin is so hot," he groaned, forcing my head back against the wall, his lips on my throat.

His mouth sealed to my skin felt so much better than good. I couldn't help jolting under him.

"You like me all over you."

There was no denying it, and as his hands moved higher, circling my pebbling nipples before he pinched them, a hard throb of desire washed through me.

"Jackson," he murmured.

I bent and kissed him, the deep whimper from the back of his throat making me smile against his lips. I put my hands on his face, holding him, and devoured his mouth. My tongue tangled with his, sliding over his, sucking, licking, and pushing, seeking dominance.

Walking him backward, I eased him through the doorway of my bedroom and then tore my mouth from his at the same time I tackled him, driving him down under me onto my bed.

My bed.

I had never thought I would get the man in my bed. I never thought I would want him there.

"What was that?" He was laughing, and the sound was deep and husky.

I loved the deep lines around his eyes, the smile that lit his face, and the way his hands slid up my thighs. He enjoyed touching me, just the simple act, and I had missed that, as well.

"You're mine," I growled, and the way his eyes fluttered shut, the way he savored the declaration, was another epiphany.

I reached for his belt buckle, and wonder of wonders, the man was ticklish.

"Big, bad-ass demon tracker," I muttered as he giggled, rolling off the bed so I had more leverage to yank off his jeans and the boxers underneath. They had blue stripes.

"Cute," I told him.

He flipped me off but gasped in the middle of his show of bravado as I dropped to my knees beside the bed and took the enormous uncut penis that had been inside me so many times down the back of my throat.

He had no idea what he'd been missing. I gave head like a rock star.

"Jackson!"

Oh yes.

"Jacks… baby," he groaned, his hands in my hair. "Your beard feels amazing."

Yet another sensation he had been missing out on.

The mantra of my name began.

I wrapped one hand under my mouth; the other went to his balls as I coated him, sucked, smiling around his leaking shaft, hearing his breath catch in his chest. I made the suction strong, let him feel my tongue swirling over the head, down the side and up, my lips sliding fast and fierce. When I raised my eyes to his, I saw his mouth open in a frozen gasp, saw the bliss on his face and how clouded with passion his eyes were. I nearly came right there.

"Want you inside," he begged me, hand in my hair, trying to get me to stop, tugging. "Need you inside. I claimed you. Please."

I pointed to the drawer in the nightstand at the same time I let his saliva-coated shaft slip from between my lips.

He rolled over fast, and it was a treat to watch his perfect ass lifted in the air as he crawled across my bed. Finding the bottle, he scrambled back to me, handing it over before turning and getting into position on his hands and knees.

"Not a chance."

He looked over his shoulder, and when he spoke, his voice was hoarse and full of sand. "Please, baby."

"Come here."

He didn't understand and then suddenly did.

"Oh yes." I grinned, noting the surprised expression. "You will look at me when we do this, the whole time. Do you understand?"

He nodded, but he was overwhelmed, and it was there on his face, in his eyes.

"Put your legs on my arms."

He slid his icy feet up my chest and then scooted forward, his knees in the crooks of both elbows as I opened the bottle with a quick snap and dribbled cold, slippery gel into my palms. I warmed it in my hands and then fisted his rock-hard shaft that was straining for me.

"Feel good?" I asked as he arched up off the bed.

"Just turn me over and fuck me," he pleaded.

"Look at me!"

His eyes flew open and locked with mine as I slid a finger deep inside him. The rapture on his face, the wince at the same time, was captivating. In seconds he was pushing down on my finger, begging for another. I complied fast, stroking his cock at the same time, scissoring my fingers inside him, letting him get used to the intrusion.

When he was squirming under me, trying to increase the pressure, I slid out of him, changing my angle, hands on the firm, round ass, spreading him, aligning my cock with his fluttering hole.

He lifted, inviting me, and I slid into him easily, burying myself to the hilt in his tight, quivering heat.

His back bowed, he raked claws through the sheets, and I smiled because my bedding was shredded. His eyes glowed bright topaz, inhuman, and when I saw the gaze full of me, only me, I eased out and plunged back down into him as hard as I could.

"Jackson, please... please."

The panting, the growling whimper, and the muscles in his ass squeezing me so tight all worked together to drive me right out of my mind. I grabbed hold of his hips and hammered into him, pressing forward, spreading his legs apart.

I felt my body tighten, and then the orgasm surged through me, powerful and blinding, and there was not the quick flash of climax but the euphoria I got when it meant something, when it was a joining, when it was more than just sex and mutual satisfaction and instead love.

Love.

There was no way.

But when I filled his channel, when I was left sated and empty, he pulled me down on top of him, over his warm body, and wrapped arms and legs around me. He didn't let me pull out; he told me I could stay inside of him forever.

"Oh yeah," I said, my voice a low rumble in my chest. "You sure?"

"Very," he promised, and I heard his complete and undeniable need.

I stayed where I was.

VIII

I COULD tell when I walked in that Ryan was surprised to see me. The look got even funnier a minute later when Raphael walked in behind me. His face went completely blank. Julian's reception had been warmer, as always, and after he hugged me, he had gone ahead and hugged Raphael.

"What're you guys drinking?" the hearth of my fellow warder asked us.

It was Phoebe's idea. It was just an open house. Nothing important, nothing formal, just an *"everyone come on by when you can drop by and say hello and see the new baby"* party. Her voice on the phone had been upbeat, casual, but there was an underlying thread in her tone. I knew mom guilt when I heard it, still missed my own, so when she said it was up to me, show up or not, I heard the order clear as day.

My ass had better be there.

I figured I would multitask, unveil the new guy in my life and see the baby at the same time. I was looking for her in the house, and when I finally saw her, I was surprised at how wrung out she looked. She was still beautiful, but her radiance had dulled, her glow faded. And I understood, new baby and all, but after observing for a few minutes, I realized it was even more. The cherub from heaven, Gabriella, Gaby, immediately started wailing if anyone but her mother had her. As a result, Phoebe was holding her while she tried to eat and talk and visit with friends and family.

She had been so happy to see me, had chided me for not coming to the hospital, but understood, or thought she did, when she saw Raphael.

"That is one beautiful man you have there," she told me when I took a seat beside her on the couch as she was trying to burp her daughter.

"Why did you go in the other room?" I asked her.

"When?"

"Just a little while ago."

She thought a minute. "I was breast-feeding, you perv." She giggled, reaching out to run a hand over my cheek. "And you should get rid of this beard of yours and cut your hair. What are you hiding from?"

I ran the backs of my knuckles up the side of my face over the close-cropped hair. "A man with a beard and mustache is trustworthy; a man with a goatee is scary."

"And who told you this?"

"I think I read it on the Internet."

"Uh-huh." She wasn't listening, staring at Raphael as he crossed the room to us instead. "Your man is making Ryan really twitchy."

"I know."

"You're enjoying it."

"Just a little."

"But why?"

"Why do I enjoy annoying Ryan?"

"No, I get that. Why does Raphael freak him out?"

"It's because he's a kyrie."

"A what?"

"Demonic bounty hunter," I told her.

"Just like you."

"I don't hunt, warders don't, we protect, and I'm human and he's not."

"Really." Her face lit up.

She watched way, way too much TV.

When Raphael sat down beside me, his hand went immediately to my knee.

"Aww." Phoebe sighed, and then her eyes popped open. "Crap."

"Crap what?"

"Crap, I'm supposed to call my sister and give her directions to the sushi place. She's picking up sashimi and the edamame for—"

"Eda-what?" I asked.

"Soybeans," Raphael educated me.

Oh. It was food. "We can go grab it for you," I offered.

"No," she said, getting up and presenting her daughter to me. "I know she's fussing, but just hold on to her until—"

"No no no," I told her. "Just—"

"I'll hold her," Raphael said confidently, rising up out of the seat and taking the squirming infant like he did it every day of his life. He put the blanket over his shoulder and then gently tucked the baby against it, patting her back softly.

I was stunned.

Phoebe was stunned.

Gaby was not stunned. She burped, scrunched up her face, blew out a tiny baby fart, yawned, stretched, and fell asleep.

"Holy crap," Phoebe said flatly.

"No poop, just gas," Raphael corrected her.

"No, I mean—holy crap, she's not screaming."

"Oh." He was unimpressed. "I didn't think babies cried if you held 'em."

She scoffed.

We drew spectators.

Cash was there, and so were Ryan and Julian, and moments later, Phoebe's mother, Lila. She volunteered to put Gabriella down in her crib and went to take her before anyone could say a word. The second she put her hands on the infant, the little girl squawked.

Grandma let go like Gabriella was the hot potato in the kid's game.

Cash tried with the same result.

All eyes in the small group were on Raphael.

"What?"

"You and the baby." I grinned up from where I was still sitting on the couch.

"C'mon, there's nothing safer than a bounty hunter that can kill demons," he told me. "And she must know. Babies know who to trust."

It was so sweet what he said, so gentle and—

"What did he say?" Phoebe's mother asked.

Crap.

"What'd I say?" The man was at a complete loss.

I bumped his knee with my foot. "I can't take you anywhere."

His smile, because I had touched him, was brilliant, and Phoebe finally saw the fangs. "Awesome," she breathed out.

"He has your child," Cash reminded his wife.

"And what's he gonna do, eat her?"

Ryan looked at her in complete astonishment.

"You won't, will you?" Phoebe asked Raphael.

"Kyries don't eat babies, just full-grown men."

I bumped him again, even gentler the second time.

"What?" He chuckled, moving closer so he could stand between my knees.

"What did he say?" Phoebe's mother asked again.

"So this is, what, permanent now?" Ryan asked.

"Do warders drain kyries?" Julian wanted to know, and I got the feeling the thought had just occurred to him.

"No," Raphael told him, "only humans," before turning back to look down at me. "Answer him."

"What?"

"Answer the warder."

I looked back at Ryan. "Yeah, we're gonna date, see how it goes."

"How do you date a kyrie?"

I coughed. "He moves in."

"Oooh, he moved in already?" Phoebe purred. "That's so hot."

"I thought he said demonic something," Gaby's grandmother asked again.

"Mom, go get a drink," Cash suggested to his mother-in-law, hitting Raphael in the arm hard as soon as the older woman turned away.

"What the fuck was that for?"

"Don't swear in front of the baby," Phoebe cautioned him.

"She's two weeks old." Cash defended my... boyfriend? "How does she know, Phoeb?"

I still wasn't really sure what Raphael and I were. Fuck buddies? Friends with benefits? He had been living in my house and sleeping in my bed for the past three days. The truth was that if I wanted to see him I had to add a line on my phone plan and move him in permanently. The man had a place he slept, not a home, just a room, he told me, in another dimension. It did not have electricity. It did not, in fact, even have running water. In my world, he stayed in seedy motels that he paid for by the night. If I wanted to see him, if I wanted to meet him for dinner and drinks, he had to live with me. He had no home beyond the one I would, or would not, decide to provide for him because he did not technically exist. He didn't have a credit rating or a social security number or a birth certificate. He could not even rent anything. If I wanted him around, he had to move in. He had asked to stay, and I had told him he could. Beyond that, there was nothing more substantial or concrete.

Every day I liked that arrangement less.

I had told him that I wanted him to go wherever he needed to, collect his things, and bring them back.

"Why?"

"I think that would be obvious."

"You want me to bring my treasures to your home?"

"Yes."

"Even as you have claimed me, even if you make a home for me, you still won't own me," he had said, leaning forward, kissing a trail up the side of my neck to my ear.

"No?" I shivered as he had sucked my lobe into his hot mouth.

"No, I do as I like. I return only if I want to."

"Do you want to?"

"Oh yes," he said, his hands sliding over my hips, drawing me forward. "I want nothing more."

"Jacks?"

My head snapped up to Ryan, and I realized they were all looking down at me because my mind had been drifting and I had been all the way across town, back in bed. "Sorry."

"Don't say that shit in front of Phoebe's mother," Cash warned Raphael.

"Cash Vega!"

"What did—"

"You're swearing in front of the baby," I told him, gesturing at Gaby, who took that moment to squeak.

We all watched as Raphael took her off his shoulder and cradled her in his arms. Her eyes blinked open, she looked up, gave him the face that was either gas or a smile, and promptly fell back to sleep.

"She really likes you," Julian said.

"I'm likable," Raphael told him.

I had to agree.

I HAD called Jael while he was in Scotland and given him my weird news, so I was not surprised when I was summoned, along with the new man in my life, to his home when he got back from his trip. My phone had beeped as we were leaving Cash and Phoebe's, and Ryan had overheard me talking to Raphael.

"Julian and I will come along," he said and left no room for argument. "I'll drive."

"Is he gonna test me or try and kill me?" Raphael asked worriedly from the backseat of Ryan's Jeep. "Should we make a stop at home so I can get my sword?"

"No," I soothed him, taking his hand. "It'll be fine."

He did not look convinced but hid his concern with a topic change. "What's with this crappy Jeep, man?" he asked Ryan. "You should get it painted."

"Yes, he should," Julian agreed. "I think cherry red."

"Or darker, like blood." Raphael's eyes glittered.

"You can take the demon out of hell…," Ryan began before Julian pinched him, hard.

"Owww, shit."

I flicked the back of his ear. "He's not a demon."

"For crissakes, I'm driving!"

But it made Raphael smile, and I was glad.

When we reached Jael's home, his mansion in Sausalito that outside looked normal but inside like some medieval Celtic castle, I was surprised to find Marcus, Leith, and Malic there as well. Jael seemed surprised to see Ryan.

"I was just about to call you."

"Now you don't have to."

He opened his mouth to say something.

"I think you should have all the others go and get their hearths as well, and you should bring your lady in so we can all meet her," Ryan suggested.

I had never seen Jael so flummoxed and never, ever, heard anyone give him orders.

"You see," I told my sentinel under my breath, tipping my head at Ryan, "you're wrong, you know. The next sentinel of San Francisco won't be me. It'll be Ryan Dean."

And I saw him realize that even though Ryan didn't particularly enjoy being a warder, he understood duty and pride.

I pulled Raphael back into a corner as Malic, Marcus, and Leith all got on their cell phones to call their mates.

"I think your friend Ryan just sort of cleared a path for me when he acted like it was nothing that I was here," he said, reaching up to tuck a strand of hair behind my ear.

"I think so too. I'll have to thank him."

"You do that."

Half an hour later everyone was assembled—Joe, Marcus's hearth, still complaining about the smell of the cab he'd just been in, and Simon agreeing, as they'd shared it, that it had smelled like the bathroom at the BART station downtown.

"What?" Joe snapped, aware that everyone was looking at him even though he couldn't see them. "It did."

"It did," Simon agreed, looking crisp and polished and handsome in his three-piece suit. His dark hair and charcoal-gray eyes were a striking contrast, and I understood, as always, why he had caught Leith's eye to begin with. Watching the long-haired blond man grab the businessman's hand made me smile.

There was another knock on the door, and when Ian, Jael's butler, went to get it, Dylan Shaw, Malic's hearth, came breezing through.

He smiled big, gave Ian a pat on the arm that the older man rolled his eyes over—it was not appropriate, after all—and then saw me and

Raphael. Malic didn't even have a chance to call him before he darted across the room, bounding to a stop in front of us.

"Hey." He smiled wide, holding out his hand for the kyrie. "I missed you."

And only Dylan could have said it and made it sound so genuine. He always meant absolutely everything he said. I had no idea the amount of energy it must have taken to live that way, so absolutely in the present all the time.

Raphael took Dylan's hand, and the young man grabbed him, hugging him, as Malic was suddenly there.

"Oh hey." Dylan's smile got bigger, out of control, brimming with love for the surly warder before he leaped at him and Malic had to catch him in his arms.

"Fuck," Malic growled, turning his neck, which Dylan had both his arms wrapped around, to Jael as he entered the room with a very elegant-looking woman on his arm.

"Nice first impression, asshole," Ryan grunted.

"Me?"

"Gentlemen." Jael's voice boomed through the room. "I want you to meet Deidre Macauley."

They all smiled and waved at her. I left Raphael and walked over to her and lifted my arms for a hug.

She seemed surprised but unwound her arm from Jael's and stepped into me. I hugged her gently, gave her an extra squeeze at the end, and then let her go as I told her how glad I was that she was there and hoped she had planned on a nice long visit.

The look I got was interest and appreciation and warmth all rolled up together. "Jael, you never told me your warders were so charming."

"I had no idea they were," he answered honestly.

She nodded slowly, studying me. "How old were you when you were called?"

"Sixteen," I told her.

All warders were orphans, alone in the world, which was the reason a hearth was absolutely vital. There had to be a grounding presence in the life of a warder or they slowly went mad. Everyone wanted to be loved; to a warder it was life or death.

"I'm so sorry," she said, her hand lifting to my face, her own brows furrowing.

"It's all right," I soothed her, coming back to the present, having been lost in my own thoughts for a minute. "But I think that's another one of the many reasons it would be nice if you were here; then we'd have a family again."

She gasped, getting it, the fact that if Jael was our surrogate father, then if she was there and with him, that made her the mom in the equation.

From the look on her face, the idea held great appeal.

"Oh Jaka," Jael said, reaching out to pat the same cheek her hand had just vacated. "I should have you move in to make sure she stays."

"Jael," she whispered. "I had no idea that you—"

"I want you here," he said, turning to look down at her from his towering height.

She was overwhelmed, in a good way, but overwhelmed nevertheless.

"Is this why we were called over here?" Leith interrupted.

I took that opportunity to whisper again how glad I was to meet her before returning to Raphael. The second I reached him, he took my hand. It was nice.

"I mean, if it was, great, let's all sit down and have a drink and talk, but if it's not, can we get to it? 'Cause Malic and I have to patrol later."

"No." Jael cleared his throat. "I wanted you all over here to discuss the concerns of having a kyrie among us."

Raphael's hand clenched mine, but I leaned closer, shoulder to shoulder with him, and felt his tension ease.

"Why?" Julian asked my sentinel.

"Because you all have the right to know who or what—"

"No, we don't." Leith cut him off. "And this is crap. All those in favor of the kyrie staying with Jackson say aye. Aye."

"We're voting on that?" Julian was surprised.

"I didn't know we were voting?" Joe chimed in, his smile huge.

"Oh yeah." Dylan's face lit up. "I vote yes!"

"Oh me too," Joe agreed. "I always want new people in my circle. Bring on the kyrie."

"Joe," Marcus began, "we aren't vot—"

"But isn't that why we're here?" Simon interrupted. "It is, isn't it?"

"Not to vote," Jael began. "To understand what having a supernatural creature with us entails and how—"

"But if we vote, we could just leave," Malic said bluntly. "Right?"

"Right," Leith agreed.

"Okay, so I vote yes," Simon announced, turning to look at Raphael. As he did, I noticed that the dark charcoal-gray eyes had warmed to quicksilver. "Raphael saved Malic and me, Leith, and a lot of other really nice people, and Jackson too." He turned his head to look at me. "Didn't he?"

"Yes, he did," I told him.

"Well, then," he said, like it was a done deal.

"So then why are we voting if he's a good guy?" Julian was confused.

"I've been here five years," Joe chimed in. "How these people do anything is beyond me."

"Why are you voting, Jael?"

We all turned to look at Deidre, who did not look pleased at what was transpiring.

I noticed her hair, how dark brown it was, and the auburn highlights in it that caught the light. Her blue eyes were clear and deep, and the lashes that framed them were thick and long. I liked her face, the warmth in her eyes, and the resolute set of her jaw.

"A warder chooses his own hearth. The sentinel has no say," she told him, and I was reminded then that she herself was a sentinel, which meant she had warders of her own to care for and protect and guide. "A warder earns the right to choose his or her own path." Her brows furrowed thoughtfully. "You don't try and choose mates for your charges, do you?"

He looked cornered.

She was suddenly wary, and I could tell it was a deal-breaker for her. "All warders have free will, Jael. You know that."

"I—"

"Jael?" She looked very concerned, concerned like maybe he better say something really fast or she would be taking the next flight back to Edinburgh.

"Hold on," he soothed her.

Blue eyes flashed. "It's unheard of for a sentinel to ever—"

"No no no," he told her, hands up, trying to settle her down, and all of us, the whole room, at the same time. "I merely, because he's a kyrie, wanted us to all be on the same page going for—"

"A kyrie is just like a warder," she told him. "One hunts and one protects. It's practically the same thing."

"But kyries are born in purgatory."

"So was I. It's just called Ferguslie Park."

"Which is where?" Julian asked.

"In Scotland. That's where she's from." I explained.

"How was I supposed to know that?" Julian squinted.

"Doesn't Ryan tell you anything?"

He turned to look at Ryan, who in turn flipped me off.

"Who are we talking about?" Deidre snapped at Jael. "Which of your warders is taking up with a kyrie?"

"That'd be me." I waved at her.

"Oh, well." Her eyes slid over Raphael. "What's the problem?"

Jael cleared his throat. "Jaka's judgment has been in question lately. His old hearth was attacking demons—"

"Frank fought demons?" Joe scoffed. "With what? His calculator?"

"With the branding touch," Leith informed him.

"We have superpowers too?" Dylan sounded excited. "Nobody told me. Malic, how come you didn't tell me?"

"I didn't," Malic began. "You shouldn't," he growled, before his head swiveled to Leith. "You fuck!"

"Gentlemen!" Deidre yelled, but her smile crept in there. "Wow. Okay, Jael, the actions of Jaka's former hearth can in no way be attributed to him, any more than one person leaving another causes the first one to jump off a bridge. Everyone is responsible for their own actions. If the warder chooses a hearth too unstable to understand the importance of being the omphalos, the center of their world, normally you can tell right away. It sounds like this Frank is in love with the idea of warding, not, and I'm sorry, Jaka, with the warder himself."

"Exactly," I told her.

"Well, then, the judgment to have loved the hearth initially is not faulty, simply, in hindsight, regrettable."

"But I don't regret it," I told her. "How could I?"

"Because you learned something." She smiled.

"Yes."

"Oh I like her." Joe grinned wide. "Can she stay, and Jael can go back to—where?"

"Scotland," I told him.

"Yeah, Jael's got the groovy name. He'd fit right in there."

"Joseph Alan Locke!" Marcus scolded him.

"What? I'm just saying."

"You need a ball gag."

"Don't I have one already?"

"Kinky." Julian chuckled, arching an eyebrow for his own boyfriend's benefit.

I saw the muscles in Ryan's jaw flex, heard the sharp exhale of breath. Julian had a very carnal effect on him, that was obvious.

"Quiet!" Jael barked out before sighing deeply. "My only concern was due to Jaka's state of mind lately."

"I'm fine," I assured him.

"He's fine," Malic growled, shoving Dylan off him before the smaller man could get his hands up under the sweater he was wearing. Malic's hearth tended to be all hands where his warder was concerned.

"He does look better," Ryan agreed before squinting at me, "although the beard and the mustache have to go."

"I think the beard's hot." Simon winked.

"Yeah, me too," Dylan chorused.

"Come over here and lemme touch the beard, baby," Joe called over to me.

I laughed because of the look on Marcus's face.

"Really?" He scolded his mate.

Jael growled. "Kyries can become true demons, so I wanted everyone to be aware of—"

"But only the unclaimed ones," Dylan said brightly, and his voice that always sounded good, husky and low, caught everyone's attention. "Isn't that right? That's what Malic said. As long as the kyrie is claimed, then they never go—what's the word?"

"Evil?" Simon offered.

"Oh-oh, rogue," Joe said dramatically, drawing out the word.

"Demony?" Julian threw in.

"That's not a word." Dylan laughed.

"Why isn't rogue good?" Joe sounded insulted.

"It's good, love," Marcus assured him.

"You're patronizing me—patronizing the blind guy."

Malic couldn't stifle his snort of laughter. "You just called yourself the blind guy."

"Why is that funny?"

It snowballed from there. Jael looked over at me, and I waggled my eyebrows.

"I guess I shouldn't have worried," Raphael said beside me.

I turned to look at him.

"It's like a damn frat house around here. How do you people inspire any fear at all?"

"Because when we're out there doing our thing, we're sort of lethal."

"Uh-huh."

But we were. We were scary if you were the bad guy. I let out a quick breath. "Now we can just concentrate on figuring out what we're gonna do without worrying about them."

"Thank you."

"For what?"

"Giving this a shot."

"My pleasure."

"Raphael."

The room went silent as Deidre stepped in front of us.

"Are you the kyrie that killed the demon lord Saudrian?"

He cleared his throat. "I am."

"That was well done." She nodded, and I saw her eyes fill suddenly as she reached up to put a hand on his cheek. "Saudrian, he took my warder Glenna from me, and because of that, her hearth David, later, as well."

"He couldn't make it without her, huh?"

"Sometimes the bond is too deep." She smiled through her tears.

Raphael's hand, still in mine, squeezed tightly. "I get that."

She took a breath. "And his mate, the blood witch Moira. Does she live?"

"Yeah, I couldn't get to her in time before I would've changed, and the portal…. I just, I didn't want to get stuck and not be able to get back to—to see if maybe…." He stopped suddenly and shrugged.

"To see if you could claim a warder for your own."

He lifted my hand, kissed the back of it, but never stopped looking at her. "Yes."

"Well, you have my protection, the protection of a sentinel of the Labarum, as well as all my warders. They will be thrilled to know who severed the head of Saudrian."

"Thank you."

"No, dear, thank you," she breathed out. "But you must be careful. Moira is a formidable enemy. I have faced her myself many times. She will try and break you before she comes for the kill." She pointed at me. "You need to be mindful of your warder."

I saw the truth of her statement hit Raphael, and instantly he tried to pull his hand free.

He was going to run. He was going to go back to my loft, grab his sword, and go find Moira. He would kill her, or she would kill him, but while he was hunting her, in the time it took to locate her, he would stay away from me, put distance between us so the witch would not come after me and I would be safe.

I held on and, with my other hand, grabbed hold of his jacket. "Don't be stupid. She knows who I am. Whether you're with me or not, she's coming, and if you're with me, you can protect me. So stay right here. Don't run. You're done running."

He nodded fast, unsure, and I pulled my hand free and grabbed him. I hugged him tight, pressed against him, head down in his shoulder. I kissed behind his ear, in the spot I had found the day before that made his knees weak.

"Jackson." He sighed out my name.

"And besides," I told him, whispering, "you've got help taking care of me."

"Yes, I do."

He wasn't alone anymore.

IX

IT WAS wet and cold, and I wanted to be home cooking, but instead I was outside in the rain because Rene Favreau had come to my office. I had looked up and found him, and then Cielo was there, too, not looking happy, looking really annoyed, and right before I opened my mouth to ask Rene why the hell he was in my office, he started talking.

Frank had changed so dramatically, was not himself; he was worried that maybe the man had endured some sort of nervous breakdown. I needed to check on him. Would I please just check on him? And I didn't understand why he couldn't just do it himself until he explained that he and Frank, just like Frank and I, had broken up. Rene was no longer in his life either. Funny.

So against my better judgment and over Cielo's very loud objections, I went to check on Frank Sullivan for perhaps the last time. He had moved, again, but I found people all the time, so it wasn't hard to track him down. The old warehouse, now converted lofts, was in an up-and-coming yuppie neighborhood in the city. As I stood in an alley, looking across the street at his window, I was trying to figure out the best way to get a look at him without him seeing me.

"What're you doing?"

I smiled but didn't look over my shoulder. "I thought you were hunting that fox demon for Mr. Sugitani."

"Found it," he grumbled, walking around in front of me. He smiled when he saw my grin. He couldn't stop himself, and the fact that he couldn't, that his reaction to me was automatic, thrilled me. "Now tell me what the hell you're doing here when you're supposed to be home cooking my dinner."

We had developed a routine in a little over a month and a half, and even though neither of us had broached the subject of permanency, it was starting to feel like that anyway.

"I gotta check on Frank."

His eyes went flat, and when he spoke, his voice ran cold. "Why?"

"Rene thinks he might be possessed."

It was not what he was expecting, and the slow squint told me as much. "I'm sorry, what?"

"Okay, see, Rene came to the office today. You remember Rene—you were there with me when I saw them the first time."

"Yes, I was there with you."

"Yeah, so today Rene pops in and tells me that he and Frank are over but that he's worried that there's something really wrong with him. Well, I know that Frank's not psychotic, but maybe, just maybe, something did follow him home, and now he's possessed."

"So you're here to check."

"I'm here to check."

"But nothing else?"

I put a hand on his chest. "Nothing else." I shivered.

He moved closer, hands on my face. "You're gonna catch pneumonia."

"No." I sneezed suddenly, having started feeling like crap earlier. My bones were achy, and I was a little stuffed up. "I'll be fine."

"How is it that human beings can fly to the moon but not figure out how to kill a virus?"

"I don't know." I coughed. "Now go home and start dinner, and I'll be right there as soon as I—"

"Shut up. I'll check on him," he said, flipping up the collar on my peacoat, taking off his own scarf and wrapping it around my neck. He pulled me back down the street, under an awning, and out of the drizzling rain.

"Thanks," I said, lifting to kiss him, and then stopped, thinking better of it.

"Why don't I get a kiss?"

"'Cause I don't wanna make you sick."

"Warder," he said, having gone back to calling me by the name when we were alone. It turned out that he liked calling me that, more of an endearment than anything else. It didn't matter to me; it was the tone of his voice, soft, sultry, that flushed me with heat. His voice made me think of sex every single time. The dark-haired, dark-eyed man turned me inside out.

"Warder," he repeated.

"Sorry."

"I told you before, I don't get your stupid human diseases," he told me, bending to capture my mouth.

I whimpered, and he smiled as he claimed my mouth.

It started slow and gentle and quickly became teeth and tongue and hands under clothes.

"Fuck," he growled, shoving me off him. "I gotta get you home."

I waggled my eyebrows.

"No, idiot," he snapped, "your skin is burning up."

"'Cause of you." I leered.

He was scowling. "No, not because of me, because you have a fever, dumb-ass. Which one is his goddamn apartment, so I can check and we can go home."

Home.

He was coming home with me.

Home to bed. Home in bed. Home where he lived with me.

"I wanna go home with you," I said, my vision clearing with that shiny clarity you get when your fever spikes way up, right before delirium. "I want you to live with me and stay with me because I love you so much it hurts."

His gorgeous, smoky, topaz eyes lit up like I had never seen. "You love me?"

"Yeah, kind of a lot. Really, really a lot."

He sucked in his breath and grabbed me and crushed me to the wall of hard muscle that was his chest and squeezed the air right out of my lungs.

I managed to get loose enough to free my arms so I could hug him back and sigh long and loud.

The man was ferocious and dangerous and untamed and just... perfect for me. I was head-over-heels crazy about him, and from the way he was when we went out, guarding me like I was made of gold, snarling at anyone who got too close, I understood that he was just as nuts about me. And now he was getting ready to nurse me through whatever I was about to get and seemed damn happy about it.

"I love you back, warder, more than you know, more than you can imagine."

But I had a good idea.

He shoved me off him, glaring at me. "Which fucking apartment?"

I chuckled and told him. And I was going to make him promise to keep out of sight, but before I could get the words out, he was gone, having bolted down the street, charging through the rain. I watched him leap up from the ground to the second floor and higher until he landed on a balcony and climbed over the railing. It was too hard to see what happened next, too dark, the rain a distracting drizzle around me. Leaning back, I shivered in the cold, having done myself a disservice by not wrapping up in more layers. I inhaled the scarf around my neck and realized that what I was smelling was me. The man smelled like me, like our home, like our bed, like us. I tipped my head back so I didn't cry.

I would never have another hearth, because he couldn't be that.

He would be more, because we were equals.

In minutes he was back, and he took hold of my jacket and pulled me off the wall where I had been leaning.

"God, you're burning up." He was worried and put his arm around me to lead me down the street toward the next one where the cabs ran.

"So what?" I asked.

"He's not possessed."

And I hadn't really entertained the thought. I had been checking more for Rene's benefit than mine. "I didn't think he was."

"He is, however, entertaining more than one man in his apartment right now."

"Oh." I nodded, grinning. "Well, there ya go. I'll report back to Rene that all is well and Frank's just having fun, and after a while I'm sure he'll settle down with just one—"

"Or two."

"Or two guys." I smiled. "I guess he'll need a bigger house than he thought he would."

"For the dungeon," Raphael teased me.

I laughed. "Maybe I should call Rene tonight so—"

He cleared his throat. "I will speak to Rene. You're done."

"Whatever you say."

"Really, whatever I say," he said, pressing a palm to my forehead. "You're hot."

"Am I?" I smiled, leaning in, kissing under his jaw. "You wanna take me home and get in bed with me?"

"Oh that's the plan, though not how you're thinking." He chuckled, tucking me close to him as we walked.

"Just so long as you come home with me, I don't care what we do."

"I don't care, either."

"Promise you'll always come home."

"You won't be able to keep me away."

And his fierce promise was all I needed.

nexus

1

SOMETIMES there were just not enough hours in the day, and no matter what I did, I could not get everything done. I had gotten extra pressure when my boyfriend—partner, the man I would take a bullet for—had told me we had to go out of town to his grandfather's eightieth birthday party. Due to the fact that I was a senior associate at the law firm where I practiced, I had to work extra long and extra late to clear my schedule so I could get away. As a result of that, we had not been able to fly out together, but I had made sure we would be sitting side by side for the trip home. Holding the man's hand during takeoff and landing—he was a nervous flyer—was really something I enjoyed.

Getting off the plane at the Blue Grass Airport in Lexington, Kentucky, I made my way down the stairs toward the baggage claim. I turned my phone on as I walked and called my sentinel, Jael Ezran. Along with practicing law, I was also a warder, which meant I hunted and killed things that went bump in the night. I stood between people and the demon horde along with my fellow warders—five of us altogether—with our sentinel Jael Ezran. Every city had five warders and one sentinel to lead them. Every night we took to the streets in pairs, one of us rotating to have a night, or more than one, off. If there wasn't much going on, only two went out. If there was a lot of activity, then Jael patrolled with us and we'd be out in teams of two or three. It just depended on the creatures from the pit.

But in the light of day, I would normally be at work doing the lawyer thing at Kessler, Torrance and Price. I would be a partner soon, Mrs. Kessler had told me. She liked me, the board liked me, and the fact that my caseload was the heaviest of the associates and my win record was close to perfect had put me over the top. And I was pleased—tired but pleased—that I had proven myself beyond a shadow of a doubt to be one of the men who would see to the firm's enduring legacy. And now I had been told to catch my breath.

It was not in my nature to rest on my laurels once I had shown what I was capable of, but to my surprise, it was what the other partners at the firm wanted. Everyone strongly suggested I take on fewer clients, the consensus being that they wanted me around for the long haul, not burned out at thirty-five. They hoped I could now enjoy my time off, so that when I was at work, I would be 100 percent invested and not worried about missing out on time with my partner, the wonderful guy they got to see and talk with at every company function. Lately I had been offered time-shares, cabins in Aspen, villas on Lake Cuomo, and a cabana in Tahiti. They wanted me to stay, and they knew me well enough to know that if Joseph Locke was happy, I was happy too. Over the years, after seeing how everyone at the firm responded to the man I loved, I was so glad I had gone with my gut.

I had been courted by many firms out of law school but had decided on a smaller, more prestigious one many of my peers had promised would never promote me. I was gay, I was black—it would never happen. But I had sat with the managing partner and owner, Helene Kessler, and looked in her eyes, and her gaze was unwavering when she spoke candidly about my future and what she could see for me if I worked hard and made a believer out of her. She wanted me because of my brain. The rest—color, sexual orientation, even the car I drove—meant nothing.

As time passed, I saw that my decision had been the best one I could have made. I was proud that I worked for a law firm that had no concerns with the fact that I lived with and loved another man. I had heard horror stories from some of my fellow attorneys at other firms and could only say that, in my experience, there had been no problem with my homosexuality. Helene Kessler ran her firm based on performance, end of story. She didn't really give a damn *who* you slept with... except for her brother-in-law Ray. The man in question was who I had just finished defending, and the people in his bed were of paramount importance to her.

I had been called to her office two days ago, and unlike our usual meetings, she was not sitting at her desk and inviting me to do the same. She was instead standing at her window, watching the rain pelt the glass. When she turned and looked at me, her eyes were clouded.

"Mrs. Kessler," I said softly, gently, crossing the room to her side.

"Helene," she corrected, as she had been lately.

It would be strange to start calling her by her first name, but as she had become insistent, I had to honor her wishes. "Helene," I acquiesced.

Silently, she passed me a file folder, and I was surprised to realize I was looking at the arrest sheet of her sister's husband. I started flipping through it immediately.

"He needs to seek treatment for sex addiction and drug addiction," she told me, her voice flat and hard like it never was.

I skimmed the contents. Her brother-in-law had been found with copious amounts of cocaine and with one—no, two— prostitutes, and—

"Ray was discovered with three escorts...." She trailed off.

"Where was—oh," I said, because I finally saw the name of the third girl, woman—no, girl, just barely eighteen. Christ.

"Passed out, all four of them. The hotel manager called the police when there was no answer in the room after check-out time, and when he went in no one would wake up." She took a breath. "Ray needs to be confined to a hospital so he can be treated," she sighed. "His wife, my sister, is just...." She looked at me, saw me squinting at her. "Oh God, Marcus, we both know I was thinking of a judgeship, and now this? Jesus, I just need it to go away. I got it on Judge Rojas's docket for the morning, so.... Just keep him out of jail, throw him in a psychiatric facility, and have them try and cure him of being a sex addict. Lock him up and throw away the key. I don't give a damn, just—"

"I'll handle it," I promised, hand on her shoulder.

She nodded, covering my hand with hers for the briefest of moments before she started rubbing the bridge of her nose under her glasses, a quirk of hers when she was nervous.

"It won't go away," I said honestly. "But we'll deal with it as quickly and quietly as we can. I promise you won't have to deal with it. I'll take care of everything."

"I know you will," she said. "You're the only one I trust."

I was pleased to hear it, and when I had gone straight to her office after court that morning, she had been waiting for me.

"It's done. He's in a treatment program, and he'll do his time, six months, at that facility."

She nodded, waiting.

"Your sister was there," I said gently. "She cried a lot."

"She's an idiot."

"You can't help who you love."

"Oh no?"

I shook my head. "You married the perfect man, and he died too soon, and I'm going to say this to you because we're friends, aren't we?"

"Of course," she snapped. "Do you think I spend my holidays with just anyone?"

I smiled at her. "Now listen. It's time, you know. Woman does not live by work alone."

"Time to do what?"

"Date."

"Bite your tongue," she chided me, getting up and walking to the huge window in her enormous corner office.

"We'll work on it."

She made a dismissive noise.

"Don't push me. I'll have Joe call you."

Her head turned so she could see me over her shoulder. "You and I both know that he's irresistible. Please don't sic him on me."

"Well, then, I want to see you take a man to the opera fund-raiser in two weeks. If I have to go, you have to have a date."

She grunted and did a quick turn so her back was against the glass. "What else about Ray?"

"If he messes up again, he's going to do time, and there's nothing you'll be able to do about it."

"Okay."

"I talked to Weber Ford at the *Chronicle*, and he said he'd bury it as far back as he can."

"Thank you."

"You can't be blamed for your family."

"Oh, yes I can. Everything they do reflects on me."

"It'll be all right."

"Or it won't, but I refuse to just cover it up and end up owing the wrong people too much. It's not worth my soul."

"No. It's not."

"Thank you, Marcus. I'll look forward to having you as a senior member of this firm."

My gaze settled on hers in question.

"It's time. We both know it is. Everyone here knows it is. You've worked hard; you're the only one at this firm that every board member believes in. We're voting Friday. I'll have good news for you when you get back from your trip to… I'm sorry. Where are you going again?"

I chuckled. "Kentucky."

Her face scrunched up tight. "What on earth for?"

"It's great there, actually, and Joe's grandfather is turning eighty."

"I suspect he's not the draw, but instead your charming partner."

I arched a brow. "You think Joe's charming?"

She laughed then, for the first time in days. "Yes, Marcus, I certainly do."

"Huh."

"Marcus."

A voice saying my name brought me from my thoughts and into the present. The phone had been picked up on the other end, but not by Jael, because he would have called me by my warder name, Marot, and not my given name. There was also the voice itself to take into account. What I was being treated to was a sound much softer, smoother, richer, a smoky tenor in comparison to the usual growl of my sentinel.

"Ryan," I said, knowing the man's voice as well as my own. He had been my fellow warder a long time.

"Hey."

"Tell Jael I landed in Lexington and I'm good, all right?"

"Will do." He yawned first and ended with a sigh.

"Why're you there?"

"Jael is thinking he wants to cook when Deidre's warders come to visit next week."

I wasn't going to touch that one. "I'm sorry?"

"Well, you know that Deidre Macauley, the sentinel he's been seeing from Edinburgh? She is having her warders fly over here to meet Jael, and he was thinking it would be a good idea to show them how well he could take care of her, so he was going to cook."

"Okay."

"Yeah, see, Malic thought the same thing. He thought Jael should have the dinner catered or take everyone out, and then the warders could see that he actually has money and can provide well for their sentinel."

Being a sentinel, being a warder, was not a paid gig. Some sentinels and some warders were nowhere near the top of the food chain. Because of Jael's inheritance and some very shrewd investing, his family fortune had grown tenfold in his lifetime. He could provide Deidre with quite a nice life, if that was what she wanted. Having met the lady, however, I knew that no man would ever have to take care of her. It would be nice for him to show off for her warders, though.

"I don't get the cooking."

"Neither do I, but whatever."

"So you're there teaching him how to cook something."

"Yep."

"Should I even ask what?"

"No, don't ask. You don't wanna know."

I laughed because he sounded so pained. "Sorry," I chuckled. "Just tell the big man I'm okay, and I'll see you in a week."

"What are you doing there again?"

"Joe's grandfather's birthday."

"Oh, that's right."

Something occurred to me. "Maybe Deidre's warders would like the idea of him cooking, of her being more involved with a man who treated his own warders like family—maybe that's what's up with the cooking."

There was a moment of silence before he answered me. "Christ, it must be exhausting to be you, thinking about everything all the time."

I grunted.

"I'll call you if anyone dies," he said.

"That's not funny," I told him.

"Did you pack your swords, or did you leave them at home?"

"Why would I pack my swords to come to a birthday party?"

"It *is* Kentucky."

"So lemme get this straight. You've been all over the world, *Mr. I-Used-To-Be-A-Model*, but you think Lexington is some hick town where packing hook swords would be a good idea?"

"I have no idea."

"I know you don't. You're just talking out of your ass."

He huffed. Normally he wasn't like that; he was thoughtful, not prejudiced against a place he didn't know. Something was wrong.

"Are you going to tell me?" I asked.

"Tell you what?"

I stayed quiet and waited.

"It's nothing."

"Sure."

"I'm just irritated." He sighed deeply, breaking down. "One of Deidre's warders, Collin something, artistic type with A Flock of Seagulls haircut, is already here, and I'm thinking from the looks of things that he finds my boyfriend somewhat appealing."

If I were there, I would have wished Collin with the '80s retro haircut good luck. No one was taking Ryan Dean's hearth away from him... no one. And since Ryan was the kind of gorgeous that people stopped on the street to watch walk by, he really had nothing to worry about. But he loved Julian Nash desperately, so it wasn't all that surprising that he was worried. It was, however, needless.

"You know, I've actually met Julian," I soothed him. "He's kind of the loyal type."

"No, I know. It's just... where does Collin get off disrespecting me?"

"I doubt he realizes he is. He just sees an attractive man he knows has the strength to be the hearth of a warder, and so he's interested. I'll bet you it's no more than that."

He grunted on the other end.

As a rule, Ryan was not volatile, but having a hearth was still new for him. He and Julian had yet to hit six months.

"How do you not try and kill anyone that comes near Joe?"

"You trust your hearth, Ry. The man is my home just like Julian is yours."

He exhaled, and I understood that he had been more upset than I realized, and now he was calmer. "Okay."

"Good." I smiled into the phone. "Call me if you want to talk some more or if you need help hiding the body."

"Will do," he sighed, and he hung up.

I turned the corner, putting my phone back in the breast pocket of my suit jacket as I crossed the baggage claim area.

"Marcus."

I stopped and looked around but saw no one I knew.

"Honey, maybe that's not—"

"It is, El. I know his walk."

"But the only guy there is a black guy."

Black guy?

"Ohmygod," I heard the man I loved say in mock-shock. "Marcus is black?"

"Joey!"

I finally saw a woman peeking out at me from behind a large pillar and began walking over to her. As the room opened up, I saw more pillars and benches beside them. My partner, Joseph Locke, was sitting on one and across from him were his mother and father and sister.

"Marcus! Honey!"

They could have been on a poster for all-American wholesome goodness, the Locke family in all their glory.

"Marcus," Joe called to me, louder than his mother.

"I hear you," I called over to him so he'd know.

"Then hurry the hell up," he grumbled.

Had he been able to see me, he would have seen my scowl, but he couldn't, so I had to wait and smack him once I got there.

"Christ, Marcus," he growled when I clipped him on the shoulder.

"You deserve that," his father rumbled, an older, taller version of the man I loved. He had dark brown hair and the same pale eyes that had been gifted to his son. "Learn some patience."

"I haven't had coffee," I warned Joe, "so don't screw with me."

He grunted.

"Yes," his mother agreed, standing up to hug me. "Leave Marcus alone."

Her, I liked. It was my boyfriend who was the grouch.

"How ya doin', Deb?" I asked as I enfolded her in my arms.

I loved to look at my boyfriend's mother: her dark blue eyes, short, wavy blonde hair, and sweet smile. I could see her in Joe, and I liked that.

She squeezed me tight, arms around my neck, and kissed my cheek, breathing out some tension. We had always gotten along well, even at our first meeting. I was always a big hit with parents; the word "lawyer" worked wonders.

"How was your flight?" Deb asked, leaning back to look up at my face, her arms dropping off my shoulders and resting on my chest. She was comfortable standing there in the circle of my arms. I was as much her kid as either Barbara or Joe, and that had been making me happy since I met her five, almost six years ago. I had lost my own mother when I was fifteen, so she was the only one I had.

"I had 'the guy' sitting next to me, you know, that 'guy', the one who wants to chat."

"On the red-eye." She was annoyed for me. "My goodness, why didn't he just let you get some sleep?"

"I know why," Joe grumbled.

"Shhh," I shushed him.

"Oh, honey, you didn't tell him you were a lawyer, did you?"

"That's not the reason, Mother," Joe snapped irritably.

"It was," I lied, smiling suddenly, leaning to kiss her cheek. "I think he overheard me on the phone before we boarded."

"How rude," she continued.

"I'm never letting you fly alone again," Joe muttered.

I ignored the love of my life in favor of his mother. "You look great, by the way."

"Guys hitting on you—what the hell, you wear a ring, for crissakes!"

"And I really love the haircut," I continued.

"Finally!" she almost shouted. "Somebody noticed."

"You got a haircut?" Barbara asked, sounding shocked.

Deb's exasperated snort made everyone laugh as she gave me a last squeeze before releasing me to her husband, who came up behind her to hug me as well. I liked that my boyfriend's father didn't just shake my hand; it was nice that he had to hug me too.

"How are you, Marcus?" he asked when he let me go and looked up at my face. "You took the red-eye out, huh? Tired?"

I groaned. "Yes, sir, but just get some coffee and food in me, and I'll be ready to go."

"Good." He smiled before he stepped sideways so Joe's sister Barbara could hug me.

I lifted Barbara Locke off her feet and crushed her against me.

"God, Marcus." She giggled as I put her down, her hands on my face. "Why can't I find one like you?"

"Oh, sweetie, don't worry. There's the perfect guy out there just waiting for ya."

And there was. Barbara was smart and funny and classically beautiful with big blue eyes and high cheekbones and full lips. If I were straight, she would have been mine. But as it was, her brother was the one I pined for.

"Suck-up," Joe said under his breath.

"Joseph," Barbara snapped as she stepped back beside her mother.

"Did you guys at least give him a snack this morning?" I asked his sister.

"No, so that's why he's like this. He needs food, and coffee too."

"Marcus, honey, let me introduce you to Ellen—"

"Wait," Joe snapped, reaching for me.

I grasped the questing hand, wrapping mine around it, noticing as always the warmth and the strength of his grip. This was not a man who sat in an office all day. He worked with his hands and he worked hard. As the owner and operator of Bumpy Road Limited, he could have taken a less physical role in his company, but he considered himself and everyone he employed to be part of the same team. He stocked shelves, talked to vendors, and called on accounts. He did every job in his company equally, which was why, I was certain, he was so beloved.

I squatted down beside the bench, hand on his knee as I looked up into his gorgeous clear blue eyes.

They were the first things I had ever noticed about him. They were pale, almost opaque cerulean with flecks of India ink in them. I had been out drinking, had turned to head back to the table from the bar—there to buy the last round—and he had suddenly been in front of me, and I was swallowed up in his gaze.

I had forgotten to breathe.

"You have a great laugh," he'd told me. "I've been listening to it all night."

I had tilted my head, realizing almost instantly that he was blind. "That's the worst pick-up line I've ever heard." I smiled.

"Are you sure?" he teased me. "The very worst?"

The arch of his eyebrow was wicked, his dimples were sweet, and his plump parted lips, wet now as he licked them, were making my cock hard. The man made my mouth go dry.

I'd noticed the way the light hit his auburn hair, a play of brown and red. I'd appreciated the splatter of freckles across the bridge of his short, upturned nose and had seen the way his eyes narrowed seductively, the long, thick feathery lashes hooding them. I'd heard the soft moan under his breath. I'd wondered, with the part of my brain that was still working, why someone had not put a ring on the man's finger. That fast, I thought I might want to keep him.

He knew what he was about, because standing there, head tilted, waiting, cute and sexy all at once, he'd had an agenda. I liked that. Men who played games, who weren't sure what they wanted, were not for me. With the no-nonsense attitude he had going, already he had my undivided attention. I'd let my gaze go everywhere, missing no part of him. He was smaller than me, leaner-muscled, prettier, but solid and strong. I liked the daring tip of his head, his lips that were pale and pink and full, and the effect I had on his breathing. He was holding onto the back of the bar stool beside him, flexing and unflexing his hand, waiting to see what I would say. As if there were ever any doubt. I wanted to *eat* him.

"I'm Marcus Roth," I said hoarsely.

He let out a breath and thrust his hand at me. "Joseph Locke."

I took the offered hand in mine, holding tight. "Pleasure to meet you."

"And you," he said, stepping forward, inhaling me.

I had thought that because he couldn't see that he would be timid about his desire, as well as reticent to trust. But the man knew what he wanted, and when he'd asked me to get something to eat with him, I'd found that I couldn't say yes fast enough. I liked the laugh lines in the corner of his eyes, found myself charmed by his rakish grin, and felt my pulse jump at the way he laced his fingers into mine. I was a big guy, six six, two hundred and fifty pounds of hard, heavy muscle; I was normally not on the receiving end of possessiveness. But Joe couldn't see me, and so he didn't know that he didn't need to stake his claim in front of other people. He was all of five ten, trying to yank me after him wherever we went. I had been charmed completely.

Now five, almost six years later, he still had to show anyone who was looking that I belonged to him.

"I knew it was you," he sighed as his hand slipped around the nape of my neck, pulling me closer to him. "I told my cousin, but she didn't believe me."

The man's sightless eyes were really the most beautiful shade of blue I had ever seen. And I could gaze at them endlessly and enjoy them without him ever flushing with embarrassment and looking away. His eyes warmed me, and I was certain, everyone who ever met him.

"Yeah, well, it's a damn parlor trick that you can tell a person by their frickin' walk, so who could blame her?"

She gasped, but Joe and his family, the people who knew me and got me, started laughing instantly.

I arched an eyebrow for poor Ellen, who was the only one not getting the joke.

Deb was snickering as she looked at me with smiling eyes. "I'm so glad you're here. Joe's been missing you," she finished, patting my shoulder.

"I'm so embarrassed."

I turned my head to look at Ellen, who was now standing on the other side of Joe.

"I didn't mean to imply that—I just, no one told me that you were—"

"Black?" I asked.

"Oh God," she groaned, head in her hands.

Poor girl, she was turning a very vibrant shade of red. Joe's father Elliot started laughing. Deb put her hand over her mouth, and Barbara giggled.

"What I meant to say—"

"Is that you were not expecting me to be black," I teased her unrelentingly.

She opened her mouth to say something but shut it fast.

"I'm kidding." I smiled wide. "You know that, right?"

She looked horrified.

"Oh, sweetie," I soothed her, standing up, lifting out of Joe's embrace. "I—"

"Marcus's friends didn't expect me to be blind," Joe cut me off, sounding annoyed. "But he's the catch, not me, so if everyone could just drop it, I would love it."

The area went silent, and I shook my head. It had been playful until he made it not so, and that wasn't usual. There was actually something eating at him.

I leaned forward, offering my hand to his cousin. "Marcus Roth, pleasure to meet you."

She surged forward, grasping my hand in both of hers. "I'm Ellen Rowe, and the pleasure is all mine, Marcus."

I smiled at Ellen to reassure her and saw her stare at me. I forgot sometimes that to some people, an interracial couple was cause for surprise. For Joe's parents and his sister, it had never been an issue. And they didn't need to understand why I wanted to date him; the question was why more people didn't. They got that Joe was a catch and loved me because I realized it as well. There was no dysfunction in my boyfriend's family, and I was thankful for them all.

"Everyone in your family is nicer than you," I told my boyfriend to make him smile.

He just scowled.

I could see how uncomfortable he was making everyone feel, so I reached out and put my fingers through his thick hair, dragging it back from his face. "Lighten up, Joey."

"Sit down for a second," he almost whined. "Dad, can you get Marcus's garment bag, please, and his duffle? They're the Louis Vuitton ones, and the tag has his business card on it. If the tag came off, there's another one in a pocket in the back in Braille."

"'Course," the older man said, turning to go.

"Elliot, I'll get it," I called out to him.

He waved at me to stay put, though, and then mouthed words. I read that Joe was upset? I looked up at Deb.

She cleared her throat. "This weekend has a lot of outdoor activities like horseback riding and a touring distillery and dancing at a friend's house. I think Joe was slightly concerned about all that he would be able to do."

And even as I nodded I realized that there was no way that this bit of news was what had my boyfriend in a twist. Joe was always up for anything, and he accepted help whenever he needed to. Something else was wrong.

I sank down onto the bench beside him, and instantly his knee was against mine.

"I'm so glad you're here."

"Me too, baby," I told him. Normally, at home in San Francisco, I would have put my arm around him and given him a kiss, but we were not there, and I didn't feel comfortable here.

"Marcus?" Ellen smiled.

"Yes, ma'am?"

"How long have you and Joe been dating? He didn't get a chance to tell me."

"We don't date," Joe answered before I could. "We live together, have lived together for over four years. We're partners. We have a civil union and rings." He held up his left hand for her so she could see the thick gold ring. It was engraved inside, just as mine was, with our initials and the date we had made our love official in front of a crowd of our best friends and Joe's parents and sister. So far, it had been the happiest day of my life.

"Oh." She looked suitably educated.

"We dated for a year, and then he begged me to move in with him, and I said yes."

"Begged?" I groused.

His lopsided grin, the one he gave me often, was suddenly there doing the wicked thing to his eyes where they heated and softened at the same time. I noticed that he hadn't shaved and found the face I knew even sexier than usual.

"And what is it you do, Marcus?" Ellen asked.

Joe supplied the answer before I could. "He's a criminal lawyer at one of the biggest firms in San Francisco. He will make partner this year, the youngest in the firm's history."

And that was it. She was impressed.

I leaned sideways as the women started talking. "Could you stop being an ass now, please?"

Joe ran his fingers over my jaw, and I watched him suck in his breath. Someone had definitely been missing being in bed with me.

"What's with you?" I asked, dropping my voice low, making it sound sultry on purpose.

"I just... I don't like it when I don't touch you every day. I think my mind started playing tricks on me, and besides, it's really hard to sleep without you."

Which I liked more than I would confess.

"I'm used to having your hands on me at night."

And that fast, as it always happened, I felt the blood rushing to my groin. "Jesus, Joey," I groaned softly.

"When we get back to my folks' place, promise you'll hold me down and fuck me."

I was suddenly awash in memories of his head thrown back, eyes closed, his skin moist and feverish, pale against the dark that mine was. I was seriously uncomfortable. "Baby, please, you're gonna make things awkward for me if you don't stop."

The throaty laughter didn't help.

"I wish we didn't have to meet everyone for breakfast," he told me, hand slipping under the collar of my sweater to the skin underneath. "I'd rather just go back to the house with.... God, your skin's warm."

I loved him all squirmy and needy, the ache in his voice, the way he clutched at me.

"I'll make it up to you tonight."

"You don't have to make anything up," he sighed, fingers like the touch of butterfly wings over my face. "Just make sure you get in bed with me. Stay with me."

"I will. I'm all yours," I said, sliding my thumb over the silky curve of his bottom lip. I released a deep breath as what he said finally registered. "Wait, what do you mean your mind is playing tricks on you?"

I got the "Joe face," the squinting, the head tipping, all of it designed to make me drop whatever I had asked about.

"Joseph," I pressed.

He scoffed. "Fine. I think I hurt this guy at my dad's shop."

"What guy?"

"A guy who came in to try and get money."

I was so lost. "What?"

"I gotta fill you in later. Dad didn't even want me to tell you at all because he's worried that you'll want him to go to the police."

What the hell was going on? "Joe," I growled. "Tell me now."

"I can't," he insisted, "not in front of my folks or Barb or El."

And he wouldn't tell, no matter what I said or threatened him with. But I could skip to the second problem. "Hurt him how?"

"Hurt who?"

"You said you hurt some guy at your—are you listening to me?"

"Of course."

"So how did you—"

"I accidentally touched him."

"You touched some guy at your dad's store and hurt him?"

"Yeah."

"Hurt him how?"

"You *know* how, Marcus."

And just like that, I was tense. "Honey, we both know that there would only be one reason why you touching anyone would hurt them."

The branding touch.

A warder could hurt a demon just by touching them. The same was true for the hearth of a warder. As a hearth carried the heart of a warder in their hand, that same hand touching a demon made their skin sizzle. It was a demonic litmus test. If my boyfriend touched you and it burned, you were a preternatural creature from the pit. There was nothing else you could be.

"How do you know?" I whispered.

"On the way out, the guy bumped me, and when I reached out to get my balance, I touched him, and he yelled," he said, his fingers curling into mine. "He scared the crap outta me."

"Okay." I took a breath. "And this guy was there to extort money from your father."

"Marcus," he said sharply.

"Fine, but he was, yes?"

"Yes."

"And what did you do?"

"I told him not to come back."

"You threatened him."

"This is my father we're talking about, Marcus."

"Were you scared?"

"Terrified."

But I would bet the guy had no idea. "You're amazing."

"Yeah?"

"Yes," I said, taking his hand in both of mine, holding tight. "Who's the guy?"

"His name was Arcan," he said. "I heard my Dad say it."

"Arcan what?"

"Just Arcan. He told me after that that's all there was."

One name, unless you were Cher or Madonna, was not a good thing. A singular name, a guy that Joe had hurt just with a touch of his hand, added up to demon.

"Did this guy say anything to you?"

"He told me he would find out who I belonged to."

Which meant he had not mistaken Joe for a warder but knew exactly what he was.

"I told him to go to hell."

"Baby." I took a breath because he was scaring me. "Why would you—"

"Because you were coming, Marcus," he cut me off. "I'm not scared of anything when you're with me."

God, the faith the man had in me. I put an arm around his shoulders, leaned him against me, and breathed him in.

"You deserve every bit of it," he told me, turning to wrap his arms around my neck. "You've never done anything for me not to trust you or believe in you."

My heart hurt just holding him, looking at him. "I need you to stay close to me, you understand?"

He nodded.

"Okay," I said, calming.

"Maybe he won't come back." He was trying to soothe me further. "I mean, maybe he's scared, huh?"

I saw him swallowing down his fear, forcing a smile for good measure.

"Right?"

"Yes," I assured him.

"All right, everybody, let's go eat."

Elliot came back with my bags, and I stood and took the garment bag from him as Joe rose and leaned into me. With one arm around him, we followed his father toward the parking lot.

ll

THE person who provided a home for a warder, the one who loved them and grounded them and centered them, was their hearth. Being the hearth of a warder was not something to be taken lightly, and while a warder could seal their home, keeping his mate safe within their sanctuary, if a hearth was attacked outside, he or she had little defense but the one they could offer with whatever skills they naturally possessed. Added to that was the branding touch. If a hearth was truly loved, when a demon came to take or harm them, they could burn the demon. It was the same power a warder had, but where a warder used it to inflict pain and then go in for the kill, a hearth used it for surprise so they could run. Joe was telling me that with the defense of a hearth, he had accidentally hurt a stranger.

Or thought he had.

"I might be crazy," he told me as we sat together in the back of the van. His parents were in the front, Barbara and Ellen behind them, and Joe and I were allowed to have a little privacy after four days apart.

"We both know you're not. Just spill it," I ordered him, taking his hand in mine, lifting it to my lips, kissing his knuckles.

He whimpered softly, and I could not help the smile. Here we were talking about something scary, and all I could think about was getting him under me and how good he would feel.

"Say you missed me."

"I told you on the phone last night," I sighed, leaning sideways against him, my breath on his ear, my teeth biting down gently on the silky lobe.

"Tell me again." He shivered as I kissed behind his ear and then sucked the delicate skin.

"I missed you," I told him, pressing my lips to the side of his neck. "So very much."

He made a noise in the back of his throat that made his sister turn around and look at me.

"Hi." I smiled at her.

She shook her head. "You two are so damn cute."

I waggled my eyebrows at her, and she blushed a beautiful shade of red.

"Me," Joe demanded, pressing my hand down onto his thigh. "Concentrate on me."

"Jesus, Marcus." She sighed heavily. "I had no idea my brother was such a diva."

"No?" I chuckled. "Really?"

Joe growled, and we both laughed.

At the restaurant, I got out first, helped Joe down, and then passed him his cane before I took his hand.

"Oh."

I looked at Ellen and saw how tense she looked. "What?"

"You're holding his hand."

"Yes, I am." I flashed her what my assistant, Lolita Powell, called my lion grin: all teeth, heat, and power.

"It's fuckin' freezing out here," Joe groused at us, tugging on my hand. "Let's get inside."

"Joseph!" Deb scolded her son.

"It's okay, baby," I soothed him, lengthening my stride and slowing him down at the same time. "Don't get upset."

"First you're black, now you're gay," he grumbled as he walked. "Fuck this, Marcus. Why are we even here?"

"Because you love your grandfather and that's what families do: deal with sometimes-uncomfortable situations together."

"I can deal with anything when it's me, but not when it's you."

And I knew that. Joe had the patience of a saint in all areas that did not pertain to me. He was a little protective.

"Ellen didn't mean anything. She was just making an observation. You gotta stop being so sensitive, okay?"

He only grunted, making no promises.

"Joey!"

I stopped as a man came jogging toward us. He was tall with golden-brown hair and striking blue-gray eyes and fine, chiseled features.

"Ohmygod, Kurt, is that you?" Barbara squealed, her mouth dropping open in surprise.

"Barbie." His smile for her was huge, and when she flung herself at him, he caught her easily.

I stood there and waited as Kurt hugged everyone before he turned to Joe.

"Joey," he sighed, and there was a lot of affection in the single word.

"Hey," Joe said coolly, tightening his grip on my hand.

There would be no hugging.

"It's good to see you," Kurt said, moving forward, arms out, closing in.

Joe knew my body as well as his own, he knew how tall I stood, how much space I took up and how far he had to move around me to put distance between him and other people. He didn't have to guess. He also knew that if he was retreating, no one would get by me.

"Mom!" he called out to Deb, taking one step back and sideways, hands fisting in my suit jacket. "Do they serve Hot Browns at this restaurant? I want Marcus to try one."

"Of course," she called back, but I didn't see her; my entire focus was on Kurt as he stopped his forward momentum before he plowed into me.

It was perfectly clear to me that Joe did not want to hug him, but because Joe was Joe, he had given the appearance that because he was blind he had simply missed the motion. It was extraordinarily thoughtful but clear at the same time. And it was strange.

It wasn't like him. Joe hugged and kissed everybody. He even hugged my fellow warder Jackson's new boyfriend, Raphael, and Raphael wasn't even human. Something was really wrong.

"Joe," Kurt chuckled, "you accidentally hid behind your bodyguard buddy."

"Kurt," he said quickly, clutching at me, "this is my boyfriend, Marcus Roth. Marcus, this is my cousin Kurt that I told you about."

Cousin.

That he told me about.

That he... told... me.... I felt my stomach twist, and my eyes narrowed.

"It's a pleasure to meet you, Marcus," he said, offering me his hand.

If I took his hand, I would crush it. My eyes locked on his as I clenched my jaw tight.

He withdrew his hand, grabbed Barbara's, and told us that his mother had reserved a big table in the back of the restaurant. Ellen followed after her two cousins, and Elliot and Deb turned to face me and Joe.

"What was that about?" Joe's father asked.

"Nothing. Let's just go in," Joe assured them, tugging on my hand.

Elliot put a hand gently on his son's shoulder. "Please, Joe."

He let out a quick breath. "It's no big deal. I'm just being oversensitive because I'm tired since I don't sleep well in a strange place."

At home, even though he didn't like to, Joe slept fine without me. He could wake up in the night, know exactly where he was, where everything was, and what had not moved. In a new place alone, if a noise woke him, he had no one to shake awake and ask what the noise was. He slept lightly when he wasn't home. At home, the man slept like the dead.

"Honey?" Deb prodded him.

His exhale of air was sharp, exasperated. "It was just a prank, but when I was fourteen we came here, out to Uncle Glenn's farm in Irvine, and I went swimming with him that time. Remember?"

"Do I remember," Deb snapped. "Yes, Joseph, I think I remember you getting lost and staying out all night and taking ten years off my life. It rings a bell."

"Well, the reason I was out there at all was because Kurt said that he was going to show me this great spot where we could swim that wasn't deep, that I would love."

"Kurt said you wandered off."

"He lied because he lost me, Mom."

"Are you kidding?"

"No, but who cares. It was, like, a million years ago, right?"

"I'm gonna kill him," she said, whirling toward the front door.

"Dad," Joe said fast.

Elliot caught his wife, who promptly fell apart in his arms. And even though, as Joe said, it had been a million years ago, for his mother the scare was still very real and well remembered. And he had only told her a very small piece of it.

Kurt had told Joe that he had a friend who thought Joe was cute. He had then lured my boyfriend down to a creek and introduced him to this friend. What Joe did not know was that there was not just the three of them. There had been six, counting Joe and Kurt. Joe was young and trusting and horny at fourteen and so had dropped his pants because the other boy was going to as well. And he had gone to his knees, but once he heard another voice tell him he was pretty, he got scared. He didn't know who was there, and when someone tried to shove a cock in his mouth, he tried to get up, only to have his shoulders held. The laughter unglued him, and when he fought to be released, they all took turns hitting him, calling him a faggot, before pushing him into the water.

At that point Kurt's brain had apparently kicked in, but the water was higher than it should have been that time of year because of the rain, and there was just enough current to suck Joe under and pull him into a connecting stream that was swollen from a rise in the river. He lost his pants as he tumbled around and swallowed enough water to drown him. But he made it to the bank, and there he stayed all night, freezing, with only a T-shirt to keep himself warm. They found him the following morning, bruised, scratched up, with a mild case of hypothermia. He had never offered a good explanation as to why his clothes were off, but everyone had figured the poor kid was out of his head at the time. The bruises were credited to his ordeal, and while Kurt had been in trouble for not looking out better for his cousin, nothing more had come of it.

"I'm gonna drop him in a well and see how he likes being cold and wet all night long," I promised, my voice low.

"No, you're not." Joe smiled and turned toward me, sliding his arm under my suit jacket and curling it around my waist, his head notched under my chin. "You're gonna leave him alone. But make sure he doesn't come near me so I don't have to make a scene and tell him off."

As always, Joe worried about making other people uncomfortable.

I clutched him to me, because just thinking about the fact that the dear, sweet man I held in my arms could have died at fourteen, and therefore never been at the club the night I met him, and not have been able to love me dearly and desperately for the past six years hurt my heart.

What if there were no Joseph Locke for me to love? I could not imagine me without him; it just wasn't possible anymore. He was my home, my whole life. Without him, nothing worked. I could be me out in the world, both professionally and as a warder, because I had a sanctuary to return to.

"Baby?"

I shivered hard.

"I can't breathe." He laughed against my throat, his warm breath tickling over my skin.

"Okay," Elliot said as I let Joe go. He pulled his wife around in front of me, and Joe's mother grabbed him, crushing him again.

"Christ," he muttered. "Mother, come on."

But she needed to remind herself that it was in the past and that she had her son safely in her arms before we could go in. Mothers were like that. Because Joe was the same way, he hugged her back tight and whispered into her hair. Everything was okay.

Inside, the hostess led us to a large room in the back of the restaurant where two long tables were set up side by side. Each table sat twenty-five, and that was enough for just the family. For the party on Saturday, they were expecting a good three hundred people, but for the rest of the time, fifty was the high end.

"Are you the only nonwhite guy in the room?" Joe asked.

"Yes."

"Am I the only blind guy?"

"Yes again," I said, squeezing his hand.

"And are we the only gay people here?"

"For the third time, and the win," I teased him, scanning the crowd. "I'm gonna go with yes."

"Oh thank God, I wanted us to be special."

"No worries about that, love," I assured him.

"Awww, thank you, honey. I—hey, wait a minute… that's not a compliment."

I tugged him after me, and we went to speak to his grandfather.

You could tell that when he was younger Henry Locke had broken hearts. The man was still stunning at eighty with his thick white hair, ruddy complexion, broad shoulders, and strong build. I was certain that women had swooned when he walked down the street at twenty-five.

"Marcus!" He greeted me loudly, standing up, big grin on his face, arms open to receive me. "So glad you could make it."

"I wouldn't have missed it," I said as I stepped into him.

He hugged me tight, pounded my back with his fist, and let me go before turning to his grandson. Unfortunately, he was careful with Joe—which my boyfriend hated— always treating him like he was fragile. Henry liked me better, and we all knew it, because I could do all the things he could, but mostly I had won him over when we took turns target shooting two Christmases ago. I had stood outside for hours with him, never tiring, never complaining, and we had bonded. Now whenever I visited, I was received warmly.

After he spoke to Joe for a few minutes, we walked down the table to where Barbara had saved us two spots. Unfortunately, Kurt was sitting beside her. When my eyes flicked to his, he looked away, so I figured we were all on the same page.

People kept stopping to see Joe, put their hands on his shoulders. The women leaned down to kiss him, and the men patted him affectionately. Everyone shook hands with me. The women hugged me when I stood, and the men clasped my hand as well, making me feel welcome.

"So," one of Joe's cousins asked from the other side of me. "What do you do now, Joey?"

He cleared his throat, hand on my thigh under the table. "I own my own company. It's called Bumpy Road Limited, and we make plastic pieces that are in Braille that go over laptop keyboards and phones and watches and other things."

"What do you mean?"

He pulled out his phone and everyone saw the clear plastic piece over the top that had Braille bumps on it.

"That's so cool," another cousin told him.

"Well, we have a lot of orders for them, and we're adding new designs as new pieces of hardware—phones and stuff—come on the market every day. They work just like a gel skin, maybe a little heavier, so they can be peeled off and put on, and they're durable, so they last a long time."

"How do you manage all that?" Ellen asked.

"I do most of the on-site selling, and I have four outside sales people and then clerks and an office manager and of course an accountant and a lawyer and—"

"Isn't Marcus your lawyer?"

"Marcus is a criminal lawyer," he told her. "He doesn't do boring contract work; he saves people's lives."

I rolled my eyes.

"Stop that," Joe snapped. "Your work is very important."

Ellen was startled—it was all over her face.

I winked at her, and she was thoroughly flustered. "Everything I do, the man knows."

She nodded fast, touched by that for some reason.

The waitress showed up, and I thanked her for being a goddess for bringing me coffee. I was quiet after that, letting Joe order my food, sitting there, taking in the conversations around me, listening.

I realized how tired I was—exhausted, really—and my body was starting to sink into the chair. But I smiled and leaned my knee against Joe's and talked to his father about my caseload. When the food was delivered to the table by several waitresses at once, I registered how hungry I really was.

"Marcus." Joe said my name to draw my attention.

"Oh, you have magic eggs. I got bacon and nifty toast." I yawned as I rubbed my eyes. They were watering, I was so tired.

"Okay." Joe smiled. "And coffee?"

"Coffee's good." I yawned louder. "God, I gotta go to bed."

"When?" he teased me.

I snorted out a laugh. The man had a one-track mind.

"Joe," his mother began, "honey, your eggs are at—"

"Oh, no, Mom, it's okay," he cut her off. "Marcus already said."

"I'm sorry?"

"He already told me where everything is on my plate."

"When?" She was surprised.

I turned and looked at her. "He hates the clock thing. Has he never told you that?"

She was looking at me with a bemused expression on her face. "No, dear, he never has."

Of course he hadn't. Joe only ever told *me* the truth about everything. All the other nice people in his life, he shielded and protected and let them do whatever the hell they wanted to make them think that they were helping him. It was thoughtful and wildly distrustful at the same time. With everyone but me, Joe worried about being a burden. And his family was wonderful, but still he was careful with them, never wanting to cause a stir or rock the boat. His relationship with me was the only one that was different.

"Well, Deb, he hates it." I smiled at her.

"Oh. And so what did you—"

Joe's laughter was deep and husky, one of the many things I loved about the man. "Mom." He coughed, still chuckling. "It's *Schoolhouse Rock*."

"I'm sorry?"

"The numbers are—"

"Oh!" His cousin Ellen smiled wide. "That's right. Three is a Magic Number and—"

"Nifty eggs." Barbara nodded. "That's right... naughty, nasty, nifty, number nine," she sang softly.

When she stopped, all eyes were on her.

"What?"

Ellen giggled. "That was quite the show of dorkiness there, Barbie."

"Yeah, I know, but—I got?" She looked at me, confused.

I grinned at her. "You know, I got six, he got six, she got—"

"Six." She drew out the word as she smiled wide. "Yeah okay."

Deborah Locke was beaming. "I love that."

"I like it too," Joe told her. "And Marcus usually does it fast just like he did a minute ago when we're out places, so it's not a thing, ya know?" he said, reaching for his coffee.

"Eleven?" she asked.

"Good-good-good-good, good eleven, never gave me any trouble 'til after nine," Ellen sang for her, off-key.

I laughed at her. "Must you sing?"

Everyone close to us lost it.

"Oh." Deb caught her breath, her eyes filling fast. "I just—"

"Mother," Joe cautioned her.

She cleared her throat. "Okay—okay, sorry."

I chuckled, leaned sideways, and kissed her cheek. She turned to look into my eyes, her hands lifting to frame my face.

I smiled at her. "You can cry whenever you like."

She nodded, leaning in close to kiss my cheek before letting me go.

"Mother, you're not kissing my boyfriend, are you?" Joe grumbled. "You have no idea where he's been."

"Quiet," his father scolded him. "Your mother can kiss him if she wants."

The looks I got after that, from everyone except Kurt, let me know I was golden.

EATING when you're tired is never a good idea. The last of your energy gets sucked away to help digest food, and then you're really screwed. I fell asleep in the van.

Joe's parents' house in Nicholasville was a beautiful two-story Georgian Colonial in red brick. During the holidays there was a wreath in every window with an electric candle in the center. As it was early

December, Elliot had not gotten around to decorating yet, but I was sure it would be on the agenda soon.

As I trudged up the stairs, everyone else assembled in the living room, I considered taking Deb up on her offer for me to take a nap. She and Barb were going back out to run what sounded like a million errands before the dancing at the country club later that evening. It sounded so good, the nap, but I just splashed water on my face instead. Then I felt better, more alive, less like a zombie. As I was getting ready to go back down and join the others, the door to the bedroom opened and Joe came in.

"Hey, you," I sighed.

"I know this is short notice," he told me. "But my Dad is running over to his shop because he got a call to meet someone, so could we... go with him?"

I saw the grimace, knew he would have much rather we climbed into bed together, but he was worried and I couldn't have that.

"'Course. Let's go."

The relief on his face was a joy to see.

III

I HAD gotten myself pumped up for some kind of altercation during the half-hour ride from Nicholasville to downtown Lexington, but by the time we got there, whoever had been there was gone, leaving Joe's dad looking at me as he had during the entire trip.

"It was nothing, like I said. You guys didn't need to come with me," Elliot said.

I studied his face.

"I have no idea what Joey thought he heard the other day, but if there was cause for any concern, you know I would tell you."

"Why didn't you want Joe to tell me what was going on? You told him you didn't want me calling the police."

"I didn't want him to give you the wrong idea, because I know you're an officer of the court and so it's your duty to inform the authorities if you think something is amiss. But they were just some punk kids, Marcus. If I couldn't take care of it, I would have asked you."

I nodded, not believing a word of the rambling explanation.

"You could be sleeping." He smiled. "You guys really didn't have to come with me."

"No, I know," I covered, chuckling. "But I enjoy walking around down here, and this way you'll take me for a beer before we head back, right?"

"Absolutely." His smile grew wider. "Why don't you and Joe spend some time, just the two of you? I'll answer some e-mail and check on the orders, and then I'll meet you over at Dunbar's in a couple of hours."

I agreed, and Joe and I headed out.

"Shit," he said, stopping suddenly on the sidewalk.

"What?"

"I forgot my scarf back there." He made a noise of disgust. "Walk me back, 'kay?"

"'Course." I smiled at how red the cold made his nose.

"Stop it," he grumbled. "I can hear you smiling, and I'm not cute."

"You can't hear me smiling." I sighed as my grin got bigger. "And you're adorable."

"I am not."

But he *so* was. There were freckles across the bridge of the man's small button nose; his lashes were so long and curly and thick that when his hair fell forward, it caught in them, and his smile was mischievous and sheepish at the same time. He was devastating.

"I'm sorry I dragged us out here for nothing," he sighed, his head tipped back as he breathed me in. "God, you smell good."

"Oh yeah," I rumbled. I touched his face, loving the feel of his skin under mine, the wicked gleam in his eyes, the sly curl of his beautiful lips.

"Let's go get a hotel room for an hour."

"That's classy," I teased, bending to kiss him because I couldn't help it.

He tasted like the spearmint lip balm he always used and the hot chocolate he'd had at the restaurant, and the flavors together when I sampled them made me a little crazy.

His moan was deep and sexy. His lips parted and his tongue darted out to meet and claim mine. I grabbed him and turned, pulled him into a dark alley between buildings, and shoved him up against a wall, pinning him there. Normally my control wrapped around me, made me the cool guy, the rational guy, the guy who never gave himself over to impetuous action. But I had no buffer where Joe was concerned; he alone could pull down all my walls.

"Oh," he moaned, his breath catching, stuttering, before his hands fisted in my sweater and held on.

He just fit me like no one ever had. My mouth on his, my thigh nestled against his groin, one hand buried in the thick, wavy auburn hair, the other kneading his ass as he pressed forward—all of it a dance we had perfected years ago. He always wanted to be closer. I couldn't wait to have him there; being entwined was always best.

The first kiss quickly became the second and the third with nothing but a panting breath to mark one from the next. His submissive whimper, so sweet, so heartfelt, infused with wanton need, made my balls ache. Every time, *all* the time, my lust for the man was like brushfire, consuming me, leveling me.

He started to rub his bulging erection into my thigh, the contact making him shudder, and I was helpless to stop him, wanting instead to make him come apart faster.

My fingers worked his belt loose, undid buttons, slid his zipper open just enough to get a hand down the back of his dress pants, slide over elastic and underneath. I had wet them, shoved them inside with our dueling tongues to make sure they were coated with saliva before I began my campaign.

I lifted his hard, leaking cock from his briefs and gripped tight as I pressed slippery fingers slowly inside him from the back.

"Marcus!" He gasped my name, whispering it fiercely as I stroked him and curved my fingers forward, pushing deeper, looking for the spot that would make him howl.

"You're so hot, so beautiful. Show me, baby. Come for me. Come in my hand."

His breathing changed to panting, and when my fingers pegged his gland, my name came out as a cry.

"I have you. You're safe in my arms, Joey. You know you're safe."

"Yes." His eyes fluttered with the sensations rolling through him.

He rocked forward, pushing in and out of my grip, the friction, the pressure too exquisite a temptation. His hands were like claws on my sweater as he held on. His head tipped back, his eyes closed tight and mouth open. The orgasm built until I bent and kissed him, taking the roar into my mouth as his body went rigid with his release. He came hard, spurting into my fist, semen oozing through my fingers as he shuddered in my arms.

The man trusted me implicitly, and that was all over his face. He knew wherever we were, no one else could see, because he knew that I wouldn't share the sight of him. I would not allow anyone else to ever see my love's surrender.

I watched him finish, buck forward into my hand, press back on my long fingers, and the ache that had welled up inside me blossomed and became hunger.

"Don't you want me?" he asked, his breath stilted.

"Always."

"Then?"

"I can wait," I breathed.

"I could have too."

"But I had to put my hands on you," I growled, leaning forward and kissing down the length of his throat.

His low whimper was very sexy. "You could have put me up against a wall."

"This was better."

"You didn't even get off."

"But I got to watch you lose yourself with what I was doing to you, and we both know I'm the only one that you trust enough to abandon every inhibition you have."

"Yes."

"Kiss me," I ordered.

The way he lifted for me, parting his lips, licking them…. His desire to submit was intoxicating. I ground my mouth down over his and laid claim. I devoured him.

I kissed him until he shoved me off, breathless, his lips red and swollen, and as I nibbled down the side of his throat, licked and sucked, he began to writhe in my arms. In seconds the movement, the pressure, the friction would be too much. I stepped away fast, leaving him gripping the wall behind him, and I wiped my hands on my pants.

I stared, certain that I really would have him there in the alley if we didn't stop.

"Marcus," he said between breaths.

"Sorry." I managed to get out. "We need to just—"

"Is there a mark on me?" he asked, twisting his head so the cords in his neck bulged.

I shook my head, trying to get my racing heart to calm down and my cock to stop throbbing. Anywhere else, with anyone else, never,

ever, would there be a problem. Only Joe released this wave of lust that I couldn't contain.

"Use your words, Marcus."

Shit. "No." I cleared my throat, shivering. "There's no mark."

His eyes became narrow slits of heat. "Then make one."

I almost swallowed my tongue.

"Please," he whispered.

The idea of shoving the man deep into the alley and bending him over and fucking him hard and fast had me choking on my own desire.

"Let's go get your scarf," I rasped.

"Fuck the scarf."

"Let's just go get it and then find a hotel like you said," I grumbled, pushing back against the wall, counting in my head, willing my body to calm to be cool, normal and thoughtful Marcus Roth.

"Look at me."

I was. He looked debauched, pants down around his ankles—underwear as well—and hooded eyes, standing there with his flaccid cock still leaking at the tip. He should not have been in control of any part of the conversation. But he was so self-possessed that even though he was the one who had been ravished, it didn't matter.

"When you fuck me back at home, I want you to leave marks, you understand?"

"Yes."

His face brightened. "Good."

I growled and he beamed back at me. He loved to win.

When I walked back into Joe's father's hardware store five minutes later, I left Joe outside to wait for me. The jingle of bells again announced my arrival, and I was surprised that the two guys I had seen leave when we arrived earlier were back. What was even more interesting was that one of them was behind the counter with Elliot.

"Marcus." Elliot smiled. "What brings you back, son?"

"Joe forgot his scarf." I squinted at him.

"Oh." Elliot forced a smile, looking around. "Isn't that it right there?"

He pointed and I saw it, the primary-color knitted beacon of a scarf one of his employees had made him. When I picked it up, I looked back at Elliot and saw again how uncomfortable he looked.

"Who are your friends?" I asked.

He opened his mouth to speak, but apparently the guy on my side of the counter had had enough of my presence and the interruption.

"Why don't you get out of here before I put you out. We have things to discuss with Mr. Locke here."

I nodded as I moved forward. "Oh yeah? Like what?"

"Marcus," Elliot interrupted, tipping his head toward the door. "Go on and catch up with Joe, son. This doesn't concern you."

"Oh, but it really does," I said, moving forward until I was beside the counter and turning my head to the guy beside me. "What's your name?"

"Why the fuck you wanna know?"

I arched an eyebrow.

"Arcan."

My head turned to the guy beside Elliot.

He scoffed. "Emir."

One name. Both of them only had single names. Interesting. I returned my gaze to Arcan. "Okay, tell Emir to come out here and talk to me. Him being back there with my father-in-law is making me nervous."

"Who the fuck are you?"

"I asked nicely," I told him, moving fast—faster than either Arcan or Emir could track—and cleared the counter to stand in front of Emir in seconds. I was in his space, nose to nose, so he had no choice but to take a step back. "I really did."

"You have no idea who you're messing with," Arcan barked.

"Marcus, please just go," Elliot pleaded.

"Whoever you're collecting protection money for," I told them, "Mr. Locke is done paying."

"Marcus," Elliot's voice cracked. "You have to go or they'll hurt—"

"They won't hurt anyone," I promised him.

"Oh yeah, we will," Emir assured me, and I saw his eyes suddenly change from the ugly dishwater blue they were to an even uglier blood red.

"No!" Elliot yelled. "Please don't hurt him."

I felt Joe's father pleading for my life all the way down to my soul. The man really did love me.

"Too late," the second guy said as his eyes changed too and he reached for me.

I took a breath, held it for one heartbeat, two, and then released a pulse of power that froze both men in their tracks.

"That's bullshit," the first guy said.

It was not exactly the response I was expecting, but they stopped moving nonetheless.

"Breka paid fuckin' Tarin this month; you ain't supposed to be here."

Tarin? "I don't know him."

"How?" Now Arcan was confused.

"I'm visiting," I told him. "And I'm not alone, and I can assure you that when my sentinel finds out what's going on here, the council will be notified."

They both went even paler than they were to begin with.

I wanted them out because I had calls to make, because I knew I needed backup. "Go now."

"Or?" Emir asked.

"Or I can make you."

I was not the scary warder. My friend Malic, with his growl of a voice, bulging muscles, and arctic blue eyes—he was spooky. Even though I was big, I normally came off as benign. But the two demons tripped over themselves getting out of the hardware store.

When the door slammed behind them, the bells having never been so loud, I turned to look at Joe's father.

"How do you not tell me that you had demon trouble, Elliot?"

His eyes, that wondrous cerulean blue he shared with his son, were huge.

"You need to tell me what's going on."

The man was speechless, just staring at me.

"I can help, but you have to tell me everything."

"Marcus." He finally breathed out my name, grabbing hold of my arms. "What are you?"

"He's a warder, Dad," Joe said, and when I turned my head, I realized that he was there along with his mother and sister. The bells had been loud, and it made sense that Elliot's family had been coming in while the two demons were running out. I just hadn't noticed. "And I'm thinking you need one."

"What are you two doing here?" I asked Joe's mother and Barbara, scared for them, startled because I had not prepared for them. I had been ready to protect Joe—I always was—and his father at that pivotal moment, but I had not anticipated the women, and it made me nervous that I had not.

"I forgot to get the zip ties to hold up the banner, and I thought we'd stop and grab them, and... what in the world is going on?" Deb yelled.

"They ran from you." Elliot said, all his focus locked in on me, holding me so tight.

"Which was smart on their part," I told him. "Because I would have sent them both back to the pit if I'd had my swords."

"You didn't bring your swords?"

I looked over at Joe because I heard the alarm, the indignation. Joe didn't get upset and reel with pain or worry, he yelled. And he was mad.

"Why the hell would you leave your swords at home?"

"Think about what you're saying," I reminded my boyfriend.

"No, Marcus!" he shouted. "You should have brought them! You should always bring them! Being a warder is twenty-four-hour, seven-day-a-week job, and we both know it!"

Shit.

"You know I'm right."

He was right.

"Say it, because I can't see the look of resignation on your face!"

I crossed the room and grabbed him instead. His arms wrapped around my waist as he pressed his body against mine.

"Please," he spoke into my throat, his breath warm and his mouth on my skin, causing a shiver of anticipation anyone could see. "Baby, you have to be more careful. I can't lose you, okay?"

I nodded. He clutched me tighter.

And we stood like that with my cheek resting on the top of his head, one hand in his hair, the other around his back and both his arms wrapped tight around me. He always liked listening to the steady beat of my heart.

"Marcus Adam Roth!"

I started and looked across the room at Deb.

"Oh, you're in trouble." Joseph chuckled, lifting his chin. "Gimme a kiss before you die."

I growled, kissed him, and then turned my head to his mother.

"How dare you keep a secret like this from us, from your family!"

"I—"

"And you!" she roared at her husband. "How dare you not trust me with this?"

"I thought you'd think I was nuts talking about demons and such."

"We have been married for forty-five years, Elliot Locke. There is nothing that would come out of your mouth that I wouldn't believe!"

He stared at her because he had no excuse to give her.

"All of you," she said fast, "need to go get in the car so we can go home and have us a talk."

Joe groaned.

I pressed his face into my chest before his mother killed him. "His stomach hurts," I told her.

She leveled me with her look. "Marcus Roth, I'm about ready to skin you alive."

But the thing was, she was mad, really mad, and I loved it. There was no talk of how scared she was and how I was putting her son in danger or how I should get out. She was just mad that I hadn't confided in her.

I moved fast, crossed the floor, and grabbed her, hugging her tight.

"Marcus," she whimpered against me, her arms around me, and her hands digging into my back.

"I thought you would hate me or not want me near Joe, and I'm so sorry, but I love you all so much and the thought of losing you, any of you, just—"

"Marcus, don't be stupid. We're your family. Families don't turn their back on their own."

I clutched her tighter and put my head down in her shoulder.

Seconds later she pushed free. "But you, Elliot Locke!"

"Yeah, you're toast." Joe laughed at his father.

"Joseph Locke!"

And it was a free-for-all after that as Barbara started yelling too. It was nice to be part of a family that cared.

IN THE van it was quiet, so I took that opportunity to call Jael.

"Marot," he said, and I realized he sounded annoyed.

Marot. It was my warder name.

Some of us had special names, some of us didn't. The more public a figure you were, the more likely you would get a call sign to protect your identity, and while I understood, it was also confusing at times.

"What's wrong?"

"Nothing," he grumbled.

But something was, and I could guess. "Your warders and Deidre's not hitting it off?"

There was a long silence.

"What leads you to that?"

I grunted. "Ryan and Collin, right?"

"How did you know?"

"I know."

"And?"

"And it's simple. Collin's taken an interest in Julian, and Ryan and Julian are like a minute old as a couple. Ryan's jealous, that's all."

"Ryan Dean used to be a model. Why in the world would he—"

"Have you ever known Ryan to be logical?"

"No, that's Leith's job."

"There you go."

"Well, Marot, let me go put my house in order and I'll call you—wait, you called me. What's wrong?"

"I have demon trouble."

"Pardon me?"

"And maybe warder trouble as well."

"Start at the beginning."

I explained, and he listened and grunted. I heard him cover the phone to talk to someone, and when he came back he told me that he was having Deidre make some calls as we spoke. It was nice to have two sentinels as backup.

"What should I do?"

"For starters, I'll send someone to you immediately. It sounds as though you've disrupted the flow of things around there, and I don't know if Tarin is a demon or a warder, but there's a warder in there somewhere, and he's either doing this himself or the corruption stems from his sentinel."

"How likely is that?"

"Not very, but we still have to act on the assumption that this is the case."

"Okay."

"Let me do this. Let me contact the council now and see what I can find out about the sentinel, and I'll call you back in a few minutes. Meanwhile I'll send Leith to stay with you."

I would have preferred my best friend. "I think I'll just call Malic to—"

"No."

But he'd said it too fast. "What's wrong?"

He didn't answer.

"Jael?"

He cleared his throat. "Malic and Jackson are on another plane with Raphael. He found Moira. She was the demon lord Saudrian's mate, you remember."

I remembered that Saudrian had tried to turn Leith into his champion and that Raphael had killed him. And I knew that Moira had vowed to kill Raphael, who was my fellow warder Jackson's hearth, for being the one to take her mate's life.

"Why would you let Raphael get anywhere near her?"

"As you know, Raphael is a demonic bounty hunter, and apparently one of his contacts let him know where Moira was. Since Jackson was not going to let him go alone, he went with him. But Malic wasn't letting Jackson follow without backup, so he went to keep both of the others safe."

It was just like Malic to go. He would never say he cared; he would just show it instead. I felt a pang of guilt for being away.

"Ryan and I are here to guard the city, so Leith can come assist you."

"I should be at home."

"You should be with your hearth, and especially now, as it sounds like both he and his family—your family—are in danger. Let me know if you need Ryan to come as well."

"I won't."

"I'll send Leith to you shortly."

"Thank you. Ask him to bring my swords. Please keep me apprised of the other situation."

"Of course."

"You say that like you would have told me if I hadn't called."

"Malic made me promise not to. He wanted you to enjoy your time with Joe."

Which again was just like him. Malic never came out and said that my happiness, or that of my hearth's, meant anything to him. But he showed it.

"Please keep me in the loop."

"I will."

I hung up and let my head fall back.

"Are you all right?"

Turning to look at Joe, I exhaled deeply. "There's trouble at home."

"Like what kind?"

"Like I should be there."

Joe took a breath and squeezed my knee. "Let's just deal with this problem with my dad, and then we'll fly home."

I shook my head. "No, Joe, that's not what I—"

"Marcus." He cut me off, taking my hand. "Everyone will understand a work emergency, and why would I stay here if you couldn't come back? I need to be with you, especially if you're going to be putting yourself in danger. A warder has to be able to return to his hearth and home to be cared for and find sanctuary and draw power. I understand my role, and it's as vital to me as it is to you. I love you and I know my value. But I can't leave my family in danger, and I know you can't, either. So let's handle this and then go home so you can fight alongside your brothers."

He was decisive and firm and absolute. It was hard to contain my love for him, because really, the man was phenomenal.

"Just say, 'Yes, Joe, I agree.'"

"Yes, Joe, I agree," I sighed.

"I go with you, Marcus. Don't be stupid."

Of course he did.

IV

WE WERE all sitting in the living room when the doorbell rang. Barbara went to get it, and when she came back less than a minute later, she had a strange expression on her face. The reason was obvious a second later; Leith Haas was trailing after her and she seemed a bit overwhelmed.

I understood why.

He was shorter than me—most men were—but not small. At six two, long and lean-muscled, the man was not someone you looked at and thought *delicate* or *fragile*.

"Hey," I greeted him, rising from the couch.

He didn't hold out his hand or try to hug me. He simply passed me a scabbard with dual sheaths, and I took it, feeling instantly calmer now that I could defend myself and everyone I loved.

"Thank you."

"You're welcome." He smiled as he moved beside me to bend over and hug Joe.

Everyone saw him do it, and their faces all broke into similar smiles.

"This is Leith Haas," I explained to the room, "and he's a warder just like me. Leith, this is Joe's family: his father, Elliot, his mother, Deb, and his sister, Barb."

Leith smiled, and I watched Barbara, especially, react to the dark aqua-blue eyes, the way he curled a long piece of hair behind his ear and the play of muscles under his clothes. There was no missing the man's beauty, but what I had always admired more was his gentleness, the quiet and calmness that he spread, and how thoughtful he was. Leith tended to think before acting, and I appreciated that quality about him.

"How's Simon?" Joe asked after the man's hearth.

The shy smile got big and out of control. "He's good, Joe. Thank you."

"Oh." Barb sucked in a breath.

I watched her eyes roam over Leith, from the long dirty-blond curls that fell to the middle of his back to the broad shoulders and muscular legs. Between the golden tan and his hair pulled back into a queue, you thought "surfer" not "warder," but unlike her, I knew the man was deadly. When the doorbell rang, he excused himself to answer it.

"Your friend is gorgeous," Barbara breathed.

"He's got a really hot boyfriend too," Joe told his sister.

"How do you know?" I growled.

"Don't be jealous, baby," Joe teased, patting his lap.

He had no idea how badly I wanted to lie down so he could pet me.

"Marcus, Leith is gay?"

"Yes, ma'am," I told Barb before my eyes flicked back to Joe.

"Simon has a voice almost as sexy as yours, Marcus Roth," my boyfriend teased again.

I really wanted to be alone with my man. I was almost thrumming with need.

"Marot," Leith called to me, and when I looked up—because he'd used my warder name, names we never called one another—I found myself looking at two men.

I turned and stepped in close to Joe.

"This is—"

"Shane Harris?" Deb said, looking at the man on the left.

"Mrs. Locke," the man said, his eyes passing over her as he looked for—"Joe!" he cried.

"Shane?" Joe lifted his face.

"Ohmygod," Shane gasped, crossing the room preternaturally fast, going down on one knee so he was at eye level with Joe. "Holy shit."

Joe reached up and put his hands on the other man's face. When he did, he smiled. "Shit, Shane, how long's it been?"

Apparently Shane Harris was more than content to stare into my boyfriend's eyes for the rest of his life.

"Joe," he finally breathed, his thumbs grazing over his cheeks.

"Marcus," Leith said under his breath dangerously.

I turned and found my friend with narrowed eyes, a clenched jaw, and his hand on the pommel of his sword. He very much wanted to separate Shane Harris's head from his body. This was my hearth Shane Harris was touching, and that made my friend nervous. And not just for me, more for himself. Warders losing their hearths, for any reason, was cause for panic. To lose your hearth to another, as our fellow warder, Jackson, had, was close to unbearable. But I had more faith than that.

My relationship with Joe was the longest that existed in my clutch—my group of five warders. Ryan and his hearth Julian had not yet made six months, Malic and his hearth Dylan were even more new, Leith and Simon had just hit seven months, and Jackson and Raphael were verging on three. So they all reacted to the very idea of losing their hearths as cause for deliberate, violent action. Joe and I, the old married couple at just shy of six years, were the anomaly, and so instead of reacting, Leith looked to me to guide him. I had to let him see what faith and trust looked like.

"What are you doing here?" Shane asked, absorbing Joe's face with his eyes, tracing over it with his hands, utterly, completely, entranced.

"I'm here for my grandfather's eightieth," he replied, smiling as he leaned back, away from Shane's touch, done now with the reunion. He tipped his head back, up at me, reaching at the same time. "And my partner Marcus Roth came with me."

I took hold of the questing hand, squeezing lightly, smiling over Joe's happy sigh.

Beside me, Leith exhaled as Shane Harris finally looked at me.

"You're a warder?" he asked as he stood up, his tone and his stance were both combative.

"I am."

"Joe"—he cleared his throat—"is your hearth?"

"For six years now." I added the five months in that it would take us to reach the milestone without thought.

He was visibly stricken, and no one said a word.

"I never told him what I was."

Which was his mistake and not mine. I had trusted Joseph Locke after the first night I had him in my bed. What was Shane Harris's excuse?

"So what the hell is going on here?" Leith asked, uncharacteristically brash for him. Normally, he only raised his voice around people he knew well, but I was guessing that Joe being thrown into the mix—or the question of a hearth—was what was rattling him.

"Hello," the other man who had come in with Shane said.

I turned to look at him and found myself smiling. He reminded me right away of my friend, Jackson Tybalt, a fellow warder. There was similar brown hair that spilled to his shoulders, familiar brown eyes though Jackson's were darker, and the smile, warm and inviting, was also like my friend's.

"I'm Kyle," he said, moving forward, offering his hand to me. "Kyle Riggs, and it seems that all of us are long on tempers and short on manners since none of us introduced ourselves proper."

He was right. We had gone directly to anger and assigning blame.

"Like I said." He smiled as he squeezed my hand. "I'm Kyle. Who're you?"

I told him my name and introduced Leith, and then Shane also presented himself properly. Once all the handshaking was done and we had all calmed down a little, Leith asked Shane and Kyle what they were doing there.

"We're here on behalf of our sentinel, William Boyd, to find out what happened today at Mr. Locke's store," Kyle told him. "He got a call from the council about a concern from your sentinel, Jael Ezran. Our sentinel would have come himself to address the matter, but he's in Portland at his daughter's wedding to, and I quote, 'the wrong guy'."

And with that, the tension in the room dissipated, and everyone was talking at once.

Joe got up, put a hand on Shane's shoulder as he had still not moved, squeezed gently, and then leaned sideways into me. The show of solidarity, without him even thinking about it, made me flush with happiness.

Shane rose slowly and lifted his hands for quiet.

"Last month our sentinel stripped one of our number, Tarin, from our clutch. He had been conspiring with demons."

"Why?"

"He needed money," Kyle chimed in. "His hearth, she wants things, and we all knew it was leading down a bad road, but there is nothing you say to a warder about his hearth."

No, there wasn't.

"I would do whatever my hearth asked of me, as well," Kyle said.

"Are you married?" I asked.

He nodded. "Yes, sir, just as long as you all—six years."

And in his mind, his marriage and Joe's and mine were exactly the same. A hearth was a home, and a warder's home was not to be trifled with. When I saw his eyes flick to Shane, I realized that his fellow warder was making him uncomfortable with the way he was looking at Joe. I wasn't all that crazy about it either.

"The demons, Arcan and Emir, they said that Breka had paid Tarin so that I shouldn't have been there in my father-in-law's store," I said to both of the warders.

"I have no idea who that is, but just like you all, we don't chat with demons. We kill them."

And that was good to hear.

"So where is this Tarin now?"

"We'll find him; it's not your concern."

"Oh, the hell it's not," Leith said quickly. "We need to speak to Tarin and find out what he promised these demons, and we definitely need to track down—" He turned to me. "Who?"

"Arcan and Emir."

"Yeah, them." Leith returned his attention to Kyle. "And I guess their boss, Breka, and kill them all."

"Tarin—"

I cut Shane off. "What's his real name?"

"Tanner. Tanner King."

"So Tanner," I said, humanizing the warder so we all understood what it was that we were talking about, "is no longer a part of your clutch, correct?"

"Yes."

"So basically you have to find him first and protect him, because once the demons find out that they paid him for a service that doesn't exist, they're going to hunt him down and kill him."

"Yeah," Kyle agreed. "I know where he hangs out. We can go pick him up first."

"But he's no longer a warder, and he's corrupted himself," Shane reminded us. "He should reap what he's sown."

"Meaning what?" Leith asked.

"We cannot be expected to—"

"Oh, the hell we can't," Leith snapped, his eyes firing even as he turned to Joe's parents. "I beg your pardon, folks, but—"

"No, no." Deb smiled. "It sounds like you need to say *something*."

"I do," he told her before turning back to Shane. "That's bullshit! Tell Marcus and me where this guy lives, and we'll take care of it."

Both Shane and Kyle looked at him like he'd grown another head.

"What?" he asked sharply.

"We'll all go," Kyle soothed my fellow warder. "Shane didn't mean to imply that we would not take care of our own. Did you?"

"Shit," Shane hissed, defeated.

I put a hand on Leith's shoulder. "We need Ryan."

He nodded and dug into the pocket of his jeans for his phone.

"You don't need another warder here," Shane told me. "There are all four of us here. We can handle a—"

"You're down a warder because there's no way you replaced one that fast. Am I right?"

"Yeah, you're right."

"Okay, so, because I want to see Tanner and the demons he's trafficking with, Leith has to go with me. No warder ever goes anywhere alone, and I'm sure as hell not counting on one of you guys to watch my back."

"Absolutely not," Leith agreed from beside me.

"So since both Leith and I need to go with you, and because this house can't be sealed, I need another warder I trust to come and guard my family and my hearth."

No one said a word because, really, what argument could they offer? I needed my own backup, and I needed a guard for the most important person in my life.

"Any questions?"

There were none.

THE two warders were on their phones while Leith and I sat in the living room with Joe's family and answered the million questions that were volleyed at us.

Demons were real?

Yes, very.

We killed them?

Yes, we did.

Was it a full-time job?

Definitely not.

Did we get paid?

Never.

How long were you a warder?

Until your body wouldn't let you be one anymore.

Did a lot of warders get killed?

All the time.

At which point Deb moved from where she was next to Elliot and came and sat down beside me and held my hand.

It was very telling.

Elliot explained how the first demon had come and shown him eyes full of blood and clawed him and basically scared the crap out of him.

"I had no idea what to do. I was afraid everyone would think I was nuts."

"In San Francisco," I said, "my friend Malic works with the police. My friend Ryan has a local television show he hosts, and he makes a point of visiting all kinds of businesses, and those include those that are owned by Wiccans, psychics, Gypsies, and the people that others go to for help with occurrences that would seem paranormal in nature. Our sentinel checks the paper, follows anything odd or out of the ordinary, and sends us to check things out."

"Plus," Leith told them, "we patrol, every night, two to three of us."

"We don't do any of that," Shane said, having entered the room at the tail end of the conversation, walking around the couch and taking a seat beside Joe.

"You don't patrol?" Leith asked.

Shane shook his head.

"Well, I, for one, think it's dangerous not to be visible to the pit creatures." Leith shrugged, gesturing at Joe's father. "Case in point."

The doorbell rang then, and Kyle asked Elliot and Deb's permission to go get it. When he returned, he had two other men with him. Here were the rest of William Boyd's warders.

They seemed like nice guys, pleasant, but as I looked at them, even at Shane and Kyle, I was struck by how different they seemed from the guys I normally hung out with dispatching demons back to hell. In comparison, they were lacking.

"So we have news," Daniel, one of the newly arrived warders, began. "I guess this demon, Breka, already found out about Tanner and grabbed him out in front of his house earlier today. I talked to his hearth, and she said that he was taken right outside of their home."

"Too bad he didn't make it inside."

Leith turned to me. "So even if you're not a warder anymore you still have all the power?"

"I think your sentinel can strip you of the title," I said, "but the strength is there until you die." I looked over at Shane. "Although I've never heard of a warder being stripped and then not returned to the labarum council. I thought warders were placed in prison until they died if they were guilty of corruption." I squinted at him.

He stared at me.

I waited.

"Shit." Shane groaned.

"Shane?" Kyle prodded.

"Okay, so, the guy the demons took, that's a doppelganger. It's not really Tanner."

The other two warders turned in stunned silence to look at him.

"William said that only I could know," Shane told the other three warders who belonged to his clutch. "We had to try and draw the demons out. We had to know who they were."

"That's horrible," Joe said suddenly, his voice full of revulsion. "All this time you guys have been letting that woman think that her warder is still sleeping in her bed, and now that he's taken, you're just gonna let her believe that right there in front of her was the last time she'll ever lay eyes on him." A hard shiver passed through him. "That's vile."

And it was. The warder's hearth thought he was dead, and he had to deal with knowing that she thought that, and she had to deal with that being her reality. I couldn't think of a more horrible price to pay.

"You need to tell her the truth and let her see him." Joe's voice splintered. "That's obscene."

"It is," Kyle agreed—his eyes, his face, everything about him having gone cold. "You let some... *thing*... sleep with the man's hearth." He took a breath. "I can't believe William would condone such a thing."

I wondered about them then, about their clutch. Jael kept no secrets from us, and we had none from each other.

"We're so lucky," I said under my breath.

"Yes, we are," Leith agreed, his voice low.

"Do we know where this demon, this Breka, lives?"

"Yes," Daniel said, turning from Shane with some effort, his brows still furrowed, his jaw still tight. He had, it seemed, the same reaction that Kyle had. "But his house is over a dimensional door. It's not actually a house; it's just an entrance to another plane."

I frowned. "Do you guys not have experience with crossing dimensions?"

He shook his head.

"Okay, Leith and I can go alone, then. It's not a problem."

"But the problem is that Breka only allows people entrance to his home if they bring him a sacrifice."

"I'm sorry?" I was aghast that they would allow something like that to happen in their territory. "What kind of warders are—"

"No, not a sacrifice like that." Daniel shook his head. "Not one for slaughter or blood, but like a beautiful man or woman who he can sleep with if he wants."

"Sleep with?" He had said sleep and not defile or rape, but I was still confused.

"Not hurt in any way," Leith clarified.

"No, just screw," Daniel clarified.

"Wait, people bring him dates?" I still wasn't sure I understood.

"Sort of, I guess. Like when you take a hot girl with you to a club, you know you're gonna get in because the doorman's gonna wave you to the front of the line."

"But you don't normally leave the hot girl with the club owner."

"Yeah, but I bet that goes on."

I cleared my throat. "So the sacrifice is what—drugged or something, and this Breka, he sleeps with them?"

"No, it's not even that sinister. The demon only glamours the willing, and they always leave the next day."

"You guys check."

"Yeah."

"Okay," Leith sighed. "So you need a regular person, or someone they think is ordinary, with you or they won't even let you in the door."

"Yeah."

"And they have to be hot."

"Like, smokin' hot, yeah."

"All right, then," Leith said, turning to look at me. "So I can look like the regular person, and then once we're in we can cut our way to Breka and the other demons and kill them. It's just getting through the front door."

I smiled.

"What?"

"You just basically said that you were hot."

"Marcus, no one's gonna believe that I'm the guy and you're my arm candy."

I chuckled. "Arm candy."

"Seriously?"

"Shit," I groaned. "You know this isn't a two-man job."

"No, it's not."

"We need help," I told him solemnly.

"It can't be helped, Marcus."

"But if they're close to killing the dark witch—"

"You know I hate that we're calling her that," Leith cut me off. "I know a lot of witches and none of them are like this demon's mate. I want to call her something else."

"Just her name, then," I soothed. "Moira."

"Okay."

"Okay, so, if the guys are close to—"

"This is more important," he assured me. "This is the family of your mate." Leith was right. There was no argument.

"Can you find them?"

His smile was warm. "I can. It would be easier if it was the other way around and I was there and had to find you, but I can do it."

I reached out and put a hand on his shoulder.

"Your energy is like a beacon, you know." Leith patted my hand on him before he stepped away. "I can always sense where you are."

I heard that from my fellow warders all the time.

"Come right back," I ordered.

He nodded, then walked out of the room and out the front door. I noticed the looks from the other warders then. Surprise, astonishment, from all of them.

"What?"

"He can come back?" Shane asked.

A wormhole was how we traveled when we had to get to one another over any great distance. We opened up a channel from one warder to the other, and we jumped through what was basically a swirling vortex of wind. It took a great deal of energy and concentration, and I was guessing that none of them could do it more than once a day.

"Didn't he wormhole here to you?"

I nodded.

"And," Shane said slowly, waiting, "he's gonna do it again?"

"I'm guessing," Joe said as he stood up next to me, "that you guys don't travel to and from other planes like the clutch in San

Francisco does on a consistent basis, exercising that vortex muscle, huh?"

They didn't say anything.

"Marcus's sentinel told me that a warder builds power by being in a clutch of other warders that are dependent on one another. Did you know that?"

No one answered Joe.

"Warders have to spend time together every single day like they do in Marcus's clutch. Do you guys do that? Are you guys even friends?"

He was listening for a word from any of them.

"Speak up," Joe scolded them. "I'm blind."

"No, we...." Shane stopped, then began again. "We don't work like that, Joe. We all check in with our sentinel, but we all do different things and don't talk to each other much. We're all very strong warders. We don't need to partner up the way they do in Marcus's clutch."

I was suddenly very happy that my sentinel was the kind of man he was. Jael had insisted on building a family, not just a team. He always said that together we were strongest, not individually.

"When do you want us back to go with you to the demon's home?" Kyle asked.

"You don't have to go at all. Just tell me where—"

"No," he insisted. "We'll be there. When will your warders be here?"

"Give them at least a couple of hours."

"Okay, so it's six now. We'll meet here at eight," Shane said, getting up from the couch to stand beside Kyle.

"We'll see you then," I agreed.

Shane moved forward to reach Joe, but I instinctively clutched him to me, and just like always, the man turned and folded in tight.

"You're very lucky," Shane said.

"I know," I told him. "And keep your distance when you return."

"Why?"

I cleared my throat. "Leith is the rational one."

And Shane understood then that coveting my hearth when my friends could see him might not be all that good for his health.

JOE stayed downstairs with his parents and talked about warders and hearths and when he had found out and why they didn't need to be afraid and how safe they all were now that everyone knew. I went upstairs to shower and try to wake up. When I fell asleep on my feet, I realized that maybe it was time to get out of the water.

I was yawning while walking from the bathroom to the bedroom I shared with Joe. My eyes were watering when I fell down spread-eagle on the bed, and I closed them for a minute, just for a quick rest.

The shaking woke me.

"Awww, crap," I grumbled, rolling over on my stomach.

"You gotta change soon," Joe told me, hand massaging the back of my neck.

"Oh God, that feels so good," I almost purred, lifting up to move into his lap.

He was chuckling softly. "I wanna go with you."

"What? No." I yawned.

"Please, Marcus."

"How 'bout *hell no*," I reiterated. "Not gonna happen, Joseph."

"Why not?"

"You don't go with me to fight demons. I—"

"But if I go as that offering they were talking about, then—"

"You heard him. It's a dimensional door. There's no telling what he's got in there, and you are not going to be guessing with me. No."

"Marcus, I—"

"No," I said loudly, lifting up, grabbing him, and pinning him under me with my weight.

"Marcus, goddammit, don't manhandle me!"

But he loved it, and we both knew it. I shifted over him to press my thigh between his legs and began suckling on his throat.

"Stop." He jolted beneath me, hands on my chest, clutching at my skin as I kissed over the line of his jaw back to his earlobe.

The whimper that came out of him sent blood rushing to my cock.

"Shit," I groaned, realizing too late that I was playing with fire.

"Marcus." He moaned my name, arms lifting, wrapping around my neck, pulling me down to him.

"Joey," I sighed, trying to lift up off him.

"No," he whispered, swallowing hard, wetting his lips, his breath warm on my face. "I missed you. You need to fuck me now."

And the way he said it left no doubt in my mind that he needed me just as badly as I needed him. We were locked into the same mindset, had been for years, so I didn't have to guess what felt good or where to touch him. Words were unnecessary.

I lifted myself up, loosened the towel around my hips, and tossed it at the chair by the desk. He rolled over under me, passed me a tube of lube from under the pillow that would have been mine—I slept closest to the door wherever we were—and I watched as he hurriedly stripped out of his jeans and briefs and climbed back onto the bed.

His beautiful ass, so taut and round, beckoned me. I couldn't help bending to take a bite out of it.

"Oh, please," he whimpered, pushing back against my mouth.

He was gorgeous on his hands and knees in the middle of the bed. Head back, eyes closed, waiting, trembling, spreading his legs apart so his pink hole was there, ready for me.... I could not even imagine anything more bewitching than my man.

"Jesus, Joe," I groaned, leaning forward, my tongue gliding over his puckered entrance.

"No," he hissed. "I don't want you to lick me or suck me or do anything else but *fuck* me. I want you inside me now."

"I don't want to hurt—"

"Marcus Roth, when have you ever hurt me?"

Never was the answer. Not once.

"You're the only man who has never hurt me in any way."

Which basically answered any question I'd ever had about Shane Harris.

"I'll tell you if you want me to," Joe asked, because he knew what I was thinking. He always knew.

"Please."

"We hid things in high school," he told me as I opened the flip-top lid of the lube. "And then the summer before college, he told me he couldn't see me anymore. He didn't want me to get hurt."

I understood why and now so did Joe.

"So he became a warder then, Marcus, and he—oh!" Joe's voice cracked as I slid a slippery finger inside him. "Figured that because I was blind that I wasn't strong enough to be the hearth of a warder."

"You don't know that."

"The fuck I don't. What else could it be? He looked at me, just like everyone has done my whole life except you, and saw someone that had to be taken care of, not the other way around."

But why? "He knew you guys could go to bed together," I said as I added a finger inside him, scissoring them apart slowly and gently, stroking at the same time, pushing in, easing out, back and forth, over and over, going deeper with each press, finally reaching his gland.

"How would he know that? All we ever did was suck each other off."

"But even that would have told him you were strong enough to be a hearth."

"Oh, fuck, Marcus!" He gasped, his body going rigid for a second. "He didn't think I could be the hearth of a warder. All he saw was my blindness, not the home I could make, not the partner I could be. You're the only one who ever saw an equal."

It wasn't true. I had met Joe's exes at the supermarket, at restaurants, at concerts, out at clubs. There had been a lot of them, the man having been a serial dater before me. Joe bored easily, and because he was blind, most men felt like they had to take care of him, and Joe would simply not have it.

He kept his own apartment for a year after we got together because he didn't want me to think he needed me. He wanted me, but I wasn't necessary—until I was.

"Do you remember what you said when I invited you to move in?" I asked, adding a third finger, spreading them, stretching him.

"Yes," he replied, his voice barely above a whisper, pushing back, wanting me deeper. "I said I didn't need to move in; we could just be fuck buddies."

"And what did I say?"

"You—Marcus," he whined. "You didn't say anything. You just got up and walked to the door."

It was all or nothing with me, which scared the hell out of most people. I loved hard and possessively, and for every man before Joe, it had been suffocating and simply too much. But for Joe, who always spoke of freedom and independence and no commitments, the wall that broke that day was the one around his heart.

"And what did you say, Joseph?" I delved as I grabbed hold of his perfect ass and spread his cheeks.

"I said 'stay'."

"Is that what you said?"

"I said, 'Marcus, please stay. Don't leave me, don't ever leave me…. I'll be with you forever, but please stay now—don't go.'"

"You said 'stay'," I growled, sliding my lube-slicked cock deep inside of him in one powerful forward thrust.

"Fuck!"

I remained still for a second, buried in his ass, letting him adjust to me, savoring the feel of his tense muscles rippling around me, squeezing. He was so tight, so hot, and looking at my groin flush against him, the paleness of his skin contrasting to the darkness of mine, I was struck, as I always was, by the merging of our flesh.

"Marcus, you gotta move."

Reaching between his legs, I stroked him from balls to tip until he shuddered.

"I'm gonna come with how full I am," he confessed, shivering some more. "And I want you to just have me—God, Marcus, why are you holding back?"

Because normally I made sure he was close before I pounded inside of him. I wasn't small, the opposite, actually, and so I was careful to never—

"Marcus, you know better."

And I did.

I pulled out partway and then grabbed hold of his hip, anchored myself, and drove inside hard and fast.

He swore and babbled, and the filthy words coming out of his perfect mouth drove me right out of my mind.

"Marcus, baby, please, could you just fuck my brains out already?"

I smiled and eased out again only to plunge back inside, beginning the driving, rhythmic thrusting that would bring us both to a shuddering climax.

"Jesus, Marcus, you feel so fucking good."

A lot of men couldn't swallow my cock, instead choking on the length and the girth, and many didn't want me buried to the balls in their ass, terrified of being hurt. So I was careful and respectful and had always made sure that my lovers were ready and willing to take me in. It was only with Joe that I had ever just let go. The man loved my dick. He could take me down the back of his throat, sucking hard, and would straddle my hips and impale himself on my shaft with his head thrown back in ecstasy as I brought him to release. He looked delicate and small, but in bed, the man was demanding and vocal about his needs. Big and thick and hard was how he liked his ass filled. I was perfect for him.

"Marcus," he cried, writhing under me as I thrust into him, so close, barely breathing, loving him wrapped around me.

"Joe, I'm gonna come."

I felt his muscles bear down, felt him tighten, and then I fucked him through his orgasm even as my balls tightened and I came deep inside him seconds later.

The man annihilated me.

He was shaking hard, and when he collapsed, I crushed him under me, both of us panting and sweating, aftershocks spilling through us even as I stayed where I was. Joe liked me there, inside, until his muscles released me. When the spasms eased, I could slowly, gently, withdraw, but I had to wait until his body was ready for me to go. I loved the closeness at the end, loved feeling his heartbeat from the inside, the last bit of our joining.

When he stilled, I slid free and rolled over on my back. Instantly he was there in my arms, claiming my mouth. I opened for him, and the kiss was as hungry as the lovemaking had been. He tasted so good that when he tried to pull free, I bit his plump bottom lip to keep him there.

"Quit." He laughed softly, the grin on his beautiful mouth stopping my heart.

"Kiss me some more," I urged.

"This is not helping you wake up." His smile widened. "Jesus, Marcus, you're gonna pass out on the drive over there."

Oh, but it was worth it. "Just let me have you."

"Don't whine."

I growled, my hand around the nape of his neck easing him back down.

"Marcus."

His lips were turned up into a wicked smile that made my stomach flip over.

"Are you looking at me?"

I grunted.

"Baby."

I stopped staring at his mouth and looked up into the pale blue I loved, marveling as I always did at the flecks of cobalt in them.

"There was a time that I loved Shane Harris."

"Yeah, I figured."

"But you know that since the day I took you home with me that there's only been you."

I knew that, because as hard as I loved, as completely and possessively, as all-consuming, Joe was worse. With me—and from what I understood, only ever with me—he was like a tiger in the body of a man. Once he claimed you, God help you if you tried to get away. I had understood when the man moved in with me that I belonged to him body and soul and nothing was taking me away from him, not even my own jealousy.

"I love you," he said before he kissed me.

But I didn't need to be told.

V

IT WAS so nice to see them. As soon as I walked into the living room, Malic levered off the wall he was leaning on and crossed to me. He didn't hug me—it wasn't what we did—but his hand went to my shoulder and held me. There was a time not too long ago when even being affectionate with my best friend in front of my hearth was problematic. Joe had mistakenly thought Malic wanted me. It was not the case. Even if they wanted to, warders getting together did not end well. Malic and Ryan had even tried, to no avail.

Sometimes warders—and it happened to a lot of them, because warders could be women or men—were drawn to one another. They fought together, bled together, and so the camaraderie that came with that sometimes got mistaken for more. The problem was that another warder could not provide a sanctuary. Another warder could not provide a home, a place where you were loved and cared for and welcomed with open arms. If two warders were together, they would fight side by side, go home, and fuck all the adrenaline out of their systems. But afterward, when that was done, when the pulse-pounding rush had dissipated and you needed to be held and kissed and even be something as simple as fed, you were both looking at the other, waiting for them to deliver. A warder, simply put, needed a caretaker, and another warder could never be that.

Coming home bruised and bloody, carrying the weight of what I'd seen with me—the gore, the horror—I was normally not even capable of speech. But I was met at the door each and every time by a man who gave me a quick kiss before having me step onto a garbage bag to strip off everything from head to toe and then pointing me toward the shower. As I lurched through our living room, I could feel the warmth of our home, smell the food, and hear the soft music. Joe liked a lot of alternative bands, so the sound reminded me of him, which was good. It was all so comforting that sometimes, just for a second, I thought I would fall apart. But he would check my progress, put a hand on the small of my back or give my ass a pat or take my hand and lead me to the shower. And then he'd leave me under the steaming water, and all of it, the blood, the memory, and the pain, would just roll off me, down the drain.

Sometimes, if it wasn't so bad and he could see that it had not been, he would join me in the shower and run his hands all over my skin before dropping to his knees and taking my cock down the back of his throat. Those were the best starts to my homecoming. But other times, when he would touch me and I'd shiver, he'd wait until I finished my shower, dried off, changed, and returned to the living room. There I would find him, normally reading, his fingertips skimming over the page, because he knew I didn't like the television on when I got home from warding. Any loud noise would make me cringe. So the music was low, and the only other sound in the room was his voice… and that was really all I wanted to hear.

"Come here," he would call, and I would move fast, lay down on the couch, and settle my head in his lap.

Joe always sat on one end so I could stretch out completely and wrap my arm around his knee as he petted me. He would then tell me what he made for dinner, point at the enormous glass of ice water on the coffee table just waiting for me, and tell me that after dinner he was going to have his wicked way with me. At which point I would get up, sit back on the couch, and he would climb into my lap.

"I bought this new wine today too," he'd say as he smiled. "Gonna get you drunk off your ass."

And I knew I was home and loved and safe… and now Malic knew what that was like, too, because he had just found his own hearth. When Joe met Malic's man and heard them talking, he'd realized that he was jealous, had been jealous for five years, for nothing. Now, when I stepped back from Malic, Joe was there to walk into his arms and hug him.

"Thank you for coming to protect him," Joe said adamantly, clutching at my best friend.

"Of course." Malic's voice rumbled low in his chest. "Always, Joe."

Looking up, I wondered where the rest of Joe's family was. Why weren't they there with me meeting Jackson and Malic and….

"Where's Ry?" I asked.

Leith rolled his eyes and then tipped his head toward the kitchen. I understood at once. Ryan Dean was holding court.

It wasn't just that my fellow warder used to be a model and was now a television host. It was more than that. People saw him and just fell under a spell of charm and beauty and warmth. The man was irresistible and surely had Elliot and Deb and Barb completely riveted with whatever he was talking about.

I looked back at Jackson and Malic. "I'm sorry that I had to pull you guys from chasing Moira, but—"

"Marcus," Jackson said, his deep, dark-brown eyes soft as he gazed at me. "Your hearth and the family of your hearth takes precedence over everything else. You know that."

"In our clutch it does," I told him.

"Whaddya mean?" Malic asked, his voice, even after so many years, still carrying a hint of his homeland that had been transported with his parents when they immigrated to the United States from Stockholm. His grandmother, his parents, all had the same accent, he'd told me, and growing up in their house, there was no way for him to miss adopting it as well. I hoped he'd never lose it.

"You won't believe what the sentinel here did to one of his warders," Joe interrupted, moving forward to hug Jackson at the same time.

Malic and Jackson listened to the story, and they were both frowning by the end.

"They let this fake warder bed his hearth." Jackson swallowed hard. "That's as much of a betrayal as what the warder did to his sentinel and his clutch."

"I agree," Leith said, his voice icy. "And I think when we're done here, we go see her and tell her the truth. She deserves that."

"How long have you guys been here?"

"Couple minutes before you came down," Malic answered me. "Jacks and I came together, and Ryan before that."

Which explained why my fellow warder had begun entertaining Joe's family.

"Where's Raph?"

"He's home watching Jules and Simon and Dylan."

"And Jael is okay there alone?"

"He has Deidre and her warders visiting, remember?"

"Then who's watching their territory?"

"Apparently there's a lot of small towns there, and some have warders and some don't, but there's a lot of crossover between the territories that do have warders, so it's all covered for the time they're gone."

I smiled at Malic. "Lucky."

"Fortuitous," he agreed. "Now what's your plan here? Once we get through the front door, we just start hacking our way in there until we reach this Breka and then send him to the pit as well?"

"Yes, they all die tonight."

Malic squinted at me. "I talked to you before you got on the plane last night. Have you slept yet?"

I shook my head.

"Oh for crissakes, Marcus," he groaned. "This can—"

"It can't," I told him. "You guys need to get back to hunting Moira, and I need to get home and help you. So this needs to be taken care of right now."

He nodded as we all heard voices and turned.

Ryan was leading Joe's family back into the living room. "Hey." He greeted me with his megawatt smile and kaleidoscope gaze. His hazel eyes changed all the time, sometimes green, sometimes brown, sometimes a mixture. They switched with his mood, and at that moment I was swallowed in a clear olive that was something to see.

"Thanks for coming, Ry," I said.

"Of course," he said, like, where else would he be?

"Did you feel that?" Jackson asked suddenly.

"Feel wh…?" I asked even as I heard feet on the stairs.

"Who else is in the house?" Malic asked, drawing the spatha from behind his back, startling Joe's family even as he stepped in front of them.

"Hey," Raphael said as he charged into the room.

"Oh, for fuck's sake," Malic growled. "Yell, asshole. I could've taken your head off."

"Yeah, right," Raphael scoffed, crossing the room fast to reach Jackson.

"What the hell are you doing here?" Jackson snapped at the man—creature—he loved.

Raphael Caliva was a kyrie, a demonic bounty hunter born in purgatory. He was not a demon, but he wasn't human, either. He still scared me just a little. I was wary, but Joe found him fascinating and never missed an opportunity to ask him a million questions. Watching Raphael when he sat with the man I loved, smiling lazily and talking to him, had gone a long way to helping me accept him.

"Nice to see you too." He grinned evilly and leaned in to brush a kiss across Jackson's mouth before he turned to look at me. "I'm going right back to guard your hearths, but Moira is here somewhere, so Jael said to get here and warn you."

"What're you talking about?" Leith asked.

"I just told you."

"How the hell do you know who's here or not?" Malic barked.

"Ask him nicely," Jackson ordered the bigger man. "That's my mate you're talking to."

At which point Raphael almost glowed. He lived to hear Jackson be possessive of him.

"Tell us what's going on, please, Raph," I interceded.

He shrugged. "Okay, so, to me, the planes of hell are like a giant spider web. Each ring has its own pulse, and everything that crosses a ring leaves a footprint. So she came this way toward Jackson as soon as she felt him move."

I turned to look at my friend. "She's after you."

"Because of me," Raphael said. "She's going to kill my mate because I killed hers."

My eyes returned to the kyrie.

"So." Raphael took a breath. "I'm going home, and I'm taking Joe and his family with me, and you guys find her, kill her, and find this demon and kill him, and then I'll bring them all back."

Everyone started speaking at once, but I raised my hands and called for quiet. I had no idea why they all responded, but as normally happened, the room fell silent.

"That is the best idea I've heard all day," I told Joe and his parents and his sister. "And you have to understand: he's trusting me to protect Jackson, who is all he has in the world, and I'm trusting him to do the same. So… that's exactly what we're going to do."

"Marcus," Elliot began. "I—"

"You guys better call Henry and tell him you're not coming to the dance tonight," I told them. "I don't want him to worry, but you're all leaving with Raph."

"I'm not going," Joe assured me.

I grabbed his bicep and dragged him into a far corner of the room before whirling him around to face me.

"No!"

"Oh yes," I said flatly. "You need to go home and keep your family calm while we sort this out, Joseph. I need you safe, and thank God for Raph and his displacement wave. He can move all of you, and there's no way any of the rest of us could. Jael will be there, too, I'm sure, but I need you to go and ease them through it. Think about them, how scared they must all be, how freaked out they must be, and—"

"I have to stay with you!"

"Not this time," I said. "It's gonna be bad, Joe, really bad."

He sucked in his breath. "Even more reason for me to—"

"I forbid it," I insisted and bent and kissed him.

He fought and pushed and dug his hands into my T-shirt to try to get me off him, but I had a hand on the back of his head, fisted in his hair, and my mouth was sealed over his. I pressed against his lips until he opened them, and my tongue snaked over his, and when he moaned deeply, I knew I had him. I kissed him until he went limp in my grip, hands now holding on for dear life, wanting me closer.

"You," I said, parting our lips, both of us softly heaving for breath, "will go with Raphael and keep him calm. Do you understand? Imagine what this is doing to him. Leaving Jackson? He *just* got Jackson, and now this? C'mon, Joe, I need you now. I need you to show him that he has to have faith."

He growled. "Why didn't you say that in the first place, you stupid ass?"

I hugged him tight, and he wrapped his arms around my neck and squeezed back just as hard.

"I love you."

"I love you too, Marcus Roth. Come get me as soon as you can."

"You know I could never stay away."

"Good."

The hug went on until Malic cleared his throat, and I let go. Walking over to join the others, holding Joe's hand in mine, I was faced with Deborah Locke.

"You'll be safe with Raphael," I said.

She nodded before lifting her hands to my face. "You be safe, Marcus. You're my son too, you know."

I turned my head to kiss her palm, and I saw her eyes suddenly fill.

"Jesus, Marcus, way to make my mother cry," Barbara said, sniffling.

"Your family is nice, Marcus." Malic smiled. "I hope mine will be too." He was going with Dylan for the first time to Atlanta for Christmas.

"It will be."

"Families are good," Leith sighed, thinking, I was sure, about the one he shared with his hearth, Simon Kim. They had, by all accounts, welcomed the man with open arms.

"Let's go," Raphael said, moving forward, taking Joe's other hand.

Joe squeezed mine tight before he dropped it, trailing after Raphael toward the foyer.

Elliot hugged me and thanked me, turned and thanked my friends, and then led his wife after Joe and Raphael. Barbara was the last to leave, wanting to kiss Ryan good-bye.

Leith cleared his throat.

"What?" Ryan asked.

"She knows I'm gay. What about you?"

He frowned at Leith. "I'm sure she knows, but watch, she'll meet Julian and forget all about me."

Leith shrugged and Ryan scowled.

"Jesus, we're all so fuckin' lucky," Jackson said suddenly.

All eyes were on him.

"I mean, I feel lucky," he sighed. "Don't you guys?"

We all agreed that we were.

"Okay, so, since we're all blessed and all"—I smiled gently—"let's make sure none of the guys we go home to ever have to live without us."

"Absolutely," Ryan agreed first. "I don't plan to let anyone else have Julian Nash, ever."

"So let's be careful," I said as the doorbell rang.

It was Shane and Kyle, and I really wasn't all that surprised that they were the only ones who had come. The other two had not struck me as fighters.

"I suspect," Jackson told the two men, "that your sentinel will be in the market for more than one new warder."

Malic made the tsk sound in the back of his throat and eyed them coolly.

"They're good men," Shane assured us. "They just think this is a suicide mission."

"You disagree?" I asked.

"No, but we won't let you go in there alone, either."

And I appreciated that, even though with my team with me, I really wasn't worried.

"Where are Joe and his family?" Shane asked.

"They were taken back to my house," Jackson told him. "Or your place, Marcus." He looked at me. "I'm not totally sure where."

"How?"

"His mate is a kyrie," Ryan said, tipping his head back at Jackson. "So he can use a displacement wave just like your sentinel."

"Your mate is a demon?" Kyle was aghast.

"A kyrie is not a demon," Leith spoke up before Jackson could get a word out. "Everyone knows that."

"Fine, whatever," Shane growled. "Have any of you given any thought to how we're going to get into the demon's home?"

They all looked at me for some unfathomable reason.

"We need a diversion," Leith offered. "In the form of someone 'hot', you said. The sacrifice, right?"

"Exactly," Kyle told us. "Every night is like some big party out there. Daniel and me, we go out there a lot to check that the number of people going in is the same number that walked out in the light of day."

"Okay." Ryan shrugged. "So we can blend if we look like we're just going into a party there?"

"Yeah."

I looked over my fellow warders, all of us. "And um, who brought club clothes?"

"Like, how dressed up are the people that go?" Ryan asked Shane.

He tipped his head like he really didn't want to say.

"It's not club clothes." Kyle grimaced. "It's more fuck-me clothes."

"You couldn't have said this before?" Malic griped.

"You said we were cutting our way in," Kyle reminded him.

"Cut our way to the head demon," Malic said. "We can't fight all the way from the front door; we have to be let in. We have no idea how many are in there."

"Especially if it's over a dimensional door," Jackson chimed in.

"Okay, so then if you guys go in as couples, it should work."

"And you guys?"

"Two couples and one threesome," Ryan suggested.

Leith groaned.

"It's okay, honey." Jackson grinned, wrapping an arm around Leith's neck, his mouth close to his ear. "I'll be gentle."

Ryan snorted out a laugh, and I started grinning.

Leith told us all to go to hell.

"We're already going," Malic reminded him.

I THOUGHT Shane was going to swallow his tongue. Even Kyle, who was straight—who had, from what he said, the most beautiful woman in the world at home—could not take his eyes off Ryan Dean.

"Why did the rest of us even need to change?" Leith grumbled, squirming in his black leather pants, uncomfortable in the skintight, brushed silk dress shirt he had on. It was clinging to his biceps, triceps, and his rippling abdomen. He did not, as a rule, wear anything remotely like what he had on. Ever. Leith was quiet, reserved, and liked cargo pants and denim shirts, jeans and cotton T-shirts. In his current outfit, complete with black leather boots, he looked stunning but really out of his comfort zone.

"Because we all need to fit in," Malic growled, dressed like I was in a suit, his Prada, mine a Hugo Boss.

"Why do you guys get to be dressed like that?" Leith was really irritated, and I was on the verge of smacking him.

"Because we're tops, sweetheart," Malic informed him. "The rest of you do both, right?"

"You know what, Mal—" Leith began.

"Just," Jackson chuckled, grabbing Leith, yanking him up beside him, "don't get all in a twist for nothing."

Jackson himself was dressed in the kind of leather pants that laced up the sides and up the crotch. I couldn't tell if he was wearing underwear or not, and it wasn't my place to ask. The black Lycra T-shirt he was wearing did not reach the top of the red pants, instead showing off the treasure trail from under his navel to right above his groin. The pants hugged his slim hips, riding sinfully low and seductive. His hair was tousled like he'd just gotten out of bed, and the beard and mustache were very sexy.

"Who do I get?" I teased.

They all pointed at Ryan.

"You're the only one people are gonna believe," Malic yawned, moving to stand between Jackson and Leith, separating them, hand fisting in each of their hair. "He overdid it."

"He's right." Jackson laughed softly, pulling free of Malic's grip. "Who knew that store even had stuff like that in there?"

I rolled my head to look at Ryan Dean. What the hell...?

He was in chaps, and they were not like any I had ever seen in my life. They were red with some swirling design down the sides embroidered in gold, and they belted around his hips. He was wearing a thong so that his cock was nestled inside, most of it covered, but his perfect, round, taut ass was on full display. The chaps were hot, ridiculously so, and the fact that it was all he was wearing was enough to make him the absolute focus of any room he walked into.

"How are you gonna fight in that?" I called over to the man preening in the kitchen, admiring his own reflection in the sliding glass door.

He turned to look at me. "What?"

"Fight. You. In that," I said irritably. "Jesus, Ry."

I had been surprised at the store Shane had taken us to at nine o'clock at night. Kyle was not.

"Lexington is a very cosmopolitan city, you know. We're not out in the damn boondocks."

But I didn't know.

"I can do a lot of things in this." Ryan waggled his eyebrows.

I threw up my hands, turned, and bumped into Shane.

"Can we go?" I barked, annoyed for whatever reason that he was leering at my friend.

"He's really beautiful," Shane said under his breath. "His hearth must be really hot."

Julian Nash was a handsome man, but not beautiful. He was tall and muscular and had dark blue-black eyes and glasses. He was not the kind of man you saw first; he was the one you noticed last. He was the guy interested in talking to you, learning your secrets.

"Julian's...." What could I say? "Hey," I said to Ryan as he joined us. "Describe Julian to Shane."

He turned and smiled warmly. "Julian is the only man who I get down on my hands and knees and wiggle my ass for."

Shane caught his breath, and Leith finally let go of his tension and laughed.

I grabbed Ryan's hand and tugged him after me toward the front door. "C'mon, pretty boy. Let's go."

We had to take two cars for the long drive from Nicholasville to Fayette County. The ride down the two-lane country roads was long and lulling, and I gave up and fell asleep. When I was finally shaken awake, I realized that we were parked and everyone was out of the car but me.

After getting out, I put my jacket back on to cover the sheaths on my back. I was not carrying my swords—Kyle was, under his leather duster—but I had Ryan's katana and Jackson's rapier. Malic was packing his spatha and Leith's kilij under his jacket. My hook swords were not discreet, small weapons. I normally carried them crisscrossed on my back in a double scabbard. Kyle, who was dressed like someone out of the Matrix—which amused the hell out of Jackson for some reason—had offered to carry in my swords. There was no guard at the door checking for weapons. It was Sodom and Gomorrah in there. There were demons throwing the party, after all. Weapons were not a consideration. And besides, I was certain, as I eased Ryan forward in front of me, my hand on the small of his back, that no one would be giving anyone but my fellow warder the time of day.

As I suspected, the doorman took one look at Ryan Dean and waved us forward to the front of the line.

Ryan did his walk, the runway stride, the strut, head back, wet lips parted, glittering eyes forward, doing the glide that made him look fluid and boneless. It was impressive, and I wondered, just for a minute, how Julian dealt with everyone wanting a piece of Ryan Dean.

He reached the front and tipped his head up, his eyes drifting slowly open, the look wicked and hot and molten.

I saw the doorman shiver.

"Welcome," the man barely got out. I was sure that with his tongue sticking to the roof of his mouth was making it hard to articulate. "Please step inside."

"Thank you," Ryan purred, moving by him.

No one saw me, no one saw Malic, and most importantly, no one saw Kyle. We moved through the crowd and people made a path for Ryan.

"What the hell," Leith grumbled behind me.

Apparently he and Jackson were groped quite a bit as we moved through the mob, especially Leith with his long hair trailing behind him.

"It's 'cause you're pretty." Jackson smiled even as hands slid over him, grabbed his ass, and tried to stop him.

"How come no one's grabbin' at Ry?"

"It's the walk." Malic was grinning when I looked over my shoulder. "It's the 'I'm too good for you' walk. No one would dare put their hands on him."

And it occurred to me that he was right. Ryan was movie-star handsome, so no one even tried to touch him. Maybe before Julian he had been lonely instead of busy.

Once we reached the back, I helped Ryan up on a low platform to dance. The trance music was not something I had ever liked, but Ryan had been gyrating in clubs for years, from New York to Paris to Rome to Tokyo and back at home in the city by the bay. It was second nature to him.

The hostess came, and we ordered a round of drinks. She offered other things, party favors, and Malic smiled at her and said maybe later. She looked concerned until Jackson took her hand and stroked over her knuckles, smiling up at her at the same time. She was charmed by the time she left.

"I wasn't charming?" Malic asked.

"You sound like a cop," I told my friend.

"How?"

"I don't know." I sighed, smiling. "But you come off like a vice detective or something."

"I'm just not pretty like the rest of you." He smirked.

I wasn't, either, not like Leith and Jackson and Ryan. They were stunning. Malic and I were more handsome, if one needed to apply an adjective to us. We sort of blended into the background, forgettable, but neither of us a breathtaking beauty.

"Don't kid yourselves." Jackson yawned, smiling.

I had no idea what that meant.

Shane looked uncomfortable, and so I took a seat next to him. Malic sat and pulled Leith down into his lap. It looked odd to me, but it wouldn't to anyone else. The only one who belonged in the big man's lap was his hearth, Dylan Shaw. Dylan would have been wriggling around, trying to wedge Malic's groin between his cheeks. I liked watching my friend get all flustered by his young, irrepressible mate.

I wasn't sure what to expect, but it didn't take long. Again, Ryan was like a beacon, and there wasn't a lot of him left to the imagination.

"Here we go," Jackson said under his breath as one man, flanked by another two, approached our table.

He stood for a minute, looking Ryan up and down, leering, before he passed him to face… me. Why it was always me, I had no idea. Yes, I was the oldest at thirty-five, but the stranger didn't know that.

"Hello." The man extended his hand, "I'm Breka. I own this club. I would love to have you and your friends join me for a private party."

"Breka," I said, getting up, Malic moving in behind the other two men, Jackson beside him. "I have a lot to talk to you about."

He squinted at me at the same time the man behind him gasped.

When he tried to turn, I grabbed his bicep and yanked him sideways, throwing him down onto the suede-covered sectional I had been sitting on a moment earlier.

Malic stepped back and, wielding the spatha powerfully, he easily cleaved the demon in half before a hole opened in the floor and he dropped the creature into it. Jackson's movement was similar but more artful, with finesse. The demon's throat was torn open with a quick slash of the rapier before he too was dropped into a black hole that swallowed him fast.

Between the thumping, driving music, the ferocious wall of conversation, and the crowd, no one saw a thing. I stood towering over Breka, and I saw him trembling. Squatting down, I took the scabbard Kyle passed me at the same time.

"Holy fuck," Shane said beside me. "What the hell was that?"

"That's the warder void," Jackson told him. "Just like you—"

"I have never seen anything like that." Shane's voice was shaky. "We…. no one dies like that. It's bloody and messy, and… now I get why you thought we could get in and out of here without creating a huge scene. I had no idea."

"Jesus," Kyle said, and I could feel his eyes studying my profile. "Our sentinel said that some clutches were more powerful—the older the warders, the longer they stay together—but I ain't never seen the likes of you all."

"Breka," I addressed the demon now quivering before me. "I want to talk to you about Elliot Locke and about Emir and Arcan, and I want to see the warder Tarin that you have in your possession. Do you understand?"

He nodded.

"I won't touch you if you do what I say."

More furious nodding.

"Now, which way are we following you?"

He pointed left.

"Okay, you tell Ry which way to walk, and then we'll follow him, all right?"

"Yes." He almost choked on the word.

Breka rose first; I walked at his side with Ryan leading the way. We moved as a single unit through the crowd. No one bothered to ask Breka where he was going. They could all see. He was following the guy with the gorgeous ass.

"Tell me how you do that."

"Do what?" I asked Shane as we walked.

"The warder void, you called it. Tell me how you make it appear."

"We don't. It just is. I thought all warders were the same. I thought they all dealt the same death to every demon: the hole to the pit."

"No, not every clutch is as strong as yours, Marcus. Did you know that every clutch has a center? Just like every warder has a hearth who is their omphalos, *their* center, every clutch has the same thing in a single warder. Kill that one warder, you destroy the clutch."

I stopped walking because, really, there was just no way he was suddenly this font of information. Turning, I found a woman, not Shane Harris at all.

"Moira," I said at the same time I saw the dagger.

I spun as she thrust forward, felt the blade drag across my arm, and watched, helplessly, as it was buried deep in Malic's chest. He had moved fast to put himself between the lethal stroke and Ryan's vulnerable back. The witch had aimed for me, her momentum had carried her toward Ryan, and she had ended up catching my friend.

"Malic!" Leith yelled, and there was screaming around us instantly.

I dove forward and caught him as he dropped to the floor, Leith's kilij and the spatha flying free, clattering away from us as we fell together. The blood was all I could see.

"Marcus!" Leith roared, and I turned my head to see the witch coming for me. Her blade was raised, she had talons instead of hands, and I had no way to defend myself from either. My swords that Kyle had thrown toward me before he ran were on the other side of Malic, and I couldn't reach them. I had one arm under his back, the other over the gaping hole in his heart, pressing down to stem the flow of blood out of his body, but I moved as far as I could trying to grasp one.

She reached me, for me, and I did all I could.

I took a breath and released the pulse of power.

She screamed and tensed, slowed just enough, hesitated for a second, and I saw the flash along the blade, the outline of the steel, the way the light slid over the length as my hook sword, wielded by Ryan Dean, came and took the head of the witch.

Hot blood hit me like a sprinkler, and then the body flew into me, knocking me back and away from Malic under its weight.

"Marcus!" Jackson cried out my name, and I shook my head, trying to get my bearings. It was like I was in a dream, not in control of my muscles, my speed, or my strength as everything moved around me.

There was so much blood pumping from the headless torso of the witch, and I slid through it, slipped over the marble floor as I scrambled back to Malic's side. I peeled off my jacket as I moved, drew Ryan's katana from my back, and tossed it to him, then did the same with Jackson's rapier, throwing it to the other warder. I yanked the scabbards off that had held the blades, then my shirt, and bunching it up, shoved it over Malic's wound and pressed down hard. I grabbed him, cradled him tight, held him close, terrified because he was turning gray, because of the fall of his head, the heaviness of his limbs.

I opened the channel, screamed my need for my sentinel, and prayed even as I heard the shriek from the other side of the room.

"Hurry, Marcus," Jackson yelled again, dropping into his stance, the rapier gleaming in the low light.

I looked for Kyle and saw him running with the rest of the terrified crowd for the exit. I had no idea when the witch had traded places with Shane, had no idea if he was dead or alive, and didn't really even care. Only Malic mattered.

"Jackson, call Raph!" I roared, but I heard the shriek then and knew there was no time.

I had seen no traces of a dimensional door until that second. But we all saw the flood of creatures skittering across the floor toward us on their insect-like legs, their bodies all claws and teeth. The witch had brought racer demons with her from the pit, and they would tear us to shreds just by their sheer number.

I saw them come like those ant hordes I watched on the Discovery Channel once, army ants, and they devoured everything in their path. I remembered the demons Emir and Arcan from Joe's father's shop and saw them briefly before they were attacked and consumed by the racers.

And then my stomach lurched and everything started to roll: the air, even the floor, with the strength of the displacement wave Jael was arriving on.

"You have to move back," Leith said as he gagged and retched, "or we're dying right now."

The wave, usually not lethal, would throw off our equilibrium enough that we would be overrun by demons.

"Leith!"

He turned and I grabbed his arm, yanking him down as I rose up.

"Marcus!" he objected.

But I was right: Leith could move Malic, he was the one who could use a wormhole whenever he wanted—he had that strength—and just across the room was enough.

I took my place between him and Jackson. "Together, and don't stop."

Ryan was fastest, Jackson was second. I was like Malic, stronger, more brute force than speed, but I had to be the anchor, catching whatever they missed. It was necessary to keep the demons off Leith until Jael came and then away from Jael until he could move Malic. Once they were gone, we could get to the door just like everyone else had and lock them in and close the portal. We just needed to give Jael some time.

"Marcus!"

I couldn't turn. I only heard, blessedly, my sentinel's voice behind us.

"I have him! All of you come now!" he commanded.

But he knew there was no way, I knew he did. It was like a wave broke on us, the three of us hacking at a never-ending enemy. The demons that faced us died, but they were replaced in the same second by the next and the next. We had to move back, get out the way we had come in, and close the door. But the longer we stood there, the more I realized it was hopeless. We could inch back, but in the time it would take, we could not keep up the pace. The depths of hell could empty on us there, and eventually we would be overrun and eaten alive. All that could be hoped for was that Leith and Malic and Jael would live.

"Save him!" Ryan screamed, and I heard the tears in his voice, knew he was crying, even as I saw the sword carving up creatures in the corner of my eye.

"Go!" My voice boomed out of me, the pulse again slowing the onslaught for a moment, just enough for Jackson to regain his footing and not go down. We had a moment as the bodies in front of us began to make their own barricade, stacking up, the stench, the blood, the gore making my stomach roll.

"Marot! Jaka! Rindahl! Come to me!"

Jael's voice called to me, spoke to the primal part of me that was all defender, guardian, warder. But I held my ground because there was no choice.

"Go!" I ordered my sentinel and again felt the rise of nausea as the displacement wave threatened to overwhelm us.

Gathering my strength, I leaped high, taking Ryan and Jackson with me, just enough to lift up over the torrent of creatures flooding the floor and escape the effects of Jael's removal of Malic and Leith.

"He couldn't have moved us without being overrun," I yelled over to my fellow warders. "We saved Leith and Malic."

"Which is good," Jackson said before he went limp, dropping like a stone back down toward the demons.

They looked like piranha beneath him, and I knew he was already dead as he plummeted. I had not noticed how much blood he had lost, but I imagined Ryan in that instant, his body shredded, pieces torn away. I could tell, suddenly, by how cold I was that I had to be the same.

"So proud of you," I managed to yell at Ryan.

But his head was back, and I realized I was cold because I was in the middle of a swirling vortex, the icy wind blasting my skin, the tiny shards of ice flying at me. Ryan, having the same strength as Leith, would take us.

But it was funneling closer and closer, closing, and there was no time. His strength was fading so fast, and I knew, in that second, that all of us could never go. The size, what he could do, was him and one other. He was losing control of it and any second it would snap back like a giant rubber band and suck him, and whoever was closest, through the vortex back to the strongest source of warder power. Back to his hearth. As warders, when we moved it was from one warder to the other, but with lack of consciousness or guidance, the wormhole would empty to the heart of a warder... to their hearth.

Ryan would return to Julian.

Diving, tumbling, I reached Jackson, let go of my swords, turned, wrenched around with all I had left, and *pushed*.

It was like a sonic blast tore through the room. The wormhole reached, spun, crackled through the air, and sucked up Jackson along with Ryan and was gone.

I took a breath, that content one, the one you take when you know everything is going to be all right, and let it out.

Burning hot razors hit me like a wall. I dissolved. The pain was all there was, and then there was no air, no light, nothing.

VI

I FELT liquid slithering down my throat and opened my eyes. I saw gold lupine eyes, but I was just too tired to worry about it.

"Warder."

I rolled my head sideways and saw a man.

"Do you know who I am?"

It was hard to keep my eyes open, but I could see jet black where his eyes should have been. He was an empty vessel, no soul in there at all.

"I'm made, yes?" the man said.

My brain, my lawyer brain, never stopped working. So I understood I was looking at a copy of someone else. And if I followed a logical thread, it could only be the missing warder.

"Tarin," I rasped.

He nodded and gently placed a cloth swollen with liquid on my face. I sucked the fluid from the material, not letting the color or the odor bother me. I couldn't be made to care. It was wet; that was all I cared about.

"You fell through a hole, warder, and there were lots of those creatures with you."

Racers. I nodded.

"You're in pieces," he told me. "Your face, body—but you don't need all those things here."

"Where?" I managed as he moved the cloth, dipped it in a wooden bowl, and let it soak up whatever was in there again.

"The road to Nebo," he said.

I shook my head. I didn't know.

"If I can pass through all seven rings, I can ask to be real," he said, and it was only then I noticed the clothes, the burlap pack, and realized that beside him sat an enormous wolf. "That sentinel, he made me to take Tarin's place in the world when he locked him up. I was with his hearth, and now I want my own."

I stared.

"The sentinel, he let the demons take me from the hearth, and then the demons threw me away when they saw you and your friends."

It all seemed logical.

"The water is all you need for now, and there's a well down the hill. You will have to get to it, because I can't stay."

I looked around, and there was nothing but what looked like high grass as far as the eye could see. I was lying beside a fire, small but warm, in a patch that had been burned, maybe. It was a small area.

"You've been here, dead, a week, warder."

A week.

"I can't wait. I have to go. The wolf says when the hunter comes that I can't be here."

He lifted to go, but I reached for him. It took all the strength I had, but I did it.

"Thank you," I said, my voice broken and full of sand.

"If we cross paths again, you'll remember this, yes, warder?"

I nodded.

His face was smeared with dirt; his clothes looked sturdy but old. He reminded me of the pictures in the textbooks of the people on the road during the Great Depression. He looked like he belonged to another time, human and in need of help. All except his eyes. His eyes were solid black, no iris, nothing.

"We're brothers now, warder, yes?"

Again I nodded, giving him my promise.

"The hunter's coming. I'm sorry to run, but there's only me and the wolf, and we have far to go. I hope you live, warder."

I did too.

"I think if you rise from this ring, from Nebo, you'll die, warder. Just rest, regain your strength, and maybe follow me." He pointed, and I saw the dirt road that cut through the grass. "If I see you on your feet, you may join us."

I stared at his eyes.

"The wolf said to kill you, eat you, take our sustenance, but I said no. I will be a man someday, warder. Men don't eat other men."

"No."

He rose then, hand on the wolf's ruff, and I watched them walk away. They didn't look back, and when they walked around a small bend, I lost sight of them. The wind, I realized, was slowly rising, making it impossible to hear anything.

I closed my eyes.

The hunter was coming.

Christ.

I just hoped it would be fast. I didn't... want... to....

Joe.

My body jolted painfully, and I realized that broken did not cover it. I doubted that I could move at all.

I had fallen through a warder void. I must have killed racers on the way down, and so the hole opened and this time instead of me stepping aside to drop a dead demon in, I had been sucked in. But Tarin, the fake warder, the doppelganger, had seen me fall. He and the wolf. They had dragged me away from the racers and put me beside the fire.

A week.

And from one level of hell to the other, time moved differently. There was no way of telling how long I had been there, what I had missed.

From what he said, I was broken, had been dead. Maybe there wasn't enough to look at. Maybe I couldn't pass for human anymore. Maybe Joe couldn't love what was left.

There were no tears; I had nothing to make them with. I could only lie there, limp and lifeless, and wait.

I closed my eyes.

IT WAS dark in a way that I could not see my hand in front of my face, and with the fire gone, it was cold. But I had been colder in a tent in Yosemite. I had been in more pain when I had fought at Jael's side when we cleared a nest of creed demons and a tusk had been driven through my back. I had been more scared when I thought Malic was going to die in my arms. There were worse things, so I concentrated on my own breath. In and out, rise and fall. I just needed to get up. I would either die or I would sit. One or the other would happen. That was just logical. Leith would have been so proud.

THERE was no mistaking the sound of footsteps, and as frightened as I was—I didn't want to be devoured, it hadn't been any fun the first time—I was really only focused on how empty my stomach was.

"Marcus!" came the scream, and I could hear the fury in it, the anger, the hopelessness, and the pain.

I could not imagine a better sound.

"Marcus!"

I had to swallow hard, had to get my voice to work, to rise.

The hunter was there.

In the predawn, the gunmetal-colored sky, I saw huge black feathered wings, felt the stirring of the stagnant air, the breeze on my face.

Only a whisper the first time, all I could do.

"Marcus!" he called again in frustration, the sound rising to a shriek, the struggle to hold onto the very last desperate shred of something.

I waited, gathered myself, breathed out, in, and used my voice for the second most important time in my life, the first being when I said *I do* to Joe.

"Raphael!" I called and just for a second I thought he was a fallen angel and so was I.

The darkness was like rain clouds over me, and then they parted, and an enormous black feather was caught between falling and floating before it drifted down, down, and came to rest beside me. And so did he.

Looking up, I found myself swallowed in smoky topaz, glittering and dark. I smiled slowly. "Wings?"

He cleared his throat. "Don't tell Jackson."

"I think," I whispered, "he'd love them."

He was squinting, working hard not to break down. Big, badass demon hunter, he shouldn't have cried.

"Can you take me home?"

He nodded as the tears rolled down his cheeks.

I would have reached for him, comforted him, but I had done so much already. I had to rest.

He told me to.

IT FELT like being dropped into the deep end of a pool. I hit, went under, and was swallowed in liquid. When my eyes finally fluttered open, I saw Jael.

"Don't drown me," I groaned, knowing instantly where I was.

The bathtub in the castle masquerading as a house that he had in Sausalito, in the master bedroom; it could pass for a small pool. The man had me submerged, and he was purifying the water, pulling God knew what out of me.

I growled.

You would have thought I gave him a million dollars the way he smiled, dropped to his knees beside the tub, and put his hands on my face.

"Son of a bitch," he barked.

I grunted.

"Marot."

I shook my head. Not today.

"Marcus," he exhaled, hands so gentle on my skin, holding me like I was fragile. "You are an extraordinary man."

"All"—I coughed to get my voice working—"all warders are."

He shook his head. "No, Marcus, you have strength that I've never seen. There are reserves in you I didn't know a warder could have. You saved us all: you put us all before yourself, and then you lived on top of it."

The big question. "How long was I gone?"

"Six months."

Jesus.

"Everything will be all right," he promised, which was not even logical.

"Joe," I said.

"Joe is well, we check on him."

"You don't see him?"

"He doesn't want to see us. It's been very painful for him. He knows you're alive because the house is still sealed, the branding touch hasn't left him, but the not knowing...."

That would have been hardest for Joe, the uncertainty and the fact that I had put others before him. Because I could have reached him, could have been safe, could have left and gotten home. But I had placed Malic before him. Jackson and Leith before him. Ryan. How could I ever say that he was all there was... when he had not been.

"Did you tell him you found me?"

"No, I wanted you to tell him when you were ready. Or I can go get him right—"

"I'm disfigured, right?"

He frowned.

"Just tell me."

"No, but why would that matter? Joe loves the man, not the wrapping."

"You think just because Joe's blind that he doesn't care what I feel like when he touches me?"

His smile was warm as he rose and left the room. He returned with a hand-held mirror, and when he turned it on me, without warning, I realized instantly that I was looking at my own face.

I looked like me. My wide-set dark-brown eyes, and my long, straight nose, full lips, high cheekbones, and thick eyebrows were familiar, and it was a relief. I could look down at my own body and see the gouges, the scars, the tears, and the bruises. It would take time, but I would be perfect before I laid eyes on Joseph Locke again.

"We should call him now, Marcus."

I shook my head. I didn't even have the strength to protect him. What use was I to him?

"You're wrong," was all Jael said.

But I didn't want to fight. My life had to wait until I was ready.

VII

I TALKED to Jael, but I wasn't ready to see anyone else. Even Raphael, who I had already seen, I didn't want to visit me again.

Jael and I walked his property with his Irish wolfhounds, and after two weeks I could throw a stick for the dogs, and after one more I could run with them. Food, water, exercise—it took time, but I built back up.

Malic had done an amazing thing and gone to Helene Kessler and told her that I needed an extended leave of absence. When she had asked for particulars, he told her only that I was missing. Would she accept that? Apparently she had. He would update her when he knew anything. There was nothing she could do. All the appropriate authorities had been contacted, and that was all. Her willingness to take his word and wait had impressed him, Jael told me. Helene Kessler, Jael thought, could handle the truth when I was ready. She already had faith in me; he felt that was an excellent foundation to build on. She was quite a woman, quite a human being, period. I was betting on her being able to handle the truth.

The demon base in Lexington, Breka's home, and everything that happened that night had been covered up under the umbrella of a gas leak, and everyone had bought it. What else could it have possibly been?

Jael spent time catching me up, and it seemed odd, but his company, though not welcome, was all I could seem to accept. Just the thought of talking about it all made me not want to see anyone. And Joe, especially, what could I say about my weakness, my inability to get back to him? What rationale could I give? I was supposed to protect him and his family, and I had instead disappeared, not been there. The failure was great.

"You're insane, you know," Jael told me as I stood on the back deck of his guesthouse, staring out at the bay. "If you just let them, they would all tell you what you did."

"But I just want it to all go away," I said, breathing in the warm summer air. It was August now, and I had left them all before Christmas. I had been gone six months and had been holed up at Jael's for another two. It was so strange.

"Can you return, Marcus? Would you prefer to start over somewhere else? Go where no one knows you? I'm sure it would be easy to do at work, and I can recommend you to another sentinel."

Start over.

"Maybe," I exhaled, finally faced with the reality.

"But Joe," Jael said softly.

I had to see him. "If he's waiting, I'll see."

"You don't throw away six years, Marcus." He didn't understand. "Explain what you're thinking."

"What happened to Deidre?" I asked suddenly, desperate to change the subject.

"Nothing happened; she was here three months ago. It's my turn to visit her next."

"She's not going to move here?"

He cleared his throat. "She's not ready to give up being a sentinel, and neither am I. It was boorish of me to think that because she's a woman that it would be her sacrifice to make."

I studied his face. "So quit and go to her."

"You say the same idiotic things as Jaka. One doesn't just leave."

"I think one does." I smiled, sighing. "If you love her."

"Love is complicated, isn't it?" He had brought me right back around to my problem. It was clever. "Talk to me."

"Just—"

"Marcus—"

"You know, that's weird already," I cut him off. "Coming from you, it's…. Just go back to Marot."

"Fine, Marot." He took a breath. "I want to hear what you're thinking."

"About what?"

"About Joe!" I could hear the frustration in his voice. "Please."

"I just… why would he want me anymore? I'm supposed to protect him, and I didn't, and he's supposed to be my whole life and then what—I just forgot him? What he means? He must hate me. I would hate me if I were him."

"Mar—"

"Just thinking about how he's going to look at me…. Why have that scene? Why not just spare us both?"

"You're scared."

"It's more than that." Simple fear would not have kept me from my hearth.

"You're resigned."

It was closer to the truth, probably a little of both. "I…. Jael?"

He looked strange, lost in thought, a million miles away.

"You okay?"

And I watched the light sort of turn on in his eyes. "I'm an idiot."

"Jael," I began. "You can't fix—"

"To your mind," he cut me off, "you were on that alternate plane a week but to your body and soul, the wear on both, the pain…. It was six months. And now you've been back two, and…. God, I'm really just so stupid." He turned away from me, charging into the other room and slamming the door behind him.

I had no clue what was going on, so I left.

THE five-mile run up and down the hills of Sausalito felt good. My body would never be the same, there were scars in hard-to-reach places, but I was strong again, and I could feel my muscles respond when I asked.

When I got back, I took a long hot shower and had changed into basketball shorts and nothing else when I wandered into Jael's kitchen for dinner.

"How dare you," the cold, flat voice said.

My head snapped sideways, and I saw Joe standing by the dishwasher next to the sink. He didn't look like himself, and I wasn't sure why, and then it came to me. I had never seen the expression he had on his face before in my life.

I waited.

He trembled just slightly, and I restrained myself, stamped down the urge to go to him.

"Marcus Roth, explain yourself right fucking now."

He looked thin, his coloring was off, and his hair was shorter. He was wearing thick black-framed Buddy Holly glasses with yellow lenses that made the blue of his eyes a strange lime green. It was odd.

"Marcus!" he barked.

I cleared my throat, holding onto the back of one of Jael's barstools for dear life. It was easier to articulate as I had said it earlier to my sentinel. I wondered briefly if that had been the point. "When push came to shove, I didn't think of you. You weren't right there. The guys were there, and so I put them first. I sacrificed myself, and in so doing put you in jeopardy. I'm so sorry, Joe." My voice bottomed out. "I let you down like I said I never would. I'm so sorry."

He nodded, and I saw the clench of his jaw, heard him take a breath, saw the shiver run though his body.

"So you think that you've let me down."

I nodded.

"Use your words, Marcus."

"Yes," I managed to get out, feeling my knees go weak, my power deserting me when I needed it most.

I did not expect the plate—and this was Jael's house, so who knew what the damn thing cost—to narrowly miss me and shatter into a thousand pieces behind me.

"What the fuck are you doing?"

"You stupid ass!" he screamed as he began emptying the cupboard above him. The plates flew toward me, and I had no idea how, but he knew where I was, and he had great aim.

"Joseph." I tried to calm him, tried to get closer at the same time.

"You idiot! This hurt me! You not coming for me the second you got home! You not sending for me the minute you could—that is fuckin' killing me, not the rest of this self-serving martyr bullshit!"

Martyr? "Now wait!" I yelled, and then I saw that the plates were gone, and he moved to the next cupboard full of glassware.

"How dare you not send for me!"

"Shit," I growled, coming around the island even as he retreated.

"Stay the fuck away from me!"

And it hit me—all the pain, all the longing, all my need, all of it. My hearth. I couldn't breathe without him.

"Joe," I gasped.

"No!" he roared, walking backward.

"I need you."

But he was furious, and hot, angry tears were running down his cheeks as he unloaded on me, screaming, yelling, and calling me every name he could think of. Mostly I was a bastard. Over and over.

"Baby," I soothed.

"Fuck you!" he railed. "You did what you had to do, Marcus! You didn't just save me and my family, you saved Malic and Jacks and Ry and Leith and all the hearths too. We don't work without our warders; do you even fucking get that? You did it all, Marcus, and then you're gonna do what, punish us all, stay away from all of us—leave us?"

I inched closer to him.

"Fuck you, Marcus Roth! I fuckin' hate you, and I'm gonna leave you like you left me, and I hope you cry yourself to sleep every night like I did and miss my smell on your sheets and my hands on your skin and just fucking rot!"

The crystal punch bowl missed me by inches. The matching ladle bounced off the copper pots hanging from the ceiling, but because he'd really flung it, put his back into it, he upset his balance just a little.

It was enough.

I moved fast, faster than he could or would ever be able to, reached him, and wrapped the man up tight in my arms.

"No," he screamed.

I held on, squeezed tighter, and the flood of relief was overwhelming. All of it, everything was just done. Nothing mattered; I had Joseph Locke in my arms.

"I hate you, Marcus," he sobbed, face pressed to my collarbone, hands flat on my bare chest. "I'm gonna leave you."

I sighed as I rubbed my chin in his hair. It was so soft, his thick auburn hair, and it smelled so clean. He was shaking so hard, pressing into me so close, struggling now to free his arms.

"I thought you'd hate me, and I couldn't bear to see that on your face."

"I'd never hate you for doing what was right, Marcus," he said, his voice nasally, stuffed up, full of tears. "I never once thought you made a decision, them over me. It never occurred to me that saving them would keep you from me. You forgot who I am; you forgot that I understand every part of you, your heart especially."

I had been so lost, and the epiphany took me literally to my knees.

"Marcus!"

He was dragged to the floor with me, and I was kneeling with him, still holding on tight, tucked against my chest.

"Forgive me," I begged. "Please, baby, forgive me. I'm so stupid. I was so wrong. I thought…. I didn't give you credit for being the man you are, for knowing what you know, for loving me like you do."

"I don't love you anymore," he told me, wrenching free, scrambling away, and turning, searching for a door, any door.

It was the back deck, which, if he got out, would strand him there as there were no stairs down. Jael lived on a cliff.

I didn't mention that he was walking out onto the lanai. It was too dear. Instead I slammed the door shut before he could get it open further, held it closed, my hand braced beside his head.

"Put your hands on me."

"You threw me away." His voice shook because crying and talking was hard to do.

"I was terrified of what you'd do, and that was stupid," I told him, my voice low and husky, coaxing, seductive. "I'm so sorry, baby."

His teeth were chattering with the welling emotion, and the trembling was obvious.

"Please, Joey," I begged. "How long have you waited?"

"Waited for what?"

"To put your hands on me?"

His breath stuttered, caught.

"I'm right here," I whispered, leaning forward, my forehead pressed to his. "Joe."

"I hate you."

"I know. Put your hands on me," I ordered, my voice hardening.

"How could you do that to me? Leave me?"

I would go out of my mind if he didn't touch me, if he didn't need to anymore.

"Me? You're supposed to love me."

"You have to forgive me. You just have to."

"Marcus," he whispered.

"This will kill me when nothing else did."

He gasped as he slid his hands up my abdomen, his fingers sliding over muscles, exploring new scars, touching me everywhere, mapping new terrain and old. His hands were so sensitive, his fingertips, his palms, and I watched his lips part with the sensation.

"Promise it's okay," I pressed him. "Swear we're still us. Joey, I'm so sorry. I can't be more sorry. Please."

The whimper, the sweetest sound I ever heard, let me know I had him.

"Your skin is like warm silk, Marcus, smooth and made to be touched. And I know you, you're worried what I'll think of these scars," he said as he bent and kissed one, tracing the next with his tongue, then following with his teeth.

My cock hardened so fast it hurt, swelling with blood, with my need for him. "Fuck, Joe."

"I love these marks. I love every single part of you, Marcus Roth, always."

I took his face in my hands, tilted his chin up, and took the glasses off, dropping them onto the kitchen counter. Here were the eyes I knew, welled now with tears, red-rimmed, full of hurt. I swallowed hard.

"Swear on my life right this second. Promise and I'll believe you."

"What?" I asked, even though I knew.

"That you will never, ever, stay away from me again," he said his breath warm on my face. "If you can, if you're able, you come home to me."

I nodded furiously so I didn't break down.

His smile was breathtaking. "Use your words, Marcus."

But there was no way. I ground my mouth down over his instead, kissed him ravenously, my tongue pushing inside, claiming what was mine, what I had to have.

His arms wrapped around my neck as he whined in the back of his throat, pushing against me, rubbing, toeing off his black Chuck Taylors at the same time.

He hung onto me, kissing me back just as passionately even as my hands flew over him, unbuckling his belt, working his zipper, rough as I disrobed him, wanting him naked as fast as I could get him that way.

When his jeans and briefs were gone, when there was only bare ass under my hands, I wrapped an arm around his waist, lifted him up, and pulled and yanked at the clothes bunched around his ankles. I left them in a pile in the middle of the broken glass in the kitchen.

His legs were tight around my hips as I walked him to my bedroom. He lifted his lips from mine to gulp air and then reclaimed my mouth with first a bite before the sucking, devouring kissing began all over again.

Our tongues slid together, over and under, around, and he wanted deeper, more, and when I fell over him, down onto the bed, pinning him under me, his arms tightened around my neck so I couldn't pull away.

He wanted me that close, and I understood. Any farther away was too much. At home we…. But we weren't at home.

I pulled back, and he lifted up to recapture my mouth, but I moved out of his reach.

"Marcus!"

I tried not to smile. "Lube."

"What?"

I was so glad he couldn't see my grin. "Um, we don't have any lube, Joey."

"Are you *kidding*?"

He was indignant, and I put my head down on his shoulder and laughed. And it felt so good. I felt so much like me I was giddy.

He shoved me off the bed, and I couldn't stop laughing. When he pulled the comforter off the bed, wrapped himself in it and stomped out of the room, the tears were rolling down my cheeks. The ridiculousness of it, passion done in by lack of Astroglide or any other slippery substance, was hysterical... and normal.

I was okay.

Joe was okay.

We would be us again.

I was laying there, sprawled out, still chuckling when he came back, chucked a small tube at me, and then slammed the door.

"Where did you get this?" I asked, smiling crazily at how annoyed he looked, how his hair was sticking up, how red and swollen his lips were and how flushed his skin was.

"From my backpack!"

"Carrying lube around, are you?" I asked even as I saw it was brand new, the seal unbroken.

"Shut up, Marcus," he said, dropping the comforter and walking over to me.

He reached for my hand, and I lifted mine toward him, the action so ingrained, so ordinary, and when my fingers curled around his, I felt it in my heart.

"I was stupid," I said as I guided him down to me, on top of me, straddling my hips.

"Yes."

I let go of his hand as I pulled down my shorts and briefs, letting my hard cock bounce free, letting Joe reach behind him and ease the clothes down to my ankles.

My shaft loomed between us as he fisted it in his hand.

It felt incredible.

"Pass me the lube."

I placed it in his hand, riveted, watching as he opened it, squeezed a glob into his palm, and then used that to slick my hard, rigid, leaking cock.

"There's no way I'll last longer than a second," I confessed. "I've got zero stamina. You're gonna have to settle for a blowjob, baby, 'cause—"

"No," he told me, lifting up, leaning forward, again reaching behind him, this time for my dick.

"Joe." I stopped him, grabbing him tight. "You're not ready. You need to—"

"I've been ready for ages; I've been waiting for you to come home to me."

"Baby—"

"Marcus, I've been working my own ass for almost a year waiting to be stuffed full of you again! You should see the fucking dildo I have at home!"

"You've been fucking yourself, thinking of me?" God, that was hot.

"Every single time, yeah."

My breath became shallow with how bad I wanted to be buried inside of him.

"And now you think I'm gonna wait? Are you insane? All I wanna do is ride you."

I let him go, because really, Joe knew his own mind, knew his body better, and absolutely understood his own limits. It was one of the many reasons I was enthralled with him.

When I felt the head of my cock at his entrance, I gritted my teeth and held on. I would make it if it killed me.

It nearly did.

He was so tight, and he was easing me inside him so slowly, inch by inch, his muscles clenched and unyielding against the persistent pressure. He felt so good, the silky rippling walls, and then he dropped down onto me, impaled.

"Joe!"

"Oh God." His body twitched, and I was squeezed in a vise of wet heat.

"Did I hurt—"

"Ohmygod," he moaned, lifting up only to slide back down my slippery length, seating himself deeper, harder.

"Joseph," I managed to get out.

He rose again only to lower himself back down, rising and falling, riding me, chanting my name, begging me to touch him.

I wrapped his dripping cock with my hand and stroked him from balls to head, holding tight like I knew he liked, my lube-slicked fingers gliding over his velvet skin.

"Marcus, I need you to fuck me, I need to feel you deep. I need to know you're home because it hurts to fuckin' sit down."

I would never do that, never be that rough, but as I slid slowly free of him and rolled over, pinning him to the floor under me, yanking his legs up and folding them in half, I realized that I wanted to.

"For once, just use me up, Marcus. Just forget yourself."

But my control….

"Let go, Marcus. Have faith. Trust me. I deserve it. I've earned it."

I bent down into the openmouthed kiss, sucked on his tongue, getting the last taste of submission before I leaned back and lined my cock up with his pink puckered hole. I sheathed myself to the hilt in one long, smooth stroke.

Joe yelled my name, and I understood from the sound, the bliss that infused it, that he needed me right where I was, hammering into him, driving deep and hard and fast.

My hands would leave marks where I was holding his hips. Watching him jerk himself off was putting me right over the edge.

"Joey, gonna come."

His moan, the way his inner walls clasped around me, bearing down, let me know that his release was imminent.

I rammed home, buried to the balls in his ass, feeling his heartbeat and mine together, the throbbing, sizzling heat rolling through me without warning. I came hard, pumping hot come deep inside my lover, frozen over him, holding tight and making sure he couldn't move.

After long minutes, I finally let his legs unfold from where I had them trapped against me, and he slid them over my arms, resting them, allowing blood flow to commence.

I was panting, covered in sweat, utterly spent, ready to drop down onto him at any second.

"Get in the bed."

I whined.

"Get in the bed now."

"Don't want to pull out."

"*Now.*"

I eased carefully from his still-clenching hole and climbed up onto the bed and dropped down like a rock on my belly, my head on the pillow.

"Shit, you need help?" I asked.

But he answered with his skin sliding over mine, lying down, his weight of no consequence to me.

"You going to sleep on top of me?"

"Yeah."

His wet, flaccid cock was pressed to the small of my back, and I could feel his cheek resting between my shoulder blades.

"Okay."

"I wish I could see you, Marcus, just once. Everyone tells me that you're a stunning man, but all I know is that touching you is different from touching any other."

I purred under him. I couldn't help it.

"Your skin is always warm and sleek, and your body is so hard and strong. I love touching your muscles, feeling them move under my palm. I love holding your cock in my hand and feeling your body vibrate with power. I love your soft mouth and your big hands and how you grab me and tug on my hair and hold me down. Your weight on me, always, is like home."

God, I loved him.

"So please, please don't ever leave me again. I can live without you. I know that now. I can. I just don't want to."

I wanted to roll over, but he pressed me down, and I was weary and so ready to sleep. I could finally, completely rest. I had Joe in bed with me.

"Stay with me."

"Yes," I agreed.

"Never leave me."

"No," I promised.

"I love you so much, Marcus, never wanna sleep without you again for the rest of my life."

Amen.

VIII

THE next morning the kitchen was already cleaned up when I walked in to take care of it. Jael was having coffee.

"I'm so sorry."

"It's to be expected. Reconciliation is messy."

I had to agree.

I promised my sentinel that I would replace all the dishes (simple), and the punchbowl (harder, as it had to be ordered online from some place in Glasgow), and he smiled and nodded and said it was fine. When his hand went to my face, cupping my cheek, I grumbled that he had been right.

"Of course," he said, like I was an idiot. "I always am."

I made omelets and served Joe breakfast in bed. Before I could take the dishes back to the sink, the kiss I got sent a wave of heat through me. I had the man pinned under me seconds later. When he arched up to meet me, I forgot about everything else.

My stomach growling brought me from the bedroom hours later, and Jael suggested that instead of eating, I shower and change.

"Why?"

"They're coming."

"Who's coming?" I asked.

"Who do you think?"

And even though I had wanted to simply go home with Joe, see it, stretch out on my California king, and watch him make dinner, I understood. It was time.

Malic got there first. I would have been disappointed if he hadn't. Your best friend should always be the first one through the door.

I was standing on the back deck; Joe was stretched out on the chaise sipping a mojito, which I had teased him about.

"Since when do you drink before lunch?"

"Since you went away."

I rolled my eyes because I knew he had years of rubbing it in my face.

"Marcus."

I turned, and Malic was standing there staring at me, eyes clouded like they never were, holding onto the doorjamb, jaw clenched, the muscles in his neck corded.

"Marcus," Joe prodded quietly. "He could die from you not calling to him."

But Malic and I didn't do words. They weren't necessary. I nodded, and he breathed, and I saw him straighten, ready to walk to the railing, and I knew that this time, it wasn't enough.

I lifted my hand, and he moved very fast. Normally, just us, no life and death situation imminent, there was no need for such a display of speed. But one second we were apart, the next second he was on me, one arm over my shoulder, the other under my arm, hugging me the way I normally only held Joe, so close I could feel his heart beating. His face was pressed into the side of my neck, and he inhaled me, breathing me in, making his body understand that I was safe so his brain could process it.

"Don't stay away again," he mumbled against my skin.

"No," I promised. Not him. The others I could never swear to, but him I could, him I had to. He was my brother.

I felt the final clench, and then he pulled away the same instant I let him go.

"All good now?" Joe asked snidely. "All hugged out?"

I laughed when Malic lunged at Joe, attacking him, and my boyfriend yelled for the big gorilla to get the hell off him. I was still smiling as Ryan and Julian, Jackson and Raphael, and Leith and Simon came through the door. Dylan came last, followed by Jael.

I took a breath and Ryan ran. I didn't expect the leap, arms and legs wrapped around me, the kiss on my cheek, my jaw, and the hug with the shivering.

"Sorry," I apologized, realizing that I had been an idiot a moment ago. I loved them all, and they were all my brothers. Malic and I were more, but that did not diminish what I felt for the others. "Forgive me."

"You saved my life; you protected me. What the fuck is there to forgive?"

When I let him go, he slid down my body, and I had Julian there to fill my arms. The mantra of the *thank you* began.

Leith and I hugged briefly, but it was hard, and his whispered words were fervent and sincere. The kiss, his lips feather-light on my own for just a moment, was unexpected.

I was out of my depth. How had I missed that they all loved me?

Simon smiled, and the dark-charcoal eyes glowed quicksilver before he leaned in to hug me.

"Don't you know, Marcus? You're the guy that holds everything together. Without you, they're just fighters. With you, they're a family."

But there was no way.

Jackson was taller than Ryan, but I was still bigger than he was, so I was again engulfed, arms and legs, and I apologized to Raphael for putting my hands on him as I held him to me.

"It's okay." Raphael smiled dangerously, his possessiveness tempered just for a minute.

Jackson kissed me and hugged me, and I got my hands in his hair and pushed it back from his face. I had grown accustomed to the beard and mustache.

"Can we sit and talk about what happened now? Please?"

We could.

Raphael came close after I put Jackson down, after he could bear to be near me as my hands were no longer on his man. We were all the same. We were protective, kind, strong—until you tried to take something from us. Then you saw the scary, primitive warder. I never liked anyone to see that side of me, the side that could be cruel and merciless. For a kyrie, the distinction between angel and devil was even thinner. So as I saw the flicker of rage rise and dissipate just as fast, I said a quick prayer for the man stupid enough to ever try and take Jackson Tybalt from the creature who loved him.

As I looked over the men who inhabited my life with me, I realized that Malic was looking away. Following his gaze across the deck, I saw Dylan leaning on the railing, contemplating the setting sun.

He was purposely standing apart.

I looked back at Malic, and he shook his head. He wanted me to not worry about it, whatever *it* was.

But how could I, after everything?

Taking a breath, I walked over toward Dylan. His eyes flicked to mine, and the second I saw the anger, I understood. Joe had looked much the same way. My hearth had been mad at me. Dylan was mad *because* of me.

I stopped close enough so he had to tip his head up to look at me. It was a lawyer tactic that I realized I used subconsciously to give me the upper hand. "You don't love me anymore?" I teased, thinking it was safest. He was just a baby, after all.

He sucked in a breath.

"Can I guess?"

His brown eyes were so big and so pained, vulnerable.

"I hurt your man."

He tried so hard, but the tears were inevitable.

"I'm sorry, Dylan. I had to deal with things myself, and—"

"No." He shook his head.

"No?"

He cleared his throat and reached out to put a hand on my chest. "Marcus, you're the guy that holds it all together," he said softly. "You don't get to be alone. You don't get to run away or decide to go on a vision quest or something."

"Dylan—"

"I thought it was Jael, you know? I thought he was like the father and you guys all thought of him like that, but no one does but Jacks. Everybody else, he's like a big brother and a boss rolled into one."

I stayed quiet because he had a point to make, and it was obviously eating him up, so he had to get it out. Peripherally I was aware that the others were closing in on us, but I was focused on my friend's hearth more than anything.

"But you, Marcus…." He took a breath, "I didn't know who you were until you weren't here anymore."

A second hand joined the first, and then both hands slid down my sides to my hips, holding on.

"When you were gone, it was like Malic lost his family. I asked him how Ryan was, and he didn't know. I asked about Leith and got the same answer. We tried to come here and visit Jael, all of us, but no one could talk. Ryan killed that witch, you know? He—"

"I know." I smiled, turning my head to look back at Ryan. "That was amazing."

His eyes sparked, and I realized that I was the only one who saw it, because everybody else was looking at me instead of Ryan Dean.

"I was dead if you hadn't taken her head off, Ry," I told him. "I knew you were fast, but I had no idea."

He nodded, and it was obvious that the man was overwhelmed.

"Jael," I told him. "You would have been amazed."

"I'm sure I would have."

"And Malic." I exhaled. "There was no way Ryan would be alive if you hadn't taken that blow for him. Jesus, man, you scared me to death."

He was staring at me hard, as though he was memorizing my face.

"And you held the line even though you were shredded, Jacks." I smiled. "When you fell… I think my heart stopped."

His dark eyes were locked on me.

"I just thought, at least Leith is safe, and Jael and Malic. It sustained me, and I think Jacks and Ry too."

No one said a word, and after a moment I became aware that all eyes were on me.

"Marcus."

I turned back to Dylan.

"This"—he gestured at all of us—"does not work without you. I didn't know. I didn't understand, but I do now."

"We're all in this together, all of us, warders and hearths, and we're a family, yeah?" I asked.

"We are now." He took a quivering breath. "Because you're home."

I took his face in my hands as he broke down into tears.

"Goddammit," Malic growled as he came toward us. "Why you gotta go all soft and mushy on him?"

I chuckled, grabbing Dylan, crushing him against me, hoping to squeeze all the tears out in one shot.

"You're suffocating him," Simon laughed.

"He's loving it," Julian sighed, "so it's okay."

"Can we drink now?" Leith whined.

I let Dylan go, released him into Malic's arms, but even as my friend took his small, young hearth close, he put a hand on the back of my neck and squeezed gently.

"I know," I told him.

"Just fuckin' stay."

"I'm not going anywhere."

"Don't leave us," he muttered under his breath. "Me."

And I understood, for us, for warders who had lost their whole families, a hearth was all they had. But for a few clutches, a lucky few, there was even more created. There was a family.

"Who's hungry?" Jael asked.

And since we all were, he started barking out orders. I was thrilled to have the spotlight off me as I sank down beside Joe on the chaise.

He smirked at me. "So what did we learn?"

I groaned.

"Maybe, jackass, you should think a little more of yourself and realize that in the big picture, Marcus Roth, you're fucking vital."

I leaned sideways and put my head down in his lap.

"I'm not petting you."

"Please, Joe," I whined, closing my eyes.

His hand slid down between my shoulder blades, and he rubbed gently, caressing, finally bending to kiss my temple.

"Say it."

"I love you, Marcus."

Always good to hear.

AS WE all scarfed down steaks and corn on the cob and potatoes wrapped in foil, all cooked on the grill, I was filled in on events.

"Raph went and found the doppelganger," Jackson told me. "You told him that he helped you, so we wanted to see if we could help him."

I looked at Raphael. "And?"

"He and his wolf are on the road, and I gave him a way to contact me if he needed. I told him that your debt became mine because while I can travel the rings, Marcus, you should not."

"Why?"

"Your energy, more than any other warder I've ever known, is tangible and traceable. You don't want something to follow you home."

"No," I agreed.

"I followed you home," Joe snapped, and I realized, as I had an hour ago, that he was really drunk. The ratio of food to alcohol in his system was way off. We had missed lunch, and whereas I had waited to drink, Joe had started before anyone even arrived.

"That was a good thing," I teased him, leaning sideways, kissing his cheek. "Now be a good boy and eat your potatoes."

He grunted. "Did you all know that Marcus is crisscrossed with new marks from fighting those racer demons?"

Dead silence at the table. It was guilt that no one needed.

"So," I said brightly. "You sure do track quickly, Raph. How do you do that?"

All eyes on the kyrie.

He glared at me.

I smiled back.

He growled. "You promised."

"I didn't mean to promise."

He was disgusted with me; that was clear.

"What's going on?" Jackson asked us.

I leaned forward to deliver the news.

Raphael took Jackson's hand instead. The solemn look on his face, the trepidation in his eyes—both, I knew, were so unnecessary.

"I have wings when I'm in other dimensions."

"What?"

"He has these huge black feather wings," I told Jackson, who turned to look at me. "They're beautiful, you should see them."

He looked back at Raphael. "You have wings?"

The kyrie nodded slowly.

"That's so cool."

Instant surprise.

"What?"

"I thought you would think it made me more demon than human and—"

"No," Jackson cut him off, leaning over to press a kiss to the side of Raphael's neck. "I can't wait to see them, and you should never be afraid to tell me anything."

"That's how you found the edge of that dimension I was in," Simon said excitedly. "You had a lot of ground to cover in every direction, and you did it so fast.... I wish you would have let me see them while we were there."

"We were inside," Raphael said softly, and I realized that he was more than a little touched by the reception over this latest development. "No need to fly in there."

"Yeah, but still." Simon smiled warmly. "I bet they're amazing."

"They are," I assured him, looking over at Jackson. "Raphael saved my life."

Jackson nodded.

"And you saved Jackson's," Raphael told me. "We're even."

Another looming silence seemed inevitable.

"So Shane's not dead," Ryan chimed in. "We found him walking down the side of the road the next day. The witch had wiped his mind, but otherwise he's well."

"The spell didn't lift when she died?"

"It did after a month." Ryan smiled, so obviously happy just to be looking at me. "He's with Kyle and the other two warders and their sentinel in Rome being... what?" His head turned to Jael. "Educated? Tortured? What?"

Jael sighed deeply. "Tortured? Really? This is what you think of the labarum?"

Ryan shrugged. "Pretty much, yeah."

"The council is not in the habit of hurting their own warders," Jael told him. "They are all being retrained in their duties. The sentinel has been stripped of his rank and is now a warder again. He will be assigned to a new city."

"That sucks," Dylan said. "I bet he has his whole life in Lexington, and now he's gotta move because he was stupid."

"Very stupid," Leith agreed. "But you don't let an incarnation sleep with the hearth of a warder. If you ask me, reassigned isn't enough."

"So what happened to the real Tanner and his wife?"

"They were reunited in Rome," Jackson said. "And he's been stripped of his warder status and his power."

"How?"

"The sentinel," Jael answered.

All eyes went to him; we were all interested in this part.

"A sentinel calls for a warder and a man or woman answers that summons. At the same time, the power within the warder is awakened by the sentinel. The presence of the sentinel speaks to the dormant power in the individual. The sentinel sparks the gift, and a warder is created."

Malic squinted. "I don't remember it being that romantic."

Dylan found that statement hysterical. Julian pushed his face down into the table, which just made Dylan laugh louder.

"But the sentinel can remove their 'recognition', I guess you'd call it, and it's as though the warder was never *seen* in the first place, never discovered, never made."

"Okay," I nodded. "So Tanner and his wife are free to be regular people."

"Yes."

"But after being a warder, won't that drive him nuts?" Julian asked. "Once you've been something extraordinary, it would be hard to go back to being a normal person."

"Which is why Lexington's new sentinel will keep an eye on Tanner and his wife," Jael instructed us all. "And the labarum council is very pleased with all of you for uncovering corruption in another territory. You're to be commended."

"Lucky everyone lived, then, to be commended," Joe said sarcastically.

"I'm glad Tanner and his wife are back together," I told Jael.

"They're getting a divorce." Joe cackled evilly. "She doesn't want a *regular* man; she only wants a warder. She's like the blonde bitch in *An Officer and a Gentleman.* She wants to marry a pilot, she doesn't want an enlisted man, she just wants to see the world…. The guy working at the grocery store ain't cuttin' it, you know?"

Everyone was looking at me.

I turned to look at Joe. "Baby, maybe you should eat something, huh?"

"I'm not hungry, Marcus. Thank you."

"At least," Malic began, picking the conversation back up, "when the new sentinel takes over, he doesn't have to worry about Arcan or Emir or any of those other demons. All of them are dead, and the portal between Breka's club and the hell dimension is closed."

"And we burned the house down for good measure," Ryan said.

"There's nothing left," Leith added. "We razed it."

"You enjoyed saying that," Simon teased. "Very barbarian of you, the pillaging."

"I do have that in me," Leith said playfully. "Right, baby?"

Simon leaned forward and kissed him lightly, then sat back and looked at me. "Joe told us that his family is well."

"Yeah." I smiled. "Joe told me that, too, and I got to talk to all of them on the phone this morning. It was good."

"Hey, Jael, could you strip Marcus's power from him? I'd love him to be just a partner at a law firm and nothing else."

I rolled my eyes.

"Don't patronize me, Marcus," Joe snapped, draining his third mojito, jiggling the ice in the glass, and then loudly slurping the last of it.

"So I guess tomorrow I gotta go see my boss and see if she'll take me back." I tried to ignore Joe. "You gotta tell me exactly what you told her, Mal."

"I need another one of these," Joe said. "Or maybe just a gin and tonic. Whatever."

"Start from the beginning," I told Malic, prodding him as I reached for Joe.

My hearth tried to pull free when I took gentle hold of his wrist, but I was insistent, and so when I eased him sideways, into my lap, he moved of his own volition.

"Nobody cares that you could've died," he whispered under his breath. "So Dylan's upset because you hurt Malic's feelings, so the fuck what? I could give a shit."

When he finished, his voice had risen and again, there was a silence.

"Why're you mad?" I asked, stroking his hair, kissing one of his beautifully arched brows.

"You could have died," he repeated.

"But I didn't, and I'm right here."

I felt his deep breath move through his whole body and calm him. When I looked over at Malic, he smiled at me.

"Your boss, Helene, I really like her."

"Yeah, me too," I agreed, appreciating the fact that he had simply changed the subject without making Joe own up to how he was feeling in front of everyone.

"I know your assistant and the associates that work for you will be thrilled to get you back too. It's Lolita, right?"

I sighed. "Yeah, Lolita. I miss her."

"Well, she misses you too. I saw her at the park not too long ago, and she grilled me about you. They have her working with—" He thought a second. "Douche-man?"

"Dutchman." I chuckled. "She just calls him Douche-man."

"Well, apparently the second you get back, she gets released, and I quote, 'from the idiot box', and will be allowed to return to sitting where she belongs at the desk outside your office."

I smiled wide. "Okay, I better get my ass over there first thing tomorrow morning, then."

"No," Joe barked loudly. "Tomorrow you're gonna spend the day home with me, just the two of us. That's what I want."

"Okay." I hugged him tight, loving the way he turned in my lap, arms around my neck, holding on tight. "Whatever you want."

He sighed loudly as I nuzzled my face into his hair, and I felt everyone around me take a breath and calm.

"What are you doing?" I heard Malic say.

"Joe's in Marcus's lap. I wanna sit in yours," Dylan replied matter-of-factly. "Just 'cause he's drunk off his ass doesn't count."

At which point Joe snorted out an indignant hiccupping laugh, hugged me tight, and turned around to face the others.

"Sorry," he sighed.

"Nothing to be sorry for," Ryan said.

And it was the truth.

IX

I WASN'T sure what to do—call or simply show up—so a day later, as Joe had requested, I went with just showing up at my office because I had always been the guy who dove into the deep end. It was really the only way to be. So, swaddled up in Armani, I rode the elevator up to the twenty-fifth floor but could get no further than the double glass doors. A woman I had never met before leaned out ten minutes later.

"Hi." She smiled wide, looking me over with an appraising eye. "You must be Marcus Roth."

I cleared my throat. "How do you know?"

"My boss said that if a tall, handsome man should get to the front doors and not come in, but just pace outside, I should call her right away. I'm thinking it's you."

It was time to breathe, so I tried. "It's me. Who are you?"

"Suzie, Suzie Jones."

"Nice to meet you, Suzie Jones." I smiled, offering her my hand.

She took it, squeezed it, and beamed up. "I called Mrs. Kessler. She's coming."

I straightened my tie first, then my cuffs. "She said handsome, not gorgeous?"

"She should have said 'hot', Mr. Roth." She smiled big. "Or edible."

I arched an eyebrow for her. "Thank you," I said as I saw Helene trotting toward me. I had never seen her move so fast, and from the stunned looks of people leaning out of their offices, frozen as she passed them in the hall, I was not the only one who was surprised.

"I didn't know she could run."

"I didn't know she would," I sighed, opening my arms.

Helene rushed past the cute little receptionist and flung herself into my arms. It was wildly unprofessional, which meant the display came right from the heart.

"Who knew you liked me this much," I chuckled as I held her.

She squeezed tighter so I understood.

WALKING into my brownstone after six that evening, I opened the door and was hit by the heavenly smell of garlic. I realized instantly that I was starving. Lunch had been at noon, and even though I had not planned to stay all day, I had ended up doing it anyway.

"Hello," I called out.

Joe leaned out of the kitchen. "Hey."

I dropped my keys on the shelf, locked the door behind me, and put my laptop bag on the couch as I passed it on my way to him.

He smiled as I walked up to him. "How was your day, baby?"

I slid my hand around the back of his neck, stroking over his nape before I tipped his head back so I could kiss him. "Long. Yours?"

"Hectic, but I wanna hear everything about your first day back."

I took his hand and led him back into our large, newly renovated kitchen. Joe had put all his energy into the house while I was missing, and the improvements, ordered by him, supervised by Julian, were extensive and stunning. All the new stainless steel appliances, especially the refrigerator big enough that Joe could hide in it, were amazing. "What'd you make?"

"Roast chicken, garlic mashed potatoes, steamed broccoli with fennel, and salad. I hope that's okay."

"Jesus, Joe, of course it's okay. I don't deserve you."

"Sure you do," he assured me, lifting his chin for another kiss that I willingly bestowed.

After I changed, we had dinner and sat at the table and told each other about our days, the friends, the crazy people, and the little things that didn't matter to anyone else. While I was doing the dishes and he was drying, he told me that he'd gotten an e-mail from Shane earlier that day.

"Oh? What did it say?" I was interested.

"Can I say first that you need to fix the voice-activated software on my laptop."

"Why's that?"

"Ryan thought it would be funny to screw with it, so now every time I read e-mail it gets read to me by some Eastern European call girl."

My iced tea went down the wrong hole.

"It's not funny, Marcus."

"No, not at all."

He growled.

I laughed softly. "Tell me what Shane said."

"Oh, well, he told me that he was sorry for everything from being so weak that a witch could possess him—that wouldn't have happened to one of you guys?"

"No," I told him. "And it wasn't possession. She made a doppelganger and inhabited it, but still, if you know yourself, if you're confident, a clone cannot be made. It's too hard."

"Oh."

"Go on."

"Well, he just said that he was really sorry and that he wished that things could have been different with us."

"What else?"

Joe arched one beautiful, thick eyebrow for me. "That if I ever left you, to please let him be the first call I made."

I leaned sideways and sucked his ear lobe into my mouth, inhaling at the same time. "You're never leaving me." My voice rumbled deep in my chest.

"No," he agreed, holding onto the counter as he shivered.

Six years—it had officially changed while I was gone—and the man still got weak in the knees when I kissed him. I was so lucky.

When I was done with the kitchen, I flipped off the light and just stood there a minute watching him. He was folding laundry that he'd done earlier and was listening to some baseball game that was on TV.

"Marcus," he called over to me distractedly. "Remember tomorrow night is that charity benefit Ryan's hosting, so you have to pick up both of our tuxedos from the cleaner's before three and be home no later than five."

"Yes, dear."

He grunted, immersed in what he was listening to.

I went into the bedroom, and after a while, he poked his head in.

"Whatcha doin'?"

"Crossword."

"I can turn off the TV. We can play cards or something."

"Nah."

He slid into the room. "You want something for dessert?"

"Like?"

"I dunno. We could take a walk for ice cream or pie or—"

"No, I'm good here."

"You feel okay?"

"Yeah, just sore."

"We could go get a drink."

"You drank enough the other day," I reminded him.

He flipped me off, and I started laughing.

"We could call some friends, go out if you want."

"You wanna do that?"

"Not particularly, but I will."

I yawned. "That doesn't sound real good."

"So, what, then?"

"Baby," I smiled. "You're not here to entertain me. You know that."

"I know. I just don't wanna take you for granted."

"You're not. I'm home. I'm safe, so are you. We're fine." He looked good in his jeans and a rugby shirt. "We'll find our old rhythm. Don't worry."

"I'm not worried."

"But listen, I don't expect you to cook every night all of a sudden."

"No, I know, but I like cooking for you, and you appreciate it, and talking while we do the dishes is probably one of my favorite things in the whole wide world."

"You're very easy to please."

"No, I'm not. You're the only one that I want to do this stuff with."

"Come here."

"What?"

"I was gonna attack you later when you came to bed, but could you just pretend it's later and let me have you now?" I grinned slowly, dropping the newspaper and the mechanical pencil I was using to do the crossword on the floor.

"Uh, yeah." He laughed, climbing onto the bed.

I reached out for the collar of his shirt. "I missed you today."

"Bullshit. You were too busy to miss me."

"I wasn't, I swear. I missed you."

"That's kind of romantic, huh?"

"Don't get used to it. Just kiss me."

He chuckled against my lips before I grabbed him, rolled him over onto his back under me, and kissed him breathless. When I was sure I had him at my mercy, I went to work on his clothes.

The bite was unexpected, hot but surprising, and I lifted up to look down at him.

"Why am I stopping?" I grumbled irritably because I just wanted to take his clothes off and ravish him, and why was he being difficult?

"I just"—he took a shuddering breath—"love you, is all."

"Yeah, I love you too," I said quickly, bending to reclaim his mouth. I got his chin.

"Marcus!" he squealed.

I growled.

"I'm serious." He started laughing. "Stop being an ass."

I whined loudly, taking his face in my hands. "I love you too, baby, more than anything. You're my whole life. Now can I please just do you?"

His face was alight with happiness, and his eyes, the beautiful pale blue I was a slave to, were dancing. "Yes, Marcus, I'm all yours."

It was always nice to be reminded.

Cherish
Your Name

1

1 THOUGHT people only went nuts over Christmas in the movies. It had never occurred to me that in real life, people put giant fake snowmen on their lawns, put life-size Santas and the reindeer—complete with Rudolph—on the roof of their house, and draped lights over every square inch of available space that a staple gun could be maneuvered into. Even the trees and bushes were threaded with lights. It was insane, and I had no idea. And that was just the outside.

Inside, the place looked like Santa's workshop. I had never seen so much kitsch in my life. All the red and white, it was like shopping at Target. The candles made the whole house smell like pumpkin pie, and the decibel level with the visiting family—uncles, aunts, cousins, kids, and Dylan's parents and their friends—everyone sitting around talking, visiting, and sharing details about their lives… I had never wanted to go home so badly. It was like being in a blender with the switch stuck on mince: I was just chewed up and spit out.

I was supposed to be cheerful and friendly and invested, but there was just no way. I hadn't been raised in loud; I had been raised in quiet. My mother stayed home and gave piano lessons to help pay the bills. My father was a college professor who taught biology. They had both been older when I was born, my mother in her midforties, my father fifty. There had only been the three of us after my grandmother passed away, and our celebrations, all of them, were small. After they died in a terrible car accident when I was ten, I was all alone. It had taken me a long time to even interact with my first foster family, and then the second and the ninth…. It had been just me for so long. And then one day when I was sixteen, I had turned a corner down at Fisherman's Wharf and been compelled to walk forward, lift my hand, and touch a man's back gently so he would look at me.

Jael Ezran, my sentinel, had turned and seen me, and the weight of his stare felt scary and safe at the same time. It seemed like I was supposed to be there, and when he reached for me, I moved forward so he could slide his hand around the back of my neck and draw me closer. That night I had met the other warders in his clutch of four and become the fifth, and from that day on, I had never felt alone again… until now. I was supposed to be bonding, but that was not happening at all.

It was important to my boyfriend that I interact with his family, so I tried. I had missed going the year before because my best friend had been missing and I could not be expected to run through the motions of being happy when I was sick at heart. But since the rite of passage that is spending the holidays with your partner's family could not be ditched two years in a row, I was there, smiling, nodding, and quietly slipping into a coma. For days on end, I wondered how much eggnog I could possibly be expected to drink. It wasn't even spiked.

"Don't be a dick," Marcus told me over the phone. My best friend and fellow warder was in Lexington, Kentucky, with his boyfriend and his parents.

He had not gone the year before when he had been fighting for his life, as in trying not to die in a hell dimension. I told him that would have been preferable to where I currently was.

"You don't think you're laying this shit on a bit thick?"

I grunted.

"People have history and traditions. You should respect them."

"There is a big stuffed elf in every room of this house."

"That's festive."

"They string garlands out of popcorn."

"You need to try and not be a self-righteous ass right now."

"I could die from this."

He cleared his throat. "Family is what's important."

"There is snowman-shaped soap in the bathroom, Santa towels, rugs, decals on the mirror, and a little plaque that says to flush the bad and not the good."

Silence.

I snickered.

"Really?"

"Uh-huh." I drew out the word.

"What's good that would be in the toilet that wouldn't flush?"

"This is what I'm saying."

"Whatever," he snapped. "Just stop being a dick."

"Why are you getting on me?"

"Because you're not even giving it a chance."

And so I tried then, I really did.

The problem was that I didn't do small things. If you needed something heavy picked up and moved, I was your man. If there were errands to be run, carpets to lay, walls to be painted, I was so there. But sitting around talking, snacking, watching movies, and just spending quality family time was beyond me. I didn't do stationary well; I had to move before I started climbing the walls.

My inability to sit still did not go over well with Dylan's parents, who already thought that a thirty-one-year-old man was far too old for their twenty-year-old son. And they were probably right, but there was nothing I could do about it. I loved the man already, and there was no way I was giving him up. Even meeting his annoying friends couldn't get me to change my mind.

He was young, so of course he had a whole gang of guys who had graduated with him and gone off to college the same time as he had and came home for Christmas every year, making the pilgrimage from different schools all across the country. They descended on the Shaw house that Lily, Dylan's mother, had made into a mini North Pole, complete with a motion-activated four-foot Santa who yelled "Ho-ho-ho, Merry Christmas" at you constantly. She had greeted them warmly, kissing and hugging them all as she had not me. It wouldn't have mattered what Dylan's mother did, if Dylan had given me a second thought.

It wasn't Dylan's fault he forgot about me; this was his family. These were his friends from high school he was catching up with. I had not been there the year before to cramp his style, and suddenly I was thrown into the mix. But I was the constant, that part of his life he could take for granted because I was unchanging. And because I was smart enough to understand that, it stung just a little, but not a lot. Not enough to matter. It was an oversight—*I* was an oversight—and he would never do anything to hurt me intentionally.

I had faith.

Mrs. Shaw was laughing at how much growing boys could eat. Dylan's buddies—Lance, Jason, and Cole—had stories to tell, news to fill each other in on, and conquests to compare. I hovered in the background, forgotten even to the point of not being introduced.

I went out on the back porch, where it was cold.

It would have been selfish to interfere, to make him acknowledge me, so I didn't. I was surprised when he left without a word to go have drinks at house parties. His sister Tina, short for Christina, said he was visiting old haunts, hitting a coffeehouse where he was sure to know everyone.

"You can't expect him to just hang around here with you and my folks and their friends on a Friday night," she said, smirking.

The accusation that I was old was there, thick, in her voice. I heard her loud and clear. I was even older than she was, thirty-one to her twenty-four, and since she was Dylan's older sister, of course, to her, I was a fossil. She thought of me being more like her parents and less like her, Dylan, and all their various friends.

If I had looked like an Abercrombie & Fitch model, I could have gone to the party and had everyone falling at my feet and showed my boyfriend that if he ignored me, I could get a replacement damn quick. The difference was that I was a warder and Dylan was my hearth, so he was not replaceable—he was the man I was building my life around. I had to wait patiently for him to return when he was ready. If I had been home, it wouldn't have mattered. If I had been home, I would have had other things to occupy my time. A warder could always patrol.

Every city had a sentinel who protected the populace from demons, ghouls, and all other creatures from the pit, and every sentinel had five warders he commanded. I lived in San Francisco and was one of the five who served Jael Ezran. I was hoping that he would call me home because of some emergency, but when none materialized, I was going to call to see if they needed me at work before I remembered that everyone was already off. Running a gentleman's club—a strip club— was normally hectic, but during the holidays, we were never all that busy. It seemed sort of strange to have hot women stripping out of elf costumes, so I had closed the place down as I did every year. With absolutely no one needing me at all, I decided to do what I always did when faced with too much time on my hands: I volunteered for chores.

"Are you sure, Malic?" Mrs. Shaw asked when I told her I would clean the rain gutters on Monday.

"Yes, ma'am."

Her smile almost reached her eyes.

"You don't have to," Mr. Shaw said when I offered to clean out the garage for him on Tuesday.

"I'd like to."

He had nodded, worried about my sanity, I was sure.

"But, Malic, it's a huge job." Dylan's snarky sister squinted at me as I started raking up debris in the backyard on Wednesday.

"It's fine," I assured her. She just gave me a flippant shrug and walked away.

At night, Dylan always came and gave me a kiss before he invited me out with him.

"No, you go." I smiled. "Have a good time."

"Just come on," he said as his friends lingered in the background.

I shook my head, and he left with them, off to another party, coffeehouse, the mall, movies, someone's house, just hanging out, getting reacquainted. He came home early in the morning, passing out beside me in bed reeking of cigarette smoke, alcohol, and stale air. Other scents clung to him as well, like men's cologne and sweat. And while I knew he wasn't kissing anyone but me, never mind screwing around, it was still hard to know he was dancing with others, letting them put their hands all over him.

"You have no one to blame but yourself," Marcus told me over the phone. "When you get invited out with your man, you go, idiot."

But I didn't want to. I was a little worried about what it said that Dylan had not slowed down since we had arrived five days ago for our two-week visit with his family in Marietta, Georgia. Maybe he wanted to spend more time away from me at home, too, but I was keeping him from his joy. The nagging concern of our age difference got bigger and bigger with each passing day.

"It was a mistake to give in to my selfish desire for him," I told the only person whom I didn't feel like a tool confessing my insecurities to.

"You're so stupid," my friend and office manager Claudia Duran told me. "I wish I was there to knock some sense into you."

"He's happier with his friends," I insisted.

"He invites you and you don't go," she volleyed back.

"If I went, I'd cramp his style."

"Or he'd be all over you."

But again, I wasn't hot, wasn't pretty like he was; I was big and scary and mean. I was not someone the other boys would love. I was a man, and I did not dance and hang out and wear jeans that were too big and shirts that were too small.

On Friday—it had taken two days to do the yard—I was cutting back the hedge that was overgrown beside the fence along the driveway when I looked up to find a man holding a large bottle of water out for me.

I smiled. "Thank you."

He lifted his right arm, which was in a cast supported by a sling, and asked me if I could do him a huge favor.

"Sure."

"I've seen you out here working like a dog, man," he said with a chuckle, and the sound soothed me. "And since you seem to be kind of into it and I'm suddenly laid up, I was wondering if I paid you, if you could help me do some stuff around my house."

He was a handsome man, older than me—maybe midthirties, early forties—with a nice face: straight nose, full lips, laugh lines in the corners of warm blue eyes, and a daring grin I liked most of all. He was just slightly shorter than my own six four, maybe six two, and leaner than I was but heavily muscled, with broad shoulders and long legs.

"I promise I'm harmless." He smiled steadily. "I'm just hurt."

"What'd you do?"

"I work construction, and you know how it goes. There's always that one fuckin' idiot that's gonna get hurt if you don't step in and save him."

I chuckled. "I know that guy."

He nodded. "I figured you did."

"I'd shake your hand"—I tipped my head at the cast—"but doesn't look like you can."

He nodded.

"Malic," I said.

"Brad."

"Pleasure."

He stared at me a long minute. "So I've got a TV to set up, a garbage disposal to replace, and a tree to pick out and bring home before my family descends on me in three days."

It sounded great. I would be very busy. "I'm your man. Count me in."

His smile was wide. "What's it gonna cost me?"

"Pizza? Beer?"

"Are you shittin' me?"

"Nope."

"Oh hell yeah, you're on." His eyes gushed warmth.

"Lemme finish this and I'll be right there."

"Thank you," he said sincerely.

"Oh no, thank you."

He snorted out a laugh. "Climbing the walls in there?"

"How'd ya know?"

"I can see the signs of a wolf caught in a trap."

"I look like a wolf, do I?"

"Ready to bite off his own foot, yeah."

I laughed then, and the look I got, like he appreciated the sound, was really nice. No one had been looking at me like I was anything but a nuisance for almost a week, so it was a welcome change.

I replaced the shears in the tool shed and almost ran into Dylan's father when I was coming out. "Sorry," I apologized automatically, stepping around him.

"You know," he began, which stopped me. "You don't have to work around the house to impress me, Malic. The things you're doing won't influence me. The way you treat Dylan is all that matters."

I nodded.

"He seems happy to be around friends his own age, and I wonder if he has any out there in San Francisco."

"Yes, sir, he has many."

He grunted. "I don't mean to be judgmental, Malic, and you seem like a nice man, but you and Dylan are at different places in your life."

"Agreed."

He looked surprised.

"C'mon." I shrugged, tired of ignoring the elephant in the room. "The fact of the matter is that this will probably be the last you see of me, sir, so I wouldn't get all racked up about it."

"Malic—"

"Excuse me," I said, brushing by him on my way toward the back fence. I vaulted over it easily and found myself liking the layout of Brad's yard. The golden lab that came to greet me, tail wagging even as the barking began, was welcome.

I went down to one knee, and the dog was all over me.

"Oh, she likes you." Brad laughed. "But she's always had good taste."

"What's her name?" I asked as the dog licked my eye and made circles beside me, wiggling close, wanting as much attention as she could get.

"Rita."

"She's gorgeous."

"She knows."

I stood up, and when I did, I saw the rainbow license plate frame on his Lexus SUV. My eyes flicked to his, and I saw him take a breath.

"You don't need one of those in San Francisco," I teased. "It's redundant."

His smile, which had been great before, became dazzling when his eyes joined in. "Jesus, Malic, where ya been all my life?"

I tipped my head toward his house. "Show me the sink."

Brad Darby was a construction manager, and his crew was good except for the new guy, who was trying to kill him.

"Little fucker just doesn't listen," he told me as he sat on the floor beside me, talking to me while I installed the new garbage disposal.

I was chuckling as he told story after story. When I was done, he made lunch and told me that now I had to go with him to get the TV.

"I thought you had it here," I said, laughing as we walked out to his car.

He squinted. "How was I getting it in the house?"

I liked him a lot. He was so easy to talk to; it was like we had been friends for years.

"You want me to drive?" I asked, smiling. "Since you've got a broken wing and all?"

"I manage," he assured me with a shrug. "It's just a little bit of a pain."

I held out my hand. "Lemme drive. Please."

He handed over the keys. "It's a mistake. You're gonna get me used to you."

But that was okay. I liked him.

When we were out, we ran into one of his buddies at Best Buy, and when Randy invited both of us to his private club later to play some poker, I told him it was up to Brad.

"He might be sick of taking pity on the homeless."

"If you're homeless, you can come stay with me." Randy gave me a grin.

"I've got first dibs," Brad said, turning me around and shoving me forward. "We'll be there around what? Seven?"

"Seven's great."

As we walked toward the electronics area of the store, I smiled at my new friend.

"What?"

But he knew how he'd acted.

"I just don't want you to get molested, is all."

"Thanks," I said.

"Don't mention it."

"Seems like you've got friends who would've helped you," I said softly. "You didn't actually need me."

"Most of my friends are busy during the week and have their own crap to get done on the weekends. Believe me," he said, chuckling, "I need you."

At least somebody did.

Brad picked out a TV he wanted and made arrangements for delivery. In the parking lot, he asked what I wanted for dinner.

"Shit, I get dinner too?" I teased.

"You can have whatever you want."

But I didn't take that to heart. I was not the guy everyone wanted. I was the fallback choice.

I had to run back to the Shaw house to shower and change for dinner. When I got there, Mrs. Shaw informed me that they—all of them, including her—were going out to dinner. She said *we*, which named everyone except me, so I understood, since I wasn't stupid, where exactly it was that I stood. They had all worked hard to let me know that I was not welcome, that I was an outsider. I received the message loud and clear. But she didn't have to worry about it; I completely understood that Dylan's family did not approve of me. And as I had explained to her husband that morning, I was never coming back. Dylan could visit his family alone; this was the first and only Christmas I would be tagging along. I had people who actually liked me who would be happy to share some eggnog with me for the holidays.

"I'm going out, ma'am. It's fine."

"Oh," she said, seeming startled.

I smiled at her and hurried up to my room. Half an hour later, I came downstairs in black jeans, boots, a heavy gray sweater, and my leather jacket on over that. I was fiddling with my watch strap when I stepped into the living room.

"Wow."

Looking up, I saw Dylan's bitchy sister staring at me with wide eyes.

"Wow what?"

"You, um…." She cleared her throat. "Look nice, Malic."

"Thank you," I said, walking around the couch she was sitting on toward the sliding glass door. It opened out onto the back deck overlooking the newly cleaned yard.

I slid the door open to look at Dylan, his friends, and his parents.

"Sorry to interrupt," I apologized, looking at my hearth. "I'm leaving, so I'll see ya later. Have a good dinner and enjoy whatever else," I said, ducking my head back into the house.

"Malic."

I leaned back out, looking at Dylan's father.

"Thank you for cleaning up the backyard. It looks like it never does this time of year."

"You're welcome." I moved to leave.

"Malic," Dylan's mother said.

"Yes, ma'am?" My eyes flicked to her.

"You should—" She cleared her throat. "—actually join us for dinner. It would be nice."

Since when? "Oh, no thank you, but I appreciate the offer."

She nodded fast, looking like she was going to say something else, but she didn't.

I went to close the door again.

"Malic."

I was getting annoyed. "Yes?" I asked Dylan, my voice holding an unintentional edge as he got up and walked over to me.

He looked me up and down before his big, beautiful chocolate-brown eyes locked on my face. "Where are you going?"

"I made a friend, and we're gonna hang out."

"Oh, okay." He nodded. "Who?"

"Who what?"

"Who's your new friend?"

"Oh, your neighbor Brad."

He stared.

I waited.

There was coughing. "Brad Darby?" Dylan asked.

I was guessing there was only one neighbor named Brad, but that was okay. "Yeah."

He shook his head, but nothing came out.

"I'll probably be late. You have a good time, okay?" I smiled at him before I slid the glass door closed and headed back across the living room.

Dylan's call stopped me at the front door.

I turned and waited for him.

He ran. "Um." He swallowed hard, taking hold of my leather jacket. "What's going on?"

"How do you mean?"

"Brad Darby?"

"Yeah?" I squinted at him.

"He's, um." He squeezed my jacket tight. "Kinda hot, huh?"

"Yeah, but I'm sure all the boys you've been hangin' out with have been plenty hot too," I said playfully.

His breath was shaky. "Yeah, but that's the difference, right? They're all boys. I mean, I'm just having fun, being here visiting, but I know I get to go home and get back to my real life, the life I love with you, as soon as it's time."

"I know that." I put my hand around the back of his neck, pulling him close to me, pressing my forehead gently to his, closing my eyes, breathing him in. "I won't lie and say that this hasn't been educational, and we should probably talk about that."

"Talk about what?" He shivered.

"Your father had some really valid points earlier today about what you need, and I just wanna make sure that you're not missing out on anything because you're not dating someone your own age."

"No, Malic," he told me, his voice cracking. "I'm not missing out on anything, and I'm not dating you. I live with you."

"No, I know," I soothed, leaning back, staring down into the melting brown eyes I adored. They were huge, fringed with long, thick curling lashes. "I just don't want you to have any regrets about—"

"Oh God, no," he whined, now fisting his hand in my sweater. "Malic, are you kidding? Not again."

"Just don't worry about it right now," I said, raking my fingers through my thick blond hair. "We can talk once we get home. I want you to enjoy your holidays with your family, okay?"

"Malic—"

"Your father seemed very relieved earlier when I told him that he wouldn't ever have to see me again after this."

Dylan looked like he was going to throw up. "What are you"—his face went white—"talking about?"

"I'm gonna skip this scene next year, baby. You can come alone."

"Mal—"

"Have a good time tonight. I'll see ya tomorrow," I said, easing out of his grip and going out the front door.

Brad was already on the street in his SUV. "What the hell? I'm fuckin' starving. I have reservations at this great steak place that's also a microbrewery. You're gonna love it."

I whined in the back of my throat.

"Oh yeah, see?" He laughed. "You're dying for some good food and better beer. Get in the car, son."

I went around to the driver's side and opened his door so I could trade places with him.

"I can drive, you know," he assured me even as he got out.

"It'll be easier this way. Just lemme help you."

"Whatever you want," he sighed, getting out, patting my shoulder as he walked around to the passenger side. I got in and waited for him. Once he was buckled up, I pulled away from the curb.

As I was driving away, I thought I saw Tina waving from the front porch, but since she hated me, it probably wasn't her. Not that it mattered. Only having a nice night did. I was really looking forward to it.

II

THE evening was perfect. Dinner was amazing, the restaurant was outstanding, and the two glasses of beer I had were good. I was certain the brandy I was offered afterward, at the club Randy belonged to, would have been even better, but I was driving, so the two beers I'd had hours before was my limit. We played poker, some Texas Hold 'em, and I told Randy how nice the atmosphere in the club was, both relaxed and elegant. He appreciated it, told me he was trying to get Brad to join as well.

"You should," I told Brad, accepting the mineral water from the server and thanking him.

"If you stick around, I can bring you," he said with a smile.

It was very flattering.

Brad's four friends reminded me of the guys I played cards with at home. I had missed the camaraderie of other men, and it was nice. We smoked cigars, which I never did; they drank like fish, which I sometimes did; and we all laughed and swapped stories. They wanted me to do some shots, but I just shook my head and reminded them again that I was driving. I watched them as I drank another Perrier. Once they found out I owned a strip club, I was the belle of the ball. Three of the guys were straight, and they wanted all the details about my club, Romeo's Basement.

The other guy, Tyler, wanted to know more about me. "How long are you gonna be here? Because I'm thinking Brad wants to know."

In the SUV hours later, close to one in the morning, I turned my head and smiled over at Brad. "I'm sorry your friend embarrassed you."

"He didn't embarrass me," he sighed as I parked the car in his driveway. "I had the best day in I don't know how long. It was completely unplanned. It just happened, and I don't want it to end. Please come in, Malic," he said, his hand tracing up my jacket sleeve. "Come in and come upstairs and get in bed with me."

I stared into his eyes because I had known all along where this was going, and just like the talk I would have to have with Dylan when I got home, I didn't want to face it. I enjoyed having friends and had hoped that it was all Brad wanted, even though from his glances, the smiles, the look in his eyes, I had known better. I was not a perfect specimen of manhood, but I was fuckable.

"I'm thinking top, right?"

I just stared.

"I'm good with whatever, so, please." His voice cracked as he leaned forward.

"Here's the thing," I told him, turning off the car and passing him the keys. "There's already a man in my life."

"Well, he can't be all that bright if he's letting you go out with me." Brad smiled evilly.

He hadn't put it together at all: why I was at the Shaws' to begin with, what I was doing there, and who I was with.

"Call whoever it is and tell him you're getting in bed with me. That will clear everything up really nice."

"Would it?" I said with a small smile.

"Fine, I get it. You're loyal and honorable and shit."

I snorted out a laugh. "Nice."

"So how 'bout a kiss to send me off to bed. Can I have that?" he asked, his eyes soaking me in.

I cleared my throat. "I'm in the market for friends, Brad, nothing else. Can I have that?"

"I already told you—you can have whatever the fuck you want."

It was nice that he was so great about everything and didn't call me a cocktease. I thanked him and told him I would be over in the morning.

"I'll make you breakfast." He smiled warmly. "And you better tell your guy to look out, Malic. I don't give up."

But it wasn't about what he would do or even what Dylan would do. Loyalty resided in the individual, and even though Brad Darby was tempting, I wasn't in love with him. And my body followed my heart, not the other way around.

I gave him my number, and we decided that whoever rose from his coffin first would call the other. I didn't linger; I just got out of the car.

The front door at the Shaw house wasn't open, but the sliding glass door in back was. Inside, I was surprised to find Dylan's mother awake in what looked like a warm fuzzy robe and bunny slippers.

I forced a smile as I slid the door shut. "You look cozy."

"Oh Malic, I'm so sorry."

I turned to look at her. "Sorry for what?"

"Sweetheart, I had no idea that this was anything more than a fling that Dylan was having. I mean, he's been talking about you for a year, of course, but he's so young that I thought it was just a phase even though you all are roommates and—"

"He lives with me; we're not roommates," I cut her off.

Her eyes locked on mine.

"You understand that, right? He moved in with me, I'm his boyfriend, he sleeps in my bed."

She looked *so* uncomfortable even as she nodded.

"Just so we're on the same page."

"We are."

"Good."

"I just… I had no idea he was in love. He's always been one to bring home strays, and so I thought—"

"I'm not a stray." I bristled, because her son was *it*. He was my world, my sanctuary, the center of everything. "I have a family."

"I know—he's it, he told me." She reached for me, and I allowed her to take hold of my hand. "I just had no clue that you're the man Dylan plans to spend the rest of his life with."

"Because he's young, you think he doesn't know his own mind."

"Yes."

"I made that mistake for awhile myself."

She took a breath, patting my hand with hers. "When you left tonight, Dylan was very upset and very angry with all of us, but mostly with himself. He didn't go out tonight. He's been in his room, and I think he's still up because I heard him in the shower a little bit ago, but… if you could go up and see him, I would be very thankful."

"I have to take a shower, too, I reek of cigar smoke, but I'll see him in a minute."

"I'd like to talk to you in the morning, if that would be all right?"

"Sure."

She nodded and let go of me.

Upstairs, I was surprised when I opened the door to Dylan's old room, the room I was sharing with him, and found the man himself sitting up in bed.

"Hey." I smiled, crossing toward the opposite side of the room to dump my leather jacket on the chair and my cell phone on the nightstand.

"What's going on?"

I turned to look at him because the voice was not his. It was low and nasally like he'd been crying. Studying him, I saw that his eyes were raw—red-rimmed and brimming with tears—his hair was tousled, and he was shaking ever so slightly.

"I'd come hug you, but I smell like a—"

"It's okay." His breath hitched as he lifted his arms to me.

I walked around the bed, sat down, and reached for him.

He moved fast, scrambling out from under the covers, sweats hanging low on his lean hips, and climbed into my lap. I loved the fact that because the man was only five nine to my six four, he always fit so perfectly in my arms.

I framed his face with my hands. "What's with the tears?"

He didn't answer; instead, he leaned in and kissed me, hard and deep and urgent, his tongue sliding between my lips to mate with mine. His arms wrapped around my neck as he whimpered in the back of his throat, grinding his growing erection against my abdomen. Normally he kissed me passionately and hungrily but never roughly, never demanding submission. It was a huge turn-on. When I grabbed his ass, pulling him forward, he moaned sweetly.

The kiss went on. I didn't want it to end and neither did he, both of us heaving for breath when he finally pulled back, his nose against mine.

"Not that I'm complaining," I told him, my smile, I was sure, just decadent. "But, baby, what the fuck?"

He took a shuddering breath. "Malic, I love you."

"Yeah, I know." I laughed gently.

"I don't want a guy my own age. I just want you. It'll always be you. I swear to God I'm not missing out on anything. You know I have my own friends at home that I see at school and do shit with all the time. And when I wanna go out dancing or whatever, I go, but who's to say what's normal and what isn't? Why do I have to live my life by rules that don't apply to me? I'm the hearth of a warder—I'm so much more than your boyfriend—I don't want that to change."

I put my hands on him, into the loose curls that framed his face, pushing them back so I could see the big, beautiful eyes now locked on mine. He was so fragile and delicate in comparison to me, it was like holding a bird, and I loved it more than I could articulate.

"Please, Malic," he said, and I heard in his voice that he was on the verge of fresh tears. "Don't doubt me just because I was a dumb-ass and took you for granted. I was just happy to see the guys, is all. It means nothing, I swear."

I nodded.

"Forgive me for being clueless. Please."

"There's nothing to forgive. You didn't do—"

"Then tell me everything's fine and don't make me prove anything to you."

"Dylan, honey."

"No," he snapped. "I don't want to *talk* when we get home, fuck that. We're good, we're fine; now say we are. Nothing's changed."

"Love—"

"No," he growled a second time. "No argument, no big talk, nothing. All I wanna hear from you is that everything's perfect."

"Okay." I gave in because I wanted to and because I believed him. "Everything's perfect."

Hadn't he proved that he loved me when he tore down all my walls when we first got together? He had seen me attacked by demons, and still he loved me. We had fights about me being an unforgiving bastard because he wanted me to make up with an old friend and I said no. He was not afraid of me, never had been, and that was rare, because of my size and strength. Dylan didn't see a brute, he saw a man. I was so thankful.

"Malic," he whimpered, shifting on my lap until he slid his crease over my now painfully hard cock.

"Baby," I said softly. "Lemme take a shower. I smell gross."

"You smell great," he promised before he kissed me again.

I was a goner.

His hands were all over me, pulling, yanking as he kissed me voraciously, sucking, biting, licking, making his claim, showing me that even though I was bigger and stronger, I belonged to him. It was a bruising kiss, and the pressure he was exerting was not gentle. He wanted me badly.

"I do not want you near fuckin' Brad Darby," he warned before he bit down on the spot where my shoulder met my neck. "He's not getting you."

"Dylan…."

"No." He was adamant, and I saw a fire in the brown depths of his eyes I had never seen before.

I smiled slowly, amazed. "You're jealous."

He growled as he shoved me down on the bed, arching over me, hands on either side of my head as he stared into my eyes. "I'm telling you what you can and cannot do. So just fuckin' deal with it."

He wasn't just jealous; he was pissed off, and the knowledge tore a blazing trail through me. I could not imagine anything hotter. He was possessive of me. He wanted me. I could barely breathe.

I moved fast, grabbing him, flipping him over on his stomach, and driving him facedown into the bed. Hands on his hips, I lifted him to his knees, ass in the air as I bent and took a quick bite of one smooth, firm ass cheek.

"Malic!" he yelled.

I couldn't resist, and spreading his cheeks, plunged my mouth down over his pink puckered hole. As he was fresh from the shower, his skin was still dewy and warm from being under the covers. He smelled clean and musky and tasted even better. He went limp in my arms as I licked and stroked, pushing in, nibbling, swirling my tongue in and out, deeper each time, making a meal of him.

"Oh God, harder," he whimpered, panting, writhing under my hands. "Please, Malic—put your fingers in me."

I eased him down on the bed, rolling him to his back, and curled over him, attacking his mouth, ravaging it as I thrust two fingers inside his saliva-slicked ass.

He arched up off the bed, and I reached with my free left hand for the nightstand. I had to end the kiss, and he was heaving for breath as I did, whining at the same time, wanting me back even as he lifted to make sure my flesh stayed impaled in him.

I drizzled the lube over his grasping entrance, then withdrew enough to coat my fingers before adding a third, stretching, pressing, scissoring, sliding over the spot I knew, making him jolt from the pressure, drawing a deep and sexy growl of need from the back of his throat.

"I'm gonna come all over you if you don't put your cock in my ass," he moaned, shoving his hips upward, begging.

I grabbed his legs, lifting them, dragging him forward, and then tucked a pillow under his bottom to adjust the angle. When he wrapped a hand around my swollen erection, squeezing, fisting, tugging, I nearly came.

"This is so fuckin' huge," he said, and his voice was full of awe and a sultry tone that only ever infused it when we were in bed. "It amazes me that I can take this inside me."

Watching it slide into his hot, tight little ass was a continual source of delight for me.

"Oh God, Malic," he whined, smearing the precome over the tip, lifting his hand away to taste it, lick it off his fingertips. "Either fuck me or let me suck you, but you're killin' me." His eyes were heavy-lidded, cloudy with passion, and his parted lips were red and swollen from my savage attention.

It was too much.

I grabbed hold of his beautiful, round, firm ass, parted the twin globes, and thrust inside the man who belonged to me.

The idea that I could ever, would ever, voluntarily walk away from him was ridiculous. He was too precious, too dear for me to even consider leaving.

And he was screaming my name.

I clamped a hand down over his mouth—because I really didn't want his parents banging on the door—and pounded into him, over and over, again and again, my hips pistoning fast and hard as Dylan's back bowed off the bed.

Moving my hand, I got a fierce whisper of promised silence before his drugged eyes met mine, the melting brown gorgeous to see as he begged me for deeper, harder, faster.

"Baby," I groaned, because he was so tight, so hot. I wanted to devour him, mark him, show him who he belonged to.

"Yours, Malic," he gasped, knowing, like he always did, like only he ever did, what to say and when to say it. "Forgive me… was stupid… yours… only ever yours."

"Fuck!"

His grin was like a gift, as was the love that went with it. "So eloquent."

The muscles in his ass had tightened like a fist, clasping, clenching, the squeeze so powerful that my orgasm came without warning, exploding through me as I filled his rippling channel. I coated his insides, thrusting into him as deep as possible, to the hilt, my balls slapping against his ass.

He yelled my name again as I fisted his dripping cock and tilted my hips, making sure I pegged his gland, slid over it, and jerked him off at the same time. Seconds later my abdomen was splattered with thick cum.

It took long shuddering minutes for us to descend from the adrenaline high. I stroked his skin, whispering how much I loved him even as tears filled the beloved eyes and rolled down his cheeks.

"Baby," I soothed him, slowly pulling out as gently as I could, flopping down onto the bed and lifting him into my lap.

He shoved his wet, sticky cock against the gooey mess on my stomach, pressed his sweat-covered body to mine, and kissed the side of my neck, licking, nibbling, frantic to get closer.

I held tight and still he wriggled closer, the smells of sex washing over me, the moist heat of the room making me light-headed even as his lips touched mine.

He kissed me so hard our teeth clicked together, and he bit down hard, drawing blood that he sucked, along with my bottom lip, inside his mouth.

I threaded my fingers through his hair, yanked his head back, and grabbed a handful of his gorgeous ass at the same time. I let a finger slide over the still fluttering semen-and-lube-slick hole and felt him shudder in my arms.

"You want it again?" I asked, studying him, his beautiful face.

"I just want you to fuckin' want me so bad you go crazy with it."

He needed to fall asleep, was what he needed, but he was still scared, and it was my place to show him how stupid that was. He never had to worry.

I grabbed the covers that had been pushed to the bottom of the bed, not caring that we'd be lying in a mess. The only thing that mattered was wrapping him back up in my arms. I crushed him to me, notching his head under my chin as I lay down, making sure that all of him was plastered against me.

He trembled hard, and I felt the tears on my collarbone.

"I'm not going anywhere, and I'm not letting you leave me, so we're good, all right?"

He took a shaky breath.

"Forgive me. I forgot for a second that you're my whole fuckin' world," I told him.

"Swear?" His voice sounded so hopeful.

"Oh God, baby, yes, I'm so sorry. I should have just told you how I felt."

"Yes, you should have, and then I would have realized that I was being an ass."

"I just missed you," I assured him. "That's all there was to it."

"But you still love me, only me, you only want me."

"Oh yes," I said before I bent and kissed him so hard and so long that when I was done, he was limp and flushed with heat under me. I rose over him like a hungry beast.

"Use me," he panted, his body spent and sated, shivering in anticipation of what I was going to do to him.

I crushed him under me instead, pinning him to the bed, and he cried silently as I held him tight, rolling over on my back so he was draped over me.

"I love you," he whispered, his face buried in the hollow of my neck.

"I know, baby," I sighed. "I swear to God I know."

"Then never doubt it," he rasped, and I knew he was struggling to lift his head, wanting to look in my eyes, but he was wrung out from fear and sadness and sex. He had attacked me, but I ended up devouring him.

"Baby," I soothed, stroking the sweat-dampened curls, feeling his body get heavy, loving the way he clutched at me, the way he inhaled my scent and nuzzled under my jaw.

"Smell amazing." He yawned softly. "Malic."

I was quiet, just running my fingers through his glossy curls, slowly, tenderly, and when his breathing evened out, I knew he was asleep.

Slowly, I eased him off me and spooned around him, pulling the down comforter up over us, snuggling tight. His sigh of happiness could not be missed, and I found that I could not stop smiling even as I reached back and flipped off the light.

248 |

III

I WOKE up late, close to noon, and of course Dylan was gone. I noticed that my phone was missing, and since I was almost completely positive I had left it on the nightstand, it was safe to assume that it had been swiped. Since I was on vacation, without an alarm, my body had just stayed in hibernation. Rolling out of bed, I went to take a much-needed shower.

Half an hour later, clean, shaved, and changed into jeans, a black T-shirt, and motorcycle boots, I made my way down the stairs. I would have gone into the living room, but I stopped before I turned the corner when I heard the raised voices.

"Of course we're going to be nice, Dylan," I heard his father, Jeff, say. "You told us how important the man is to you."

"But you knew that before and you were still mean."

"Yes, but after your display last night before we left for dinner—"

"Dad—"

"He just seems so cold to me," Lily Shaw chimed in. "He's nothing like Ethan."

"No, Mom, he's not, thank God."

"Dyl—"

"I will not talk about Ethan Burke," he said quickly, and his voice was as I had never heard it: hard and icy. "And besides, that was a hundred years ago."

"It was three years ago, before you moved to San Francisco," his father corrected him. "That ain't a hundred years, kiddo."

"Honey, you never told us what hap—"

"Let it go, Mom," he told her. "That's ancient history."

There was a long silence.

"I'm sorry, love. I know Ethan hurt you when he took up with his friend Gordon."

"I don't want to—"

"I'm sorry," she began. "But, sweetheart—"

"Why don't we just not talk about any of it?" Mr. Shaw coughed, obviously uncomfortable from the sound of his voice, having cut off his wife before she could finish her thought.

"Jeff, we should be able to talk about your son's love—"

"I don't want to hear about either of my children's love lives," he told his wife. "I just don't want to know!"

"Dylan," Tina began, "we just want to know if this guy loves you."

"He does." Dylan cleared his throat, and I wondered what had happened that made his voice not his own.

"How do you know?"

"I know."

"Does he tell you?" his mother asked.

"He has."

"But not a lot," she prodded. "Right?"

"Mom."

"He's the strong, silent type," she offered as an out.

"It's not that."

"Then what is it? A man should tell you he loves you," she assured him. "Mike tells Tina. I hear her say it back to him all the time on the phone."

"Yeah, but Mike's a piece of crap."

"Dylan!"

"Oh, c'mon, T, you know he is. Along with the other—"

"Don't start," Tina ordered.

"Fine, then, we'll go with the obvious… your man's a dog."

"And Malic isn't?"

"Not at all."

"Honey." His mother was trying to soothe him. "You should have the same interests with the person you love. You should be at the same place in your lives so that you can grow together and make plans and have goals. You—"

"We do."

"How? He's so much older than you."

He was quiet, and my stomach twisted into a knot. There was nothing he could say to convince them, and I knew it hurt him that he wouldn't be able to make them understand our—

"He picks me up," Dylan said suddenly, breaking the silence.

"I'm sorry?" his father asked.

"When I work graveyard." Dylan cleared his throat. "Sometimes I get off at seven in the morning, or sometimes I get off at six. It depends when someone decides to show up to relieve me. But whatever time it is, Malic picks me up, takes me to breakfast, and then drives me home and puts me to bed before he starts his day."

He forgot the sex part in the middle. Between the "got home" and the "put to bed" there was usually what started with a kiss and ended with us both breathless and panting and covered in sweat and semen. After the full-body hug when I picked him up, it was my favorite part of the morning.

"Oh," his mother said, bringing me back to the conversation I was eavesdropping on.

"Every single time, Mom," he told her. "He *never* isn't there."

"Well, yes, that's very nice."

"It's not nice, it's amazing."

"Honey—"

"Every time, Mom, without fail."

"Okay."

"And yeah, T, you're right," he told his sister. "He doesn't go out dancing with me, but he trusts me to go, sends me off just like he did here, telling me to have a good time."

Silence.

"When was the last time you went out, just you and your girlfriends, without Mike having a goddamn seizure?"

"Dylan Walter Shaw!"

"Mom, c'mon! You should be way more worried about Tina's psychotic boyfriend than the stable, dependable guy I live with who wants to buy a house with me."

There was a pause.

"What?"

"Yeah." He exhaled sharply. "Malic has this great house in Pacific Heights that I love, but he doesn't want me to feel like I moved into his house, so he's gonna move just so we can buy something together. And I keep telling him that I love the house we're in now, that I think of it as our house—I mean, you should see it, Mom, it's like this great summer cottage that would fit perfect in a beach town in Florida—but he's worried, so I gotta move, and I'm trying so hard to get him to hear me, but—"

"Dylan."

"He just won't lis—"

"Dylan!"

"What?" he barked at his mother, who had interrupted him.

"So what you're trying to tell us is that man upstairs *shows* you he loves you instead of telling you."

"Yes." He sighed.

Long, long silence.

"Why are you looking at me?" Dylan's father said after another minute.

"Think about it a second, Dad." Tina sounded like she was on the verge of tears. "It'll come to you."

"Oh." Dylan's mother's voice trembled the same way her daughter's had.

"Crap," his father groaned after another minute or so, and I smiled because the longer I knew the man, the more I liked him. Hell, Dylan's whole family was growing on me. "He's just like me."

"He's *just* like you," Lily agreed. "Jesus."

"So lemme get this straight." Tina was starting to giggle. "You went out and found someone just like your father? Would that even be called Oedipal? Is there even a name for that?"

"Oh God," Dylan moaned. "I'm gonna throw up."

"Here's a tip: don't use the wicker trash can."

"Eww." He made a low noise of disgust.

"Damn it." Jeff was beside himself. "I'm not like that. I tell you guys I love you all the time!"

Tina scoffed.

"I do!"

"That's amazing," Lily sighed. "Your son went out and found someone just like you."

"It sounds worse every time you say it," Dylan complained.

"Oh, shut up," Jeffrey Shaw grumbled at his son as the front doorbell rang.

"I'll get it," Tina chuckled.

I came around the corner at the same time Mrs. Shaw's sister and her family arrived for dinner. Apparently they came every year the night before Christmas Eve to eat, visit, drop off their gifts for Dylan and his family, and pick up the ones from Dylan's family to theirs. What was nice was that as soon as I cleared the stairs, Lily was there to take my hand and lead me into the living room to have me meet her extended family. Apparently when I had been meeting cousins and aunts and uncles before, that had been Jeff's family. This was hers. It was a lot of people to get to know in such a short amount of time. But she introduced me like she liked me and as though this was how things were between us. Friendly. I hoped it stayed that way.

As I was not good with names on my best days, I gave up trying to retain them all, but I found myself smiling over the screaming kids running around the house, the hugging and kissing and happy squealing. I realized that I had been missing out on the big family gathering for my whole life. Funny how having Dylan back, knowing we were solid, made everything else enjoyable.

"Good morning." Dylan smiled, unsure for some reason.

"Come here, baby."

He moved fast, and I understood as he sprang at me, arms wrapping around my waist, face in my chest, that he was scared.

"What's wrong?"

Quick shake of his head.

I put my hands in his hair and tipped his head back so he had to meet my gaze. "Tell me."

"Later, okay?"

What was I going to do, twist his arm? "Okay."

He leaned forward and just breathed. I loved it. There was just something about holding the man in my arms that centered me and grounded me like nothing else. I was *better* when he was near me.

Dylan offered to cook lunch, and after a moment of surprise, his mother agreed. She had no idea that I'd starve if the man didn't cook for me, and she really had no clue that he was really good at it.

An hour later, as the production line for Ryan's huevos rancheros was in full swing, Lily leaned on the counter to ask her son a question.

"Why do you call this creation Ryan's huevos rancheros and not Dylan's?"

"Oh, 'cause Ryan taught me to make them."

"And who is Ryan?"

"He's a friend of Malic's. He used to be a model, but now he's a television host in San Francisco."

"Really?" she teased her son. "A model?"

He nodded as he whipped out the iPhone I had given him when he moved in. He fiddled with it a moment and then handed it to his mother. "There, see? Ryan."

She caught her breath. Tina, who was standing beside her, did as well.

"Ohmygod, D, you know this guy?"

He smiled wide. "Yep, Malic used to date him."

"Oh for crissakes," I growled. Dylan cackled. "We're friends," I told the two amazed women. They were staring at me like I had grown another head. Really, was I so vile that a man who looked like Ryan Dean would never even give me the time of day?

"Wow, D." Tina whistled. "How are you supposed to compete against that?"

His voice dropped low in warning. "You know what...."

I put a hand around the nape of his neck and drew him back to me, tucking him against my side.

He leaned against me more heavily than usual, like he craved the closeness, as the noise rose around us. After everyone was sitting and eating, balancing plates on knees on the floor, in the living room or at the coffee table or the dining room table with the extra leaf added, Dylan's folks and his sister joined my hearth and me at the kitchen table. I was surprised when Lily leaned forward and took my hand.

"I'm so sorry I didn't believe my son when he told me you were special to him, Malic. Please forgive me."

"Nothing to forgive."

"He told me all about you. Don't think for a minute that he's been quiet. He's been singing your praises for over a year now."

"He never stops," Tina confessed from her seat beside her mother. "You know how the Eskimos have like seventy-five words for snow?"

I nodded.

"Well, D has, like, the same number for the color of your eyes. It's revolting."

I turned and looked at my boyfriend, who was sitting on the other side of me, eating.

His smile was big and out of control. "I told Brad Darby your dance card was full."

"What?" I chuckled.

He made his eyes wide. "When your buddy Brad called early this morning to see if you could come out and play, I told him that you were busy and would be for the rest of your life."

"You did not." I smiled because he was adorable when he was all pissed off and jealous. Like he had anything to worry about.

"The hell I didn't," he growled. "He can go right to hell, Malic, and I know people who can give him directions."

I grinned. "Do you now?"

He tried not to smile. "Yeah," he said, lowering his eyes, like I wouldn't be able to see how pleased he was with himself.

"Dylan, he's a really good—"

"Brad Darby is gay?"

We all turned to look at Mr. Shaw. Poor guy, he was having a hell of an afternoon. First, he had to talk about his son's love life, and now his next-door neighbor was a homo.

"Yes, Dad, I've told you that a million times."

"The man was a Marine, for crissakes," Jeff complained.

I chuckled.

"Ohmygod, Dad, please crawl out from under your rock." Tina laughed.

"He's so big!"

"Malic's bigger, and he's gay," Tina said. "He could hold the man down and make him scream uncle if he wanted."

"Which is probably what Brad dreamed about last night," Dylan grumbled.

"Oh dear God!" Jeff Shaw barked out, and we were suddenly all laughing together instead of them without me.

"He's disgusted with you, you know," Dylan said under his breath so I had to lean sideways to hear him.

"What are you talking about?"

"Brad, he thinks you're a jerk because you've got a boy toy instead of a real relationship. He told me to tell you how disappointed in you he is."

"I see," I grunted.

"Don't you care?"

"Why would I care?"

"You guys are friends."

"We're acquaintances, and now I know we'll never be friends."

"Why not?"

"Because friends don't judge you before they know all the facts. That's why they're your friends."

"Really?" he said snidely.

"Don't start," I warned him.

"I'm just saying that Rene Favreau deserves a pardon."

Not again. "Let it go."

"The man was one of your best friends for years, and just because he slept with Jackson's ex doesn't—"

"He wasn't his *ex* when they slept together," I reminded him. "That's the problem. Rene was my friend, but Jackson's more. And Rene—"

"Is Jackson happier now than when he was with Frank? Yes or no?"

"That makes no difference."

"Answer the question."

Of course my fellow warder Jackson Tybalt was happier; he finally had someone to love as hard as he wanted with all the passion and possessiveness he had to give. Jackson had needed an equal in power and strength. He just hadn't known it. But that was not the point. Jackson had been living with and loving Frank Sullivan when my friend—one of my best friends—Rene Favreau stepped between them. He had been the other man, and I found that no matter how I tried to forgive the trespass, I simply could not. It was made worse because Rene had unwittingly come between a warder and his hearth, but truly, that part shouldn't have mattered.

"Malic?"

The man I loved was being deliberately obtuse to try and push me to reconcile with Rene, and had been for over a year. I, however, was not about to change my mind.

"It doesn't matter," I told Dylan for the ten thousandth time. "Lying is lying, cheating is cheating, and Rene knew who he was getting in bed with when he did it. What Jackson's life looks like now is—"

"You're being so stubborn and—"

"I'm inclined to side with Malic on this," Dylan's father chimed in, and we both turned to look at him, having forgotten that we weren't arguing in a vacuum. The other three people at the table had apparently been listening in rapt attention to our discussion.

"Dad," Dylan whined, "you don't even know what you're—"

"If a man cheats on a stranger, he will cheat on a friend. It's about character."

I looked at Dylan and pointed at his father. "Exactly," I agreed.

"Rene didn't cheat on anyone," Dylan told me.

"He knew Frank belonged to Jackson, and he slept with him anyway. He cheated, Frank cheated. The only one who did nothing wrong was Jackson."

"You cannot fault the heart for where it needs to go," Tina told me.

"Yeah, you can," I assured her.

"You can't help who you love," Dylan's mother seconded her daughter.

"The two people who were doing the cheating on my friend...." I shook my head at Dylan's mother. "They broke up four months after it started."

There was a long silence as Lily Shaw considered her next point. "Oh, well, then that was just crap, wasn't it?"

I laughed at her, and she smiled and swatted my arm. Even Dylan ended up smiling at the look of absolute disgust on her face.

AFTER lunch, I sat with Mr. Shaw and some others watching a college football game, as I had been invited by Dylan's father to join him on the couch. Dylan was with his cousins, talking, laughing, and I was enjoying listening to his father argue with two of his brothers, my boyfriend's uncles, about quarterbacks and defensive lines and how they were both full of crap.

When the game was over and people started just talking, busting out cell phones and cameras and connecting the video camera to the TV, I was going to excuse myself, but suddenly I had a lap full of Dylan. He had basically fallen down on top of me and startled his mother, who was sitting beside me.

"Dylan, be careful," she gasped, because it had been a violent movement, fast, bruising.

"I don't have to be careful," he murmured, pressing his face into the side of my neck. Normally he would have kissed and bitten me, sucked hard to leave marks, and even though I was too old for hickeys, I found that every now and then, a love bite from my man was a welcome mark of his passion for me. But his mother was there, so he contained himself, simply inhaling deeply, breathing me in.

"He doesn't have to be careful," I echoed his words. "I won't break."

Dylan nodded, his hands on my chest, clutching at me.

"Or leave you."

"I know." His voice faltered.

"Or not keep you safe."

The whimper came fast, and he wrapped his arms around my neck and buried his face down in my shoulder as he pushed against me, trembling hard. When I turned to look at Lily, her eyes were huge.

"What's going on?" I asked softly.

"I have no idea," she assured me, patting Dylan's back. "Sweetheart, why don't you and Malic go upstairs and talk, all right?"

He nodded, slid out of my lap, and was on his feet in seconds. "Come on."

I stood, towering over him, and took his hand. He held on really tight. "Whatever this is, I will make it all right."

He shook his head. "It's no big deal. I'm just being stupid."

Whatever it was, I hoped nothing I ever did would create the pain I was seeing on his face.

It took everything in me not to yell and make him confess his soul to me right there. Instead, I followed step by step back up to the second floor to his room. When the door closed, he tried to dart across the room, but I held his hand and sat down on the bed.

"You have to let me go," Dylan said.

So I did, because he looked like he was on the verge of tears. I took a breath. "Please tell me already, because you're killing me."

"It really is nothing," he assured me. "It's just my folks, this morning, and… I was just caught off guard, is all."

"Please."

He cleared his throat. "Okay, so when I was seventeen, I thought I was in love with Ethan Burke." He took a breath and smiled at me through now watering eyes.

Shit. I realized that this thing he was going to tell me was so far from being nothing that I felt my stomach flip over.

"And he really wanted to have sex." He coughed, starting to pace. "But I was seventeen, and I wasn't sure I was ready to, even though I really wanted to, you know?"

"Sure."

His eyes flicked to mine, checking, seeing what I was doing, and I wanted to yell at him to hurry the hell up and talk. I nodded instead.

"Yeah, so, Ethan, he was a big deal. He was on the swim team and the soccer team, and he was captain of both, so he couldn't tell anyone that he was gay."

"Okay," I said, because he had stopped talking, waiting for me to say something.

"Okay," he echoed, "so I didn't know, but he was friends with this guy, Gordy Horne. He was one year ahead of us, so when Ethan was a senior in high school—"

"Gordy was a freshman in college."

"Right."

"Go on," I prompted. "So what did Gordy do?"

"Well, so Gordy, he invited us to this party at a frat house, and I guess he was pledging there or whatever, and he could bring two guys, or girls, with him, and he took us."

"And?"

"And so Ethan brought me a wine cooler or something, and after just one, I'm wasted, and I know that's not me, and I asked him if he put something in my drink."

Everything in me tensed.

"He told me he did, just to loosen me up."

Oh God, please no.

"At the hospital, the doctor said I tested positive for Rohypnol."

"Come here."

He moved fast, and I had him in my arms and then under me on the bed seconds later. As I stared down into his eyes, I saw how intently he was looking at me, searching my face, checking for something.

"What happened?"

He swallowed hard. "Could you lie down next to me?"

I lay down with my head on the other pillow, facing him, and he turned on his side to look at me. It was nice; we talked that way in bed at night a lot.

"So," he said, reaching out, tracing my eyebrow. "I ended up in a room with Ethan and Gordy, and all of a sudden Gordy thanks him for bringing me, and Ethan's telling him that it's not a problem and that he's welcome to me."

I concentrated on taking small breaths as I listened to him.

"Ethan... he gave me away." His bottom lip trembled. "He didn't stay with me. He just left me with this guy, and he's all hands, and I... God, Malic, I don't know what would have happened, but then I'm naked and there are all these guys in the room and.... Now, in retrospect, I know Gordy wasn't supposed to be where he was, and he was a pledge, and—it was such a mess."

"What happened?"

"I still don't know, but I guess those guys were all for hazing and making Gordy fuck me in front of them as an initiation or whatever, but they couldn't find my wallet."

I exhaled a deep breath. "I'm sorry, what?"

"I guess they don't give a shit if you're eighteen and they fuck with you and take pictures and blast them all over the Internet, but if you're underage, they freak out."

It was all becoming clear. Hazing, all the tests, "brothers" seeing how far they could push the pledges. Would they suck cock or take another guy up their ass to get into the fraternity? How far would everyone let it go? And no one cared as long as everyone in the room was a consenting adult and the word *yes* was audible. No one was getting raped because everyone got asked if it was okay first. When they had found Gordy in bed with Dylan in one of the rooms used for fucking, everyone had been excited to watch two pledges go at it on camera. It was a big deal, there were whole websites devoted to gay hazing and seeming violation. Everyone was all for it, and they all knew Gordy, but no one remembered Dylan. As pretty as he was, as much as the voyeurs wanted to see Gordy do him, first they had to see his driver's license.

"So what happened?"

"I guess my wallet with my learner's permit was in my jeans, and when they found out I was only seventeen, they carried me downstairs and threw me outside, naked, with all my clothes and my shoes."

Jesus…

"So I didn't get raped." He gave me a trembling smile. "Ethan just gave me away. I got molested a little by Gordy and then thrown out onto the middle of the frat house front lawn."

… Christ.

"I think I threw up, like, a billion times walking home. I finally passed out at the mailbox. Tina found me when she got home from choir practice, and my folks took me to the hospital to make sure I was okay."

"And were you?"

"Except for the roofies, I was fine."

I stroked his hair back from his face over and over, looking at the big chocolate-brown eyes, the long lashes, and the thick impish brows. Just looking at the man was a gift. How anyone could ever hurt him was beyond me.

"Did you press charges against Ethan?"

"I just wanted to forget it ever happened, and besides, it was his word against mine that he ever gave me the drink."

I bet the truth would come out if both his arms were being broken.

"Malic?"

"What?"

"Do you know you're growling?"

"Just—what did you tell your folks?"

"I told them that Ethan broke up with me to go out with Gordy."

"Why?"

"Because I was so ashamed and embarrassed… I just wanted it to go away."

"What happened after?" I asked, putting my hand on his thigh, bringing him closer to me until he got the hint and slid his leg up over my hip.

"Ethan told everyone at school that I was a whore so that whatever I said would have sounded like I was making shit up, you know? Not that I would have outed him. I remember him telling me that when he took me to the prom that everyone would see who he really loved. It turned out to be just a lot of shit."

I had no idea what I was supposed to do.

"So you know, the rest of junior year was just crap, but then after he graduated and I came back for my senior year, everything was better. I mean, it was still kinda shitty, but not as horrible, and by the time I graduated, no one cared anymore."

I nodded.

"I was lucky I had the guys."

I squinted at him. "Those friends of yours, they stood by you?"

He nodded. "They did, even though it was hard on them to be friends with a cockwhore." His confession made me think so much better of Jason, Lance, and Cole. "They didn't treat me like a leper, and for awhile, they were the only ones."

I had to process everything. "So have you ever seen Ethan again? Gordy?"

He took a breath. "Gordy and I didn't travel in the same circles; he wasn't my friend, so I never saw him again, and Ethan went off to college and never came back, as far as I know."

"Good."

"And I never think about it anymore, you know, but like I said, it just bugged me this morning because my folks and my sister, they didn't know the real Ethan. All they saw was the guy who came over and was nice to me in front of them. He told them that he was going to take me to prom and everything, and because he was a big deal and he came from one of the richest families in town, they were really impressed. When he was suddenly gone, I had to tell them something, so that's why I made up the whole 'he left me for Gordy' thing."

"So your folks never knew what you were going through in school."

"No, only the guys," he sighed.

Which explained why the guys—his friends Jason, Lance, and Cole—were so important.

"But this morning before you came down, we were talking about you, and I was trying to explain to all of them why I love you, and—"

"I know, I heard."

"You did?" he asked, sitting up, moving, climbing over me, onto me, and straddling my thighs. "When?"

"I was eavesdropping. I'm sorry."

"It's okay." He smiled wide, and seeing it, the joy that washed over his face, made it suddenly hard to breathe. "I just got sick to my stomach with them thinking that Ethan could ever be in the same league with you. I mean, I love you, Malic, and this is the first real time for me, and now I'm the partner of a superhero, and I matter."

"You always mattered," I told him, hands on his thighs, lifting him up, pressing, moving him so his perfectly round little ass was wedged over my groin. "There's only one difference."

"What's that?" he whispered, his eyes fluttering as he began to squirm, trying to improve his angle.

"Now you're mine, and we both know I don't share."

"I know," he said, stilling completely, his eyes instantly brimming with tears. "You would never let anyone touch me—ever."

I smiled up at him, and I watched him swallow hard.

"Jesus, Malic, that smile is just… evil," he said breathlessly, which led me to believe that he was more than just a little turned on by how I was looking at him. "Seems like maybe you wanna eat me."

"Even your name is precious to me, you understand that?"

"Yes."

"And you know if I ever see that guy on the street, he's a dead man, right?"

"Just leave him alone." He chuckled, then sighed deeply. "God, I feel so good."

"Yeah?"

"Yeah." He seemed almost surprised. "I feel like now that I told you, there are no secrets at all with us."

"You were afraid to tell me?"

"I just didn't want you to think of me as a victim. I need to be strong for you, and that's how I want you to see me. I never want you to question your choice like you did yesterday."

"I didn't question you. I just worry because—"

"I'm young."

"Yes."

"But you're over it now, right?" he asked, shifting at the same time, pressing against me, his eyes narrowing as he licked his lips.

"Yes, baby," I said, reaching up and sliding a hand around the side of his neck, leaning him over, drawing him down to me until his lips were hovering over mine. "Now kiss me like you mean it."

"Jesus, Malic." His breath stuttered. "I always mean it."

"Do you?" I teased, my hand moving fast, the belt buckle, snap, and zipper surrendering easily.

He whimpered as he lifted up, getting the idea of what I wanted, what I would have, as he shucked out of his jeans.

"You wanna kiss me?"

"I do, but I need... oh... I... oh."

He moaned incoherently because I had taken hold of the hard cock pressed to my hip and was slowly, gently, tantalizingly milking it.

"Could you please put—fuck!"

"Should I put that in my mouth?" I asked.

He was shivering with his need.

I flipped him, rose over him, and took him down the back of my throat as he whined and begged. He lifted up, one hand on my head, fingers buried in my hair, watching like he loved to more than anything. Having me swallow his cock, he had told me on numerous occasions, was the absolute hottest thing he had ever seen in his life. He never felt more wanted than when I had a mouthful of him, and because I loved his taste, his sleek skin, the way he whimpered and came apart, I sucked him off often.

"Oh Malic, please," he cried as I increased my suction, used my teeth, and slid a finger into my mouth to get it wet.

He twitched and jolted, and I could tell how much he needed me like this, wanting him, craving him, unable to keep myself from tasting him. When I slid my arm around and under him, letting my slick finger slide seductively between his cheeks, his back arched up off the bed.

"I can't... I want... gonna come."

I increased the friction as he buried his cock in the back of my throat.

"Oh fuck, yeah, take it all." His breath caught as his hand fisted in my hair, tugging, making sure I couldn't move. "You love my cock in your mouth just like you love putting your cock in my ass, huh?"

I swirled my tongue under his shaft, tugged, and he came hard without a second warning, filling my throat so I had to swallow fast, drink him down just like he wanted. When he was flaccid in my mouth, I let his spent cock slip from between my lips.

His eyes were wet and dark as he stared at me.

"You okay?" I asked.

He nodded, beyond words, just gesturing me close.

"What do you want?"

The aftershocks of his orgasm were still rolling through his lean frame, so speech wasn't possible. Lifting up over him, I bent to kiss him breathless, ravish his mouth, letting him taste himself on my mouth. I knew he craved that, the only thing he needed more was to mark me, show everyone to whom I belonged.

"Maybe." I chuckled, lifting so he could take in great gulps of air, and said, "I should tattoo your name on my ass, huh?"

"Across your chest," he replied haltingly. "My name." He slid his hand up over my left pectoral. "Right over your heart for everyone to fuckin' see. You're mine, Malic Sunden. Don't ever fuckin' forget it."

I wouldn't.

IV

CHRISTMAS is a time for forgiveness, or so everyone always told me. As I stood outside on the back deck that evening, leaning against the wall, Lance and Jason with me, I was certain that Christmas was also a time for people to get what they had coming to them. Even Santa gave out coal.

"Me and Lance," Jason was telling me, "we made Ethan Burke's life hell."

"How?" I asked.

"God, we had his car towed like, what, ten times?" He cackled, looking over at his partner in crime.

"Oh God, at least." Lance chuckled. "I carried a can of yellow spray paint wherever I went, and every time we saw the car out— wham, instant tow-away zone."

"What'd he drive?" I asked.

"A tricked-out Camaro." Jason snorted out a laugh. "God, I loved seeing that car up on the back of a tow truck."

"Me too," Lance sighed, pretending to wipe tears from his eyes. "Ah, good times."

"You guys really hated Ethan, huh?"

"He could've gotten Dylan raped," Jason told me. "Or worse. Fucker deserved every second of shit we gave him."

I agreed and was surprised that I would. I had no idea that Dylan's friends were guys that I could so easily see eye to eye with, but since they were his friends, I should have given them the benefit of the doubt to begin with. His friends at home were nice people too. All his art school pals were flamboyant and quirky. I did not understand their fashion sense at all, especially the girls', but they all cared deeply for Dylan. I should have known that his oldest friends would have been the same. They had lived with him through a rough patch in all their lives, when the peer pressure had to have been staggering, and they had stood up instead of caving.

"Ethan knew it was us," Jason laughed, "but there wasn't shit he could do about it."

"Remember that time the police came to question us and your mom said we were with her all night?" Lance asked him.

Jason cackled, smiling. "Yeah, so the police are like, 'Which night was that, Mrs. Flynn?' And she's all, 'Whatever night it was, officer.'"

I was impressed and I told him so.

"Like they're gonna screw with a single mother, like she's not tough, right?" Jason scoffed. "Come on."

I nodded.

"And then they went to my house another time and questioned my folks," Lance said, "and they said the same thing, that 'Of course the boys were with us.' I love that they never even thought about it, just instinctively protecting us."

"That's what you do for your kids, right?" I said.

"Absolutely," they chimed.

"You guys both have great parents."

"Yep," Lance agreed. "My dad asked them if the police department would like to start having garbage dropped off instead of picked up."

"Your dad works for the city?"

"Union." Lance's grin turned sly. "They don't wanna mess with him."

"They gave up after that. There wasn't enough to go on, and so when the car got egged or towed or, you know, when all four tires disappeared at once...."

"That was inspired." Jason sighed deeply, looking over at Lance. "Truly."

"Thank you." Lance smiled. "The time you parked it in Principal Ferriday's parking spot was also a very nice touch."

"One tries."

Yeah, I liked them both. "So you guys both went out of state for school?"

"Yeah," Jason told me. "All three of us, D, too, as you know, and we only get home for Thanksgiving and Christmas now. We all have jobs to help with school that don't end when classes do in the summer anymore. It's nice for all of us to see each other, but we're sorry we've been hoggin' up all of his time. The four of us just don't get to hang out like we used to."

"That's okay," I told them. I stopped when I heard someone walking up along the side of the house, gravel crunching under shoes.

"Hey, there he is!" Jason greeted Cole loudly. "Get the fuck up here."

As I watched them, I realized that the warmth I now felt toward them was making me see them with fresh eyes. Cole, who had just joined us, was the tallest, long and lean with sandy-blond hair and blue eyes. Jason was built heavier, stocky, like maybe he had wrestled in high school, and because his brown hair was buzzed short, it accentuated how big his green eyes were. Lance was built more like me, like a defensive lineman, and he was all muscle. When he noticed my regard, I got the dazzling smile and the crinkling blue eyes. They were all bigger than Dylan but not enough so that they would have looked like his bodyguards. I could see how they would have fit walking around together.

"We're just talking to Malic about Ethan's car."

"Figured it would come out sooner or later." Cole yawned, flopping down into the chair. "Where's D?"

"He's taking a shower," I told him, unwilling to say why he was taking one at six in the evening. Looking debauched with swollen red lips and flushed skin was not the way to meet your family or your friends. "You know, it took a lot of balls for all you guys to stick up for Dylan like you did. You were all headed for college, right?"

"Yep, all of us on scholarship."

"And what if you had been caught? None of you would have been going away to school. Your futures would have been fucked."

"Yeah, but, Malic…." Jason leaned forward in his chair. "There was no way to let that shit go. Dylan needed us. What are friends for if they don't ride to your rescue?"

Absolutely. "Do you guys ever see Ethan?"

"He went away to college and stayed wherever that was," Cole chimed in.

"If he was rich, how come he went to public school?" I asked.

"Ethan told me once that he had been kicked out of every prep school Mr. Burke could think of. Public school was Ethan's last chance or it was military school next," Lance said.

And now I knew the whole story.

"You know what the bitch of the whole thing was?" Jason sighed deeply. "I used to watch Ethan look at Dylan, and you could see it. Anybody could see it."

Lance shrugged. "Yeah, I never understood why Ethan would let that dick Gordy talk him into hurting D when it was so obvious that Ethan was crazy about him."

"Yeah, but not enough." Cole yawned again, stretching. "If you love someone, you never let them get hurt—no matter who tells you to."

"Agreed." Jason stretched too. "Fuck, I'm hungry. When are we gonna eat?"

As if on cue, Lily Shaw poked her head out the back door and told everyone that dinner was set up in the kitchen and everyone should come in and serve themselves. She had a buffet line going already.

I told them to go ahead when they lingered, waiting for me, and then pulled my phone from the pocket of my jeans and called Marcus.

"Hey," he said with a yawn on the other end. "What's going on?"

"The exciting life of a litigator, huh?"

"Are you kidding? All I did was eat today." He chuckled. "All Joe's mother does is feed us and try and make us fat."

I smiled into my phone. "She adores you."

"It goes both ways." He sighed. "But I'm glad you called, because I was going to come see you in a little bit."

"See me, like, *see* me? Why?"

As a warder, Marcus could use a vortex, like a wormhole, to travel from wherever he was to me and be there in seconds.

"I had a feeling you needed me," he said after a long moment.

"You did?"

"I did."

"Shit, Marcus, what're you psychic now?"

"Nope, just tuned in to you," he said, and I could hear how much he liked me in his tone, the warmth that infused his voice. "So talk to me."

But I had to think of what I wanted to say.

Being Marcus, he talked instead, because he knew it was what I needed. "Hey, you and Dylan are for sure coming home for New Year's, right?"

"Yeah, why?"

"Joe's putting the deposit down with the hotel today for the suites."

"What are we doing, again?"

"We're all going out for dinner, and then dancing, then up to some suites."

"That seems like a lot of work when all any of us wanna do is go home and fuck."

He was quiet, and I started laughing.

"God, you're a crude-ass bastard," he told me.

The tension felt good to dump.

"Listen, you ass, Joe had a fucked-up New Year's Eve last year—"

"Since you were missing," I reminded him.

His exasperated sigh, then: "Yes, since I was missing, and so this year we're celebrating big."

"Joe has a definite idea about things."

"Yes, he does."

"Well, tell him that Dylan and I will be there."

"Good, I will. Now tell me what the hell is going on already, because that's all the small talk I've got."

And so I told him the whole sordid story. As he listened, I realized that just letting it out, telling him, calmed me. Talking to Marcus always did that.

"So what's your plan now?" he asked cautiously.

"I don't have one. It's over. I just wish I could erase it for Dylan."

"You don't need to erase it. You just need to be there and be the man you are. Dylan's strong and smart, he knows who he is. Sounds like he just had an emotional reaction to his family thinking you were not the white knight you are. But he's not damaged in any way, Mal; he's fine."

And I knew that, but it was still nice to hear.

"Thanks."

"Don't mention it. I'll see you in a week."

"See you," I said and hung up as I heard the sliding glass door behind me. Turning, I found Tina.

"Come in and eat, okay?"

I just stood there, looking at her.

"What?"

"Nothing, just looking at you."

"Well, stop." She glowered, but I saw that she liked me; it was there in her eyes, the way they softened. She had started off thinking I was a different kind of man, and when she learned that her brother loved me and that I loved him in return, everything changed for her. I was her brother's guy now, and that meant something to her. That knowledge had wedged itself into her gaze. I liked it a lot. "Don't be nice to me, for crissakes," she snapped. "Look how I've treated you."

"You didn't know me," I reminded her.

"Just get in here," she grumbled, gesturing me in before leaving the doorway, not wanting to close it, instead letting out the warm air so I would have to do what she said.

I moved fast to follow her and reached for her arm, but when my fingers closed on her wrist, she winced and pulled away.

"Oh, I'm sor—"

"No, I... it's fine," she gasped, turning into me like it was natural and not brand new, more instinctive, before she suddenly caught herself. She froze, her head snapped up, and her eyes met mine.

"Tina?"

"I... *oh.*"

It was the whimper of the "oh" that did it. She was barely holding on, and right then, her body betrayed her, and I felt the tremor run through her. I crushed her to my chest. I was not gentle, even when I tried, and her gasp scared me for a second before she melted in my arms, molding herself to me. She needed something—shelter, safety, I wasn't sure what—but because I was big and solid, I could offer her the strength she seemed to be lacking at the moment.

"Who hurt you, Tina?" I asked, speaking into her hair.

She recovered fast, pulling free, grabbing my hand and tugging me after her into the hall by the stairs. When she whirled around, she lifted her sleeves, revealing the dark-red bruises on her wrists and forearms.

"What the fuck?" I asked.

She had been wearing turtleneck sweaters since I arrived and when she pulled it away from her throat, I understood why. There were new bruises that were purple and older ones that were yellow, and I felt my stomach twist into a knot of absolute revulsion.

"Tina."

Her eyes lifted to mine.

"Who?"

"My boyfriend, Mike, we live together in Cambridge, we go to law school together... he... he... Malic...."

I grabbed her again, and she started sobbing in my arms.

After a minute, Lily came around the corner.

"Hi." I smiled awkwardly at her as Tina shuddered and bawled into my chest, her face buried in my Henley as she clutched me tight.

"What's going on?"

I tipped my head sideways, and because the long sleeves of one of her daughter's many sweaters were finally pushed up, she instantly saw the damaged skin.

"Ohmygod." She sucked in her breath. "Tina, did Mike do that?"

"You know he did," I told her, "if that's where your mind went."

"Jesus—" Her voice deserted her.

There was lots of sniffling, more tears, and then Dylan was suddenly above me on the stairs, finally done showering and changing. He looked really good in the low-rise jeans, white T-shirt, and beige zippered cardigan. Everything about him was soft and sweet.

"What the hell's going on?" Except his tone. His tone was hard and cold and flat.

"Mike hurt Tina." His mother's voice trembled. "Oh Dylan, look at her arms."

He was horrified—it was all over his face—and then he was furious.

"I told you!" he yelled at his sister, stomping down the staircase. "I told you it would escalate, and I told you he was a fuckin' psychopath! I'll fuckin' kill him!"

"No," I said softly as he moved in beside me—wanting, I could tell, to take his sister's place in my arms. He needed me; he was raw and vulnerable from unburdening his soul earlier, and though normally a rock himself, he was a little unsteady at the moment. Even though he had felt better after telling me, the confession had still been emotionally taxing. "I will take care of everything, all right?"

Tina started hiccupping as she lifted her head to look up at my face. "He said he would hurt me if I—"

"By the time you get back home, sweetheart, he'll be gone."

Her breath was coming in nasally staccato snorts. "He will?"

"He will," I promised.

She buried her face in my chest again, clutching at my back, pushing in tighter, and I felt Dylan's hand on my arm.

"What's wrong, baby?" I asked.

He shook his head as his eyes started to water.

"Do me a favor."

"Sure," he said, and I saw him pull himself together just because I needed him to do something for me.

"Get my phone out and call Jackson for me. Tell him I need him and Leith here now."

He nodded and reached into the back pocket of my jeans. When he walked a little way down the hall, making sure he was out of earshot of his sister and mother, I turned my attention back to Tina.

"I don't know why people think they can screw around with my family," I said, taking her face in my hands and tilting her head back so I could see her swollen eyes. "But it's a mistake. I'm not a nice man."

She swallowed more tears. "Am I your family now?"

"Oh yes."

She took a quick breath. "I don't usually cry. I usually get mad."

"And I like that." I smiled down at her. "I'm the same way."

"Oh." Lily's teeth began to chatter with the welling up of emotion as she watched. "Malic, you—"

"I will take care of it," I told Dylan's mother, reaching for her, and I was not surprised that she moved forward, into my side, wrapping one arm around my waist as she stroked her daughter's hair with her other hand.

"What was wrong with Dylan earlier?" Lily asked, tilting her head back to look up at me.

"Old news, nothing pressing, he's fine," I assured his mother, not being able to tell her the truth as his secrets were not mine to tell. "I'll take care of him."

"I know." She nodded, smiling.

That she knew I was her son's safety net made me very happy.

"Jacks," Dylan said, and I could hear the smile in his voice. He liked Jackson; everyone did. He had a face that made you smile when you saw it, a warm sound to his voice that was the cadence of a drawl from growing up in Tennessee without the dialect, and a smile that managed to be wicked and warm at the exact same time.

"Malic, what are you going to do?"

"I'll tell you in just a minute," I replied to Tina, turning to look at Dylan.

He was walking back toward me, shrugging, holding my phone.

"What?"

"He told me to tell you that they'll be here soon."

I understood.

"Malic," Lily said, letting me go, stepping back, her eyes still on my face. "You have friends in the area?"

"They're on a layover, Mom," Dylan told her, thinking on his feet, covering up the warder vortex as all hearths did. Some families, like Joe's, Marcus's hearth, knew that they had a warder in their midst and that he or she belonged to a clutch of other warders. Most did not. Maybe someday Dylan and I would share my secret with his family, but not yet. "So they're just gonna stop by and say hello when they get in."

"And where are they flying through to?"

"Massachusetts," I told her, "as luck would have it."

"Oh, how funny."

"It is. So they can pop in and deliver the news to Mike that he's moving out." I smiled.

"What?" Tina gasped.

"Go wash your face," I directed, "and let's get something to eat."

She took a breath and walked away.

"How did you do that?" Lily asked.

"What?"

"Get her to listen to you?"

I grinned at her. "I have a way with women." From the way she was looking at me, she was completely charmed at that moment. I turned and grabbed Dylan's hand, yanking him after me. "Come on, let's eat."

He liked being manhandled; I knew that, so he followed fast.

"Both my kids listen to you, Malic," Lily grunted from beside me. "Amazing."

I smiled at her as I grabbed a plate for Dylan and shoved it at him.

"I'm not really hungry."

"Eat now or I'll make the plate and we know how that always turns out."

He snatched it out of my hand grumbling about my size versus his and how he could not be expected to eat the trough of food I normally piled up for him. I was careful not to snicker at his irritation.

He stomped away from me, sitting down with his friends on the couch, the plate of food on his knees, but after a deep breath, I saw him finally relax. That was the important part, for him to decompress. In minutes he was talking and laughing, and hearing the sound made me feel good. He still seemed off balance to me, and Tina was barely holding it together, but they were both okay for the moment. I made a plate and sat down at the table. Watching Dylan, watching Tina, I felt better. Protecting was hardwired into a warder, so seeing that they were both safe soothed me. When Lily returned to me twenty minutes later with her husband in tow, I stood and took hold of his shoulder and explained what was going on.

"That asshole hurt my baby?" Jeff muttered under his breath, the anger and betrayal right there simmering on the surface.

"Yes, sir," I told him.

"He's been in my home, Malic," he snapped, his eyes flicking to mine, his gaze locking there. "I trusted him with her." And he felt like a very poor judge of character at the moment.

"I know."

"How can I let her leave here and go back there?"

"Because I'm going to make sure it's safe before she goes home."

"How?"

"I have some friends who are going to speak to her boyfriend for me."

"Really?" He was surprised.

"Yes, sir."

When the doorbell rang, Mr. Shaw left me to answer it.

Whoever the Shaw clan was expecting was not at all who they got. Jackson came through the door first, with Leith behind him, and they had obviously come from two very different places.

Leith was dressed in cargo khakis, steel-toed work boots, and a heavy cable-knit sweater under a shearling-lined denim jacket. The long blond curls that fell to the middle of his back were tied back from his face in a queue. Everyone noticed him. There was no way not to; the man was very handsome even though he looked irritated.

Jackson had on a suit, and he looked crisp and polished. The only piece missing was the tie. Thick brown hair, now cut short, still kicked out around his ears, curling down the nape of his neck. The beard and mustache made him look softer than he did without them, warmer, but the glint in his dark-brown eyes was mischievous and sexy. Leith you noticed first; Jackson was the one you wanted to get up and talk to.

When they saw me, they crossed the room to reach me, Jackson grinning wide, saying hello to everyone, Leith just walking through, clearly annoyed.

"That was scary fast," Dylan said as he joined me, leaning into my side, watching the warders come closer.

I had to agree. He knew how hard it was for me to travel through the wormhole, how much energy it took, so, really, it was a huge deal that they were here already.

"My," Lily said to draw my attention, smiling when she had it, even as she smoothed her daughter's hair back from her face. "Your friends must make quite… the… ent…."

"Hey."

I reached for Jackson, giving him a brief hug, tipping my head at Leith afterward. Jackson hugged everyone; Leith mostly just touched his hearth, Simon. The only other person he was overtly demonstrative with was Marcus. But we all touched Marcus; it was just something we did, something we couldn't help but do.

"You guys hungry?" I asked.

"I'm not," Leith said as his eyes skirted over me and then Dylan. Satisfied that we were fine, he took a breath.

"Me neither." Jackson grinned. "Besides, traveling makes me kinda queasy. Always has," he said, referring to the wormhole we all used.

"So what's up?" Leith wanted to know.

I looked back at Mrs. Shaw. "Hey, Lil."

Her smile was beautiful, as she did it through fresh tears. Looking at her daughter was making her quietly weep. "It's Lil suddenly? No one calls me Lil."

"Oh no?" I teased, then I cleared my throat. "Hey there, Lil, could you please get something to write on and give my buddies the address of Tina's place in Cambridge?"

She turned to look at my fellow warders, first Leith with his warm aqua eyes and chiseled features, and then Jackson, who was standing there looking strong and stable and everything she needed at that moment.

"Are you both really going to go see Mike in—"

"Yes, ma'am," Jackson told her even though he had no idea yet what was going on, instead simply following my lead. "Would you mind getting us that address, please?"

"Of course." She smiled and got up and left the table we were standing beside.

"Thanks for coming," I told my fellow warders.

"You called," Jackson said, giving me his wide-open grin. "You never call. You normally just try and handle whatever it is alone. So if you ask Dylan to call, we're gonna get here as fast as we can."

"You guys are getting scary with that travel," I said low and under my breath since Mr. Shaw was there and we were in the middle of a living room with a lot of people who seemed very interested in us. "Dylan just got off the phone with you not too long ago."

He tipped his head at Leith. "He brought me. He and Ry, the stronger they get, the easier it is for them to do. Both of them can move one more at any time from any place now."

I looked at Leith. "Really?"

He nodded, shrugging. "It's no big deal."

"It's a huge deal," I assured him. "Jael's gonna be impressed."

"He already is." Leith squinted at me, indicating Tina with a tip of his head. "So what's this about?"

"Abusive boyfriend," I told him as Mr. Shaw sat down beside his daughter at the table and took her hand in his. "I need him gone and too scared to come back."

Dylan, who had let me go when I greeted Jackson, was suddenly back, leaning against me, his arm sliding around my waist. He was shivering just slightly, and I would have bet that seeing Tina's fear was taking him back to a time when he had been in her shoes.

Leith cleared his throat, and he mouthed the question for me when I looked at him: Did I want the guy dead?

I shook my head. "Tina lives with this guy. They go to school together. I want him to run the other way when he sees her from now on."

Leith nodded, and I noticed that his face had changed. His hearth, Simon, had a stalker of an ex-boyfriend whom Jackson had scared out of his mind. If Jackson had not stepped in and ended the volatile situation, I had no doubt that Leith would have killed his hearth's stalker and dropped him in a hell dimension to be devoured and never found. Leith was, first and foremost, logical, and removing a problem with a final solution just made, to him, good sense. If something was bad, you killed it. The end.

"He needs to find other living accommodations. I don't want him back for any reason."

"Malic." Tina found her voice.

I looked over at her.

"Mike pays half the rent, and—"

"I'll take care of his half until you find someone else to live with."

"But I can't—"

"And if you don't, you don't, and then you'll owe me, right?"

She shook her head. "I don't want to owe any—"

"Just let him take care of it, Tina," Dylan snapped at her. "Don't screw with your knight in shining armor, all right?"

No one made a sound.

Tina finally took a breath. "Thank you, Malic. I accept."

I looked down at Dylan as his hands went up under my shirt, sliding over my hips to trace bare skin. "Maybe you should go to bed, huh?"

"Come with me and I will. You can watch TV, and I'll take a nap beside you. It's one of my favorite things."

"What is?"

"I like it when it's raining outside and we're in bed and you're watching football or whatever and Fu is sleeping next to my back and I'm halfway—"

"Who's Fu?" Jackson asked suddenly.

It was jarring, but it was good for Dylan to have to answer the question because he went from being sentimental to alert, as he had to answer a stupid question about our cat.

"He's a Siamese," Dylan answered.

"Fu's a cat." Jackson nodded. "Got it."

"And he leaps at stuff all the time." Dylan was smiling now, straightening up, stepping away from me, and I was glad. I liked seeing him get his bearings. "But he doesn't just pounce, you know? He does like all these weird mid-air acrobatics, and sometimes it's like he freezes in these positions, and it's just hysterical. He goes all Cirque du Soleil on me. That cat cracks me up, so…." He shrugged. "Fu. Stupid cat named himself."

I had to smile thinking of the damn cat. First I thought he had a death wish, the way he kept jumping off things like the bookcase, and then I'd thought he needed antipsychotic drugs, and now, having never had a pet before, I realized he was pretty much just a normal cat, if that word could even be applied to such mysterious creatures. I had no idea why he had to sit on Dylan's laptop only when Dylan wanted to use it. Why he had to take naps in the reusable grocery bags, and why my lap—not Dylan's—was his favorite place to curl up on the couch, but why he slept under the covers on Dylan's side and never mine.

"He's a freak," I told Dylan even though I loved opening the front door and having the little hairball come running to greet me, followed by my beautiful boy. I was a very lucky man.

"He's our freak," my hearth reminded me.

"Well, yeah."

"I hope Julian's taking good care of him."

"Of everyone you know," I told him, "think of anyone you'd rather be on cat duty than Julian."

Dylan nodded. "You're right, Raph thought I was gonna eat him," he said pointedly to Jackson, scowling, speaking of the man's hearth, who also happened to be a kyrie.

"Well, yeah, Raph doesn't get the whole 'animal that you feed that you don't end up eating' thing." Jackson chuckled. "But I kind of understand; there are no such things as pets in purgatory."

"What?" Tina asked.

Jackson was still chuckling when Mr. Shaw cleared his throat.

"What the hell is going on?"

"I think you need a drink, sir," Leith offered.

"I think you're right," he agreed but turned to cup his daughter's face in his hands. "Now listen, all of us together will help you make up Mike's end of the rent. It's gracious of Malic to offer to do it alone, but we'll do it as a family." He turned to Leith then. "And you two don't have to get involved in our—"

"It's our pleasure, sir," Leith assured him.

"It's kind of our gig." Jackson's smile was soothing and warm. "So we're good."

I had no pity for Mike, who had hurt someone he was supposed to love and someone weaker than him as well. He was in for a shocker, and I was certain that after he saw Leith and Jackson, he would *never* bother Tina again.

"Here we are," Lily said as she returned and passed an index card to Leith. "Now what are you going to—"

"Don't worry about it," he told her, smiling gently. "We'll take care of everything, ma'am."

She turned to Tina. "Honey, we should press charges and—"

"I just want him to go away, Mom." Tina sucked in a breath. "I mean, I'm the idiot who's been letting it go on, letting it get worse and worse every time… I have no one to blame but myself."

"No," Jackson assured her. "You have the man who's been beating you to blame."

"And we'll make sure he never wants to come near you again," Leith said flatly.

She nodded and her bottom lip quivered, and Lily made a face and was suddenly crying along with her daughter. "Oh baby," she cooed, and Tina pulled away from her dad to reach for her mom.

"Christmas is awesome," I muttered under my breath.

"Stop," Dylan warned me.

"Let's go," Jackson said before he turned away. "I'll call you when we get there."

"We'll send before and after pictures." Leith snickered.

"No, we won't." Jackson shook his head. "Hello, *evidence*."

Leith nodded. "Yeah, okay, no pictures. How about just sound?"

Jackson started laughing as he shoved Leith forward.

"Are they leaving already?" Tina sniffled, looking at me. "God, Malic, I'm so sorry. What your friends must think of me."

"They're only thinking about what happened to you and what they're going to do to Mike once they find him."

"Oh, now wait a minute," Mr. Shaw said quickly, having not been listening to their earlier banter but catching what I said loud and clear. He rose up out of his seat like he was going to go after Jackson and Leith. "Malic, your friends can't just—"

"Yes, they can," I assured Mr. Shaw, getting him to look at me to give Jackson and Leith more time to get out the front door. Once they were outside, they were gone. They just had to get there without being called back.

"No, they can't." His voice rose. "We don't just take the law into our own hands, Malic."

"Sometimes you have to."

"That's it?" Lily asked. "I can't even feed them?"

"They don't need to be fed," I told her. "They came because I asked them to, and now they're taking care of Tina because of me and Dylan and because that's what friends do. And for your information, Mr. Shaw—"

"Jeff, Malic. Call me Jeff."

"Jeff." I sighed. "Jackson Tybalt is a licensed, bonded private investigator, and he owns his own security company called Guardian Limited. You can Google him and you'll see he's legitimate. He won't do anything that will hurt Mike unless Mike is uncooperative. If he's on his best behavior with Jackson, everything will be settled quickly and quietly. It's only if he creates a problem that he'll have one."

Jeff thought about that a minute, mulling it over.

"Sir?" I prompted.

"Well, that seems reasonable," he told me.

And it was, except that Leith was there too. Jackson was the least of Mike's problems.

"Jesus, Malic." Lily Shaw sighed heavily. "You're like a guardian angel, aren't you?"

"No, ma'am." I smiled, reaching for Dylan, drawing him closer, enjoying the way he molded himself to my side. "He's the angel."

"No, Malic," she said sincerely, "I'm pretty sure it's you."

And I would have argued, but Dylan kissed under my jaw, and I forgot all about what we were talking about. It was more important just to hold him.

V

I HAD never been for a walk through a neighborhood at night just to look at the lights. I had never been on a block where everyone opened up their homes to everyone else, and it was like a circuit Christmas party. Dylan's whole family got swaddled up—cousins, too, friends, aunts and uncles, and stray guests—and went for a tour of homes. We passed other people strolling, and the Shaw family, the small one and the extended one, stopped and chatted. I was introduced as Dylan's boyfriend and shook a lot of hands. There was a big Thermos of hot chocolate passed around, much discussion about how some people had just gone nuts with the decorations and how Mr. Erickson had again managed to get the entire gingerbread family up on his roof. It was an impressive feat, and when the man himself came out of his house to say hello, he was greeted with a round of applause. He looked very pleased even though he gave a dismissive wave like it was nothing.

It was nice. It was normal and warm and suburbia at its finest. Everyone liked each other on the street; everyone waved and invited us in for hot spiced cider. People were pleased that Dylan had made it home for the holidays, and they were glad he had brought me. They were all thrilled, they said, that he had met someone nice. He deserved to have someone in his life just as great as he was.

"What?" Dylan asked as we sauntered along with the others, making the trip home so Lily could open up her house to others and return the hospitality they had been shown. Apparently it was the annual Christmas Crawl on Somerset Lane, and the end of the block families, down by the cul-de-sac where Dylan's folks lived, were supposed to be ready for visitors by nine.

"I had no idea that you grew up on the Beaver's street."

"Very funny." He smiled up at me. "You're just so used to killing bad things you forgot about all the good that life has to offer."

There was some truth in that.

"Tina looks better," he said, gazing over at his older sister.

"Yes, she does."

"You were great with her."

"She just needed a shoulder to cry on."

"More like a big, strong muscular chest and washboard abs."

I shook my head, and he leaned hard, surrendered up all his weight, and just fell toward me, confident that I would catch him and tuck him up against me, which was exactly what I did.

"Hey, do you like Christmas cookies?"

I squinted at him. "How should I know?"

He stopped walking and just stared up at me.

"What?"

"Didn't you make Christmas cookies with your mom when you were a little boy?"

"No."

"Are you telling me you've never made Christmas cookies?"

"It wasn't something we did in my family."

"You didn't make Christmas cookies and then leave them out for Santa on Christmas Eve?"

"Santa," I scoffed.

"No?"

"No."

Dylan turned and yelled at his mother. "Mom, you're not gonna believe this!"

I WAS smiling at Dylan's father, who was shaking his head as he made me a hot toddy.

"The secret is the honey," he told me as he coated the bottom of an Irish coffee glass with it.

It was going to be good, I was sure, and I could smell the brandy he was using. But however many drinks he and I had, we would not be able to catch up to Lily, Tina, and Dylan. Hours after the crawl was over and people had returned to their homes, ages after Lance, Jason, and Cole had left to hit house parties, and just an hour before midnight, what was passing for cookie making was still going on in the Shaw kitchen.

What had started out as a warm family undertaking had degraded into the cookies doing terrible, nasty things to each other. There were no adorable gumdrop buttons; these cookies were decorated pornographically with too much icing and sprinkles. Dylan had used the silver candy decorations to show his mother what a Prince Albert was, and Tina had been making bondage cookies when someone dropped the flour and a white cloud covered everything. Mr. Shaw and I had been watching from a safe distance, observing the Kahlúa and Baileys that had washed down the sugar cookies. Lily, Dylan, and Tina had also consumed all the rum balls that had been made earlier in the day.

"They are drunk off their asses," I assured Mr. Shaw.

"Yes." He sighed, smiling at his family. "And I couldn't be happier." He turned to me then. "Forgive me for being an ass."

"Forgive me for being a judgmental prick."

He nodded, passing me the hot brandy and honey concoction. "Agreed."

It was really good, and sipping it, watching Lily laugh so hard she was crying, seeing Tina dissolve into a fit of giggling and telling her mother and brother that she was going to pee, and listening to Dylan heave for breath, I was content. I could see myself in that kitchen for many years to come.

"Please make sure you come next year, Malic," Jeff prodded. "It wouldn't be as good for Dylan if you stayed away, and we would miss you."

A day ago, I hadn't been able to see myself there for another minute. A day ago, I had wanted to run. Now I had a family beyond the one I shared with my fellow warders, and I was amazed at the turn my life had taken.

When my phone rang, I got up to answer it, taking my drink with me. The call from Leith took longer than I expected, and by the time I got back, I was smiling. I was surprised to find the cookie-making station deserted and only Mr. Shaw waiting for me in the living room.

"It looks like World War Three in there," I said about the dismantled kitchen.

"Yes, but that's all right. They had a good time, and I enjoyed watching them."

So had I.

"I'll get in there in a little while and clean it up," he continued.

"I can help you."

"No, you've done enough work around here for a while; you can have the night off."

"I appreciate that," I said, taking a seat on the couch across from where he was on a recliner.

"Who was on the phone?"

I explained that it had been a very disappointed Leith.

"Disappointed how?"

"Tina's boyfriend, Mike, had already moved all his things out of the apartment."

"Oh? Why?"

"I guess Tina has an upstairs neighbor named Gabe, and he and Mike had already had words the day after Tina left to come home."

Mr. Shaw leaned forward on his chair to look at me. "Meaning what?"

"Meaning that I'm not Tina's guardian angel because I'm too late," I told him. "She already has one."

"Gabe, you say?"

I nodded.

"She's never mentioned him."

"He might just be a friend," I said, "but whoever he is, he scared the holy hell out of Mike, because Leith says that there are no men's clothes left at the apartment and this Gabe gave him and Jackson the third degree until they explained that they were friends of Tina's who had come to check on her. Leith said he was very protective. He liked him a lot."

"I like him a lot, too, and I've never even met the man."

"And Jackson ran a background check on him already, and he came back clean. He's a crane operator at a construction site, and—"

"Ran a background check on him?"

"Yeah, remember me telling you he was a private investigator?"

"Oh yes, that's right. Go on."

"Yeah, so he's in construction and—"

"I'm a foreman. Did you know that?" he asked, cutting me off again.

"No, sir, I didn't." I smiled.

"So you're saying my girl is being looked after by a solid, stable guy who lives upstairs from her."

"Yes, sir, that's what I'm saying."

"Well, that's not too terrible, is it?"

I shook my head. No, it wasn't.

"Your friends were disappointed that they didn't get to beat Mike up, weren't they?"

"Leith was. Jackson likes it when things work out. He believes there's a divine order in everything, and he enjoys the occasional demonstration of that."

"Jackson was the one with the beard?"

"Yeah."

"I liked them both, Malic. They came when you called, and they were all on board to help Tina. You can tell a lot about a man by the company he keeps."

I agreed wholeheartedly.

"Tell me a little about yourself, Malic. My son tells me you own a strip club where only women take off their clothes. How come?"

It made sense that Mr. Shaw and I were finally getting around to having "the talk." He wanted to know all about me and who I was and what I did for a living. He had not given me the third degree as was his fatherly prerogative, and it was time. I was asked what my intentions were toward his son, and I answered honestly... I wanted to keep him. He thought that sounded outstanding, especially since Dylan had told him the exact same thing with a little bit of a twist. His son, it seemed, wanted to make an honest man out of me. He wanted us to get married.

We had been going around and around about marriage. I thought it was dumb. He wanted to do it. We were, as of now, at an impasse. But that he had voiced his desire to his father filled me with happiness. I couldn't stop smiling, which annoyed me to no end.

We drank some more brandy after that, no hot toddy needed, and I got upstairs a little after one. I didn't realize until I heard the giggling from Tina's bedroom that Dylan and his sister were still up. I left them alone, not wanting to disturb them, and went to my room—Dylan's bedroom—and flopped down on the mattress. Minutes later, the door swung open, bringing Dylan with it. I couldn't stifle my chuckle at seeing him lean on the door, not able to correct himself with all the alcohol coursing through his system. It took him a long moment to recover, to straighten up, and when he did, he slammed and locked the door behind him, unsteady on his feet. He was very cute, very drunk, and he looked just decadent in... whatever it was he had on.

"What are you wearing?" I asked before I could help myself.

"You like it?" he asked, grinning playfully, his eyes sparkling with mischief and heat as he came toward me.

It looked like a nightshirt out of some Victorian romance novel, complete with a ruffled neckline. It was made out of some sheer material. It fell to his knees, showing off his long, lean, muscled legs, and with the light behind him, I could see right through it.

"Well?" he prodded because I hadn't answered him. "Do you?"

I coughed. "Do I what?"

His smile was hot and wicked. "Do you like my new nightshirt?"

I more than liked it; I loved it, as was evidenced by my rapidly hardening cock.

"I got it before we left home. I wanted to surprise you on Christmas Eve and beg you to fuck my brains out."

I stayed still with great effort, because he was drunk, and taking advantage of him, even though he belonged to me, was not allowed. Whenever we had sex, he had to be 100 percent willing and ready for me. Drunk, he was off-limits.

"So...." He leered, crossing the room in a wavering line, finally making it to the bed. "What do you say?"

I made a noise in the back of my throat, aching, like I was dying, because I actually was. He was so pretty, so sexy, and all I wanted was to have him under me, begging.

"It's technically Christmas Eve. It's after midnight."

My brain needed to turn on so I could banter with him. Needed to... *God.*

It was agony watching him crawl up the bed to me, nestle against my side, drape those shapely sinewy legs of his over me. He leaned down close so he was gazing deeply into my eyes. He was warm and he smelled like sugar cookies, and the neckline of the nightshirt had fallen off his left shoulder while the hem had ridden up to reveal a line of smooth golden skin.

He was breathtaking.

I felt the tremor of need roll through me as two hands were placed flat on my chest.

"Hey, Malic," he whispered. "I put this on so I could get laid now, okay?"

There was no part of his agenda I was missing.

"I changed when you were downstairs bonding with my dad," he whispered, wriggling against me.

To still him, I smoothed a hand down his side. "You need to sleep it off, baby."

He wasn't listening to me, instead rocking forward, pressing his lean frame to mine, lifting the swell of one round buttock into my hand and touching my face at the same time. He was, of course, naked under the nightshirt, and I couldn't resist grabbing a handful of his tight little ass. When I did, he purred like a giant cat.

"Stop teasing me," I said hoarsely.

"Who's teasing?" He moaned softly, the sultry sound making my blood race as he lifted the nightshirt and his already leaking cock bobbed between us.

It was too much to say no to, so I reached down and took hold of his rigid shaft, squeezing firmly but gently, which elicited the strangled groan I was expecting. His reactions to me were always so hot, so real.

"Can I just ride you? Could you just slick up your cock and shove it up my ass?"

"Baby," I barely got out. "We—"

"Don't I smell good?"

I wanted to devour him; that was how good he smelled.

"Malic." He said my name like no one but him ever did, making it sound sexy and dirty and loving all at the same time. "Show me who I belong to," he said, his fingers tracing over my bottom lip. "You know you want to."

I groaned because it hurt not to move, but I would not debauch my angel. He was much too precious to me.

"Honey." He smiled down at me, the curve of his pouty pink lips making my mouth dry. "There's drunk like I was the first night we met, and then there's that warm buzz you have right before you overdo it." He sighed, hands in my hair. "Right now I feel good, and I just wanna be under you in this bed. Wouldn't that be nice?"

It would, but there was no way. He had passed drunk hours ago, no matter what he said.

"Shouldn't you trust what I tell you? Shouldn't we be equal partners, not you making decisions for me?"

"You're gonna throw logic at me now?" I teased, sliding my hands up his sides, feeling the sinewy muscles through the gauzy material of the nightshirt.

"Malic, lemme have you," he pleaded with his big warm eyes.

"Okay." I made the deal, my hands moving to his face, framing it. "You put your head down, just lie here with me, and if you don't fall asleep in ten minutes, I'll screw your brains out."

"Deal," he said, collapsing on top of me, coiling tight, his lips open under my jaw, kissing softly.

I concentrated on my heartbeat instead of my straining, swollen cock.

"You know, sometimes I come just with you pushing inside of me," he said, exhaling a long, deep breath.

I grunted as I breathed in and out and in again.

"You feel so... good... Malic. I... I...."

"Yes?"

"Malic."

I smiled, the smugness of winning tempered with my desire to be buried inside of him.

He was passed out another minute later, sprawled on top of me, snuggling close even as he drifted off. I had no one to blame but myself for blue balls and realized a cold shower wasn't going to fix the problem.

I got up, tucking him under the covers, and would have started undressing for bed, but my phone rang. It was a number I didn't know.

Normally I didn't answer calls from strangers, but I needed the diversion so I wouldn't attack the alluring creature in the bed. "Hello?"

"Malic!" Brad Darby yelled at the other end. "I need help!"

And since he didn't sound seductive or drunk, pretty much just terrified, I turned and bolted, dropping my phone in the process.

I flew out of the room and was downstairs fast and out through the sliding glass door that led to the back deck. I leaped down to the ground and charged across the Shaws' backyard to the fence that separated their lawn from Brad's. Vaulting over it, I made the high warder arch that we were all capable of that ate up distance faster than anything else but the wormhole. I didn't stop at the back door; I tore it off its hinges and barreled through the kitchen and into the living room.

Suddenly I felt cold and almost wet, like I had walked through fog, but it was thicker and almost slimy, like Jell-O. It felt like I had stepped through a portal of some kind or a barrier….

Damn.

I had been ambushed on Christmas Eve.

"I accept the sacrifice," a voice hissed from behind me. I wanted to run, but it felt as though I was moving through deep mud, wading in it up to my knees. "He's strong. Breaking him will be a pleasure."

"And Joanna?"

"Free."

I was going to say something, but it was like a shade slapped shut, made that snapping sound when you pulled on the cord, and my world went black.

VI

IT WAS dusk, as far as I could tell. I was supposed to be somewhere, but for the life of me I couldn't remember where that was. But I would remember. It would come to me. Walking down the street toward the corner, I wondered if I was supposed to meet friends. As I moved sideways to avoid a man who was on his phone and not watching where he was going, another man plowed into me.

"Sorry," he said, grabbing hold of my arm and then letting me go just as fast, like he had been burned. His eyes were full of fear as his head snapped up to me.

"No worries," I grunted.

"No, I hit you, and I'm sorry."

"It's okay," I said, ready to move by him.

He stepped in front of me, barring my path. "I'm Joshua. Who are you?"

"Dylan," I told him.

He smiled like I had answered correctly, and that made no sense. Why would he...?

"Sorry," he said again and moved away so fast it could almost be called running.

I turned to watch him go and then walked to the entrance of the alley, wondering at the stranger's reaction. Yeah, I was a big scary guy, but just my very ordinary first name should not have been frightening.

Dylan.

There was nothing remotely terrifying about Dylan.

Nothing.

"Dylan!"

A name should be instinctive, but when I was called, I turned because I thought I should. I didn't hear the word and look around. That was wrong, but I wasn't sure why.

A man smiled at me as he rushed forward into my arms. "There you are, baby."

I lifted a hand to keep him back.

"D?"

Gorgeous man, and from the look of him, of his face, his pretty blue eyes, I had hurt him by keeping myself from him.

"Are you okay?"

I searched my mind for his name, but came up empty. "Who are you?"

He was stunned. "You don't know who I am?"

There was nothing familiar.

"I'm Aram, your boyfriend." He smiled timidly. "We're supposed to be Christmas shopping across the street, but you were late, so…." He trailed off, reaching for me only to have me take a step back. "I came looking for you, and here you are."

I was supposed to be somewhere; I did know that.

"Are you okay?"

It was hard to tell. I didn't feel like me.

"Honey?"

The endearment felt hollow.

"Could I please touch you?"

My eyes narrowed, and I took off my black leather faux-fur-lined glove and offered him my right hand.

He hesitated. "What's wrong with you?"

"I thought you wanted to touch me."

His eyes locked on mine. "Tell me what's wrong."

I dropped my hand and stared at him.

"Do you want to go Christmas shopping?" Aram asked.

Christmas. I hated everything about Christmas… being alone….

"Maybe we should just go home," he suggested.

His words were echoing in my head, and it was like there was a pulse that I could hear, a sound, a low thrum that I just couldn't… something about Christmas, but what?

"Dylan?"

Why was there only this? Only a name? And what about Christmas? What was I...?

"Did we make cookies?" I was so confused.

He scoffed. "You? No, baby, but if that's what you want, let's run home right now and make some, 'cause you're scaring the hell out of me."

But he didn't reach for me, and minutes ago he had been ready to run right up to me. Whatever I had said, now he was wary, frightened.

"I didn't mean to scare you."

"I'm not," he assured me. "I may be a little freaked out, but you never scare me."

But it looked like I did. His eyes were not soft; he was waiting for something.

"Dylan?"

Cookies.

Sugar cookies.

That smell of them baking.

"Come on, let's go home."

He didn't take my hand, just walked to the curb and hailed a cab.

Once we were inside, he gave the driver directions and he settled back. We sat apart, on opposite sides of the backseat, and I asked, after a minute, if I could roll the window down.

There was a whir as the glass lowered and a fine mist of spray hit my face.

"It's raining. You should close it," Aram said.

"It's just drizzling," I told him, enjoying the smell of the rain, seeing the wet streets, watching the people hurry to get home.

They all needed to rush home. It was Christmas.

When the driver stopped, we both got out, and Aram stood for a second in front of the building with the doorman.

"Are we going up?" Aram questioned me.

I looked at his face. He was just perfect, the lines of him, the blue of his eyes, and his chiseled features.

"You don't feel like home," I told him.

"What?" He chuckled, reaching for me, but carefully, trying to grab my arm but not at the same time. It was so weird, like he was trying to handle nitroglycerin or something.

"This doesn't feel like home."

"Come upstairs, love," he said softly. "When I'm naked in your bed, it will feel like home."

But I felt.... He wasn't my home, and Dylan wasn't me. Dylan was who I needed to reach. I had to get home.

Sugar cookies.

His skin smelled like sugar cookies.

I couldn't breathe. I staggered away from Aram, walked past the concerned-looking doorman up to the side of the building, and splayed my fingers on the cold limestone. I needed to get home, home where he was. I needed the man with the hooded brown eyes, the full curving lips, and the skin that was smooth under my hands. When he hugged me, there would be soft curls on my face, warm breath down the side of my neck, and hands digging into my back. He would tremble in my arms, press against me, and whimper deep in the back of his throat.

Dylan.

Not me, that wasn't me, that was *him*, but if I could get to Dylan, he would know who I was, because he was mine.

Mine.

Dylan belonged to me and I belonged to him, and that was important because he knew my name and would give it back to me. He knew everything about me because he was my hearth.

And I was a warder.

"Love?"

"You fuck!" I roared at the man, snarling over my shoulder at him, startling the people rushing by as I rounded on him, grabbed him savagely, turned, and slammed him as hard as I could into the wall I had just been leaning against.

He cried out and I saw it then, the shudder that tore through him. The motion took something away from him, and he dimmed a little right in front of me.

"I'm a warder," I told him. He was darkening more and more with every second, and there were beads of sweat breaking out on his forehead because I had my hands on him and it had to hurt.

"I don't know what—"

"Warder," I reminded him and released a pulse of power and energy that made him scream.

There was a deafening roar behind me, and I turned in time to have a creature plow into me. The building I had thought was solid shattered when I was driven back against it. The fall was unexpected, and everything dissolved as I tumbled faster and faster, whole worlds streaking by me in an instant until I just stopped and landed in Brad Darby's living room.

Like coming up from the bottom of a pool and breaking the surface, I was suddenly breathing air that was not heavy and wet, air that I had not even realized was slowly suffocating me. I stumbled forward into the middle of the living room on my hands and knees.

It was surreal, the Christmas tree and the twinkling lights, and Rita, the friendly golden retriever that had met me the other day, was there to welcome me back with a lick on the face.

I sat back on my heels, one hand on my thigh as I caught my breath, petting the dog with the other. The house was quiet except for my heaving breath, the happy whimper of Brad's pet, and the telltale sounds of fucking. At least someone was getting their early Christmas Eve morning freak on.

After a minute, I stood, lurched toward the front door, and grabbed at the doorknob. I was still building my strength back up, so I unlocked it instead of going through it, opening it fast. The chain rattled against the wood with the motion.

"What the hell was that?" I heard from above me.

I got the deadbolt open and the chain off and had the lock on the doorknob undone by the time I heard footsteps on the stairs. Normally I would not have even hurried, but the man had just fed me to what I was guessing was a summoner demon, and I had no idea if that was it or if he was capable of more. I just wanted to get back across the yard to my hearth, to Dylan. I needed to see him and hold him and make sure that my life was exactly as I'd left it.

"Ohmygod!"

I turned and saw Brad Darby at the top of the stairs. He was in sleep shorts and nothing else but his sling, and the man behind him had on sweats and a T-shirt that was inside out.

"Malic!"

I flung the front door open, pushed at the screen, and was outside on his porch seconds later. Being a little unsteady, I tripped down the stairs and landed on my ass on the stone path that led to the street.

"Wait!"

I got my feet under me, turned, and altered my course. I flew forward in a hard, fast run toward the fence that separated his backyard from the Shaws'.

"Malic!"

I leaped, and for a second, my strength failed me and I had that sinking feeling in the pit of my stomach. But then I rose and rose, the arch swelling inside of me before I pushed it out. After landing safely on the back deck of the Shaw house, I went inside, horrified to find I had left the sliding glass door unlocked, and thrilled that the street was so safe that it didn't matter.

Locking myself in, I looked out across the yard. There was no movement, no one was coming after me, and so I walked to the couch and collapsed. I was heaving for breath, and I realized that "exhausted" did not do the feeling justice. I just needed to close my eyes for a second.

Just one… second.

The doorbell startled me, and I yelled without meaning to.

"Oh God, I know, me too," Lily Shaw groaned as she walked by me. She was wearing sunglasses in the house because it was morning and very bright. "Jesus."

I just stared at her.

"I think my head's going to explode," she groaned. "Don't let me drink anymore, all right?"

She was adorable with her hair pulled back in a long curly brown ponytail, hand at her temple as she closed in on the front door, talking to me like we were pals. She explained that she had been up for hours cooking and apologized for not noticing me earlier.

"Sweetheart, do you know that you're covered in dirt?"

"Oh," I said, getting up so fast that I was almost lightheaded. "Mrs. Shaw, I'm so sorry for—"

"Knock it off." She laughed and then winced loudly. "Christ, I seriously need some morphine for this headache."

I had to smile at her.

"And what happened to 'Lil'?" she teased me as she opened the front door. "Huh? Mal?"

There was a family there, and as they came in, loud and boisterous, I walked back to the hallway and hovered there, watching.

Lily was welcoming them—friends and family of her friends and coworkers—over for Christmas Eve brunch. This was another tradition she observed, sort of an open house, where people stopped by, left presents, picked up presents, snacked, and brought a potluck item to share. These were people she worked with, old friends, all the folks both she and her husband shared their lives with, to whom they were not related by blood. There were friends of her kids, too, Dylan's pals and friends of Tina's. She had told me the night before what the day would bring, and seeing the people come in, the women tease her about her Jackie O sunglasses and ask her where her martini was, I was comforted. It was normal, and I really needed that.

Walking upstairs, I turned the corner and saw him standing in the doorway of his bedroom.

"Hey," I called softly, seeing how rumpled he looked, his hair standing up and the way he was squinting suggesting a hangover of Biblical proportions.

"You shit," he snapped. "I was supposed to get laid."

I took a breath and squinted at him, holding myself together.

"What's wrong?"

Instead of answering, I shook my head.

"Malic?" He said my name softly as he took a step forward. "Why are you covered in dirt?"

I cleared my throat. "I had a rough night."

He came toward me, but I took a step back.

"What's going on?"

"I'm filthy and you look so clean and—"

"Malic," he growled, charging across the rest of the space separating us. He leaped at me, and even though I was hurt and a little unsteady, he was still so much smaller that he didn't upset my balance at all.

"Baby, it's okay," I soothed, one hand on his face, the other cupping his ass, holding tight to make sure he didn't fall.

"Tell me what happened."

I leaned in to kiss him instead.

He met me more than halfway, taking possession of my mouth, his tongue pushing for entrance as I smiled against his lips. The man was warm and he smelled like sleep and vanilla, and the way he was whimpering, trying to get closer, I could not have asked for a greater declaration of love and need. I put a hand in his hair to hold him still and used my other arm to wedge him tight against me. I didn't want to let him go.

The kiss went on, and I found myself drowning in him, his breath and his touch, in the feel of his tongue tangling with mine, of his groin pressed into my abdomen.

"Oh God," Dylan finally gasped, breaking the kiss to take a gulp of air, hands on my face. He stared at me with swimming eyes. "Baby, what's wrong? Please tell me, you're scaring the crap out of me, but my brain gets all fuzzy when you kiss me and—"

"Dylan." I sighed, putting him back down, both my hands in his unruly curls. "You just saved my life."

He looked so confused. "How?"

I dragged him back into the bedroom with me and sat him down on the bed while I paced in front of him and told him the whole weird story. When it was done, when he was staring at me with wide eyes, he told me to go take a shower.

"What?" It was not the reaction I had been expecting.

"You need to wash last night off of you, and you need to sleep. So—"

"But it's Christmas Eve. I want to—"

"It's still only what, around eleven in the morning?" he said as he glanced at the digital clock on the nightstand. "You can sleep a few hours and still be up way before dinner, go caroling with my family, and then to church for midnight Mass."

"Dylan, I didn't want any of my crap to mess up your holi—"

"Nothing's messed up. We have lots of time," he promised me, taking hold of my hand, squeezing tight. "Go jump in the shower, and I'll bring you something to eat."

He was being so strange and calm that it was a little frightening. I hurried to do what he asked.

I stayed in the shower longer than I should have, but I was exhausted and needed the heat on my body. When I emerged from the bathroom, opening the door, I wasn't sure for a second if I was dreaming or not.

"Marcus?" I said to my friend.

He was standing there in the hall, holding his hook swords and my spatha. He looked like he was ready for war except for the fact that he was wearing a very expensive designer suit.

"What are you doing here?"

He strode down the hall and smacked me hard in the stomach. I had to bend forward just a little from the impact. "Yes, it's really me, and yes, I'm really here. Why in the world would you not call me?"

"Could you not hit me?"

"Why, I repeat, did you not call me?"

"You're in Kentucky with Joe, and I—"

"For crissakes, Malic," he snapped irritably. "Dylan said you thought it was a summoner demon?"

He looked really good, and just seeing him, I felt better. Just looking at him, for me, for all of those in his clutch, brought on a sense of well-being that was really remarkable.

"Mal?"

"Thank you for coming."

"I couldn't sense you at all," he told me, and I heard the worry in his voice. "Normally I can, and I've been trying to get ahold of you all morning, so when Dylan called, I came."

I reached out and put a hand on his shoulder. If it were anyone else besides Marcus, any other warder, I would have held up and held it together, shown no weakness. The only one we were all honest with, the only one we showed our cards to, was Marcus. For the others it was newer, the realization of what they did without thought; for him and me, it was how it had always been. The trust had always been understood. Best friends from the first day I ever laid eyes on him. So because it was him, my anchor, I did what I only ever did with Dylan: I showed him the need in me. I let him see.

He stepped close, and even though all I was wearing was a towel and he was wearing a Prada suit, I grabbed him. I leaned—and I never did that, but my head went down on his shoulder—and I breathed. Only Marcus could actually support my weight when I gave it to him. At six foot six, covered in hard muscle, he made you think linebacker, not lawyer.

"So," he said after a long minute, stepping back at the same time I let him go. "You were on a different plane?"

I nodded because he didn't have to ask me if I was okay; he just talked like everything was fine and normal and good.

"That's why I couldn't feel your presence at all even when I concentrated."

"Yeah, but I wasn't deep enough for the time shift to start."

"When did you go in?"

"Sometime last night."

"You feel all right?" he asked, looking me over. "What did it do to you?"

"It washed my memory."

He smiled. "But you're a warder who has a hearth. A demon can't take the memory of a hearth. It's buried too deep."

"I had no idea that I could never forget his name."

"The demon probably thought his name was yours. That's how dear it is, how deep inside it's buried."

I just stared. "Is that how it is with all hearths and warders?"

He nodded, smiling gently, and I knew he was thinking about Joe. *Joe.*

"Aww, shit," I groaned. "Just when the man started to like me."

His smile got bigger. "He likes you."

"He's gonna hate me. I take you away from him on Christmas Eve? I'll be lucky if he ever speaks to me again."

For years, Joe, Marcus's hearth, had disliked me because he had thought I had designs on Marcus. Little did he know that the only designs I had were brotherly, not carnal. When I had found Dylan the year before, it had finally built a bridge between us that taking Marcus away from him at Christmas had probably torn down.

"I was worried," he told me. "Joe's the one who said to come, find out what was wrong, and report back. How Joe felt before, that's over and done. He cares for you; he cares for Dylan. Don't second-guess him. He won't like it."

I nodded because, just a little, I was afraid of Joe. We all were. It wasn't in a fear of his temper kind of way or a fear that he would or could hurt me kind of way, but more in a *Jesus Christ, don't let me disappoint him* way that really made no sense. We all wanted the man to be happy with us, and we all wanted his approval for reasons that were completely unexplainable.

"Malic."

I realized that my mind had been drifting. "Sorry, what?"

"Put on some clothes, and I'll meet you downstairs so we can talk."

"Did you meet Dylan's family already?"

"Yes, your boyfriend introduced me."

I tipped my head at the weapons in his hand. "How did you explain those?"

"I didn't. I left them on the roof when I got here and just now went out the window in the master bedroom and brought them in."

"Why are you carrying them around?"

"I don't know where to hide them, but because we don't know what we're dealing with, I don't want to run the risk of not being able to reach them."

"That makes sense."

"So where?"

"Give them to me. I'll put them back in Dylan's room in his closet."

He passed me his hook swords and my spatha. "No one goes in there but you and him?"

"'Course."

"Okay, I don't know." He put his hands up. "He's still a teenager, you know."

I flipped him off. "He's twenty now, asshole."

"Sorry, I stand corrected."

"You're being a dick."

He waggled his eyebrows.

"You know, Dylan wants me to rest," I pointed out.

"Well, you need to eat first, and then we need to go over and see this guy who thought trading a warder to a summoner demon was a good idea."

"He had no idea I was a warder," I told him. "I'm sure of it."

"Doesn't change the fact that if you had been weaker, I would have never seen you again."

He had a point.

"We're going over there."

"Yes, sir," I teased.

"It's not an order," he assured me.

"Of course it's not." I smiled, but as he left me, taking the stairs down, I had a moment to remember a conversation I'd had with our fellow warder Ryan the week before.

He and I had been picking up Marcus to clear a nest of verdant demons, and we were waiting outside for him.

"Have you noticed how much he's changed lately?"

I turned slowly to look at my former lover, fellow warder, and friend. "Who? Marcus?"

"Yeah."

I nodded. "Yeah, he's definitely become the leader."

"You know, I thought for a while that I would do it, become sentinel after Jael."

"You'd make a good one."

He shrugged. "I get mad fast, and that's not good. You rush in—"

"Not always," I defended myself.

"Always," he assured me. "And Leith thinks too much, and Jackson... Jacks is good, except that his power isn't increasing. Have you noticed that?"

"Yeah, I have noticed that."

"It's Raph, I think," he told me. "One of the things a warder does is gain strength to protect his hearth, and the longer the hearth and warder are together, the more power the warder gains, as he has more and more and more to lose."

"Sure. First there's just the hearth, and then there's the hearth and the home they make, and then the hearth's family and then children...."

"Exactly," he agreed. "But with Raph, he can protect himself, so Jackson's power isn't increasing to take care of him."

"But he doesn't need to; he's got an equal in Raph. That's kind of nice."

Ryan nodded. "But that does not make him a good candidate to be sentinel."

"Yeah, but let's not take away that Jackson is still one of the strongest warders I know."

"No, no, I know, but still."

"Marcus never wanted to be sentinel because he worries so much about losing anyone that he could never make the hard decisions."

"But now he knows he doesn't have to." Ryan exhaled deeply. "Now he knows, after that last stunt he pulled where he saved all of us and nearly died, that he can do all the sacrificing to keep us safe and not lose anyone."

"Yeah, that's great—the king rushing out in the middle of the battlefield to save his knight. That's fuckin' brilliant."

Ryan chuckled. "Marcus will be sentinel after Jael. There's no doubt in my mind."

"And we'll have to guard his ass all the time to make sure he doesn't get himself killed."

"I'll do it." Ryan smiled his dazzler up at me.

"Me too," I assured him.

"Malic?"

Again my mind had been drifting, but this time I was looking at Dylan and not Marcus.

"Hey." I took a breath. "I'll be down in—"

"What if you hadn't been able to get back to me?"

It took me a second to realize that he was shaking. "You know that would never happen."

"How—" He cleared his throat, and I saw it then, the tears welling in his eyes. "—do you know?"

"Because I came back because of you," I told him, striding forward, reaching him, hands in his hair, on his face as he stood there, eyes closed, his face lifted to me.

"Malic," he whimpered, "I can't lose you. I just got everything I wanted and— "

"Baby." I sighed, my breath on his skin making him shiver. "You are stuck with me forever if that's what you want."

"That's what I want," he told me, eyes fluttering open as he stared up at me. "So marry me."

Not again, I thought, and I groaned.

Instant squint as he pulled back, visibly annoyed. "What's with that look?"

"Just, really? I still can't believe you said that to your father."

"What? That I want to marry you?"

"Yeah."

"But I do want to marry you."

"Which is fine, but your dad was happy with what I said."

"What did you say?"

"I said that I wanted to keep you."

"Like a pet."

"Oh for crissakes, not like a pet! You know what I meant. I want you to stay with me forever, and I will love you and take care of you."

"Like a pet."

I growled at him. "I'm gonna kill you."

He scowled.

"Your father knows my intentions are honorable."

"Does he?"

"Of course."

"I want a ring."

He had to be kidding.

"I'm not kidding."

It was insane how well the man could read my mind. "You wanna get married and you want a ring."

"Yes."

"Why?"

Hands on his hips. "Because I love you."

"Fine, love me, but weddings are for straight people. We'll just make a promise and—"

"I want to make a promise in front of our friends."

"Dylan—"

"And a judge."

"That's ridiculous."

"Joe and Marcus did it."

"Joe and Marcus are both sentimental saps. We're not."

"Go downstairs and tell him to his face that he's a sap."

I strode to the top of the stairs, abandoned all propriety and pretense of adulthood, and yelled down the stairs at Marcus.

"What?" he barked when he appeared on the bottom step.

"I think marriage is stupid."

"I think you're stupid," he told me before he walked away.

I turned back to look at Dylan.

"I want to get married," he insisted.

"No."

"I want to be Dylan Sunden."

Oh God.

"Malic?"

Of all the things he could have said, voicing his desire to share my last name, the name my father had always told me meant the world to him when my mother had taken it, was the one thing that would change my mind.

"Oh." His smile was luminous, his eyes sparkling with mischief and happiness at the same time. "Somebody liked the sound of that."

I took a breath.

"Dylan Sunden."

"Your father...." I coughed. "Shaw is his name. You should never let Shaw go."

"But I could let go of Walter." He waggled his eyebrows, coming closer. "And then Shaw could be my middle name, and think how literary I'd sound. Dylan Shaw *Sunden*."

What the hell was up with names? Just Dylan's had saved me, and now simply thinking about him sharing mine—permanently.... People got divorced all the time, every day, so why did just the thought of him having my name make my heart hurt?

"Malic."

I had enough time to look up before he launched himself at me.

"I love you so much," he told me before he kissed me senseless.

My hands slid over the curve of his ass as he made love to my mouth. It was made for me, the perfect round globes made to be stroked and squeezed, and the way he moaned deeply into my mouth made me whimper in reply. I was a heartbeat from dragging him into the bedroom when he broke the kiss to look at me with clouded eyes.

"Baby," he said, and his voice was full of aching, drugging need. "Let's go downstairs, eat, and then take Marcus and go over to Brad Darby's house, okay? I want you to kill the demon that tried to take you away from me, and then I want to watch you punch Brad out."

I squinted at him.

"What? I can't be petty?"

"People." We both turned, and there was Marcus, scowling at us. "Let's eat."

He left before I could apologize for mauling my hearth when we were kind of in a time crunch to get him back to his own mate and his own Christmas.

"He's getting really bossy," Dylan grunted, tightening his arms and legs around me so he was plastered against my front. "Have you noticed that?"

LILY SHAW was completely charmed by Marcus Roth. She stammered a little, she made sure his plate stayed full, and she disappeared for ten minutes and came back with makeup on. Dylan could not stop staring at her.

"What?"

"I have never seen my mother act like such a girl," he told me, shock all over his face. "She's a mother; she's not supposed to do that."

"Do what? Get flustered when a handsome man is in her house?"

"Yeah." He was indignant. "What is that?"

I laughed, reached out, and put my hand on his cheek. He leaned into the caress.

"It's weird," he groused under his breath.

Marcus was his normal charming self, and after a few minutes, some of the other women—Dylan's parents' coworkers—were also hovering close to talk to him. When Lily blushed over a compliment he gave her, Dylan made a gagging noise in the back of his throat.

Watching him, how revolted he was, I was having the best day since I'd gotten there.

After brunch, Marcus insisted on cleaning up the dishes, and since not only was the man hot but also courteous and charming, Lily was basically attached to his hip. And the thing about the man was not that he was like Ryan or Leith or even Jackson—you didn't immediately notice that he was beautiful. What you noticed was his height and his build, and then slowly you heard his voice, felt the presence of a man who could protect you, and finally realized that he was all you needed. It was my conclusion, and I had asked Joe if that was how it had been for him.

"No." He had grinned at me. "I heard his laugh and had to have him."

The laugh was good too.

"And I wasn't taking no for an answer."

My impression was that Joe always got what he wanted. The man was a force of nature.

When Marcus finally joined me on the back porch, I asked him if he was done flirting with all the women in the house.

"You're funny."

The sarcasm was not lost on me. "You know Joe would be jealous if he were here."

The look I got made me spit out my water.

"Joseph is never jealous," he assured me, looking around. "He knows... he's it."

I had no doubt about that.

"Where are my swords?" he asked me since I had been in charge of smuggling our weapons out of the house.

I tipped my head toward the edge of the porch beside the potted pine that the Shaws decorated as their outdoor Christmas tree.

Marcus retrieved both his swords and my one, passing me my scabbard as he attached his across his back. I noticed that even with that task done, he seemed distracted.

"What are you looking for?"

"Ry."

"What?"

"Ryan was supposed to be here to... oh."

I felt the icy wind then, the vortex of a warder, and if anyone had been outside to look, they would not have seen a barrier go up, but they would have felt it. If a warder traveled into a closed space, everything sealed. Every lock, every window would shut tight until the warder stepped from the wormhole and saw clearly where they were. In a wide open area, a barrier was raised until the warder could safely arrive, and as soon as he or she got their bearings, the barrier dissipated.

Marcus and I both watched as a very annoyed-looking Ryan Dean stepped from what looked like a funnel of wind completely untouched, as though he had just come from a photo shoot. Each and every artfully styled strand of hair was in place. The only odd thing about his appearance at all was the presence of the katana that he was holding.

"Where's the house?" he barked, and Marcus as I heard the door slide open behind me.

"You don't have to yell at me. I told you that Jackson could have come," Marcus called back.

"Jackson already came once, and so did Leith, so you know it's bullshit to ask them to come again! I'm here, let's go already!"

"What's wrong?" Dylan asked as he leaned in beside me. "Why's Ryan mad?"

"Merry Christmas to you too, asshole!" I shouted before turning to look at Dylan, putting my hand in his hair and dragging it back from his face.

"Malic," my boyfriend scolded gently as he chuckled, leaning into my caress like a big cat.

"Fuck you, Malic. I wanna go back to my new loft and be with my boyfriend and my family!"

"Ryan!" Dylan scolded my fellow warder.

I gave my attention back to the snarling, pissed-off man in the middle of the yard.

"I want to go home!" he snarled at me and Marcus.

It was Julian's family. Ryan, just like every warder in the world, was an orphan. But the fact that he thought of them like his family… that was nice.

"Now!" he ordered us. "Julian's mother and I are supposed to be cooking in two hours. Let's go."

"It's not Malic's fault!" Dylan defended me.

"I will kill you all if we don't go already!"

"I'm coming too," Dylan told him, shifting like he was going to walk down the stairs.

"The hell you are!" Ryan roared, pointing. "Demon hunting is no place for a hearth!"

"You took Julian with you," Dylan volleyed back. "He told me!"

Before Ryan's brain could explode, Marcus put a hand up for him and then turned to Dylan.

"Listen to me," he said softly, other hand on Dylan's shoulder. "When Ryan took Julian, that was him and Malic just patrolling, and even then it almost went bad. This is Malic's first Christmas with your family, and it finally, now, took a turn for the better. Does killing their son seem like a good gift for your parents? Even putting their son in danger is not a good idea. Put yourself in Malic's shoes, Dylan. What would you do if the roles were reversed?"

"I want to see Brad Darby get hit," he told my friend. "He deserves it."

"And I understand about revenge," he assured Dylan. "Joe has a cousin, Kurt, who nearly drowned him when he was young, and after I met him, I was thinking that I would enjoy beating the crap out of him."

"And? Did you?"

He shook his head. "I didn't because it's over and done. Joe lived, and Kurt knowing for the rest of his life what he did is revenge enough. He lost Joe as a person in his life that day, and in my estimation, that's a real tragedy. For Brad there on the other side of your property, what he did was try and pay his debt to this demon, whatever that is, with Malic. Now, we don't know yet what he paid the demon for, but we'll find out. I assure you that whatever we find out, we'll let you know, but all of us need all of our hearths safe at all times or we cease to be able to function."

Dylan bit his bottom lip as he stared up into Marcus's face.

"Please, honey, just stay here," he said, his hand lifting to Dylan's face. My boyfriend nodded fast, and I found that I could breathe again. Marcus gave him a final pat and then left him. I bent and kissed Dylan and told him to stay put. Dylan didn't move, but I saw how tight he was holding onto the railing, his knuckles white as I descended the stairs after Marcus.

As soon as we stepped onto the grass, Ryan yelled at me for directions.

"It's right there." I pointed across the backyard to Brad Darby's house. "God, you're an ass!"

He whirled around and started charging over the lawn toward the fence that separated the Shaw property from Brad's.

"You didn't have to come at all," I told Ryan when we caught up with him. "Marcus and I can handle this."

"If it's really a summoner demon, one warder has to guard the passage back, Malic, while the other two push through the barrier and face the demon."

"Yeah, but—"

"I would never forgive myself if I let you or Marcus down," he told me solemnly. "But that so doesn't make me any less pissed that on Christmas Eve you are dealing with this bullshit and therefore so am I."

"Ry—"

"It's bullshit!" he growled, levitating over the fence instead of climbing or vaulting.

"Holy crap." I looked at Marcus.

"I told you," he said as he and I both jumped the fence. "He and Leith are powering up, and I gotta wonder for what."

I chuckled. "What? You're thinking that they're getting stronger to fight some epic battle?"

"Could be."

"You think maybe they're just powering up because it's time or because they can?"

"Nothing is ever that simple."

And he was right.

We came around the side of Brad Darby's porch, and I heard Ryan groan.

"What?"

He tipped his head at the large inflatable snowman. "It's creepy."

I turned to look. "You fight demons, and the snowman is creepy?"

"Yeah, it's weird," he said, stamping up the stairs before he pounded on the front door.

No answer.

He knocked again, and there was still no response even though we could hear a low wail coming from behind the door.

I was going to break it down, charge it and slam it under my weight and strength, but Ryan put both his hands up, and the door flew off its hinges.

"Shit," I remarked. "That's impressive."

"Theatrics," Marcus told me. "But I—oh crap."

Moving forward, we all saw the hole at once. There, not ten feet from Brad Darby's front door, was what looked like a funnel cloud sucking everything out of the room. It would have been funny seeing Brad, with his one good arm, and his fuck buddy holding onto the light fixtures hanging from the vaulted ceiling, but their faces were a study in terror. It was like the room had been tipped on its side so that the two men and the dog were above the twister, ready to be sucked down into it. I was mostly impressed by the dog, who was holding on with her teeth to the pant leg of Brad's sweats, her jaw clamped down.

"Help us!" Brad's friend cried.

"Help!" Brad screamed.

I found myself more irritated than anything else and amazed, as I often was, by what should not have been possible but was.

In theory, one room could not be the only one affected by a tornado. It was like the little girl's room in the movie *Poltergeist*: just not possible. But in front of me, Brad and his date and his dog were all holding on for dear life so they wouldn't get sucked into the void. It was just so strange even though I had been looking at the same kind of thing since I was sixteen years old.

Marcus spoke words in Latin, and all three of us took a step back at the same time.

The funnel collapsed and the area flipped back, but while it was in the process of righting itself, everything fell. It was like the room had been in the dryer. It had all been tumbled. It was not going to be ready for Brad's family to visit; even the Christmas tree itself was a wash.

We walked into the room as the couch crushed the TV.

Marcus and Ryan both winced, and Brad and his friend started screaming.

"Looks like there was a rave in here." Ryan smiled for the first time since he had arrived. He bent down to one knee as Rita bolted for him.

Dogs were funny; they were good and loyal until they understood in some epic way that you were not the alpha in their life anymore because you could not protect them. An alpha that could not be head of the pack was useless to them. Rita stood in the circle of Ryan's arms, her nose under his chin, and trembled.

"You guys can kill a collector demon alone, right?" he asked.

"Now that I know what it is," I said, gesturing around to indicate the room. "Now that I know it's just a collector. Of course."

A summoner demon would never have revealed itself with a display like the twister in the middle of Brad's living room. Summoner demons dragged souls to hell, slowly made you insane, and fed off that emotion of the terrifying decay of a fraying mind. When you were completely gone, you were devoured by whatever creatures you were thrown to. A summoner demon was terrifying and required three warders to kill, as Ryan had said earlier. Marcus, Ryan, and I had killed many. But this was not that kind of demon, as evidenced by the hokey display from a low-budget horror flick. We were dealing with a collector, and that was all.

I felt stupid. "I can kill this myself," I told Marcus. "I feel like an ass dragging you and Ry here for this."

"No," Ryan snapped. "You still need two, Malic. There should always be two warders, and if a collector gets the jump on you—"

"Like this one did by pulling you through a barrier and onto another plane," Marcus said, "then it's bad news. You never, ever, hunt alone."

"Never," Ryan echoed.

Marcus nodded.

"But since it's a collector demon," Ryan said, rising from the floor, Rita beside him, making sure he put no distance between them, "I'm going home."

"What am I, chopped liver?" I asked the dog, who was obviously preparing to follow Ryan Dean to the ends of the earth. "You saw me first."

Her head tipped sideways like she didn't understand the question.

"You like pretty boys too, huh?" I teased her.

Her tail started wagging, but she didn't move. My guess was that she wouldn't ever be moving from the man's side.

"I hope Julian likes dogs," I told him.

"Julian likes all animals," he said. "The man was raised on a farm, after all."

"He was?"

Ryan nodded, his smile getting even bigger now that he was talking about his hearth.

"Who the fuck are you guys?" Brad's friend roared.

We all looked over at him standing there, shivering, eyes glazed, staring.

"Ohmygod, what happened?" A woman had walked in through the open door, a man with her. He was holding her hand.

Ryan stepped sideways so that his back was to us and then opened his hand. She had startled him, and Ryan hated to ever be caught off guard. The front door lifted from where it had fallen and slammed into place. Everyone jumped except me, Marcus, and Rita. I understood then why the dog had chosen Ryan: she could tell who the strongest guy in the room was, and she wasn't about to be wrong twice in choosing an alpha.

"Oh no," the woman gasped, hand over her mouth. "Brad, what did you do?"

He moved quickly across the destruction that was now his living room and grabbed the woman with his one good arm. She was obviously his sister, as they looked so much alike. His hand on her arm, he looked down into her eyes.

"The demon gave me until midnight last night to find another sacrifice, or he was taking you away, Jo. I couldn't let that happen. After all you've been through, after finally beating the cancer... I just... I didn't know what to do."

He bent his head forward, into her shoulder, and sobbed. She put her hand on the nape of his neck and gently stroked, crooning at the same time, promising him that everything would be all right.

"Hello." Marcus's deep baritone turned every eye on him. "The demon is just regrouping; he will be back in a moment, so before he gets here, I need to know if I'm feeding you to it"—he stared at Brad—"or if I'm going to save you."

And of course he would save Brad—we were not in the practice of feeding humans to demons—but if they thought he would, that made for some intense conversation.

As it turned out, Joanna, Brad's sister, had been diagnosed with stage four stomach cancer. They had done everything but had eventually turned to their aunt, their deceased mother's sister, for help. She had performed a ritual and traded her life for Joanna's. It was a selfless act, or so it seemed. Unfortunately, their aunt was a practitioner of dark magic and had just wanted to return to one of the planes of hell. Tricking a collector demon had been easy, but when he discovered the ruse, it had been hard to remedy. He wanted a human soul for curing Joanna, not a tainted creature who was no longer in possession of one.

The demon had returned to Brad and given him an ultimatum: Joanna could return to hell with him, Brad could, or a sacrifice could be presented to him. Brad had panicked because he loved his sister, but he was terrified of trading his life for hers, and then he had thought about what was behind door number three.

"Okay." I sighed. "At least I understand now."

"I'm so sorry," he said, his eyes raw with pain. "I didn't know what to do, and I knew you'd come to help, and I preyed on your weakness... God, Malic, I'm so sorry."

"You preyed on his bravery, on his goodness," Marcus corrected him. "It's not weak to want to help, to want to save people."

"I can't tell you how sorry I am."

Ryan scoffed. "You're just sorry it didn't work, but lucky for you it didn't, or we would be here in a much different capacity."

"What do you mean?"

"Never mind. Malic's here," Ryan told him, turning toward the door, traipsing through the rubble. "And you have a small problem, not a big one. Oh, I'm taking your dog, by the way."

"What?" Brad yelped.

"I'll see you two at home," Ryan yelled back to Marcus and me. "Jules and I will be at the hotel for New Year's if I don't see you before."

It was funny, the confused look on Brad's face as Ryan did the neat trick again and made the front door fly across Brad's front yard. We all saw the funnel of wind that looked so different from the vortex the demon had raised: smaller, tighter, more directed.

Ryan stepped into it, turned, and called Rita. I would have thought she would hesitate—she was a dog, after all—but that was perhaps her greatest strength. She didn't question. Ryan was her new alpha, so she charged after him. They disappeared a second later.

"Holy shit." The man who had come in with Joanna was finally freaked out enough to speak. "What the fuck is going on?"

We all heard it then, the fluttering of wings before a flying beast about the size of a rhinoceros appeared out of thin air. It looked like a pterodactyl—its jaws were huge, and the high-pitched wail was deafening. Marcus and I both leaped back. The creature missed us both but turned fast, like a coiled snake, twisting around to strike at us a second time.

We had been fighting together so long, we were so synchronized, that the minute Marcus leaped into the air, I lunged forward with my spatha. The demon, pivoting away from me, was caught in Marcus's descent, pinned to the varnished wooden floor of Brad's living room by the twin hook swords my friend carried. I turned and brought the spatha down across its neck, cleanly severing the enormous head from the body. There was a geyser of blood that sprayed everything—me, the walls, the floor—before the ground began to shift under us.

When a warder killed a demon, a black hole materialized beneath us, a portal to a hell dimension opening up to receive the slain. I stepped behind the carcass, Marcus jumped back, and the demon was sucked through the floor and disappeared. All that remained was the splatter of blood, Normally it was small; in this case….

Marcus smiled, waggling his eyebrows. "Nothing says Christmas like dead demon."

I flicked my hand, and blood and gore fell in a soggy clump to the floor. It made that wet gloppy noise as it puddled close to my feet.

"Gross." Marcus chuckled.

"How are you not covered in demon?"

"I jumped free of the splatter zone, man," he teased, touching the lapel of his suit. "This is Prada, you know."

I rolled my eyes before I turned to Brad, his sister, her boyfriend—I still wasn't positive about that and didn't care enough to ask—and Brad's fuck buddy. "You need one of those power washers,"

I said, gesturing to the gore on the walls, the mantle, and the staircase. "Or a new house."

"You killed the demon." Joanna's eyes were huge as she stared at us. "Won't another one just come in its—"

"No," Marcus cut her off. "The covenant is only with one creature. The debt is a singular transaction. None other will ever come."

"But I got a miracle from that demon," she told him. "I have to pay my debt."

"We don't pay debts to demons," I said flatly.

"But neither do we normally make deals with demons in the first place," Marcus clarified.

"I don't know how to—I don't... thank you."

It wasn't her fault—or it was, but wasn't. It was their aunt's fault for putting the horrific cycle in motion. I didn't really care; I just wanted to take a shower.

"I feel soggy," I said to Marcus as we walked toward the opening where the front door used to be. As I moved, I made a wet squelching noise that made my friend smile.

"You look like hell," he said, chuckling low as he made a show of allowing me out first.

Every now and then warders lost pieces of clothing to the hunt, and I suspected that my boots were goners. "I bet I look like I've been dipped in forty-weight."

"You look like a whale blew up on you."

I made a noise of disgust as I walked toward the edge of the porch with him.

"Malic!"

I turned, and Dylan was there.

"Don't come near me," I warned. "I'm covered in demon guts, and I don't want it on you."

He never listened to me.

Bolting forward, he leaped, and I had to catch him so he wouldn't fall. Safe in my embrace, he hugged me tight with arms and legs, squirming for closeness as he looked into my face.

"You scared me to death! Did you hit Brad?"

"No, but look," I said, walking back to the doorway with him. Inside, the three people—I wasn't sure where the bed warmer had gone—were surveying the damage to the one room for the first time. Realization that Christmas at Brad's house was impossible was finally dawning.

"Oh." Dylan's smile was radiant, and everyone heard the happiness in his voice. "Awesome."

"My home is destroyed," Brad cried as the man who had been with him, his fuck buddy, squeezed by me, careful not to get any of the blood that covered me on him. He had obviously ducked back upstairs for a second to grab his clothes and was now running for the hills. Not that I could blame him. He bolted down the steps, yelling at Brad to never, ever, call him again.

Dylan and I both watched him run and then turned back to the remaining three people in the room that looked like it belonged in a slaughterhouse.

"How am I going to explain this to my family?"

"You need a power washer," Dylan suggested, logically.

I chuckled over the comment.

"What?" my hearth asked, turning to look at me.

"That's exactly what I said."

Dylan laughed softly. "Walk me back to my house so I can hose you off."

"Wait," Marcus said, striding by us, walking through the rubble of the living room and up to Brad.

I wasn't sure where he was going. "What're you—"

Marcus nailed Brad on the jaw, sending him crashing down over what remained of his coffee table. It was only hard enough to stun him—Marcus didn't use a quarter of his full power—but still, it was scary.

"Brad!" his sister Joanna yelled. The boyfriend yelled, too, as he scrambled over to them. He stepped in front of Marcus, which was pretty brave; I gave him a lot of credit even though he blanched as he did it.

"Don't even look in the direction of the Shaw house," Marcus warned, shoving the boyfriend out of the way easily so he could hover threateningly over Brad. "Don't speak to them, don't go over to borrow something—in fact, I would move as soon as possible." He took a breath. "You fucked with my brother because he wouldn't fuck you, you asshole piece of shit. I should drop you into a small dark place and let you be eaten alive."

All three people had tears in their eyes, all were shaking, all terrified. Even though I felt some pity for Joanna and her boyfriend, it wasn't enough that I was going to call Marcus back to me.

"If I ever hear from Dylan that you spoke to him, his folks, his sister, or any of their friends... you're dead."

They stared at Marcus as he turned and stalked back to Dylan and me. On the porch, Dylan thanked him.

"No thanks necessary." Marcus grinned, heading down the steps as I followed with my hearth still in my arms.

"So you'd really go back and kill a man?" I teased my friend.

"No, Mal, you know I don't kill people." Marcus sighed deeply. "But he doesn't."

And he was right.

VII

MARCUS went inside and grabbed towels from the upstairs bathroom for us, telling Lily, he recounted, that Dylan and I had both fallen into mud outside. She probably would have questioned the story from anyone else, but this was Marcus smiling down at her from his towering height, and she was smitten with him. I was certain, when he hugged her good-bye, that she had shivered just a little. Once he was back outside with us, he gave me a head tip as Dylan prepared to hose me off around the side of the house. He wasn't about to hug me, or my hearth. The suit was expensive after all. We watched him as he stepped into the vortex and vanished.

Dylan had just stripped out of his blood-smeared clothes—it was only the fronts that were stained, and the handprints on the seat of his jeans—before proceeding to hose me off. Just before I froze to death, he quit, pronouncing me gore-free, and then bundled up both sets of clothes and ran them back to the garbage can in the garage. I was shivering when he came back, but so was he, and I yelled at him to get his ass inside. He was laughing as he led me through the living room. His father reminded me that it was too cold to be running through the sprinklers outside in the yard.

"You're a riot, Jeff," I called to him from the stairs.

"I know," he said, sounding like he had amused himself.

"I don't know about this being accepted into the family thing," I grumbled as I followed Dylan, trudging behind him.

He was still chuckling and walked into the bathroom before me, closing and locking the door behind us. I watched him turn on the hot water and then drop the dirty towel he had used as a covering on the floor. Seeing the lean, muscular frame made my stomach flip over. It was always a pleasure to see Dylan naked.

"Come here," he said, opening the frosted glass door and stepping into the shower under the spray.

I peeled the cold wet towel off, my pale skin covered in goose bumps underneath.

When I stepped into the cubicle with him, he plastered his warm body to mine.

"Oh fuck, you feel nice," I said, running my hands all over him, his hair, his face, down his back to his ass.

He wiggled free then turned me around and pushed me forward against the wall. I stood there, face pressed to the sweating tile as I felt a mesh sponge glide over my back. It felt good. The closeness, his hands on me, scrubbing, soaping, and his grip on my arms, pushing me down, made me smile.

When I was on my knees, he washed my hair, but with my face inches from his groin, I could not resist temptation. Leaning forward, I took the length of him down the back of my throat.

"Oh God!"

He convulsed with pleasure as I began to suck and stroke him with my tongue, my hands on his hips as I devoured him.

"Malic, I don't wanna come," he whined, pulling back, wriggling away from me, out of the shower in seconds.

I stood, smiling, and washed myself off, letting the whole experience with Brad Darby and the demon go, keeping only the love of my hearth and the support of my friends with me.

There was the snick of the magnetic latch on the door, and when I turned, a lube-slicked hand wrapped around my cock.

"You need to shower." I smiled as he stroked me. "And that is just gonna wash off, you know."

"Not right away," he told me, adding more to my dick from the bottle of lube he'd brought back from the hamper he'd hidden it in the day we arrived.

"Baby—"

"Shut up," he commanded me, closing the bottle, letting it fall to the floor before he looked up at me. "Pick me up and fuck me against the wall."

"Love—"

"Malic!" he yelled, and I realized how close he was to falling apart. "I need you."

I grabbed him, lifted him, and draped his knees over my arms as I pressed him back against the tiled wall.

"Oh, baby, please."

He was trembling with need, and when I pushed in, drove up into him with one hard thrust, he moaned my name.

"Did I hurt—"

"Fuck, Malic, you feel so good. I can feel your cock get harder and thicker, and the stretch is—fuck! How do you get my gland every... oh." He whimpered in the back of his throat.

He was so beautiful, so hot, so drugged with pleasure that he made my heart hammer in my chest. "I don't think I can... stop."

"Why the hell would you stop?" he moaned, writhing on the wall, in my hands. "Fuck me, Malic. Fill me up. I need to know you're safe and strong. I need to know who I belong to."

He was so tight, and as my cock throbbed inside of him, his muscles rippled around me, the suction fierce as I was pulled in deeper. When I eased out a fraction only to sheathe myself fully inside, his fingers dug into my back as he lifted his head for a kiss.

I devoured his mouth, taking possession, and my tongue tangled with his as I began to pound into him, the strokes hammering and hard.

He broke the kiss to breathe, head back in ecstasy as I leaned in and sucked and licked and kissed his throat, leaving the marks I knew he craved.

When he was panting, I fisted his dripping cock in my hand and stroked him as he screamed my name. Seconds later he spurted over my abdomen, the muscles in his ass clamping down so hard, spasming around me, that I came hard, buried inside of him, flooding his channel, still thrusting into him as I shuddered through my orgasm.

It took long minutes to recover, but when I did, when he did, I lifted him gently off my shaft and put him on his feet. I washed him, his hair, gently cleaned him up, and then lifted him again, this time carrying him out onto the thick rug. I was still holding onto him, afraid, from his flushed skin and glazed eyes, that he would faint.

"You okay?" I asked him, making sure he could stand before I darted to the window and opened it. The icy air blew in, and I watched him revive a little. "You look like you're gonna pass out."

He purred, and I saw his eyes flutter.

"Shit," I groaned, but I made it to him before his eyes closed and he hit the floor.

The man had swooned, and holding him in my arms, I had a minute of fear wash through me. What if he....

"Malic," he murmured, coming around that fast. "Need water, need to cool down, need to lie down... need you to suck my dick."

"That last one is crap," I growled, not wanting to put him down, but not wanting to walk out of the bathroom naked with an equally bare-assed Dylan in my arms.

"Love to watch you do it." He sighed, and I watched, amazed, as his dick began to harden again.

"Jesus, that recovery time is ridiculous."

"Twenty," he cackled. "Put me down. We need towels."

He was steady on his feet, the cool air from the window helping, and when we were both covered, we made a dash for the bedroom.

Inside, he locked the door, pulled the towel off, and ordered me to get on my knees.

"You need to eat something and drink something," I told him even as I realized how hard his cock was.

"No." His heavy-lidded eyes were on me. "I want to watch you suck my dick."

I went to my knees, because, *really*, whatever he wanted.

"Open your mouth," he told me, grabbing his cock like he never did, sliding the leaking end across my closed lips.

It was hot, hearing him make demands, seeing the need in his eyes, feeling his fingers thread into my hair and then fist tight.

I opened and he slid in, pressing back so hard I almost gagged when he hit the back of my throat.

"I'm gonna fuck your mouth, and you better suck hard."

Normally I held him, his hips, but he didn't want that. He didn't want me to have any power or control. He wanted only to make me do what he wanted.

My body was sated, but I felt the roll of desire go through me nonetheless. He was really getting off on it, watching me as he slammed his shaft into my mouth over and over.

"Malic," he whispered. "I'm gonna come. I want you to drink it all down and lick me clean, you understand?"

I growled.

"Because then I'm gonna kiss you so hard, so long, 'cause I wanna taste myself on your tongue and know I had you, know you're mine."

The man annihilated me with his desire.

"Oh, baby, I fuckin' love your mouth and your lips and your fuckin' tongue."

I hollowed out my cheeks, increasing the suction, and his head fell back as he came. It wasn't much—he had just come in the bathroom—but I sucked hard and drank it down.

As he wanted, I licked him clean, his cock, his balls, and then rose over him, staring down into his eyes.

"Kiss me," he whined, licking his lips.

I bent, scooped him up, and dumped him down onto the bed. He was staring up at me with sparkling eyes.

He sighed deeply, blissfully sated. "I love you so much."

"I love you too, baby," I chuckled.

"I need food and water," he almost giggled.

"I would agree."

"Well, go get it."

"Oh hell no," I told him, walking over to the armoire to get my clothes. "Get your ass up, and let's go downstairs and see your family."

He grunted.

"Now."

"I like you better when you're not talking," he teased. "When your mouth is full."

"I will beat your ass if you do not get up."

"Really?" He sounded so hopeful.

I had no one to blame but myself. I had created a monster.

I HAD tangled with a demon the night before, killed it the following afternoon, and then gone caroling with Dylan and his family that evening. I didn't sing—it was not at all in my skill set—but I listened and watched and held Dylan's hand as we walked.

I sat in the enormous Catholic church for midnight Mass, enjoyed watching Dylan get up and take communion and then get up again when the priest called for volunteers from the congregation to sing with the choir. He smiled at me sitting there with his family, and when we walked out, I had Dylan tucked under one arm and Tina under the other. We talked to a lot of people even though it was after one in the morning, and when we got home, we had a snack of sliced ham with spicy mustard on butter rolls and potato salad. It was nice, just us, just me and Dylan's family in the kitchen talking and laughing.

The gossip was fun to listen to, and Tina brought up the one girl who had worn clear plastic four-inch heels to Mass.

I grunted.

"You saw her too, right?"

I coughed. "She was hard to miss."

"Hooker heels, right?" Tina asked.

My smile was evil.

She smacked my bicep. "See, Mom, I told you. Debbie Riley is a whore."

"Tina!"

"What?" Tina smacked me again. "Tell her."

I turned to Lily. "You only wear those if you're working the pole."

"Malic!" Lily scolded.

"What?" I chuckled.

It was fun to watch Dylan's mom give us all the evil eye.

"I didn't say anything." Dylan snickered, slurping his apple cider.

Afterward, everyone wandered off, and I went out to sit on the couch, close to the Christmas tree. Dylan's father had made a fire when he came home, unconcerned that it would burn the house down in his sleep. Between the flickering flames, the glow of the twinkling multicolored lights, and the stockings hanging on the mantle, it was as close to perfect as it was going to get without—

"Can I lie down by you?"

I looked up and patted my knee. My boyfriend wanted to stretch out on the couch beside me with his head in my lap. I was utterly content.

When I started stroking his hair, he sighed deeply even as his eyes started to flutter.

"Don't leave me here, 'kay? If you go up and I'm asleep, take me with you."

"Of course."

He got comfortable, turned his head, nuzzled my thigh gently, and then closed his eyes as I continued stroking his hair.

"Where did you go today with my dad before caroling? You guys ditched us for an hour and a half."

"Both of us had some last-minute shopping to do."

"Oh yeah, like what?"

He did not need to know about the trip to the jewelry store. I was a spur-of-the-moment guy, and it turned out that Dylan's father was as well. When he had invited me to go with him, I had felt privileged, and then when I was there, walking around in the small, elegant antique jewelry store, I had seen it: the ring with the old miner-cut diamonds. Apparently the owner bought a lot of the pieces in her shop at estate sales, and this one, set in white gold with a two-carat stone, had been a rare find. As soon as I saw it, I knew I had to have it. What was nice was that Mrs. Gruber, the lady who owned the store, had a son who had just married the man of his dreams in New York City. She was going there to spend New Year's with them.

"Is he the love of your life?" she had asked, smiling.

"Yes, ma'am," I assured her.

And she basically gave it away, which I appreciated. The price tag had been steeper than I wanted to go, but I would have, because it would be the ring Dylan would wear for the rest of his life. Watching the clerk ring it up on my American Express card, even at half its original price, had impressed Mr. Shaw. I liked him knowing that I could provide for his son even though once Dylan graduated from art school, he might be supporting me.

"With a degree in fine art?" Mr. Shaw scoffed. "I'm thinking you're gonna be the breadwinner in your family, Malic."

In your family was nice to hear.

"Malic?"

Brought back to the warm, cozy present, I smiled down at Dylan.

"Where'd you go?"

I pointed. "You see that small red box right there?"

I could tell when he did because he jolted just a little. "Yeah." He was breathless.

"That's yours to open first thing in the morning."

"It is?"

"It is." I smiled down at him, curling a long strand of hair around his ear.

"I have to wait?"

"Yep. I promised your dad."

"My dad?" he asked, rolling his head in my lap to look up at me.

"He wants your mother to see it."

He whimpered in the back of his throat. "So?"

"So?"

"You're gonna ask me something tomorrow, then?"

"I am." I smiled. "What do you think you'll say?"

His breath caught. "I think I would say thank you for loving me, for coming here with me, for everything you did for Tina. I love you more than I can say."

"That's all very sweet, but not an answer."

"Yes." He swallowed hard. "I'll always say yes to you."

I cleared my throat. "About the house—"

"I love the house."

"If I put your name on it, too, would that be okay?"

He nodded, sitting up, climbing into my lap, straddling my thighs. "That would be perfect."

I grabbed his hips and pulled him close. "Let's go to bed."

"Oh no." He shook his head, leaning forward and kissing me before he got up, grabbed a cushion from the couch, and lay down next to the tree. "I have to stay down here and guard my gift. Go get the blankets off the bed."

"Me? Why do I have to sleep down here too?"

"You sleep with me," he told me. "Always."

So possessive lately, and I loved it. I never thought it would be such a turn-on. "You should lie close to the fire."

"That's too far away from the tree."

I rolled my eyes as I got up. "Fine, I'll go get blankets and some pillows, but you need to change."

"No thanks," he said, unzipping his corduroys to give me a glimpse of smooth gold skin. "I'm good in these or out of these." He grinned.

I snorted out a laugh. "Okay, baby, I'll be right back down."

"Hurry, 'kay? I want to snuggle up with you."

When I was almost to the stairs, he called out to me. "I love you."

"I love you back." I smiled.

"Hey, do you think we could fool around by the tree?"

"Not on your life," I assured him. In his parents' house, out in full view? The man was insane. "Hell no."

"I bet I can get you to change your mind."

His impish grin, tousled hair, dimples, the way he peeled off his sweater and leveled a heated gaze at me—God, he probably could get me to break every rule in my book.

"Hurry."

I hurried.

MARY CALMES currently lives in Honolulu, Hawaii, with her husband and two children and hopes to eventually move off the rock to a place where her children can experience fall and even winter. She graduated from the University of the Pacific (ironic) in Stockton, California, with a bachelor's degree in English literature. Due to the fact that it is English lit and not English grammar, do not ask her to point out a clause for you, as it will *so* not happen. She loves writing, becoming immersed in the process, and falling into the work. She can even tell you what her characters smell like. She also buys way too many books on Amazon.

http://www.dreamspinnerpress.com

Also from MARY CALMES

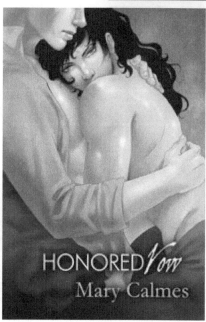

http://www.dreamspinnerpress.com

Contemporary Romance from MARY CALMES

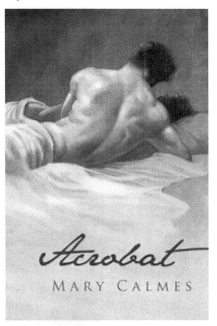

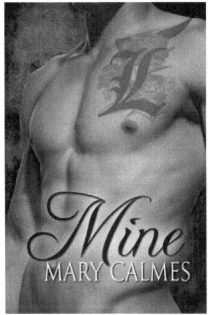

The *Matter of Time* series

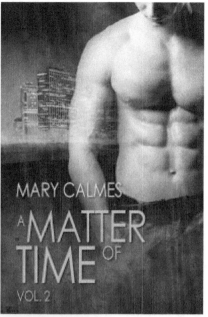

http://www.dreamspinnerpress.com

Also from MARY CALMES

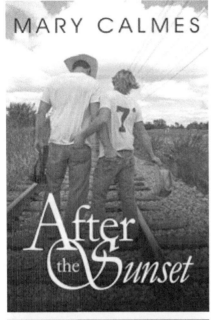

http://www.dreamspinnerpress.com

A novella from MARY CALMES

Frog

MARY CALMES

http://www.dreamspinnerpress.com

A novella from MARY CALMES

Dreamspinner Press
Fairy Tales

THE
SERVANT
Mary Calmes

http://www.dreamspinnerpress.com

A novella from MARY CALMES

Romanus

Mary Calmes

http://www.dreamspinnerpress.com